Silk or Sugar

A Novel

Silk or Sugar

A Novel

Elizabeth Pye

Silk or Sugar
Copyright 2016 by Elizabeth Pye
A Writers Lair publication
Printed in the United States

ISBN-13: 978-0998213002
ISBN-10: 0998213004

Original watercolor cover design by Barbara Parish

To Earl,

my late husband and mentor.

My soul mate.

Acknowledgments

A special thanks to my friend and perpetual critique partner, Amy Jenkins of Kansas City, Missouri, who traveled to California to encourage me to start work on Janine's story, *Silk or Sugar*, at a low point in my life after the death of my husband.

I'm grateful for my *Romancing the Page* critique friends who endured, with infinite patience, the early draft of my story. Their persistence and suggestions have greatly improved my novel. Roberta Smith, Anne Fowler, Marilyn Ramirez, and Holly La Pat, please accept my heartfelt thanks.

I'm indebted to Dave Thompson, who provided technical assistance with the manuscript and Mary Thompson for welcoming me into the Wordsmiths' critique group.

I'm beholden to my editors, Mike Foley, who did a first edit, and Jenny Margotta, who performed the final edit and shepherded the book to publication. Many thanks to Kathy Puffer for a final edit of the proof copy of my manuscript. I wish to express my gratitude to Barbara Parish for the beautiful watercolor book cover and for her talent and attention to my vision of it.

Author's Note

Silk or Sugar is a work of fiction taking place in 1803 during a turbulent time in the history of France. I have taken care to represent the historically-inspired characters of Napoleon and Josephine Bonaparte, Baron Pierre-Clement de Laussat, Georges Cadoudal, and Lazare Carnot as accurately as possible. My research included primary and secondary sources. I have read memoir accounts, historical reports, and other writings to gain useful insights. All other characters are entirely products of my imagination.

The inspiration for *Silk or Sugar* stems from my love of France, its people, architecture, and countryside. The birth of the Republic was especially difficult, testing the soul of the nation. When I walk past the Place de la Concorde, the Parisian site of the guillotine during the French Revolution, the unthinkable horror of its history is like a dark cloud carried along on a cold winter wind.

Chapter 1

New Orleans—February 1803

Janine de Fleury sat erect, her head lowered as she stitched the last pearl on an elegant silk gown. Flexing her stiff fingers, she stood and hung the garment with care—a gown worthy of her station in life. But she, the Marquis de Fleury's daughter, would not be attending the grand ball. She'd have to content herself with dressing the wealthy ladies of New Orleans and bide her time until she married Baron Dupré. God willing, they would return to France and serve the rightful king, as had her dead father and mother.

The jingle on the door of her little shop, Très Chic, jolted Janine from her musings, and she swirled around to come face to face with the painted spectacle of a wealthy plantation owner's haughty English wife. Everyone knew the woman had married him for his money and to escape from her father's pig farm.

"*Bonjour*, Madame Pugh." Janine forced a smile and humble countenance, an appeal to her customer's vanity. "May I get you a cup of tea before I ready your gown?"

"Mademoiselle, I haven't come to take tea with you." Madame Pugh stamped her foot. "If you value my business, you will see that I am not kept waiting again."

Janine's blue blood boiled. She resented the vulgar Madame Pugh's attitude toward her, seeing her as mere shopkeeper. Janine stifled a hiss and looked her in the eye, saying with aristocratic dignity, "Please excuse me while I package your gown."

Janine pursed her lips after the customer left. She squeezed her eyes closed and tried not to think of the tenuous position of her marriage contract. Madame Dupré, the mother of her betrothed, had changed toward her since they'd fled France together during the Revolution. She'd abandoned her *noblesse oblige* in favor of greed—a more grievous act than that of the uncouth pig farmer's daughter. Yet Janine could think of no better alternative to the marriage which would enable her to fulfill her role as a daughter of the illustrious de Fleury family.

Just as soon as she managed to meet her dowry.

1

⚜

Janine clutched her blue wool shawl around her petite figure and pushed an obstinate, chocolate-colored curl under her hood, seeking to lessen the effect of an unseasonably cold north wind. The swift air current whipped along St. Charles Street, but she held her course along the cobblestone walkway. The better choice because she'd make better time than following the plank sidewalks of the more sheltered routes to her destination. The icy ache in her heart far exceeded that of the wind chill promising freezing temperatures by nightfall. She felt desperation akin to that of leaving Chateau Fleury ten years earlier.

Her thoughts halted when one of two ships entered the port too fast, ramming the docks. A flurry of ear-burning profanity erupted as men gathered around to assess the damage. Janine's mind quickly returned to her stalled marriage contract with the aristocratic Charles Dupré. She wanted to have a family—to become part of his family—to soften the loss of her own parents, victims of the butchers of the Revolution. But Madame Dupré had changed from protector to impatient negotiator for payment of the dowry. And as for Charles, he was a virtual stranger in faraway lands with the deposed French royals—unlike Etienne Tremeau, the unacceptable love of her youth. She could count on the fingers of one hand the number of letters she had received from Charles during her time in New Orleans.

Janine stood for a moment, staring at the Duprés' two-story brick house on Dauphine Street. In service to the exiled French Prince Louis, her betrothed had been to New Orleans only once, three years ago, and had spent much of that time urging her to gather the necessary dowry funds to fulfill her part of the marriage contract. The ominous prospect of spinsterhood in a strange country frightened the twenty-five-year-old French aristocrat now living among the New Orleans bourgeoisie. With determination she summoned as much refined demeanor as she could before she grasped the familiar, iron lion-head knocker, announcing her presence. Footsteps preceded the scraping sound of the heavy wooden door as it opened.

"Bonjour, Mademoiselle de Fleury." The black manservant smiled at her. "Come in. I'll let Madame know you are here."

"*Merci*," Janine said, following the kindly man across the black-and-white patterned marble floor of the spacious entry hall. She dismissed the thought of sitting. She would stand to remain alert for her meeting with Madame Dupré.

The butler returned and ushered Janine to the door of the ornately decorated room. "Monsieur and Madame await you in the salon."

Monsieur, too? Janine hadn't expected he would be there. Why was he? But yes, the stony-faced, gaunt man stood like a statue by his plump wife's side. "Bonjour, Monsieur *et* Madame Dupré." Janine hoped she projected more confidence than she felt.

"Bonjour, Mademoiselle," Monsieur Dupré said, a blank stare masking his feelings.

Her head lifted high and nose in the air, Madame pointed to a chair. "Sit down." She waited until Janine obliged. "We'll get right to the point, Janine. A decade has passed without your dowry being paid. By all rights your marriage contract with our son is null and void. However, being compassionate people, Monsieur and I will give you an additional six months to fulfill your financial obligation before we enter into an agreement with another family."

"I don't understand. You know that when the royal family returns to France, I'll be . . ."

Monsieur Dupré scoffed. "Humph, the royal family, not likely. Napoleon is a powerful man—a war hero who brings glory to France."

"How can you say so? Your son, my betrothed, is with the rightful King of France, Louis *le Dix-Huitième,* serving him with the utmost commitment," Janine said without pausing for a breath, determined not to stop even if interrupted.

Madame scowled at her. "Times have changed in France. Charles will return to New Orleans by the end of summer."

Astounded at what she heard, Janine asked, "He abandons our king?"

"He *will* be married by year's end to a woman who fulfills her marriage contract! We've already spoken to several plantation owners about such an alliance."

Somehow, Janine wasn't surprised by the Duprés' threat. If they'd forsake their king, why should she expect to be treated any better? She'd have to meet their demands and take her chances on Charles being a good husband.

Madame continued, "Monsieur and I shall forbid Charles to

have any contact with you until your dowry requirement of twenty thousand *francs* is met."

Janine stood, her eyes steady with determination. "I shall fulfill my part of the contract. Good day." She left the room and the house without waiting to be shown out, her cheeks hot as if on fire. Her pent-up resentment of the Duprés turned to flaming anger and indignation. If and when they married, she hoped she and Charles would leave New Orleans; she didn't want constant interference in their lives.

Janine paced in ever widening circles in the apartment above her Bourbon Street dress shop, struggling with how best to convince her business partner to buy her out. After all, she'd invested three years in the dress design business before taking Angélique as her partner five years ago. Angie's skills with a needle had dovetailed nicely with her own design talent. Together, they'd established Très Chic, now one of the top two New Orleans dress shops. Their clientele attracted society ladies in town and from the outlying plantations.

In spite of their success, Janine had been unable to accumulate enough money to meet her dowry. Her only hope was to return to France and liquidate the remaining assets of her family's estate. Selling her interest in the dress shop wouldn't provide enough money, but there was Chateau Fleury. She'd have to sell the chateau to begin her new life with Charles and pray they'd find contentment together. Goodness knows what condition the chateau was in or what had become of the furnishings. She'd find out for herself. Fortunately, a married friend, Madame Darcy, had agreed to act as her chaperone on the voyage—a necessary consideration for a respectable young lady.

Hearing Angélique on the stairs to their residence, Janine sat in her favorite, well-worn velvet chair and waited. "I need to speak with you right away," she said as Angie rounded the corner.

Not stopping, Angélique went into the kitchen and set the basket of apples she carried on the table. "I have two dresses to complete by tomorrow. Conversation will have to wait."

"Angie," Janine continued, following her friend into the kitchen, "you know I wouldn't ask you to take time from work if it weren't important." She paused for a moment. "Monsieur and

Madame Dupré have threatened to nullify my marriage contract . . . to seek another wife for Charles . . . if I don't pay my dowry in full within six months."

"Why now?"

"Charles is leaving the service of King Louis. He'll return to New Orleans within a few months. I must have enough money to pay my dowry before his arrival."

"Where will you get the money?"

"There's only one way. I'll return to France and gather what remains of the family assets."

"It's unwise to leave our business here. You've worked too hard to establish it. You know you could forget about your miserable marriage contract and marry my brother. Antonio adores you. Angie stepped closer to Janine. "I'm not sure he'll wait for you."

"Angie, I want to sell my share of the business to you. I need the money now. Besides, when I return I'll marry Charles." The better part of wisdom dictated she not voice she had no interest in marrying Antonio under any circumstances. Truth be told, she didn't even like him. She'd heard whispers that he was involved in the slave trade.

"Janine, I . . . I can't. You're risking too much. What if your plan fails?"

"It will succeed. It has to. I'll go to the family who helped me escape during the Revolution. They'll help me."

"A lot can change in ten years. They may all be dead by now."

A chill coursed down Janine's spine at the thought. "Non, they should be safe. They're just plain peasant people."

"Why should they want to help you?"

An image flashed through Janine's mind of the ten-year-old boy of few words on his first day in the chateau's classroom. "Etienne, their son, is only two years older than I. *Père* invited him to attend sessions during my lessons with my tutor. His family was loyal and grateful to father for his kindness."

A surprised look crossed Angie's face. "Oh? What did you think of sharing your tutor with a peasant?"

A smile softened Janine's serious expression. "Etienne was clever and we got along quite well. My only worry was appearing dull compared to him. He perceived my concern and offered to help with my lessons. As we got to know each other, we shared many of our secret dreams."

"Really?" Angie said, raising an eyebrow.

"We did. So much so that he spoke freely to me. One day toward the end of the term, he gave me a serious look and said he wanted to talk to me. I hoped he wasn't going to tell me he'd no longer help with my studies. I was dumbfounded by what came next. He declared someday he would be a great military leader . . . and he asked me to marry him. I just stared at him. It was ridiculous. He should have known my father would insist I marry into a noble family."

Angie shook her head. "He dared to dream."

"I told Etienne it was not my choice—that my father would arrange a suitable marriage for me. He didn't listen to reason." Tears burned Janine's eyes as she recalled the loss of his friendship. "He became sullen and wouldn't talk to me for weeks. Quite some time passed before he relented, but we no longer shared confidences." Janine sighed. "If I'd known how it would change him, I wouldn't have been so frank. I understand *now* why he was hurt by my words."

"You still haven't explained why you think his family will help you?"

"That wasn't the end of our contact. He remained loyal to my father—and to me. He worked for us up to the time I emigrated. After my uncle was murdered, Etienne helped me escape to Bordeaux and to the home of my fiancé."

"He had come to terms with your arranged marriage contract?"

"Oh, yes. I suppose by that time he had."

"Have you had any contact with him since you've been here?"

Janine shook her head. "Please, Angie, say you'll buy me out. Everything depends on you."

"How much money do you need?"

"I spoke to a financial man about the value of our enterprise. He estimated it might fetch as much as twelve thousand francs."

"Without your designs, our shop won't be nearly so valuable."

"Angie, please. You're my only hope." Janine paused. She *had* to have the money. What could she say to convince her friend? "I'll even reduce my two-thirds share by ten percent as an incentive."

"I don't know. I'm afraid the business won't thrive without you."

"Don't worry. After I'm married I'll continue to design apparel and give you first choice." *May they be Paris-inspired.*

6

"Well, whether you marry or not, it could work. Antonio will want you to get any capital coming to you. I'll speak to him and tell him you need the funds to settle your family estate. But he'll insist you sign a note. You know how Antonio is about money. But I don't want a sales contract from you. I want you to be my partner."

Wrapping her arms around Angie, Janine said, "You'll do it?"

"I'm worried for you. What if something goes wrong?"

"You won't regret it. Très Chic has a loyal clientele."

"That's not what I mean. You're risking everything."

"I know you'll do well while I'm gone. You've learned a lot over the time we've been together. Your own designs are beginning to sell, too."

"I wish you wouldn't leave a thriving livelihood to gamble on an unknown. There may be nothing left of your family assets."

"I won't know if I don't go."

"All right, I'll see what I can do."

"Merci, you're a true friend," Janine said, squeezing Angie's arm.

Angie nodded. "Now I must get back to work."

"Thank God, it's going to be all right," Janine chanted, dancing around the room. Afterward she went into the bedroom and collapsed on the bed. She allowed tears of relief to spill down her cheeks for several minutes before pulling a tattered envelope from the nightstand drawer and removing Charles' most recent letter. She ran her finger across the fibers of the Dupré crest before re-reading his words.

My dear Mademoiselle de Fleury,

When will we marry and be able to return to our home in France, you ask? I do not have the answer.

I am losing faith that our countrymen will recall our King to take his God-given place on the throne of France. Napoleon has entranced them and they follow him as sheep to the slaughter. There is talk he will declare himself Emperor while the rightful King spends the bitter winter in exile.

7

> *Perhaps New Orleans rather than France will give us the best chance to begin our married life. With your dowry and help from my father, we can buy land and grow sugar cane, or we can expand upon your business and my father's mercantile. I'll be expected to learn my father's trade.*

She folded the letter, returning it to the envelope. *In six months we shall marry.* They had met only three times—during the signing of the marriage contract, in Bordeaux two years later, and once during his brief visit to New Orleans. She remembered little about him—not even the color of his eyes. He had remained in France to serve the exiled future king, while his family and Janine escaped to New Orleans. She hoped he wasn't like his mother, who had arranged for Janine to tutor the children of an acquaintance to pay her own room and board.

Loire Valley, France —May 1803

Janine grasped the coach door handle and willed her thumping heart to quiet. The death of Madame Darcy aboard ship had left her without a chaperone. She prayed she'd find another lady in Tours to accompany her. Desperate times required reckless action. First, she must see Chateau Fleury. The huge iron gate and the curved driveway veiled her view of her beloved ancestral home. Finally, home again. What would she find there? Bittersweet memories . . . and money needed for her dowry? Still, it was the only real home she'd ever known. New Orleans had required her to keep body and soul together by the fruits of her labor.

"Mademoiselle, shall I wait?" the coachman asked as he opened the coach door and helped her down.

"Please open the gate and take me to the house." She handed him the larger of the two sturdy iron keys she'd tucked into her bodice for the long trip to France.

After several attempts, he returned and thrust the key toward her. "This doesn't fit. Do you have another one?"

How dense could he be? The lock was simply rusty. Janine snatched the key from the man's outstretched hand and poured a few drops of lavender oil on it from a small vial she carried in her reticule. She hurried to the gate and inserted the key in the lock, hoping the generous amount of lubricant would allow it to turn. However, the lock held fast, and after several unsuccessful tries she had no choice but admit defeat.

She studied the key and then the lock. *They've changed the lock. Who?* A glimpse of a tower through the trees assured her that at least her beloved chateau was still standing—not a burned-out shell like the neighboring one. With reluctance she returned to the coach.

The driver gave her a triumphant look. "Where to now?"

"Back to town." Biting her lower lip, she made up her mind to go straight to Madame Tremeau's home. Madame and her son, Etienne, had saved her from sure death at the height of the Revolution. Madame had hidden her and comforted her while her son arranged to smuggle her to Bordeaux to her betrothed's family. Always a wellspring of information, Janine felt certain the woman could tell her what had happened at the chateau and shed light on why the gate lock had been changed.

Janine's optimism faltered as she gazed out the carriage window at the many burned-out chateaux, abandoned coaches, and battered remains of churches. Some forests were devoid of mature trees; all that remained were spindly, new-growth saplings.

As the carriage entered Tours and passed the market square, she saw a scarred pedestal where a statue of the martyred King Louis XVI had once stood. There were piles of rubble from demolished buildings, and many of those still standing needed repair.

"Stop. I'll get out here," Janine instructed the driver as they circled the square. Feeling a twinge of finality, she stepped down from the conveyance and paid the round-trip fare. Would she recognize the Tremeaus' modest home? Turning off Rue des Ursulines, she walked along the chestnut tree-lined street, passing timber and plaster houses in the old part of town, and continuing beyond the cobbled road onto the dirt one at the edge of town.

Emotions of the frightening night so long ago lashed at her heart as she approached the house with the blue-paneled door. The moment of truth was at hand. The dwelling looked as she remembered

9

it and gave little evidence of the Revolution, but would she find the Tremeaus still living there?

With a lump in her throat, she tapped on the door. Receiving no response, in desperation she knocked again and again.

Chapter 2

Inside the cottage, Colonel Etienne Tremeau looked up, irritated at the persistent knocking at the front door. With reluctance he replaced his quill in its holder on his boyhood desk. He rose, giving his chair a shove on the way out.

"Orders from Bonaparte?" the handsome, sun-bronzed soldier of the French Republican Army muttered as he neared the entrance. "Sometimes I wish he did not trust me so well." Unlatching the door, he peered through the open crack. His heart pounded and his long legs almost buckled when he glimpsed Janine de Fleury's unforgettable and beguiling gold-flecked eyes.

He wasn't prepared for the challenge. He felt the emotional vulnerability of the thirteen-year-old boy he'd been at Chateau Fleury—the gardener's son, not a suitable mate for her, the marquis' daughter, or so Janine had told him at the time. After all these years of exile, what was this aristocratic heartbreaker doing back in France? He'd thought himself devoid of feeling for her, but seeing her again, his pulse raced as it had when a youth. Lord knows, during the intervening years, he'd sought pleasure with other women—only to turn away from them at the last moment. He wouldn't allow himself to suffer such humiliation at the hands of a woman again.

Quickly donning his emotional armor, he pushed the door open then crossed his arms. "You're out of your mind, daring to come here. For what? My help with your . . . and I suppose your husband's . . . royalist espionage?" Etienne said with a sneer.

Janine stepped back while still maintaining her aristocratic bearing, her eyes flashing with indignation. "I am not a spy or here on behalf of anyone besides myself." She held her head high. "Baron Dupré and I are not yet married. I'm here to settle estate matters at Chateau Fleury in order to fulfill my dowry agreement in the marriage contract."

"Marriage contract, dowry, and goodness knows what else." Etienne's words were bitter as he stepped onto the porch and lashed out. "You *aristos* haven't changed—always selfish and greedy. You don't belong in the Republic."

Janine paled and Etienne saw she was on the verge of tears.

11

What's happened to me? I'm acting like a boorish beast. He resisted the temptation to hold her in his arms and comfort her. He would not allow her to complicate his life; neither did he wish her ill— even if she had returned as a royalist spy. Yet if so, his duty lay with Bonaparte and the new French Republic. He'd have no choice but to bring her to justice.

"Etienne, who is it?" His sister, Anne, appeared beside him. "I . . . Janine de Fleury?"

Janine moved closer. "*Oui.* Anne, let me look at you. You're so grown up."

"Janine is just leaving." Etienne grasped his sister's arm.

"Just leaving? Why . . . because you forgot your manners and didn't invite her in?" Anne turned to Janine. "Please forgive him. The war has changed him."

"No need to apologize for me." Etienne bowed in mock deference to Janine. "Mademoiselle de Fleury, I leave you with my sister. I have important matters needing my attention."

Etienne watched as Anne led Janine into the kitchen, pulling closed the heavy curtain across the doorway. He stood as if his feet were glued to the floor and ran his finger along the scar on his cheek, a reminder of his early years in the Republican Army. Wounded in a battle at Le Mans against the ill-equipped *Vendéen Militaire* led by George Cadoudal, a tenacious opponent of the Revolution, Etienne carried a constant reminder of the enemy. And through the intervening years, Cadoudal managed to elude capture and continued to plot against the Republic, remaining a thorn in his and Bonaparte's side. *How ironic if I must be the one to condemn Janine for treason.*

On the other side of the curtain, Anne faced Janine across the small oak table. "Etienne is not as you remember him. He's been away from us for too long."

The kitchen bore little resemblance to Janine's memory of it. It seemed cramped and cold without the delicious scents of simmering stew, fresh baked bread, and the comfort of Etienne's and Madame Tremeau's welcoming presence. Sipping steaming coffee, Janine wondered to whom she could turn.

"He's home for a top secret assignment for Napoleon Bonaparte," Anne whispered as she passed a plate of petit fours.

Janine rested her arms on the table and leaned closer. "Home? Where's he been?"

"After he recovered from his war injuries . . ."

"War injuries," Janine interrupted.

"*Oui*. You saw the scar on his cheek. His leg healed well but occasionally bothers him," Anne said. "And once he was well, Bonaparte recommended he serve as emissary to Governor de Carondelet in New Orleans."

"He . . . he was in New Orleans?" Janine felt as if she'd been struck in the stomach. Did Etienne care so little about her that he hadn't contacted her while there? If so, she could expect little help from him now.

"Yes, some of the time. He even bought land to try his hand at growing sugar cane."

Janine stirred what remained of the sugar in her coffee. "How's your Maman?"

"Quite well. She's at the market now."

"I need to ask her about Chateau Fleury and what has happened there."

"She'll be happy to see you."

"Does Etienne spend much time in New Orleans?" Janine asked, trying to sound casual.

The heavy curtain in the doorway shuddered as Etienne stomped into the kitchen, his thick brown hair tousled. "Mademoiselle, that's no concern of yours."

"I wouldn't have asked if I'd known you were there."

He glared at her. "Go back to New Orleans. There's nothing left for you here."

Anger welled inside Janine. "Monsieur, that is for me to decide."

"It is best you leave this house. *Now*," Etienne called over his shoulder as he left the kitchen.

What had come over him? Why was he so hostile? She looked at Anne, who said nothing and looked away. Janine stood. "I must go."

Anne rose and linked arms with Janine as they left the kitchen. With the other hand she wiped a tear from her cheek. "I'm so sorry. He frightens me at times," she said, giving a startled response when the front door opened.

Madame Tremeau entered carrying a basket overflowing with a rainbow of assorted fresh vegetables. She blinked, set down her basket, and squinted at Janine for a long moment. "Blessed saints, if it isn't Janine de Fleury," she exclaimed. "My dear, I have often wondered what became of you." She kissed Janine on both cheeks. "Come and tell me."

Janine hesitated. She wanted to stay and bask in the affection she felt from Madame Tremeau, but Etienne had left no doubt she was not welcome in his home.

Anne put her index finger to her lips and whispered, " Maman, Etienne ordered Janine to leave."

"Janine," Madame sighed as they stepped outside the house, "the war has taken a toll on my son."

"Madame, I need to talk with you."

"I will come to you. Where are you lodging?"

"In the old Grand Hotel on the Quai de la Loire."

"Oh, my dear, you shouldn't be there," Madame said, an appalled expression on her face.

"It's all I can afford." Shame scorched Janine cheeks at the reproach.

"It's no longer respectable. It caters to riffraff and ladies of the night."

"It will have to do until I can make other arrangements."

"Perhaps I can help. I think Madame Parot's son is leaving next week. I'll speak to her about your need."

"Thank you for your kindness." Janine moved toward the street.

"I'll walk with you."

"Merci. Madame, I've just come from Chateau Fleury. The gate lock has been changed."

"Could be the State locked it because of unpaid taxes." After a short pause, Madame Tremeau continued, "Umm, it seems I recall hearing that a family member returned from England and reclaimed the chateau several years ago."

"Non! That's not possible. I am the only heir who has a legitimate claim to our property."

"I don't know about that."

14

"Is the imposter a man or woman?" Janine asked in disbelief.

"A man. An uncle, I think."

"It can't be. My *only* uncle was murdered. Etienne and I were at Chateau Fleury when it happened."

"He never mentioned it. Could it be another uncle or great uncle?"

"There is no other uncle." Janine sighed. "Etienne knows."

"Unfortunately, Etienne doesn't want to talk to you."

"Do you know of anyone else who may be able to help?"

"The old priest, Father Dillon, has been here as long as I can remember. He seems to know everything about everyone."

Janine's pace slowed as they approached the shabby hotel. "Where will I find him?"

"At Saint Gatien," Madame Tremeau replied. "He spends much time at the cathedral."

"Maybe I'll find him there this afternoon." Although crushed by Etienne's negative reaction to her, she thanked God for Madame Tremeau's suggestion. The priest would be an invaluable ally and source of information.

Madame Tremeau gave Janine a quick hug. "We'll talk soon . . . as soon as I have news. You must leave the hotel before anyone realizes you are staying there. Your good name is at stake."

Chapter 3

Reluctant to ignore Madame Tremeau's admonition about being seen at the hotel, Janine steeled herself to venture out to seek Abbé Dillon's counsel. She felt she had no choice in the matter. Besides, the short walk to the cathedral wouldn't give her much public exposure.

Feeling sure no one had seen her, she breathed a sigh of relief as she neared St. Gatien Cathedral where her parents had married and she had worshipped as a child. She gazed up at its flamboyant gothic towers dominating the cerulean blue skyline and wondered if she'd find *Abbé* Dillon inside. So much depended on talking with him. After a short walk through The Cloister, the little square behind the chancel of the cathedral, she entered a small side door of the church.

The murmur of voices teased her ears and Janine spotted a woman sitting in a chair beside one of the huge stone pillars. As she drew closer, she saw two men nearby, selling walking sticks.

The shorter, rotund man ran his hand across his mouth. "I hear Abbé Dillon is to be appointed Canon of the Cathedral."

Janine approached the men. "*Je vous demande pardon.* I couldn't help overhearing you mention Abbé Dillon. Can you tell me where I might find him?"

The second man, tall and thin, wore a black hat in stark contrast to the wisps of white hair peeking from underneath it. He leaned down until his face was directly in line with hers. "And who be asking for the good abbé?"

"I'm Mademoiselle Janine de Fleury. *L'Abbé* Dillon baptized me when I was a baby."

The woman Janine had noticed earlier had obviously been listening to the conversation because she stopped knitting, looked up at Janine, and remarked, "Now that be pretty special, I say."

Jingling coins in his hands, the short man moved closer and peered at Janine. "The abbé be in the cloister garden almost every afternoon."

"*Merci beaucoup.*" Troubled by the lack of reverence for the sacred demonstrated by the people inside the cathedral, Janine moved away from them. *Such goings on—they barter with each other for goods and services.* The men even wore hats, showing a lack of respect by not removing them.

16

She reminded herself that during the Revolution, churches had been secularized and desecrated. How quickly people changed. About two years had passed since Napoleon and the Pope had reached an agreement between church and state with the signing of the Concordat. Now at least the church was open to the public.

Deciding she'd seen enough, she retraced her steps back to the side door. A peaceful respite welcomed her outside near the shady north side of the building. Janine passed along the mossy stone walls until she came to an archway leading into the walled cloister garden.

Clipped hedges, semicircular gravel paths, and bright green grass were as she remembered them—fully healed from the destruction of the Revolution. She took comfort in the serenity of the cathedral gardens, but her heart remained heavy after her encounter with Etienne Tremeau. She'd been mistaken in thinking she could rely on him to help her unravel the mystery at Chateau Fleury, but she reminded herself how fortunate it was that Abbé Dillon was still at the cathedral. He was a family friend and would surely help her.

She found him sitting on a bench under the arcade of the Psalette Cloister. His hair had turned white and he had gone from lean to rotund, but she still recognized her old friend. "Bonjour, Monsieur L'Abbé Dillon," Janine said softly.

He blinked, his red face a mask as he focused on her. An awkward moment passed before he closed the large, leather-bound book he held on his lap and placed it on the table beside him. A flicker of recognition followed by shock registered on his face. "Can it be Mademoiselle de Fleury?"

Janine noted his brief discomfiture and wondered whether the atrocities directed at the church during the Revolution had rendered him a broken man.

"Oui. It is good to see you again," Janine said in as cheerful a tone as she could muster. "How are you?"

"*Bien . . . et vous*? Please sit down and tell me how you are." He relinquished a half-hearted smile and welcomed her in a pleasant-enough manner.

She wondered whether she'd just imagined his discomfort at seeing her. She must try not to let her imagination get the best of her. "I've just returned from New Orleans to settle my family's estate." She took a seat across from him, noticing the fine leather shoes he wore.

17

Rather too grand for a clergyman in these times. Apparently, he'd recovered financially at any rate, she mused.

"New Orleans?" He gave her a quizzical glance. "I thought you'd gone to England and married the Baron Dupré."

"Non. I went to New Orleans with Monsieur and Madame Dupré while Charles stayed in service to King Louis."

He nodded. "I had it all wrong, I see."

Janine inched closer to him. "You lost track of me, but I know you keep in touch with happenings in the parish. I hope you can answer some questions."

"My child, I shall try to be of help."

"I've been away for ten years and returned just two days ago. I went directly to Chateau Fleury, but I couldn't open the gate with my key—someone has changed the lock." Janine paused and gave the abbé an imploring look. "What do you know about my home?"

He cleared his throat and broke eye contact. "Eh, during the Revolution, it was confiscated by the government. Personal belongings were sold. That's all I can tell you."

Janine shuddered. "They sold *everything* inside the house? I must establish my claim to the chateau."

"That is out of the question. Your uncle, the *Comte* de Fleury, returned from England and established the family's claim." The abbé paused. "I thought you knew."

Aghast at what she heard, Janine cried, "My uncle is dead!" Perhaps she had misunderstood. "What you say is impossible. I witnessed his murder."

"You must be mistaken. He's very much alive."

Janine moved closer and looked him in the eye. "I am *not* mistaken. I was with him when he died." She averted her eyes, fearing her scalding tears threatened to diminish her in his view.

With an unreadable expression, the abbé shook his head. "Do sit down. It seems you and your uncle succumbed to the prolonged stress of the violence of the Revolution. Your uncle grieved for you when you chose to honor your marriage contract with Charles Dupré . . . the royalist traitor."

Royalist traitor, unexpected words spoken with rancor from the mouth of Abbé Dillon. Janine sat down and swallowed the retort on the tip of her tongue. She couldn't afford to alienate him. Besides, she wanted to see the imposter. Was this cleric in league with the charlatan

18

who claimed to be her uncle? Regardless, she needed help to reach the fake comte ensconced in her chateau. "I want to meet the man who represents himself to be my uncle. Will you accompany me there?" she asked in a measured tone.

"He may not want to see you. I'll contact him and see whether he will agree. He's much opposed to royalist sympathizers."

Janine's legs shook as she rose. "I will get to the bottom of this with or without your help," she said, her voice quavering.

The abbé stood and waggled his finger inches from her face. "Mademoiselle, you best go back to New Orleans . . . or England . . . without dallying here. Royalist conspirators are the enemy of the Republic and come to no good end."

No matter how much she wanted to deny it, she realized the priest had sold his soul for pieces of silver. The question was to what degree? Was he in league with the man who'd stolen her uncle's identity?

Janine turned and walked away, saddened to realize that the old man whom she'd believed to be a friend now had a heart of stone. If she couldn't trust him, whom could she?

"Mademoiselle, wait a moment," he called.

Janine hesitated and looked over her shoulder. "What do you want?"

"I'm sorry I spoke so frankly to you. Please understand I did so out of concern for your safety. Much has changed since you've been away. I'll do everything I can to persuade the comte to receive you."

Janine considered his offer, well aware that he might not be worthy of confidence. Yet she decided to see whether he succeeded with the imposter. She shouldn't go alone, nor could she be assured of access on her own. She'd have to find someone to go with her. Who? All this ran quickly through her mind, but aloud she merely murmured, "Thank you."

"All right, my dear. I'll send word to you within a day or two. Where are you staying?"

Her cheeks burned at the thought of the hotel's bad reputation as she considered her response. "I'm in and out. It's no trouble for me to stop by to see you."

"As you wish."

She turned to leave but stopped and faced him. "How long ago

19

did the Comte return and make his claim?"

"About four years ago, if my memory serves correctly."

Janine nodded. "I've taken enough of your time this afternoon. Good day."

Her head was throbbing by the time she reached the hotel. Discouraged, she climbed the stairs to her room and flopped down on the bed. At the moment, her problem-solving skills seemed to have taken flight. Who could she turn to if the abbé didn't help her? She twisted and turned before falling asleep without getting into her nightclothes.

Aware of a bright light shining on her, Janine was relieved to see it came through the window across the room. She'd awakened from a dream of being chased by three men. One of them had caught her, and another one had held a torch in front of her face. How strange that the mind incorporated actual sounds, lights, and other sensations into a dream. She reached for her small gold brooch timepiece—her grandmother had given it to her on her twelfth birthday. *Almost nine o'clock, I better get moving.* She would stop by the market square to buy a fresh supply of fruit and cheese after meeting with the abbé.

She pinned the watch to her muslin dress just below the large, blue lace collar then picked up her satchel and opened the door just enough to see if anyone was in the hallway. *All clear.* She stepped out and closed the door behind her. After going down the stairs and entering the lobby, she greeted the concierge. "Good morning, citizen." *Citizen suits him. He's a grumpy old man.*

He made an unintelligible response.

The brisk, fresh air lifted her spirits. By the time she reached the cloister garden, she was humming and looking expectantly at each of the benches along the arcade. Where was the abbé? She was looking forward to hearing what he had to say, but she didn't see him anywhere in the entire garden. He was nowhere to be found.

Sighing, she sat down on the same bench he had sat on the previous day. As she waited she took the last piece of cheese from her bag and nibbled on it.

"*Excuse-moi.* Have you seen Abbé Dillon today?" she asked a gardener who stopped nearby several minutes later to prune the faded roses.

"Not today."

"Merci." She hoped against hope that the abbé had gone to see the Comte at Chateau Fleury.

Not knowing what else to do, she decided to go to the market square and treat herself to a cylinder of dry Cabochon du Poitou cheese. She'd wait until the morrow to return to the cathedral. It would be a long wait and patience was *not* one of her strong points. She knew she'd be well advised to work on developing it, however. She racked her brain. Was she missing any clues?

Taking little notice of the shops and houses along the way, she paused when she came to a dressmaker's shop. Her interest piqued, she went inside. A young woman with flawless skin and abundant blonde hair stood swathed in yards of ruby red silk brocade.

The middle-aged seamstress, pins loosely held between her lips, deftly fastened the fabric around her patron and acknowledged Janine with a bob of her head.

"Please, continue your work while I admire your beautiful fabrics." Janine ran her finger along emerald-green velvet similar to the gown she had worn on her fifteenth birthday celebration at Chateau Fleury—her last real celebration.

"Janine de Fleury," a strong, self-assured voice came from the direction of the yards of silk brocade.

Janine turned away from the bolts of fabric and studied the face of the woman who had spoken to her. She didn't recognize the woman, but she certainly looked prosperous. "I'm sorry. I don't recall meeting you."

A throaty laugh came from the blonde woman. "Meeting me? Why, I'm your almost aunt. I'm Minette—de Bernay now."

"Minette! Let me look at you." Janine could hardly believe her eyes. Her uncle, the Comte de Fleury, had been in love with her. Without telling him, Minette had gone to England to escape the violence of the Revolution. Janine wondered why she had behaved so, and she remained resentful of the woman's treatment towards her uncle. "What are you doing here in Tours?"

"I'm married and live here now."

"Happily, so it appears." Janine concluded she enjoyed a

comfortable life.

With a flip of her head, Minette said, "My husband is in favor with Napoleon. He's been promoted to general and expects to receive a title of nobility . . . if he continues to be successful in battle."

"But are you happy with one of Napoleon's soldiers?"

"You might say he's a diamond in the rough . . . a bit crude. But I manage to keep myself happy while he's away."

Feeling uncertain in her presence, Janine turned to leave the shop, saying only, "It's been nice seeing you again."

"Wait a moment," Minette's voice held a note of urgency. "You haven't told me what you've been doing since I last saw you. Are you married?"

"Not yet." Janine did not elaborate.

"Come to my salon tomorrow afternoon. We can catch up on things. Later in the evening I have four game tables arranged, and I do need another person. I'm sure you'll meet a lot of . . . congenial people."

"I'd like that but . . ."

"Well, then, it's settled. I'll send my coach for you at four o'clock. Where are you staying? What's the address?"

"Eh, I'll be at the cathedral in the afternoon. I'll meet the coach in front of the church."

"Wonderful."

Dare I hope Minette will help me?

Chapter 4

Janine stepped onto the rough surface of the street in front of the dress shop, gingerly making her way around puddles of amber-colored liquid. Neighing sounds came from a team of horses in front of a chemist's shop. Whiffs of ammonia assailed her nostrils. She lifted her skirt just enough to safely cross the street, warm kisses of the high-riding sun on her face. Optimism filled her such as she had not experienced since sailing from New Orleans. She felt as though a closed door had opened. Her chance meeting with Minette—a friend from her life at Chateau Fleury—could be of great help.

Janine intended to ask her why she had left France without telling her uncle, Alexandre. How could Minette consent to marry one of Napoleon's revolutionary warriors? She knew from personal experience that people did desperate things in desperate times, but still. Janine couldn't help but feel a bubbling anticipation about her reconnection with Minette. A visit to her home and being among friends felt so right—like in happier times.

Upon her arrival at the marketplace, Janine's attention turned to a vendor's bountiful display of cheeses. The eager seller urged her to sample his selection from a tray garnished with purple grapes. She selected three pieces and relished each bite, her appetite having returned with a vengeance. Pointing, she said, "I'll take that piece of Brie de Melun." The soft, creamy cheese covered with a red protective skin would keep well.

"You take this one too? Half price?" The vendor's head bobbed up and down as he offered a piece of white goat cheese.

"All right," she nodded. She'd take it to Minette.

"And the other one?" He gestured toward the third one she had sampled.

"Merci, Non. Please wrap the goat cheese separately." Janine waited just long enough to get her package, hurrying before the man tempted her further.

She didn't weaken until coming to the flower stalls. The fragrance and fresh beauty of the red carnations enchanted her. Tempted, she paused, but then she shook her head. *Too frivolous for my francs—no carnations for me.* She reluctantly gave in and moved on, stopping later to indulge in buying two large, red apples. Money well spent. She had to eat, didn't she? Resolving to buy nothing more, she continued out of the square, heading toward the hotel. During the long afternoon in her room, she'd have plenty of time to prepare for the next day. She needed to take the lace collar from the blue dress and attach it to the pink one she planned to wear to Minette's home. Bathing and washing her hair would be her final chore of the day.

The next morning Janine awoke, refreshed from a deep, dreamless sleep. After breakfast of an apple and a piece of cheese, she sat down on the wobbly vanity bench and looked into the dressing table mirror. Her heart-shaped face looked thinner and paler than when she'd left New Orleans. *I look sickly.* She sighed and reached for her remedy to the problem; the rouge she applied to her cheeks and lips created a healthy glow. She lifted her thick brown hair from her shoulders and fastened it into a cascade of curls, leaving a few loose ringlets to frame her face. Satisfied that she'd done all she could for her appearance, she allowed her mind to dwell on her anticipated visit with the abbé. Would it bring her any closer to reclaiming Chateau Fleury?

She waited until early afternoon to leave the hotel. Walking briskly along the unevenly cobbled street, she reached the cloister garden in good time and made her way to the abbé's favorite bench. She found him there by a small table, the large brown book propped up on a bookstand. Could he read it at that distance or was it simply for appearance?

"Good afternoon, Abbé Dillon." She forced a lilt to her voice.

He removed the book from the stand and laid it on the table with a flourish. "And a good afternoon to you, Mademoiselle." His lips quavered, his eyes studied her. "You have dressed with great care as if for a special occasion."

She adjusted her linen dress to avoid wrinkling it and sat down across from him. "Have you arranged for me to visit Chateau Fleury and meet with the Comte?" she asked, almost choking on the word Comte.

He raised his eyes and fastened them to her lace collar before looking away. "I'm afraid I have bad news for you. The Comte is in England for an extended time."

How convenient. "How do you know?" she said as calmly as possible, struggling with her frustration. "Did you go to Chateau Fleury?"

"I met the caretaker in town and inquired about the Comte."

"For ten years," she said, choosing her words carefully, "I've dreamt about returning to my family home. And finally, I have been able to travel across the Atlantic to realize that dream. Please help me." *I can't play cat and mouse.* "Will you arrange a visit for me before the Comte returns?"

The abbé focused on the cathedral bell tower. "I'll speak to the caretaker about it."

"Merci. I appreciate your help." Janine leaned back against the wooden slats of the bench, closed her eyes, and listened to birds chatter in the hedges. Emotionally spent, she allowed her thoughts to drift to Minette and the people she'd meet there. Could they provide useful information about Chateau Fleury? Would she even have anything in common with them?

The tolling of the cathedral bells jolted her to the present hour—four o'clock. She must hurry to meet the coach. She glanced at the abbé and saw he had turned his attention to the leather book. Janine stood. "I must take my leave. Thank you again for your help."

"My pleasure, Mademoiselle." He placed his index finger on the middle of the page and looked up at her but said nothing further.

Janine did not see him silently watching her as she hurried through the passageway between the cathedral and the cloisters and onto the street. A grand coach emblazoned with the de Bernay crest on its door waited in front of the cathedral. Janine recognized the crest from Minette's calling card.

"Mademoiselle de Fleury?" the footman in full livery asked in a deep voice. He opened the door as she approached.

"Oui, merci, monsieur," she said as he helped her into the coach. The butter-soft seats smelled of new leather. Brown suede covered the interior sides and roof. She could tell it was new, not a refurbished one. Minette's military man lived in high style.

The conveyance lurched forward and began to move slowly along the rough surface of the street behind heavily laden wagons headed for the quay. The waterfront buzzed with all sorts of shipping activity. The pungent odor, a mixture of fish and smoke, became stronger as they passed the old Castle of Tours and approached the stone bridge across the Loire. The coachman restrained and coaxed the horses along the overpass. People walked along a separate pedestrian walkway. Upon the glass-like surface of the water, boats and ships— large, small, and all sizes in between—moved cargo along this hub of commerce. Every so often a small boat of fishermen could be seen, safely out of the main passage by the far shore.

As the coach reached the other side of the river, the coachman loosened the reins, setting the horses on a trot along the road out of town. They picked up speed as they reached the forest and Janine gripped the inside strap, steadying herself until the horses fell into a smooth gallop. She relaxed into the rhythm of the ride until the horses again slowed to a trot.

Peering out the coach's window, she saw the woods had given way to open green fields. The easy trot continued over the narrow, grassy road until they reached a white stone gatehouse where the gatekeeper looked at Janine and waved the coach onward. She pressed her face against the window and watched as they progressed along the circular gravel loop around the front of the white tufa-stone chateau. Two one-story wings reached out like outstretched arms from the three-story center portion of the house. After the vehicle came to a full stop, Janine stepped out and greeted Minette, who waited on the front steps.

Minette led Janine through a garden room running the length of the main building. "It's good to have you here," she said. Her cheerful voice promised a delightful afternoon. "We have so much catching up to do."

Janine nodded, taking in the pleasant sights and scents. "It's beautiful here." Through open doors, the breeze carried the perfume of orange blossoms from a dozen tree-filled urns. Janine's lightweight skirt fluttered around her legs, but nary a ripple passed across Minette's pale salmon gauze dress, its straight skirt cut in the style favored by Josephine Bonaparte. The high waistline, accented with brown velvet ribbon just below the low-cut bodice, emphasized her bosom.

As she entered the salon, Janine noticed two men in military dress played chess at a gaming table. As the men stood and came toward them, Janine thought of her father, who'd taught her the game. She hadn't played it with anyone else since his death. She missed him so very much.

"Mademoiselle de Fleury, I'd like you to meet my husband, General de Bernay."

Janine extended her hand. *"Avec plaisir,* monsieur. With pleasure."

"Enchanté, mademoiselle." With an awkward gesture, the General reached for her hand and brushed his chapped lips across it. Appearing ill at ease, he stepped back and signaled for the other man to come forward.

"Mademoiselle de Fleury, may I present Lieutenant Louis Lenoir," Minette said in a cheerful voice with no sign of apology for her husband.

The lieutenant seemed more comfortable in the company of ladies. At least ten years younger than the general, he was much better looking in a carefully groomed way. His brown eyes were alert, and every hair on his head and moustache were in place.

"My great pleasure to meet you, Mademoiselle," he said with rehearsed warmth. He gazed into her eyes, kissed her hand, and held it a moment before moving to Minette's side. "Madame de Bernay has spoken well of you," he said as his gaze continued to hold her eyes. "Will you remain in France for an extended time?"

"A month or two, I expect."

"Lieutenant, time to get back to the board," the general interrupted.

"Ladies, please excuse us. Duty encroaches." The lieutenant bowed to Janine and Minette.

"Of course." Minette smiled in dismissal before turning to Janine. "Come this way. We won't be disturbed in the library."

The elegant paneled walls and coffered ceiling gave the room they entered a welcoming ambiance. A huge desk with bookshelves on each side was the focal point of one side of the room. A large fireplace counter-balanced the other end and invited conversation in deep leather chairs placed invitingly before the hearth. A large table and chairs separated the room into two distinct areas, one for work and one for relaxation. A large Aubusson rug with splashes of jewel-toned flowers and leaves on a rich cream blanket of fine, handwoven wool covered much of the parquet floor.

Minette offered a chair to Janine. After giving a tug to the bell pull, she sat down across from her.

Looking with interest around the room, Janine noticed that the bookshelves contained very few books. Most of the volumes appeared to be new and unread, except for a small group on one shelf.

"It's so good to have you here," Minette effervesced. "Tell me about New Orleans. It must be primitive. Oh, you poor thing . . . enough of that," she cried, not waiting for an answer. "Now that you're here, will you stay?"

"That's not my plan. Charles and I will marry in New Orleans. But I do hope we make our home here. I'll try to persuade him to resist his parents' wish that he join their well-established mercantile business."

"No!" Minette gasped. "You deserve better than a . . . bourgeois . . . life."

"Minette, you of all people know times have changed. We all must find new means of livelihood."

"Chérie, that's what I am saying, your future is here. Things have changed and France now provides many opportunities for the fortunate few who avail themselves."

"How so?" Janine asked.

The sound of clattering wheels interrupted their quiet conversation. A light tap announced the presence of a maid pushing a teacart laden with an assortment of pastries and a monogrammed silver coffee service. The scent of freshly brewed coffee blended with that of oranges.

"Merci, that will be all now," Minette said. The girl curtsied and left the room while Minette poured two cups of coffee. "Cream and sugar?"

"Just cream, thank you."

After adding cream, Minette handed Janine the cup and a small plate before offering the tray of pastries.

Janine selected a honey and grated orange rind-coated pastry and another one topped with a drizzle of chocolate. She savored the scent and anticipation of fine pastries after her meager diet.

Minette settled back in the leather chair. "Napoleon holds my husband in high esteem and determined a wife from the old aristocracy would be a great asset to him. Monsieur Talleyrand persuaded me that such a marriage would benefit me greatly and also would make use of my many social skills." She cradled the delicate cup in her hands, took a sip of the steaming, pale brown beverage, paused, and looked expectantly at Janine.

Uncomfortable with the direction of the conversation, Janine wondered what she could add. What could she say? "I hope you have found Monsieur Talleyrand's words to be true."

"Oui, my husband is satisfactory in many ways. He's quite unlike Lenoir, who is from an aristocratic family. I presume you noticed he is more polished than my François. Do you find the lieutenant pleasing?"

"Pleasing? He seems pleasant enough." *A bit too charming?* "I've only met him this afternoon."

"Pleasant . . . and on his way to becoming one of Napoleon's select group of advisors. François says he has a bright future."

Taking a deep breath, Janine asked the question that had been on the tip of her tongue since they'd come to the library. "Minette, why did you forsake my uncle?" There, she'd asked it.

Her voice quavering, Minette said, "Oh, God, *chérie*, it wasn't like that. I was in Paris, about to be arrested, when I had a chance to leave."

"I thought you just up and left . . . that you didn't care what happened to him."

"I knew of Alexandre's plan to emigrate to England with you. He insisted that I leave at the first opportunity. That's why I did. I waited and waited for him, certain he'd come. But as things got worse in France, I gave up hope that he had survived. He's dead, isn't he?" The tears in Minette's eyes revealed the depth of her pain.

Janine nodded. "Oui." Close to tears herself, Janine sought to change the subject. She didn't have the strength to tell Minette about seeing her uncle murdered . . . or about the imposter who had claimed his identity. "What time are the guests expected this evening?"

Minette raised and lowered her hands. "Not until seven. I've allowed time for our visit before their arrival."

"I'm afraid I won't be able to stay for the games and dinner tonight. I must leave before seven," Janine's anxiety about being alone after dark overrode her excitement about the social gathering. In her enthusiasm to accept Minette's invitation, she hadn't thought about the coachman taking her to the disreputable hotel. She'd have to ask to be let off at the cathedral and walk to her lodgings.

29

"Why must you be back by seven? Can't you stay the night?" Minette asked.

"I have an early morning appointment with the abbé."

"Then promise you'll come for dinner tomorrow and stay the night."

"I can't promise. I may be at Chateau Fleury, taking care of some business matters." Janine couldn't bring herself to ask Minette to go with her.

"Well then, as soon as you can, you must come," Minette said. "Let my dressmaker know. I'll see her tomorrow afternoon, and if you're free we'll ride back together."

"I wish I knew whether the abbé has arranged a visit to the chateau." Janine took a deep breath. "Will you come with me if he has?"

Chapter 5

The powdery gray of twilight slipped into the blackness of night. By the time the carriage crossed the bridge on its way to the cathedral, shades of midnight blanketed the town, pierced only by a splattering of yellow specks from gaslights on the bridge and on a few of the main streets. A flickering light to the right along the quay marked the location of the Grand Hotel. So close, yet Janine must not stop the coach. She would walk from the cathedral to the hotel this one time but promised herself to learn from her mistake. A respectable place to stay must be found before she visited Minette again.

The coach rolled to a stop and the coachman pulled open the door. As he extended his hand to help Janine alight, he hesitated. "You did say you want to be let off here, didn't you?"

"Yes, thank you." Janine turned and walked toward the cathedral before stopping to watch the carriage disappear into the night. She took some comfort from the thought that Minette might go with her to Chateau Fleury.

She shivered, although the night air held no chill. Pride had prompted her foolish decision to disembark from the de Bernay coach near the cathedral so she could walk to—the not so grand—Grand Hotel by the quay. She made her way toward her cheap lodging, taking care to seek any lighted areas she could find. A faint silhouette of a man and a woman moved ahead of her. Their voices carried in the night air until they disappeared around a corner.

She breathed a sigh of relief when the hotel came into view. No one in sight—almost there. What was that—a twig snapping? The hairs on the back of her neck rose, freezing her in place. Rustling noises came from the bushes. A stray animal or . . .

Rough hands tightened around her neck and pulled her into the bulky torso of a scruffy man. He smelled of rotting refuse percolating in alcohol. Inebriated!

"Stop struggling or I'll knock you silly," he growled as his grip tightened.

Falling, falling into blackness, no awareness until she heard a familiar voice.

"*Mon Dieu.* What is *she* doing here? Mademoiselle de Fleury . . . Janine, can you hear me?" She felt herself cradled against a warm body while hands examined tender spots on her neck and arms.

Janine opened her eyes and looked up into the sapphire blue eyes of Etienne Tremeau—the hypnotic eyes that never failed to cause her heart to flutter. "Where am I?" she murmured.

"Outside the Grand Hotel."

She tried to sit up but fell back into the security of Etienne's arms. She sensed his strength now as she had when he had helped her to escape during the Revolution. With a tremble she recalled the foul beast that had pounced from the shadows, dragged and choked her. Where was her attacker? How could Etienne have known? What would he think she was doing in such a disreputable place? She *cared* what he thought—more than she liked to admit.

From the darkness the drunkard whined to the burly man tying his arms behind him. "Citizen, don't take me to prison. I can explain. That strumpet tried to steal my bag." He called to Etienne, "Citizen, help me. You believe me, don't you? I swear it's true."

"Shut up before I have you gagged, you miserable liar," Etienne said.

Janine felt the tension in his muscular arms as he spoke, an edge to his otherwise controlled baritone voice. What was he thinking?

"There he is." A young soldier spoke to a *gendarme* who had accompanied him to the place where the drunk stood, guarded by the other soldier. The policeman pulled the prisoner to his feet, manacled him, and pushed him toward the bridge. "Keep a watch on him while I get her story," he ordered the other officer who accompanied him. Turning to Janine, he asked, "What happened?"

She felt the moral support of Etienne's hand on her arm as he guided her to a bench and sat beside her while she gave her account of the attack.

When she stopped speaking, the policeman gestured toward her then toward Etienne. "Colonel Tremeau, you know her? Shall I seek care for her or . . ."

"I'll make arrangements for the lady." Etienne thrust his arm in the direction of the prisoner, said, "Take him away," and then turned to his two companions. "Get a carriage. Also, I'll need a place to stay for a few days." The two soldiers hurried to do his bidding.

Filled with embarrassment at being found in such an unseemly location, Janine summoned her courage. At least he didn't seem to think poorly of her. "Etienne, I'm staying at this hotel. Will you help me inside?"

He stared at her and shook his head. "Absolutely not. This is no place for a lady."

Janine lifted her eyes to meet his. "I intend to leave here as soon as I find another place."

"You don't have to justify yourself to me. It will take a day or so for you to recover from this and you must have someone to care for you during that time. I will take you to stay with my mother and sister. They will tend to your needs." Etienne took her hand and gave it a squeeze. "It will be all right."

Tears threatened to spill down her cheeks; a spark remained of the Etienne she remembered. His chivalry reminded her of her father, whom she had dearly loved and admired. "I cannot. You have no place for me."

"You'll have the use of my room. I'll stay in town with my aide de camp, Adrien Fortier."

Janine felt helpless and vulnerable but didn't want Etienne to feel sorry for her. After all, he was a Republican and she an aristocratic royalist. She forced herself to sit up and move away. She couldn't trust herself while so close to him. "I don't know how to thank you."

The spell was broken. "Well, don't then." He stood and strode away from her toward the bridge, a tall figure with broad shoulders as erect as if marching in one of Bonaparte's victory parades. Suddenly, Etienne turned back toward her, his golden-brown hair highlighted as he passed under one of the few gaslights along the quay.

As he approached, Janine stood and faced him. "This is the second time you've rescued me," she said as he drew close to her. "I'm sorry to be so much trouble."

He shrugged and took a step back. "You're more trouble to yourself than you are to me."

"You may be right." She stared at him and wondered why she couldn't find words to entice him to speak more freely.

"Just remember," he said, moving closer, "the third time I may not be there. You must learn to be careful."

Janine dared to hope that he would always be there if he could. That was the kind of man he was. If only he wouldn't be so guarded with her. "I hope the next time I can do something for you instead," she said with utmost sincerity.

Upon the arrival of the carriage, Etienne eased Janine inside and climbed in beside her. He rolled up his lightweight jacket and put it behind her head. "How's that?" He leaned close and with tenderness brushed his hand across her brow. "Shall I adjust it?"

She nodded. "Umm, that's nice," she said and relaxed into the comfort of his presence. It felt so right to be with him. To her he wasn't Napoleon's colonel, but her Etienne of long ago. She chided herself for her wishful thinking. Her time in New Orleans had proven she was strong, and she realized she must continue to rely upon herself. Etienne *was* Napoleon's colonel now, whether she liked it or not.

Although they remained silent and Etienne looked out of the side window most of the way to the Tremeau home, just having him there was enough.

When Etienne led Janine into the house, Madame Tremeau and Anne stared, their first looks of surprise changing to ones of concern.

Madam Tremeau paled. "I'm so sorry. I knew I shouldn't have let you stay at that dreadful hotel. It's no place for a respectable young woman. If only . . ."

"What in God's name are you talking about?" Etienne swung around to face his mother. "It's not your fault."

She put her hands on her hips. "I let her go to that hotel." She hastened to add, "I've arranged for her to stay at Madame Parot's house after her son leaves for the army next week. But still . . ."

Etienne shook his head. "Don't just stand there staring. She's bruised and hurt. Anne, escort Janine to my room. *Mère*, bring a cool cloth and bandages," he ordered as he went into his room. His mother and sister rushed into action, doing as he bid.

Within moments Anne helped Janine into the room. Etienne pulled the sheet off the cot and grabbed a clean one from a nearby shelf, tucking it in around the mattress.

Janine lay down on the small bed, grateful to be off her wobbly legs. Her throat hurt and the cuts and bruises throbbed. In spite of her discomfort, she found interest in the orderliness of the room—a reflection of the man. The sparsely furnished room was immaculate. No clothing carelessly draped on the chair, and papers on the small writing table by the window were neatly stacked.

Madame Tremeau entered, carrying a tray with ribbons of clean cotton fabric and a bottle of fragrant lavender oil. She applied a little of the oil to Janine's temples. "This is for your headache, and it will soothe your abrasions, too." She swabbed the oil on the red, scraped skin on Janine's arm.

Random thoughts flitted through Janine's mind—thoughts of that long-ago time when Etienne and his mother had cared for her at this very house. Tonight, she had glimpsed the Etienne she remembered. She'd always have a soft place in her heart for him. But she reminded herself that this was also Colonel Tremeau, who freely gave commands he had undoubtedly learned in Bonaparte's army. It was all too tiring. She flinched as Madame Tremeau daubed more oil on her open cuts.

"In a few days, she'll be healing nicely," Madame said as she bandaged the last of the lacerations.

"I'll leave her in your care then." Etienne opened a drawer, pulled out a change of clothes, and placed them in a leather satchel.

"Where will you be?" Anne asked her brother as she came into the room. She carried a cup of lavender tea, which she handed to Janine. "Drink this. It's soothing and will help you sleep."

"At Adrien's for the night," Etienne said to his sister. He squeezed Janine's hand. "Get some rest. I'll look in on you in a day or two."

Janine opened her eyes and lifted her head from the pillow. "Thank you again for your kindness," Her voice was hoarse and filled with emotion.

"Think nothing of it." Etienne left the room with Anne, speaking to her in a hushed tone.

Janine couldn't resist comparing the warmth the Tremeau family had shown her in her time of need to the lack of compassion demonstrated by Charles' family. The Duprés had treated her like a poor relation, tolerated but with no trace of true affection. Since leaving Chateau Fleury, she'd known little tender, loving care. In those years no doubt her heart had hardened as she fended for herself in Louisiana. Perhaps she'd lost a part of herself. She didn't know. Each day she'd made an effort to appease Madame Dupré while trying to seize opportunities that came her way. She'd been desperate for a real family once again. Burning moisture gathered in her eyes as she fought the urge to give in to self-pity.

Anne returned to the room, carrying a plain white nightgown and a clean dress. She laid the gown on the foot of the bed and hung up the dress. "I brought you one of my nightdresses to wear and a clean frock for morning. Is there anything else I can do for you before I go?"

"Merci, non. I'll try to sleep now." Janine closed her eyes and tried to still her mind, hoping for slumber to steal her away.

The next morning Janine sat on the edge of the cot and waited a few moments before swinging her legs over the side. *Good.* She didn't hurt anywhere. She welcomed the light of day so that she could see and assess her bruises. The small mirror above the table revealed ugly, reddish-purple marks on her throat. She lifted the larger of the two bandages; the most serious cut had closed. With relief she removed the bandage and then decided to remove the other one as well. She slipped out of the nightgown and into her dress. A final check in the mirror reflected the ugly bruise on her neck—the garment didn't hide it. She'd have to remedy that somehow; perhaps Anne had a scarf she could use until she could buy fabric at the dressmaker's shop. And while there she would leave a message for Minette.

A soft tap at the door was followed by the sound of Anne's voice. "May I come in?"

Janine opened the door and welcomed her. "I'm much better today," she said and took the tray of tea and sweets from her, wondering whether Etienne was in the house. "Thank you."

"You're dressed already. And have removed your bandages, too." Anne shook her head and winced. "The bruise on your neck will take some time to disappear."

"I know. Do you have a scarf I may wear until I can get to the dressmaker's shop for some new fabric?"

Anne moved toward the door. "I'll get one for you." In a few minutes she returned with a scarf in shades of pinks and beige and held it up to Janine's dress. "This one is pretty with your dress. Do you like it?"

Janine wrapped it around her neck, adjusting it to cover her bruises. "Perfect. Now I'm presentable." She took another look in the mirror and turned to Anne. "I must go to town today, but first I want to help you around the house."

"Let's see how you feel after you've been up and around for a while," Anne said on her way out.

Alone again, Janine sat down, sipped her tea, and allowed her thoughts to linger on Etienne. She must not read too much into his attention to her the previous night. Still, she'd seen a man who warranted her admiration. She strained to hear a muffled conversation from somewhere in the house. *Etienne?* She placed the cup on the saucer and picked up the tray. She'd go to the kitchen and see for herself.

Alone in the kitchen, Madame Tremeau frowned when Janine appeared. "What are you doing out here? You should rest."

"I'm much better this morning. My nose led me toward the inviting smell of fresh coffee."

"Of course." Madame nodded, took the pot from the back of the stove, and poured a cup. "Just for you," she said as she handed it to Janine.

"I thought I heard Etienne's voice. Is he here?"

"Oui. He's in the garden."

A sudden impulse to see him prompted Janine to say, "I think I'll join him." She gulped the hot beverage, not waiting for a reply, and went through the kitchen into an enclosed porch leading outside. The perfume of lavender sweetened the air. Flowers hung from the rafters to dry, and lavender wreaths, bundles, and sachets in various states of completion lay on a table in a corner.

Janine paused at the garden gate, shading her eyes while searching for Etienne in the expansive, lush garden. A gentle breeze carried the scent of lavender in its wake. Opening the gate, she started along the graveled path past row after row of lavender plants on her left. To her right, raised beds of green beans, leeks, chard, and spinach flourished. Farther along the way flowers created a burst of rainbow colors. Where was he? She began to think he wasn't there, but she wandered on anyway.

As she neared the end of the path, she walked among hollyhocks in full bloom, buzzing bees the only sound heard, until she reached a shaded, verdant retreat of grass complete with three chairs. Rewarded for her persistence, she found Etienne seated there with his eyes closed.

"Bonjour," she said softly.

Opening his eyes, he stared at the scarf she wore around her bruised neck. "Bonjour. How are you this morning?" he asked with little enthusiasm.

"Much better, merci." She sat in the chair across from him, although he had not invited her to do so.

Etienne adjusted his chair so as not to face her. "You'd better go back inside. Tomorrow is soon enough to venture out."

Janine wouldn't be dismissed so easily. "You have an abundance of lavender plants here."

"It seems you plan to ignore my suggestion that you return to the house." Etienne stood and stared down at her.

"I'd feel much better if you'd humor me. Please sit down and talk to me."

He shook his head but put up his hands in surrender and did as she asked. "My sister has a lavender business," he said, keeping his eyes averted.

"She must stay busy. At least half the garden is dedicated to it."

"She's made a success of it," he said, a chill in his voice. "Her wares sell well at market."

"It's important to find a marketable talent."

Turning to look her, he challenged. "How would you know?"

Janine quelled the urge to get up and leave. "Because *I* have done just that!"

"You? What talent might that be? Hosting royalist sympathizers?"

"Do you think I am devoid of ingenuity?" How bitter he was. Did he think she had taken her silver spoon to New Orleans and lived a life of luxury? "In New Orleans I was thrust into another world far from the protection and safety of life at Chateau Fleury—the only life I had known."

"Come now. You had the support of the Dupré family."

"They didn't coddle me. Rather, they put me to work. I wanted something more than being a governess. I need security and stability in my life."

Etienne studied her for a brief moment. "So . . . you started some sort of business?"

"Yes, I did. I used my talent for designing dresses and developed my skills with the needle."

"I suppose it's a bitter pill to swallow for an aristocratic lady born to wealth and privilege. Most people are fortunate to keep body and soul together and are grateful for the chance to do so."

Why did he direct his resentment of aristocrats toward her? She gulped to contain her indignation. "You should know it's unwise to make hasty judgments."

He raised a brow. "Not in all cases. Rapid judgment is necessary on the battlefield."

"This is no battlefield. We are not enemies."

"I wager you hope for the restoration of the Bourbons to the throne." He spoke sardonically and cast a skeptical look in her direction.

"Well, I . . ."

"Are you so naïve as to not know the Bourbon princes are only interested in reinstating their privileges and that of the aristocracy? The peasants and bourgeoisie be damned!" Etienne clenched his fists. "You can't really believe things could return to the old ways. There have been too many changes for that to happen. King Louis accepted a constitution." Etienne stood, shoving his chair back against the fence. "There is no point in discussing this any further."

How had she let the conversation deteriorate so before asking the one question on her mind? Placing her hand on Etienne's arm to prevent him from storming off, Janine asked softly, "How long were you in New Orleans?"

He looked at her sharply and Janine was afraid he would not answer. But finally, after a long pause, he said, "Almost two years."

"Did it occur to you to look me up?"

"Non, it did not. Why would I?"

Maybe because you cared about what happened to me? But keeping that thought to herself, aloud Janine merely said, "And what about you, Etienne Tremeau? Are you contemplating marriage, or are you only contracted to Napoleon Bonaparte?"

"All you need to know is that my first concern is for the

Republic. I wish to be of service to protect and further the principles of equality and liberty for all citizens."

"You haven't answered my question about whether you have a special lady in your life."

"You asked whether I am contemplating marriage, *not* whether there were any women in my life."

"Why won't you answer my questions?"

"You really should not concern yourself about the women in this *peasant* boy's life." Jaw set, he rose from his chair. "You expressed a desire to pick up a few items in town today. Just for you, I'll arrange for a carriage to take you there this afternoon and have the driver wait to return you here." He turned and walked toward the house.

Janine watched him leave the garden and disappear between rows of *maïs*. She made sure to stay in the garden long enough for the family to finish their breakfast. By the time she returned to the kitchen, she found Anne there alone, stirring a large copper pot on the big iron stove.

Anne looked up and replaced the lid. "I'm making stew," she explained, wiping her hands. "Etienne said you are going to stay with us a while longer. I'm glad he's being kind."

"I am, too. I'm happy we had a short time to talk this morning. And he's sending a carriage to take me to town this afternoon. Would you like to come?"

"I wish I could . . . but I can't leave while mother is away. What will you do there?"

"I'll stop by the dressmaker's shop for threads and fabric for a scarf or two, get my things from the hotel and, if time permits, stop by to see Abbé Dillon."

"I've been saving my market money to buy fabric for a new dress." Anne blushed and looked at her hands. "Adrien, one of Etienne's officers, has been courting me. While Etienne is here, he and his lady will escort us to a concert. I don't even have fabric yet, and my dress must be ready within six weeks."

His lady echoed in Janine's ears.

Chapter 6

After lunch and the kitchen tidied, Janine sat across the table from Anne and worked on her final sketch of the gown she'd promised to make for her. She envied the young woman's joy as they decided on the style and color of her gala attire.

Janine moved her chair closer to Anne and arranged three drawings so Anne could see them. "The cornflower blue gown will bring attention to your blue eyes. Or this pale gold one will emphasize the highlights in your hair." Janine pointed her left index finger at the first sketch and then the other before continuing to put the final touches on the last one. "Either shade goes well with your sun-kissed complexion."

After a final flourish of peach-tinted chalk, Janine handed the third drawing to Anne. "This one seems to be your favorite color. You selected it from among all the others."

"I love them all, but I know I may only have one. By morning I'll have made my choice." Anne thumbed through the drawings and placed them in a neat pile. "May I keep them until then?"

"Of course. We'll take the one you pick with us tomorrow and select the fabric," Janine said as she gathered up her drawing supplies.

"I can hardly wait." Anne's smile was quickly replaced with a frown. "I can't imagine what's taking Etienne so long."

"I hope there isn't a problem," Janine replied. After a moment she took a sheet of paper from her supply and began writing.

> *My dear Minette,*
> *Please accept my deepest apology for my tardy communication to you.*
> *Unfortunately, I am recovering from minor injuries I sustained after I left your home. I will be with the Tremeau family for the rest of the week. After which time, I will be in touch with you.*
> *Best regards,*

Janine signed it and wrote Minette's name across the front of the folded sheet then stood, her head tilted to the side. "I heard a noise outside. Maybe the coach has arrived." She hurried from the kitchen to the front room, Anne following behind.

Just as they reached the entryway, the door opened and they saw Etienne holding it for Madame Tremeau to enter first. "There's been a change of plans," he said when he saw Janine. "If you're ready, we can leave now."

Although aloof, he had come for her himself. Janine lost no time with questions. It didn't matter; at least they'd be together. She gathered her bag and shawl and walked with him to the street. A small, two-person, uncovered cart pulled by a single horse stood nearby, unlike the large coach she had expected.

Etienne watched her reaction. "I hope this lowly mode of transportation is acceptable." He took her hand and helped her to the burlap-covered seat. "The blacksmith hadn't finished shoeing the team of horses when I left."

"Of course it is." Janine assured him then cast a wary eye toward the dark clouds to the west.

As if in response to her unspoken concern, he said, "I'll keep an eye on the weather. You best begin with your most pressing business. We may not get to all of the stops you'd like."

Puddles of muddy water lined the sides of the road as they drove into town. "Has it been raining in town too?" she asked.

"A shower moved through about an hour ago. It looks as though it's heading north, away from us."

"It missed here all together." She pondered whether she should check out of the hotel before going to the dressmaker's shop—while with Etienne. "Let's go to the hotel first, please. I need to get my things and leave that place."

"To the hotel," he repeated.

"Will you come inside with me?" she asked, giving him a sideways glance.

He nodded. "It is better you not go there unaccompanied."

The cart turned the corner and followed the river toward the hotel. Whiffs of rotting fish, animal waste, and other disagreeable odors wafted toward them on gusts of wind. Along the quay a beehive of activity took on a sense of urgency. Men shouted at children to speed up cleaning the piles of fish stacked around them. Others loaded wagons with hay and pieces of driftwood. In the distance the shabby hotel, with its peeling paint and dangling sign, presented a dismal

Janine felt an urge to escape as quickly as possible. "I'll be relieved to leave this unsavory hotel and the waterfront's disease and sickness. In New Orleans I go to great lengths to avoid the docks."

Etienne made no comment, merely called, "Whoa," and pulled on the reins, commanding the horse to stop in front of the hotel where he tethered it to a post.

Etienne sauntered around the lobby while Janine went to the desk and rang the bell on the counter. A man with several days' growth of gray whiskers ambled from an anteroom to the shabby but once elegant front desk.

"Monsieur, I plan to check out today and need the key to gather my belongings from the room." Janine gestured to the rows of keys on hooks behind the desk.

The man leered at her. "Your services needed elsewhere? There is no refund if you leave early."

She adjusted the scarf around her neck. Could he see her bruises? "I was assured at registration that I would be charged only for the actual days I stayed. The rest was a required advance deposit."

"There is no refund and that's that." He leaned across the counter, making no move to give her the key.

"I asked you for the key." She tried to speak with authority.

Etienne approached the counter. "Citizen, do as the lady asks, right now."

"Oui, citizen . . . monsieur." The clerk struggled to regain his balance after tripping on his chair. He took the key from the hook, opened a lockbox, removed three silver coins, and handed them to Janine.

Bang. Clang. Boom. Sounds of metal on metal preceded the appearance through the curtained passage to the anteroom of the bulging apparition of a woman carrying an iron skillet in one hand. She stomped her foot as she glared at the man. "I heard what you said . . . you cowardly little weasel." She lumbered around the counter, grabbed Janine's arm, and jerked it behind her back. "Thief, give me those ill-gotten coins. Or must I take them?"

43

Before Janine found her voice, Etienne forced the hag's hand from Janine's arm and placed himself between them. The woman raised the pan to hit him, but he knocked it from her hand. She lunged at him and grazed the side of his face with stubby fingernails.

"Stop! Citizen, no, he's Bonaparte's man," the desk clerk cried with alarm. He turned to Etienne, "Please, citizen . . . she doesn't know what she's doing. She's been sick. We don't want any trouble."

Etienne ignored him. "Let's go," he instructed Janine.

They climbed the squeaky stairs, long past their prime, and went to her room. She opened a small case and removed a thin strip of lightweight fabric and a little tin of ointment. "Let me put something on that scratch."

Etienne took the ointment from her hand. "Get your things. I'll take care of this."

"As you wish." She collected her meager possessions while Etienne cleaned his scratches. When she was ready he carried her two bags downstairs and waited for her by the door. There was no one at the reception desk, but she heard muffled voices from behind the curtain to the back room. Placing the key on the counter, Janine hurried to join Etienne. On their way to the cart, she looked up at the sky. "Is it safe to make another stop?"

"One more. The rain seems to be continuing north for the time being."

"I'll be able to complete a scarf or maybe two tonight. I'm sure Anne needs the one she loaned me," Janine said, trying to make conversation. But sensing Etienne's impatience with her chatter, she remained silent during the rest of the ride. He didn't seem to notice.

Without a word between them, Etienne brought the horse and cart to a stop in front of the dressmaker's shop. "I'll return within the hour. Be ready to leave."

Janine felt rushed as she went inside to select fabrics. "Bonjour, Madame," she said to the seamstress who rested her feet on a footstool while stitching a garment.

"May I help with anything?"

"Not at the moment, thank you. I'll let you know when I'm

ready."

Abruptly setting her work aside, the seamstress opened a drawer. "I almost forgot. I have a note for you from Madame de Bernay." She handed Janine the envelope bearing the de Bernay seal.

Janine opened it and read that Minette had been to the dressmaker's earlier in the day and was disappointed not to have heard from her. She took the letter she'd written to Minette from her bag and laid it on the table by the dressmaker. "Please give this to Madame de Bernay when you see her." Janine returned to the fabrics and selected a silk one for scarves and material for appliqués to cover the mended rips on her soiled dress.

At the counter she reviewed her bill of sale. Satisfied with her purchases, she paid for them with a silver coin.

The woman lovingly ran her fingers across the pale yellow silk cloth. "This will make into a beautiful scarf or large collar. You did say you're using it for a scarf, didn't you?" She folded the ivory-colored cotton organdy without comment.

"Yes, I did."

As she prepared to wrap the cloth in thin pink paper, the proprietress picked up the fabric Janine had chosen for appliqués. "What do you plan to make with this one? You know a scarf or collar made from this will not go well with many dresses."

"It is ideal for appliqués for one of my dresses." Janine detected doubt in the woman's eyes as she studied Janine's dress and the scarf she had borrowed from Anne. *She means well.*

Janine picked up her package and went to the door. Etienne paced near the horse and cart. She thought better of her impulse to keep him waiting. No point in irritating him further. She gave a brief wave to the seamstress, who had returned to her sewing, and went outside.

Etienne reached the cart ahead of her. He took her package, put it under one arm, and helped her to her seat. He said nothing until they were well on their way. "We have time to stop at Madame Parot's. Would you like to do so?"

"I do want to meet her, but it's not necessary today. I've already taken too much of your time," she said dryly.

"Best take care of it today." After continuing a short distance along the street toward the Tremeau home, he stopped the horse in front of a small brown house.

"This is it? Your mother and I passed it on our walk a few days ago."

Irregular shaped stepping-stones led through the shaggy grass to the maroon front door. Etienne knocked. When no one answered, he called again. "Madame Parot, it's Etienne."

The door creaked open and a small gray-haired woman with red eyes stood before them. "Come in." She led them into a small, dark sitting room. Curtains pulled across the window made it difficult to see after being in the daylight. "Please sit down. May I get you a cup of tea?"

"Non, merci. We don't have long to stay," Etienne responded for the two of them. "This is Janine de Fleury—Mère spoke to you about her."

"Oh, yes. How do you do?" The woman fidgeted with her hair. "Please excuse me. I'll be but a moment while I take the kettle off the stove." She hurried from the room, pulling a handkerchief from her pocket and wiping her eyes.

"Her son left for the army today. She's having a hard time with it," Etienne whispered to Janine.

The older woman returned, still clutching the tattered fabric, and sat across from them. "Madame Tremeau told me of your need for a room. I have one if you are interested." Wringing her hands, she blinked back tears.

"Madame Parot, I am interested in the room when it is convenient for you to have me come."

A wild look swept across the woman's face before she jumped up and rushed to Etienne, tears streaming down her face. "You're a colonel now." She sat down in his lap like a frightened child. "You must promise me you will protect my son and bring him home to me. He's just a lad."

"Madame, you know I cannot promise, but I will do anything I can for him."

A slight smile offered welcome relief from her sad eyes. "I'm relying on you." She stood up and turned to Janine, staring at her as if seeing her for the first time. "*Demain, Oui.* You may come tomorrow. We can discuss the arrangements then."

The woman was obviously distraught and Janine felt she might be suffering from a nervous disorder. "I'm not sure about tomorrow," she hedged, not ready to make a commitment. "I'll contact you later."

Etienne stared at her in disbelief. "Later? You need a room now." He stood and spoke to Madame Parot. "We'd best go now. She'll contact you soon."

Troubled, Janine wondered, *Did Etienne stop by earlier this very day and make arrangements with Madame Parot?* Perhaps he wanted his room back or just wanted her out of his house.

Janine and Etienne left the house and rode the short distance to the Tremeaus' in silence. Upon arrival, Etienne helped Janine from the cart, then without a word he climbed back into his seat.

Startled, Janine asked, "Aren't you coming inside?"

"Non." He looked straight ahead with an annoyed expression and cracked his whip.

How could Etienne want her to stay with such a nervous woman? Janine realized she had a dilemma. She had nowhere else to go and must rely upon the good graces of the Tremeaus.

Chapter 7

At the dressmaker's shop the next day, Janine had trouble keeping her mind focused on Anne and the fabric selection for the new ball gown. Two worrisome matters put a damper on what should have been a pleasant morning: Chateau Fleury and Madame Parot.

"This one! It's perfect. What do you think?" Anne's fingertips caressed the pale peach fabric and she gave Janine an imploring look.

"It's beautiful and just the right color." Janine smiled at Anne's beaming face. She wouldn't allow her problems to interfere with Anne's special day.

"Oh, yes, it's lovely," the seamstress concurred, taking the fabric from Anne's outstretched hands.

"We'll take it," Janine said. It was easy to get caught up in Anne's excitement. After she had paid the shop owner, Janine handed the package to Anne and together they left the shop. Pausing outside by the door, Janine said, "While you're at the marketplace, I'll call on the abbé. What time shall we meet?"

"Be at the square at five o'clock," Anne said and moved toward the center of town.

"I will." Janine watched Anne's slight figure, the precious package promising a fairytale evening tucked under her arm, grow smaller as she walked away. Then she started toward the cathedral, her thoughts focused on Chateau Fleury.

"Bonjour, Abbé Dillon," Janine greeted the old man, relieved to find him in his usual place."

"Good day to you. Are you enjoying your time with us?" The abbé stood and stretched before sitting again. "It seems everyone knows where to find me in the early afternoon. It is an ideal meeting place, wouldn't you agree?"

"Yes . . . on days like this." She reveled in the scents, sounds, and sights around her: the perfume of roses, bird songs, and the massive, spire-topped cathedral.

The abbé cleared his throat. "I've spoken to the caretaker of Chateau Fleury on your behalf. He says the comte's strict instructions forbid visitors at the estate in his absence."

Wondering what her next move should be, Janine turned at

48

hearing the crunch of footsteps on the gravel path.

"There you are." Minette rushed along the path toward Janine, waving her hand as she approached. "Good day, Abbé Dillon." She turned to Janine. "Your note speaks of an injury. My coachman knows nothing about it. What happened?"

"I'll tell you later. I'm better now, but I've just received some disturbing news from the abbé. He said the caretaker won't receive me at Chateau Fleury. Now what?"

Abbé Dillon looked skyward as if in supplication to the Lord. "I . . . I . . . perhaps I can persuade him to allow you to look around outside—if I come with you."

Hands on her hips, Minette said, "Don't be ridiculous. That's the least he can do. I'll take you. Abbé Dillon, you get word to the caretaker that Janine and I will be there at ten o'clock tomorrow morning."

"Madame de Bernay, I don't, eh . . . I think it will be much better if I accompany you."

"Meet us there then. Good day, Abbé Dillon." Minette turned to Janine. "Let's go."

"Perhaps we'll see you at Chateau Fleury," Janine said, wondering whether he would make the trip. She turned to Minette. "I have a couple hours before I'm to meet Anne Tremeau."

As they left the garden, Minette walked ahead of Janine like a woman with a purpose. "Where will you meet her? We'll give her a ride home."

"She's at the marketplace. But I can ride back to the house with Anne and her mother."

"The Tremeau family. Now there's an interesting story," Minette mused aloud.

"In what way?"

"Colonel Tremeau is a steadfast Jacobin. In the early days of the Revolution, his affiliation served him well. But his Republican ideals need to be tempered in today's political climate." Her eyebrows lifted and she held Janine's gaze as they passed through an arch leading to the street.

The coachman stood by the carriage and opened the door. "Where do you wish to go, madame?"

"To the townhouse."

"Oui, madame."

"The townhouse? You have a house here?" Janine asked.

"We do. François finds it convenient for meetings with his officers and other dignitaries." After they got underway, Minette continued talking about Etienne. "Bonaparte still trusts and relies on the colonel. But if he doesn't adjust to the changes in Bonaparte, he'll find himself out of favor."

Janine wished Minette would move to another topic. She still smarted from Etienne's behavior at Madame Parot's. Besides, she wanted to explain to Minette about the imposter at Chateau Fleury. "I'm sure Colonel Tremeau understands what is expected of him."

The carriage lurched as the driver guided the horses into a narrow space between two buildings.

"That didn't take long, did it?" Minette turned to Janine. The two climbed down from the coach, and Minette led Janine along a side path to the front of the house. She lifted the knocker of the large, carved wooden door and let it fall. "It may take a while for someone to get to the door. The valet and his wife are the only staff we keep here."

After a few minutes the door opened wide. "Madame. Come in." The valet stepped to the side, allowing them entry. "Will you be staying for dinner?"

"No. Just bring some cakes and tea to the salon. That will be all, thank you."

Janine chose to sit in an overstuffed chair facing a large stone fireplace adorned with gilt arrow sconces in the style favored by Bonaparte. Minette sat across from her.

"You're staying with the Tremeau family?" Minette raised an eyebrow. "Your note says you were injured. What happened?"

"I don't know where to begin. I know I shouldn't have been out alone after dark, but I was. A drunkard knocked me to the ground. Fortunately, Etienne and several of his officers were passing by and rescued me."

"Hummm, Etienne—first name basis already?" Minette clucked her tongue. "Did you hit your head or twist your ankle or . . ?"

"No serious injuries. I only suffered minor bruises, a slight sprain and cuts. That's all," Janine said. "Perhaps you weren't aware, but I've known Etienne since we were children. He was a precocious child. *Père* was impressed with his gardener's son and invited him to attend my tutoring sessions with me."

"Your father invited him to attend classes with you, and he graduated to become your knight in shining armor?" Minette's eyes narrowed speculatively.

Janine ignored Minette's pointed question, remembering the mischief in Etienne's blue eyes and the thrill of their plots against the tutor. What would her father have said had he known? "Yes, my father was fond of Etienne and felt it would be beneficial for him *and* me."

"At least Etienne benefited. He has come a long way since those days. Janine, you and I have known each other for many years, too." Minette stood and took Janine's hand. "You need to distance yourself from him. Come and stay with me in the country. You'll meet many interesting and important people. Who knows, you may renew some past friendships."

"Why, Minette, how very generous. I'd like that." *She's right, but not for the reason she thinks.* Janine knew she couldn't expect the Tremeaus to take care of her. Etienne had made himself abundantly clear on that score. "There's something you need to know before we go to Chateau Fleury," Janine said, raising her hand.

"What?"

"As you know, my uncle is dead. He was killed by our groomsman, not by the revolutionaries." Janine paused. "A man claiming to be *Comte* Alexandre de Fleury returned from England and now is in possession of Chateau Fleury."

An expression of indignation crossed Minette's face. "He can't be allowed to get away with it."

"No, he can't," Janine echoed.

"We'll get your things from Madame Tremeau's this afternoon. You won't need to impose on them any longer."

"It's not that simple. I'm going to make a gown for Anne for a very special event." Her heart lurched at the thought of the ball and Etienne with *his lady.* "Madame Tremeau has arranged for me to take a room with a neighbor."

"You? You're making a gown? Minette laughed. "*Pardonnez-moi,* it's not that I don't think you can. It is just not a

51

good use of your time. I'll have the seamstress make it instead."

"You don't understand. I promised to make it for her. It is something I am able to do, and I need to show my gratitude for all they've done for me."

"But really, the young lady will appreciate having a professionally made gown. Think how surprised she'll be."

"Minette, my dear friend, there are many things you don't know about me. I *am* a professional dressmaker. I've already designed the dress and I *am* going to make it for Anne."

"You can't mean it."

"Yes, I do. During my years in New Orleans, I established my own design and dressmaking business. Don't look so horrified. You know the Revolution has wrought many changes in people's lives— including mine."

Minette shook her head. "I'm sorry. I had no idea how difficult things were for you. It's strange to think of you as a shopkeeper. You deserve better, and we're going to see that you get it."

"Don't feel sorry for me. I've been blessed to have succeeded in my work."

"I didn't mean it that way. Take the room offered by Madame Tremeau's friend, make the dress, and then come and spend time with me. I need your creative ideas, too. We're having a ball next month, and there is so much to get done."

What have I done? Minette had given her a chance to decline the room at Madame Parot's. Why hadn't she? Would a second visit with Madame Parot change her first impression of the woman?

Chapter 8

The next morning the de Bernay coach moved slowly through thick fog as Janine and Minette made their way to Chateau Fleury. Anxiety rippled through Janine like bolts of lightning through a stormy sky—a faceless threat, menacing and mocking. Although she was silent, her mind was in turmoil. *What remains of my home?*

"You're as quiet as if waiting for the schoolmaster's rod to strike," Minette complained.

Janine shook her head and glanced toward Minette, her fingers intertwined, her knuckles white. "I hope the fog clears by the time we get there."

"Chérie, I am sure it will."

Janine returned to her vigil. She pressed her face on the window and an audible sigh of relief escaped from deep within her throat as the carriage slowed before turning from the road and passing through the open gate to Chateau Fleury.

"So far so good. The abbé must have arranged for our visit. We're inside," Minette said in an upbeat tone.

Janine remained silent as they rounded the first of two curves along the gravel road canopied by the overhanging branches of mature trees. She'd have to wait until they were beyond the second bend before she could hope to see her home. "I wonder if anything is left of the walled rose garden," she mused aloud.

As they came within sight of the chateau, she strained to see it, but the shroud of low-lying cloud cover hid it from view. How would it look? Had it been damaged during the Revolution?

"*La grande dame*—as beautiful as always," Minette exclaimed as the clouds lifted for a brief moment and the majestic limestone chateau came into view. "Do you remember the time I fell into the fountain and got soaked?"

"Oui, sort of. I forget . . . how did it happen?"

Minette shrugged. "I reached for one of the coins on the bottom of the pool and my bracelet fell into the water."

"Oh, yes. I was afraid I'd get into trouble. I looked up at the angel at the top of the fountain and prayed for deliverance—like I always did whenever fearful." Janine shook her head. "If she's still there, I'll ask for help today."

Her friend smiled. "Do you really believe prayers are answered?"

Although much had happened in the intervening years, Janine still maintained her faith in a higher power. "I do . . . more or less. When I was a child, I thought of the walled garden as my own sanctuary."

Just speaking of it, she felt as if she had been transported back in time to the idyllic—sacred to her—setting inside the brick-walled garden. Inside the garden all of her senses would awaken and everything there would blend—the sound of splashing water from the outstretched hands of the glorious angel with the golden wings atop the four-tiered fountain, the delightful fragrance of hundreds of roses and jasmine in full bloom, and the vision of pink, red, and white water lilies floating on the surface of the base fountain pool.

"It was a wonderful place," Minette said, with a faraway look.

"Merci Dieu." Janine's heart thumped as relief flooded over her at the clear view of the familiar and dear-to-her-heart slender towers and high gabled windows of the Italian Renaissance-style chateau. Its stone façade changed from gray to golden as the sun pierced the veil of cloudy vapor.

Drawing closer, the steady crunch-crunch sound of the coach wheels reminded Janine there would be no denying the condition of the house after she'd seen it for herself. Up to this point she had refused to consider what she might find upon her return.

As the clouds gave way to brilliant sunshine, Janine saw no evidence of damage to the exterior of the chateau. Turning her attention to the walled garden, she felt as if a fist had knocked the breath from her—one of the angel's golden wings was missing.

"You see, the house has been spared . . . just as I thought," Minette said.

Janine wiped a tear from her cheek. "It's a miracle."

"Is that a tear of joy?"

Janine nodded. "I'm so thankful my house is intact. But I can't shake a bad feeling about it."

"I don't understand."

"My angel's wing is broken. What does that portend?" Was the imposter a violent man? Was she risking her life by confronting him? Jaw set, she resolved not to give in to fear.

"It's not the end of the world. It can be replaced and be as good

54

as new." Minette proffered with a pat on Janine's hand. "Look over there." She pointed toward the green expanse of the vineyards. "The vines look well cared for."

Janine turned, but her eyes got no further than the limestone stables. A new red brick addition had almost doubled their size. She looked away, remembering her uncle's murder just outside the stable clock tower.

"Whoa, boys. We're here," the coachman spoke to the team. The steady crunch of the wheels on the gravel died away as the coach came to a complete stop in front of Chateau Fleury. The coachman assisted the women in alighting from the coach.

The two women started toward the house together, but then Janine rushed ahead, gazing around her as she went. Looking through the gate into the walled rose garden, she saw years of neglect, the same as that of the brown-spotted lawn. Thankfully, the chateau didn't appear any less beautiful than the day she left. Gardens could be restored or replaced.

"Wait for me." Minette rushed to catch up with Janine.

Janine forced herself to look back at the stables and the old kitchen garden. In the twinkling of an eye, she was back in time to the day when, just outside the building, she had seen the groomsman drive a knife deep into her uncle's chest. A year earlier the Revolution had stolen her parents from her, leaving her an orphan dependent on her uncle.

She pulled away from the horrible memories and focused on the familiar pattern of vineyards far and near. At least they weren't in ruin. Visions of happier times soothed the ache in her heart. She treasured the infrequent times with her father when he had come home from battles for the king. When she was with him, when she had his full attention, the world had seemed to stand still. Nothing else had mattered. They'd saddle up their horses and ride to the vineyards where he would talk to her about viticulture for a while, and then he would ask her what was on her mind.

"Come on, Janine. You need to go inside." Minette interrupted her friend's thoughts, slipped her arm through Janine's, and guided her toward the house.

Janine moved along with Minette as if in a trance until she came face to face with the cathedral-sized front door. She lifted then dropped the familiar, heavy bronze knocker, yet the *tap, tap, tap* seemed far away.

From within the oversized door, a smaller, inset one opened and a man with shaggy red hair stepped onto the portico. "Mademoiselle de Fleury, I presume." He didn't even pretend to welcome her.

"Thank you for seeing me."

"I'm the caretaker here. The abbé told me you wanted to see Chateau Fleury again. He will be arriving anytime now. We'll wait out here." He gestured for the woman to sit on the benches by the wall, then he descended the steps and spoke to the coachman.

Little time passed before Abbé Dillon arrived. The caretaker and he exchanged a few words before starting toward the house. Janine and Minette stood as the men reached the portico. With labored breathing, the abbé hesitated and cleared his throat while keeping his eyes on the caretaker. "Mademoiselle de Fleury this is Jean . . . uhh . . . O' Rourke. Monsieur O' Rourke, Mademoiselle de Fleury."

"As I agreed, you may look around outside," O'Rourke said. "I'll leave you to it."

He opened the door and started inside, but Janine dashed past him into the great foyer, her eyes sweeping its thirty-foot length until she was satisfied of its good condition. By the time the caretaker, Abbé Dillon, and Minette came inside, a torrent of questions to ask the caretaker pounded in her head. Her voice sounded eerily calm, unlike her thumping heart. "Monsieur O'Rourke," she said, stepping in front of the caretaker, "how long have you been at Chateau Fleury?"

"Get out of the house. Your visit is over," he shouted, anger evident in his red face.

"Not until you answer my questions."

The man reached for Janine's arm but Minette stepped between them. "I wouldn't do that if I were you," she said, her voice firm.

The abbé shook his head at O'Rourke. "Madame de Bernay shows great wisdom."

O'Rourke looked daggers at Janine but said nothing.

Undeterred, Janine scowled at him. "How did you hear of the caretaker position?"

"The comte and I met in England."

"I see. You mentioned the comte. Does he travel to England often?"

"Yes."

"If I may ask, what sort of business takes him to England?"

"Mademoiselle, the comte's business doesn't concern my job."

"Well, monsieur, I find it odd that you are hesitant to answer a simple question. His means of livelihood shouldn't be a mystery."

"I'll be back in few minutes," O'Rourke said, turning to leave. "You may look around downstairs only. The upstairs is under renovation." O'Rourke glared at the abbé, said, "I leave them with you," and left everyone standing in the foyer.

Janine went into the chapel to offer a prayer for her parents and uncle, as well as to ask for guidance while at the chateau. Thick dust lay on the altar and chairs. She knelt at the altar until hearing footsteps behind her. She looked around and saw the abbé approaching. How long had he been there?

He waited in silence until she arose and came toward him before starting forward to meet her. "Mademoiselle de Fleury, I am depending on you to conduct yourself with honor. You are a guest in the chateau and *must not* wander around without permission."

She stopped in front of him. "Abbé Dillon, *this* is *my* home. You are the one who is a guest."

"Mademoiselle, you must keep calm. You've been away for a long, long time. This is now the comte's home."

There was no reasoning with him. Janine made no response, walking by him across the reception hall into the blue salon. She moved around the spacious, gilt-paneled room. None of the furnishings were familiar. She stopped in front of the fireplace and stared at the de Fleury coat of arms affirming her rightful claim to the chateau.

"Chérie, where have you been?" Minette entered from the adjoining green salon.

Janine turned to her. "The furniture is gone. Come upstairs to my bedroom with me." Minette raised an eyebrow but with a shrug followed her. At the foot of the curved stone staircase, Janine stopped in front of two life-sized bronze horsehead finials mounted on the polished marble newels. "Ghastly. Why would anyone do such a thing?" she exclaimed in disbelief.

"They belong in the stables, not here. Were they originally there?" Minette brushed her finger over one of the bronze heads.

"Non, non, non. They don't belong here at all." Confronted with the stamp of the interloper's presence in her home, Janine's tone was indignant.

Minette lightly touched Janine's arm. "Let's move on."

Janine nodded and began climbing the stairs with Minette a step behind. The *click-click-click* sound of their heels on the stone stairs announced their disregard of O'Rourke's admonition. Yet there was no sign of the abbé or the caretaker. At the top of the stairs, all was quiet on the soiled but thick, maroon wool runner along the hallway. Where were the men?

Janine motioned Minette to follow her as she slowly opened the door to her bedroom. Dust motes danced in a beam of light in the otherwise barren room. The feeling of emptiness closed in around Janine. Everything was gone, even her favorite pink drapery. She stepped inside, circled around the perimeter of the room, and stopped at the spot where her dowry chest had stood.

"My dowry chest is . . . is not here." *How naïve of me. Of course not.* Her face brightened. "I hope Nanny hid it in the attic."

Minette put her arm around Janine's waist. "Perhaps."

"It's dreadful seeing my home pillaged like this." Janine stomped her foot. "I intend to get to the bottom of this. I feel so violated."

"And I will help you," Minette assured her.

"I must go to the family burial vault to look for my uncle's tomb." They moved toward the door and Janine hesitated for just a moment before exiting the room and closing the door softly behind her.

She and Minette walked along the corridor until they came to an elaborately carved walnut door. Janine tried to turn the knob; it was locked, but they could clearly hear a muffled screech, screech, followed by a thud from behind the locked door.

Janine whispered, "Someone's in there—in my mother's boudoir." She turned back and went along the hall, checking each door and looking inside the open ones.

Clomp, tap, clomp, tap. Footsteps echoed from the stairwell. The caretaker appeared ahead of the owner of the footsteps, his face ashen as he approached them from the other end of the hall. "You have deliberately disregarded my instructions. Leave this house now." He put a hand in his pocket and kept it there. "I have indulged you and have been betrayed. You are not a woman of honor."

The abbé slowly made his way to the top of the stairs. *Clomp, tap, clomp, tap.* Beads of perspiration dotted his forehead and upper lip. He panted as he drew in each breath. "We must leave . . . this good man now . . . and thank him . . . for his kindness."

"Who's in this locked room?" Janine demanded of the caretaker.

"Mademoiselle, no one."

Janine raised an eyebrow and squared her shoulders. "We heard a squeal and thump come from inside there."

"Probably a rodent. I'll let the master know upon his return."

"I won't leave until you unlock the door." Janine pointed to the key ring dangling from his belt.

"I don't carry a key to that room—the comte keeps the only key with him at all times. The room has been readied for his wife."

His wife . . . he's mighty sure of himself. Janine turned to Minette. "Let's get out of here." They hurried down the stairs, continued along the gallery, and out through the front door. "I must get to the crypt. I'm not likely to be allowed back anytime soon," Janine said.

With a heavy heart she led the way to the de Fleury family crypt—the eternal resting place of her ancestors and little Andre-Pierre, her brother. Before she left for New Orleans, Etienne had assured her that he had taken her uncle's body there and placed it in an unmarked casket.

Tall grasses and a tenacious variety of weed grew along the way to the rust-pitted, oxidized, black iron gate that separated the place of the dead from its surroundings. They followed the winding path to the entrance of the crypt.

Janine stared in horror at the stoned-in space where the door had been. The vault had been sealed with bricks. Placing both of her hands on the cold barrier, she bowed her head. "Why? Why, would anyone do such a thing? For what purpose?"

Minette shook her head. "So many unthinkable things have happened. There's no explaining or understanding it." She linked her arm with Janine's and drew her to the path. "Chérie, it's time to go."

"Minette, we must get some answers."

"And we will."

Chapter 9

Lost in thought, Janine stood before one of the gilt arrow sconces by the fireplace in Minette's townhouse salon, her level of frustration rising. She felt as though a poisoned dart had pierced her solar plexus. The caretaker at Chateau Fleury had evaded her questions earlier, despite her probing. His level of discomfort in her presence was palpable. What was he hiding? Clearly, he wouldn't be a source of information.

Minette came to her side. "What are you thinking?"

"O'Rourke. I'll get no useful answers from him."

"I agree. He's afraid of something. We'll have to find another way to solve this mystery." She sat down in one of the comfortable chairs while Janine paced back and forth in front of the fireplace, releasing a little of the urgency to do *something.* Finally, Janine sat down across from her friend.

"Do you know the whereabouts of any of your former household help?" Minette asked.

Janine pursed her lips and shook her head. "Non. Most of them were let go for their own safety after my mother was killed." She remembered with affection how her nanny had stayed with her to the bitter end. "Cecile refused to leave me. You remember her. She'd been my mother's nanny, too."

"Oui.*" Minette frowned. "Where did she go after you left for Bordeaux?"

"I don't know whether she left the chateau or . . . what happened to her." Filled with guilt for leaving her there, Janine's voice cracked. "I begged her to leave for her own sake. She wouldn't. She helped me pack, all the while assuring me not to worry about her. She said, 'I'm an old woman. The revolutionaries don't care about me.'"

"Where might she have gone? Do you know of any family or friends . . . where they live?"

"I have no idea. We seemed to be all the family she had. She had been with us for so many years . . . long before I was born. Maybe Abbé Dillon knows."

Minette nodded. "We'll make a list of questions to ask him. He does seem to know everyone in this part of the country. Anyone else?"

"No one that I can think of . . . other than Etienne. I don't want to ask him. Anyway, he's been away in the army most of the time."

"He won't be sympathetic to you. He's no friend of aristocratic families."

"Why do you say that? He helped me after my uncle was murdered."

"I know. But he became quite radical after you left. He performs his official duties well, but he avoids mingling with socially prominent families. It's clear to me he's a strict Republican at heart. His one saving grace is his bravery, and that keeps him in favor with the First Consul."

There was no arguing on that score. During their childhood, the difference in their social status had irked Etienne. Things had changed since those days. And now Etienne held a position of power and she was a shopkeeper. "I hope we won't need to speak to him about it."

"I'm glad you see the wisdom of not doing so. What I do suggest is that you and I stay in the townhouse for the next three days and gather as much information as we can about Chateau Fleury." Minette shook her head. "I'm sorry, but I can't delay beginning preparations for the ball at the country house more than a few days."

Elation turned to disappointment. Conflicted between her promise to Anne and Minette's offer to help, Janine said, "Merci. I'll have to talk to Anne about her gown. And there's Madame Parot. I need to let her know I will be delayed a few days before I stay with her."

"Chérie, I understand. After lunch I'll take you to pick up your things from the Tremeaus. You'll be able to talk with Madame Parot also."

"Very well."

"My ball is the big event of the season. Everyone who is anyone in the Loire Valley will attend, as will important people from Paris. We'll do the best we can under the circumstances. It will all work out, you'll see."

"I hope you're right. Do you have a room where I can work on the gown while I'm here?"

"Upstairs. You'll have a sewing room of your own, complete with a mannequin so you won't have to wait for Anne to come for fittings."

The valet entered. "Lunch is served, Madame."

"Merci." With a look of relief, Minette motioned for Janine to come with her.

Janine had little enthusiasm for eating, but with her stomach no longer in knots, she appreciated her pleasant surroundings and the savory aroma of the meal.

The oval dining table adorned with a yellow tablecloth rested on a herringbone-patterned hardwood floor. Six pale-green chairs offered an invitation to the beautifully laid table. Their caned seats and backs added to the casual grace of the dining area. Light poured through floor-to-ceiling windows, reflecting from the polished floor onto the yellow tapestry-covered wall panels. Minette sat at the head of the table and Janine sat to her right.

When the valet, in his dual role as butler, set a bowl of steaming onion consommé in front of her, Janine's appetite returned with gusto.

Minette offered her a piece of crusty bread before taking one herself. "We'll start with the abbé and work our way through the list of names we've gathered."

"I agree." Janine nodded as she sipped her soup. "We need to visit him first thing and begin adding names to our list."

They ate in silence until Minette edged her bowl to the side. Her face lit up with her signature carefree expression and she said, "Chérie, the ball at the country house is only two weeks from Friday. Say you'll be there." Before Janine could answer, the main course of fish arrived.

What could she wear to such an elegant event? Janine tempered her thoughts while searching for a response. *Admit it.* The best answer was the honest one. "I don't have a ball gown with me."

"I'm not surprised. You'll wear one of mine. I'm sure you can find something to your liking. My dressmaker will alter it for you in plenty of time."

A smile graced Janine's lips. "That's most generous, but I'm sure I'll have time to make minor alterations myself."

Minette gave Janine's hand a gentle squeeze. "Whatever pleasures you. It'll be splendid having you there." She slipped her chair away from the table. "Shall we remove to the salon?"

A serving cart with silver coffee service awaited them. Minette sat in the chair by the coffee and poured a demitasse cup for Janine and herself. "This afternoon we'll stop at the cathedral and speak with the abbé. Later, I'll take care of some preliminary arrangements for the ball while the coachman takes you to the Tremeaus."

By the time they finished their coffee and departed to the coach, a stifling humidity threatened a stormy afternoon. After the short ride to the cathedral, Minette and Janine walked along the north side of the house of worship, keeping in its shade as long as possible. *He's not there.* Janine wondered where the abbé could be. He wasn't sitting at his usual place along the colonnades, although it was shaded and it was his usual hour to be there.

Just then a man came into view, walking toward them. "I'll ask him if he's seen Abbé Dillon. Let's hurry to meet him," Janine quickened her steps, rushing ahead of Minette. "Monsieur, excuse me. Have you seen Abbé Dillon this afternoon?"

The man leaned against the cool stone wall of the Psalette Cloister. "Oui, about an hour ago. He said he must care for a sick uncle."

"Do you know where he can be reached?"

He pressed his palm to the side of his head. "That's the strange thing. He left in a hurry and gave no means of contacting him." Shaking his head, he said, "He seemed distraught."

"Thank you, monsieur." Janine daubed her brow with the edge of her linen handkerchief. "What next?" she said to Minette.

"You'll go to the Tremeaus as planned, and I'll take care of things here."

"I know. But when I asked 'What now?' I was thinking out loud about our next source of information."

"Chérie, you worry too much. The abbé will be back before long, especially since he went off without telling anyone how to reach him."

"It may be difficult to find Cecile. I hope we can."

"When you speak with Madame Parot, let her know you'll be spending time with me."

The coachman deposited Minette at the dressmaker's shop and continued on with Janine, passing the side streets and turning onto the main road leading out of town. As she traveled along the dusty road toward the Tremeaus' house, Janine realized how quickly she had come to depend on Minette's companionship. She enjoyed being with her and looked forward to their time at the townhouse.

Maybe, just maybe, with Minette's help she could meet her deadline to gather enough money to return to New Orleans and settle the marriage contract—if that was what she decided to do. At least she would have the money. Marrying Charles was becoming less and less desirable. Seeing Etienne again had increased her doubts about Charles and a union with the Dupré family. How foolish. Etienne hadn't been and still wasn't a choice.

The coach rocked violently as the two large horses came dangerously close to a ravine at the side of the road. Luckily, her driver's rapid action prevented them from being clipped by a small carriage racing past. Janine glimpsed two men in the offending carriage—the abbé and Etienne Tremeau—before the wake of dust obscured her view. It had happened quickly, but she had no doubt about their identity. Where were they going at a speed as if Satan chased them? Why were they together?

Chapter 10

"You damn fool. You almost collided with that coach," Etienne roared at the driver of their open, canopied carriage.

Sitting next to Etienne, the trembling, ashen-faced Abbé Dillon placed a hand over his heart and looked to the heavens. "You did say you were in a hurry to get home."

Without acknowledging he'd heard a word, the driver slowed the small carriage. At least the near accident had distracted the abbé for the moment. *I haven't time to listen to his slanderous ravings.* Etienne knew he should have ignored the agitated priest when he stopped by and insisted that Etienne go with him to hear a prisoner's story of a plot to kill Bonaparte that involved Janine. After seeing the captive, it seemed that Janine was in more danger than Bonaparte. She had the bruises as evidence.

"Colonel Tremeau, think about it . . . Mademoiselle de Fleury has every reason to want to avenge her parents' death. She's a serious threat to the Republic—especially if she works her way into the de Bernays' inner circle."

"And so are hundreds of other aristos. Abbé Dillon, your source turned out to be a common thief who refused to speak a word to either of us while we were there. You have wasted my time."

"Colonel, it's not my imagination. I have heard whispers from others about her. Why, she's to marry one of the exiled king's guards. And just how do you suppose she got the money to get here? Answer me that," the man said in a low, conspiratorial voice.

"I suggest you tell me . . . since you seem to know all about her."

"The Royalists, of course."

"The Royalists? You think they've been in contact with her in New Orleans and assigned a petty criminal to represent them?" Etienne made no attempt to disguise his impatience. The prisoner who wouldn't speak was none other than the drunkard who had attacked Janine de Fleury near the Grand Hotel. *Fear had been written all over his face. Why?*

The abbé shifted his position on the wooden seat. "You'll be remiss if you don't alert the First Consul to Mademoiselle de Fleury's return."

Etienne gave the older man a withering stare. "Citizen, you of all people don't need to tell me of my duty to the Republic."

From that point they rode in silence. By the time the carriage came to a complete stop in front of the Tremeaus' house, Etienne stood at the ready and stepped out. Turning to Abbé Dillon, he said, "You've had your say. Good day."

Glad to be home alone, away from the abbé and his prattle, Etienne removed his waistcoat, leaving on his long-sleeved white shirt, before he sat in his well-worn, overstuffed chair and sipped a glass of wine. He refused to dwell on Citizen Dillon—just yet. He relished the comfort of the old chair and regarded with disdain the *nouveau riche* military bourgeois and merchants who aspired to be the new aristocracy. They rejected their past and scorned all reminders of it. Their homes were an assortment of cold, incongruent rooms. As for the abbé, he had a weakness for finery as well. His shoes were of the finest leather and he wore an expensive ruby ring on his middle finger. Etienne gave a snort of disgust. It hadn't taken the pest long to creep into his thoughts again.

As Etienne reached for a second piece of cheese from the small plate on the side table, a thread on the frayed armrest caught a button on his sleeve. The wine sloshed over the rim of the glass, depositing a blood-red stain on the front of his white shirt. *"Merde!"* He set the glass on the table and started to unlace the ties on his shirt. As he struggled to loosen a tangled tie, an unwelcome tap on the door interrupted him. He thought better of ignoring it; most likely, his mother had returned home, loaded down with baskets of vegetables.

He made his way to the door with one arm out of his shirt and the other held fast with no space to get it out. He opened the door with his free hand and came face to face with Janine. *You're supposed to be with Madame de Bernay.* "Uh . . . Mademoiselle de Fleury . . . come in."

Janine hesitated a moment and then laughed. "What happened to you?"

Etienne edged toward the front room, struggling with the shirt. "Please excuse me while I extricate myself from this tangled mess." He stopped and turned to face her. "Better yet. Why don't you see if you can undo this infernal knot?"

Janine set her bag on the floor and grasped the offending knotted laces. "You've gotten yourself in a real bind," she said, smiling at his predicament. "I hope I can free you."

Her twinkling, expressive, gold-flecked brown eyes moved him as they had many years ago. He averted his eyes. "Come on. Get me out of this thing."

She hesitated, seeming to be undecided about what to do. With trembling fingers she pulled at the coiled strings. After untangling the loops she continued to loosen the laces. "This is my chance to help you in your time of need."

Her slow finger dancing on his chest, combined with the hint of her gardenia perfume—a mesmerizing combination—got the better of him. He leaned down, pressed his face to her hair, and breathed deeply. "Ummm. Gardenias."

"Now who's keeping you captive . . . or are you free already?" Janine tugged the shirt and pulled it over his head to reveal his upper torso. Her face turned scarlet as she backed away, still holding the shirt. "Do you remember the time the back of my dress got caught on a nail when we were playing hide and seek?" she asked as she let the shirt fall to the floor.

Etienne chuckled. "Oui. I'm surprised you do." He remembered with satisfaction—she'd had the advantage of knowing every good hiding place on the entire third floor of the chateau—but he had won. She had called out to him for help, fearing the wrath of the tutor who would arrive within minutes. Those were the days when he idolized her—before she had said, *Marry the gardener's son? You jest.* No doubt she hadn't realized the devastating impact of her thoughtless words.

She stroked his arm. "Your skin is golden brown."

"That's what happens to people who work out of doors . . . without a shirt." He watched her expression to gauge her reaction. She blushed. His resolve crumbling, he picked up his shirt. "Let's get this soaking before the stain sets. Wait for me in the kitchen while I get dressed."

In just a few minutes he returned to the kitchen, his upper body shielded under a clean shirt, and went to the porch for a pail of water. After setting the bucket on the kitchen floor, he dunked the soiled one up and down in the water before scrubbing the stain.

Janine sat at the table and watched him as if he were performing some sort of heroic feat. "You're so intent as you work."

67

He ignored her at first. But how long could a man remain stoic—while his body responded to her nearness. Giving no thought to his wet hands, he spun around and wrapped his arms around her. As he pressed her body against his, the feeling of cold droplets on his arms sobered him. Reluctantly, he released her and reached for a towel, chastising himself for relinquishing control.

"Wh-where are you going?" Janine stammered.

He shook his head side to side in mock disbelief. "To dry my hands. And then to finish the wine I was drinking when you arrived. Would you care to join me?"

She sighed. "I'd like that . . . while I wait for Anne."

He set aside the towel and removed a glass from the cupboard, carrying it to the table in the front room. He sat in the old armchair and poured the wine as Janine took a dainty chair, Anne's favorite.

She appeared preoccupied while swirling the wine in the glass, but neither of them spoke until she set her glass on the table. "I think you know why I've returned to France."

How would I know? "Tell me why?" Etienne encouraged.

"I've come to fulfill the requirements of a returning émigré to reclaim my family's estate."

"I recall hearing that you found the estate under lock and key," Etienne said.

"That's right. But even more shocking, Abbé Dillon said my uncle had returned from England and successfully claimed the property!" Janine got up and knelt by Etienne's chair, placing her hand on his shoulder, her face close to his. "Etienne, *you* know that isn't possible."

Her eyes pleaded with him. He knew something was wrong. The abbé hadn't mentioned anything about it to him. "Janine, it has to be someone else . . . another relative? Regardless, this development greatly complicates your chances to make a claim."

She stood and took a step back, holding eye contact. "No. There is no other entitled relative. How could someone be successful with such a claim? Do you know what happened at Chateau Fleury after I left?"

Her lovely face had turned a ghostly white and he wondered whether she might faint. "Come. Sit here while I tell you what I can." Etienne rose and reached for her hand, leading her to the sofa. "I returned to the chateau after I brought you here. Your uncle's body remained untouched where I left it under a blanket inside the stables." He paused and waited for Janine to speak. Her eyes misted but she remained silent. He leaned back, allowing her time to comment. She reached for his hand but said nothing as he continued, "I moved his body to the crypt, placed it in one of the empty tombs, and closed the lid. I saw no one and left for home. My thoughts were of getting you safely to Bordeaux."

Janine nodded. "I'm eternally grateful to you." Looking into his eyes, she straightened and ran her fingertips along his face and across the scar on his cheek. "Is that the last time you were there? Did the revolutionaries confiscate the property?"

"I seem to remember the property was confiscated before I left for military service . . . about nine years ago. Afterward, I was away most of the time until wounded. I spent a couple of months here during my convalescence. Since then I've been home very little and have lost track of local happenings. There have been a great many changes here."

Janine rested her face in her hands before returning her gaze to Etienne. "What can I do? Where do I begin? Will it take a long time to know the outcome?"

"I wish I could give you answers, but I don't have any." Etienne draped his arm behind her shoulders. "I'm not at liberty to help you with the process. I'm awaiting orders that may take me out of the country any day now."

She let out a slow breath. "I understand. I'm just feeling a bit overwhelmed. This is so much more complicated than I anticipated. And I can't stay more than three months . . . four at the most."

In the past he'd been able to help her in times of crisis. Although he desired to do so again, this time was different. He struggled with how to express his feelings. She just sat there, her eyes pleading with him to divine a solution.

He intended to give her a reassuring hug but instead cupped her face with his hands and gently brushed his lips across hers. She pressed her lips to his with an ardor that surprised him. He responded to her passion and sought her lips with abandon. For an instant he released his suppressed desire and probed her mouth as if searching for her very soul.

While he fought for self-control, Janine slipped her face to the side. He released her, dazed by his lack of self-discipline.

"Forgive me. I've behaved badly." Janine looked down at her hands then raised her eyes to meet his. "Please don't think poorly of me."

He struggled with his emotions. "Think no more of it. I share the blame." He stood and moved to the window, at that moment needing to put as much space as he could between them. He started toward the kitchen but stopped when he felt a tug at his sleeve. He looked down to see Janine grasping the fabric.

"I don't want to leave with this on my conscience. Let me explain before I get my things," she implored.

Etienne wanted to keep walking. He didn't want to hear anything more. There was nothing that needed to be said as far as he was concerned. He hadn't been good enough for her at Chateau Fleury, and there was no reason to think anything had changed. No matter how he longed to give her his heart, she remained locked in the past social order to which he did not belong. That was one of the reasons he fought so hard for equality and deeply resented Bonaparte's push to establish his own court of aristocrats as part of the Republic. Albeit open to a select few—including him—he wanted no part of it.

Conflicted as he was, nevertheless, he relented. He took a deep breath and exhaled slowly. "Really, you don't have to explain anything to me."

"I do and want to . . . for both of us." She moved toward the sofa with a backward glance at him before she took a seat. He remained standing while she continued. "Etienne, you have every reason to be angry with me. There is a contract for my marriage . . . to a stranger. I feel as though you and your family are my family."

Etienne took his favorite chair. "Well, that's the way arranged marriages are."

"Yes, I know. I'm so confused about what I should do. I wish I could marry for love."

"Janine, we are friends—as you say—and my family are your poor relations," he said with sarcasm.

She lowered her eyes and shook her head. "Non. I didn't mean it that way. I'm sorry you don't understand. Why do you always close me out?" She stood. "I'll get my things from your room now."

He had weakened and now he would think of her time and again. Just as he had after she went to New Orleans. Not until he had been in the Army several years did he accept that she was out of his life. At this juncture he didn't need to be connected with a rumored royalist spy or to be distracted by a hopeless yearning for her. Yet he couldn't deny his concern for her well-being. She must leave France immediately or risk accusations of being a royalist sympathizer, or worse yet, a conspirator. Abbé Dillon had made that clear.

He nodded. "I helped you get to New Orleans ten years ago and I'll help you again. If you need passage, I'll arrange it. I believe you should leave here as soon as possible. Staying any longer is dangerous." Who would know better than he? Any day now he would receive his orders to mete out justice to royalist conspirators in retaliation for the recent attempt on Napoleon's life.

"I am in danger?" Janine asked.

"Too many things have happened to you since you've been here to be coincidental. There's the mystery person at Chateau Fleury, the assault upon you at the Grand Hotel, and . . ."

"And what?" Janine peered at him.

Etienne didn't want to frighten her, but she already knew there was something more. He must inform her. "The abbé came to see me today. He told me he'd visited a man in jail recently. He claimed that the man accused you of being involved in a royalist plot."

"That's ridiculous. You know why I'm here—to settle my family estate. Who else even knows I'm here?"

"At the abbé's request, I went with him to question the prisoner. He is none other than the man who attacked you. Of course he recognized me. He panicked and lay face down on his mat, wouldn't say a word to either of us."

"How strange. My attacker knows who I am and is accusing me of being involved in some sort of plot? Who is he? I'd never laid eyes on him until the night he grabbed me."

"I don't know, but I intend to find out. Discovering his motive will be difficult." At the sound of a knock at the door, Etienne looked at Janine. "Now who?"

"I'm here to pick up Mademoiselle de Fleury," the de Bernay coachman announced when Etienne opened the door.

"Merci. I'll inform her that you are here." Etienne pushed the door closed without latching it then turned to Janine. "Your coach has arrived."

71

"May I leave a note for Anne?"

"Oui."

After writing the note, Janine folded it, printed Anne's name across the front, and handed it to Etienne. "Please give it to her."

He nodded. "When I have information for you, I'll leave a message with Madame Parot."

Her vision seemed to cloud as she paused at the front door. "Thank you. I hope to see you before you leave on assignment. *Bonne chance.*"

He gave her a farewell kiss on the cheek before again urging her to leave France—and him. "I'll get information about passage to New Orleans and let you know when you can leave."

"There's no hurry. I'll need time to think about it."

"I have to do it while I'm here. Remember, I'll leave soon," Etienne said.

"Ah, yes. I won't delay. *Au revoir.*" She opened the door and stepped outside, pulling it closed after her.

Etienne pressed his hand to his aching head and with the other hand tipped the wine bottle to his mouth and emptied it. She was gone.

Chapter 11

The de Bernay coach moved at a good clip along the dusty road, taking Janine away from Etienne, but she took little notice of the jostling ride. *Etienne . . . Etienne, do you know how my heart aches at the thought of leaving France? If I stay will I pay with my life?*

The merits of accepting Etienne's offer to arrange her return trip to New Orleans must be considered. He wasn't one to submit to fear in a crisis. If anything, he would minimize the seriousness of the risk. Why had she been attacked? Nothing had been stolen. With the brutal episode still fresh in her mind, she recoiled at the memory. Her neck and arms still bore ugly black and blue marks as testimony to the danger. She lifted her sleeve and shuddered at the sight of the ugly scab on her arm. The risks of staying were frightfully real.

Regardless, she couldn't let go of Chateau Fleury and her birthright without a whimper. Did the sting of Etienne's sarcasm reveal a truth she was loath to admit? She was proud of her aristocratic heritage. And if she retreated to New Orleans, there'd be no money for her dowry . . . all that awaited her there was the large debt on her share of Très Chic. She could stay and successfully challenge the interloper at Chateau Fleury or start over in another place of her choice.

Yes, she'd stay in France for the time being. As ironic as it seemed, Etienne had given her the strength to decline his offer to help her leave the country a second time. Relieved she'd reached a decision, she rested her head against the back of the seat and let her thoughts drift.

Etienne . . . Etienne. Images of him plucked a sad tune on her heartstrings. He had earned her respect and trust from the time they'd first met. Her opinion of him had been confirmed when she overheard the tutor tell her father that Etienne was a brilliant student and demonstrated a real strength of character. The teacher had queried the marquis about sponsoring the boy's further studies in engineering— and this from a man who rarely gave compliments.

Many a time Etienne had helped her with her math and science lessons to spare her from the acrid tongue of their teacher. Etienne had risked the man's wrath for her. She admired him for never wavering in his determination to make a contribution to his country—always a pillar of strength. He'd helped her through some of her darkest days.

As she relaxed, her thoughts became more fragmented. The Tremeaus were peasants who held values unlike her own. They were good people—just not her people. But today she had clung to him and drawn courage from him once more. There were other feelings too . . . feelings she shouldn't be having. No reasonable answer came as to why she hadn't resisted her impulsive behavior.

The gentle rocking of the coach was so soothing. She'd missed Etienne in New Orleans . . . and she had dreamed of him . . . always the same dream. *They stood close, she memorizing every contour of his body and face until their eyes met and his deep blue eyes engulfed her like a huge wave, carrying them further and further into an endless ocean. And there they drifted, together in rapt harmony.* The rhythmic motion of the coach ceased. Janine opened her eyes, disoriented. She'd dozed.

The dream again.

Janine saw they had arrived at the dressmaker's shop, and she waited as the coachman went inside to fetch Minette. Within a few minutes he returned, carrying two packages and putting them inside after Minette was seated.

Sitting across from Janine, her face aglow, Minette said, "I've been questioning people on your behalf." Janine nodded, wondering what her friend had found out. "At the marketplace I found a doctor who has lived here all his life and knows of the tragic murder of your parents, although he did not know them personally. He'd heard that a relative who emigrated from France to England had returned to claim the chateau."

"What else did he say?"

"He asked why we haven't visited the chateau. I told him we had, but only a caretaker was there. I asked if he had met or knows the occupants of the estate. He said he has not."

Janine sighed. "No clues about the interloper's identity."

"No. But he referred me to one of his patients. The woman had been quite upset about what happened at the chateau during the Revolution. She had a friend who worked there and stayed on after the family left. She lost touch with her and presumed her friend dead until years later when she turned up in a midwife's home."

"Is the midwife here in town?"

"Yes, I have the address. We'll call on her tomorrow."

"You're amazing. This is unbelievable."

"All this and I managed to picked up a new wig while in town . . . I'll show you at the house." Minette patted the round box on the seat without stopping for a breath. "Did you see Anne and Madame Parot?"

"Just Madame Parot."

With a wicked look in her eye, Minette asked, "Did you see Anne's handsome brother?"

"I left a note with him for Anne. I spent a good deal of time talking with Madame Parot. She was full of questions. I think she's lonely," Janine said, hoping to evade the question.

"What pleasantries did you and Etienne share?" Minette didn't take her eyes from Janine's face.

Janine ignored her probing remark. "The afternoon slipped away quickly."

"Did you ask him about the current occupant of the chateau?"

"He said he doesn't know anything about what's been going on there. He's been in the army most of the time since I've been gone."

Minette placed a steadying hand on her packages as the coach made a sharp turn from the street into the entrance at the back of the townhouse. After departing from the carriage, she escorted Janine along the stone walkway toward the street, pausing long enough to examine a silvery pink rose. "My new gown is this color. You'll want to select a different color for the ball." After they arrived at the front of the house, Minette knocked on the door. "I have another surprise for you inside."

The butler opened the door. "Madame, did your afternoon go well?"

"Most successful. Please see that my packages are taken to my boudoir."

"Oui, Madame. What time would you like dinner served?"

"Seven o'clock. There'll be just the two of us again. Thank you."

Minette led the way to the semi-circular stairs at the back of the long, narrow reception room. Janine followed her up the stairs to the gallery overlooking the area below. Along the wall a row of austere, dormitory-type doors broke up the plain lines of the space. Minette opened a door near the end of the hall.

Stepping into the room, Janine saw that the bedspread, curtains, and window valance were made of a green and cream *toile de Jouy* fabric, a pleasant surprise. "This is lovely." She set her small case on the bench at the foot of the bed and went to the window. Through the panes she observed the coachman polishing the coach in the shade of a large tree. Seeing no trace of the horses, she surmised they must already be inside the stables.

"Come with me." Minette motioned and led the way to the next room.

Janine stared in amazement at Minette's sewing room. Two mannequins stood near a wooden rod that extended from wall to wall. In the center of the room, moveable cabinets topped with baskets and bins of sewing supplies surrounded a long worktable—everything a seamstress could possibly need. "I can't believe my eyes. It's better than being in my own shop."

"Alas, your work here will have to wait until tomorrow. But for now, I'll send you some warm water so you may freshen up. I'll stop by about six-thirty, which will allow you time to look at my gowns before dinner."

The next morning Janine and Minette began their search for Nanny Cecile. As they approached the address provided—only a few miles from the townhouse—Janine saw an old woman sitting on the porch, resting alone in front of the tall, narrow, half-timbered house just a few blocks from the cathedral. Her head lay to one side, the supporting pillow perilously close to slipping from her slatted wooden chair. She roused long enough to swat at a fly before she closed her eyes and turned her face away from the sunlight.

Janine spoke in a hushed tone. "Is that . . . it *is* Cecile."

Minette nodded.

Drawing close to the woman, Janine saw the years had taken a heavy toll on the woman's appearance. Her hair—no longer gray, but now snow white—framed her wrinkled face. Her emaciated body revealed little form beneath her clothing. What tribulations had she endured to turn her into a shell of her former self? Guilt swept over Janine for having left her at the chateau. Her nanny hadn't fared well. She edged to her side. "Nanny Cecile . . . Cecile, how are you?"

The woman opened her eyes and brushed a wisp of hair from her face. With an expression of wonder, she tried to stand. "Mercy me. Marie, my dear Marie! Have you come to take me home?"

"Please don't get up." Janine placed her hands on Cecile's arms and leaned toward her. "Nanny, I'm Janine. Maman is not here. I'm grown up now. I've come to visit with you and brought my friend Minette. Do you remember her?"

Cecile shook her head and squinted her eyes. "Oh, my little one. Why didn't Marie come?"

"She wasn't able to come today." Janine watched her face and wondered if she remembered their last days at Chateau Fleury. She hesitated before asking, "Did you like being at Chateau Fleury?"

"I'm tired now." Cecile closed her eyes.

Janine pulled up a chair and sat beside her. She held Cecile's hand and began to hum a lullaby Nanny had often sung to her.

The old woman began to hum along. "Hush, little one." she rocked back and forth and patted the back of an unseen baby.

Janine stopped humming. "What's the babe's name, Nanny?"

"Aw, let me see. It's Marie's tiny baby boy . . . or is it Janine? I can't tell you."

"That's all right. You're a good nanny. You took good care of the babe."

"I tried. I did everything I could to save him."

"I know you did. Little Andre-Pierre was so very sick. Maman told me."

Cecile straightened with recognition in her eyes. "And then we had you, Janine. Such a blessing. I stayed at the chateau and prayed for the day you would return. But the soldiers came instead and forced me to leave." She began to sob.

"Don't cry. You were very brave. I'm sorry I couldn't come back sooner, but I'm here now." Janine released her hand and hugged her. "Where did you go when you left the estate?"

"I took a room in town . . . waited for you until . . . the day some men attacked me on the street. I don't remember."

"Had you seen them before?"

"I think so . . . in the marketplace . . . always just standing around whenever I went there."

"Do you know any of them by name?"

Cecile put her bony hand on her forehead and clenched her hands. "No." She shook her head. "I saw . . . saw . . . I can't remember his name."

"With them?"

"He talked to them. He glanced my way and dashed off in a hurry." Cecile trembled.

Janine patted her hand. "Don't worry." She sat by the old woman and hummed the familiar lullaby. When Cecile finally calmed down, Janine motioned for Minette to follow her as she moved away from Cecile. "We'd better leave her now."

"Let's speak with the woman in charge here," Minette suggested.

"Wait here while I tell Nanny we're leaving." Janine returned to Cecile's side and took her hand. "Nanny Cecile, I'm going now. I don't want to tire you. I'll come back to see you again."

Cecile squeezed her hand but her focus seemed to be behind Janine, as if someone stood there.

Their visit left many unanswered questions, but Janine was relieved to have found her old nanny. When Janine tapped on the front door, a plump, middle-aged woman with unnaturally bright red hair opened the door just enough to peer at her. She was grasping the arm of a tottery old man who stood close by her side. "Bonjour. What can I do for you ladies?" She looked past Janine to Minette.

"Madame, we saw Cecile on the porch and stopped to say hello." Janine gestured to the chair where Cecile sat.

"Cecile? Non, that's Gemma. There's no Cecile here. I care for Gemma and Sarah. And of course, Henri here." She gestured to the man by her side.

Minette moved closer to the flame-haired figure at the door. "Madame, may we have a word with you about the one you call Gemma?"

One look at Minette's fine silk dress and gold necklace spurred the woman to action. She flung open the door with her free hand while keeping a firm grip on the arm of the old man. "Certainly. Come in and sit, if you can find a place. I must fetch Gemma." She stepped around them toward the outside. "The aged are more difficult to care for than are wee babes. Always scattering things, wandering off, or getting themselves into trouble, to mention just a few of the challenges I have to contend with."

Waiting for her return, Minette and Janine picked up books and pushed aside blankets to make room to sit on the chairs draped with striped covers of mattress ticking.

The lady of the house brought Cecile inside and took her and the old man past them into a back room where a discordant, tinny sound from some sort of string instrument became louder when she opened the door. She returned out of breath and heaved herself into a chair across from them.

"As I was saying, life isn't easy here. I'm a widow and must keep body and soul together. My husband was killed eight years ago on the street not far from here by the lawless roving mobs. Dreadful."

Janine shuddered with her at the mention of the Revolution. "I'm sorry. I lost my parents to the violence also."

The woman picked up where she had left off. "Before the Revolution I was a midwife and continued to practice until the day my husband was killed. When my money ran low, I went to Abbé Dillon and asked him to help me. I took his suggestion and opened my home to several of the aged and sick without families to care for them."

"Who brought Ce . . . Gemma to you?" Janine asked.

The woman ran her fingers through her unruly hair. "Gemma was different. She's only been here five years—after the worst of the violence ended—yet she was in a bad way . . . tortured and definitely beaten . . . a head injury. Abbé Dillon made arrangements and brought her to me himself." She frowned. "He never visits her though. She had no family to pay for her, so he takes care of it from one of his charity funds."

"Now, Sarah's story is different." She gestured in the direction of the tinny sounds. "Her daughter brought her to me before she left the country, but now that she's back, she visits her at least twice a week. And Henri's grandsons come to see him when they can." She shook her head. "Such a shame about Gemma."

Chapter 12

Janine caressed the silk fabric before slipping into the gown. Studying her reflection in the floor-length mirror, the vision of the lavender silk gown filled her with hope. Few alterations were required; the waving of her magic needle would soon transform Minette's gown into her own. She had looked forward to such a day for many years—a time when she'd be the one wearing a lovely gown. In New Orleans she'd taken pleasure in making gowns for her clients and indulged in daydreams about attending such gala events with Charles.

"It's a bit too long." Minette stood at the door watching her.

"You may as well come in," Janine said with a start.

"We're having dinner guests tonight." Minette approached Janine, stopped in front of her, and grasped the fabric at the waist. "There's a little spare material here."

Ignoring what she already knew, Janine said, "Guests?"

"Lieutenant Lenoir." Minette paused. "My husband and another officer will also be here."

Matchmaking at Napoleon's behest? "That's nice." She'd have to wear the same dress she'd worn when she first met the lieutenant.

"If you'd like to wear the little green dress you admired last night, you're welcome to it." Her friend seemed to read her mind while slipping a pin into the fabric at Janine's waist.

"Uh, yes, I'd like that." *I must look my best for Lenoir.*

"Chérie, you'll look *magnifique*." Minette bent down to pin the hem. "How am I doing as your assistant?"

"You're a lady of many talents." Janine took the pincushion from Minette's hand, pushed in a dozen or so needles and pins then placed it on a small table with her thimbles and scissors.

The housekeeper tapped on the door. "Mademoiselle Anne Tremeau is waiting in the salon."

"Merci. We'll be with her shortly," Janine responded.

Minette helped her out of the gown and hung it while Janine dressed. When they reached the salon, they found Anne pacing around the room.

"Madame de Bernay, I'd like you to meet Mademoiselle Tremeau," Janine said.

Minette smiled at Anne. "I'm pleased to meet you. I've had the pleasure of meeting your brother, Colonel Tremeau."

Anne blushed. "My brother has many acquaintances, unlike myself. It's nice to meet you."

"You have one very special friend in Mademoiselle de Fleury. Please excuse me. I know you have things to discuss." Minette left the room, and a few minutes later the butler brought in a tray of coffee and petit fours.

Anne accepted a cup of coffee from Janine but raised her hand, declining the tray of cakes.

"What's the matter, Anne? I can tell something is wrong." Janine picked up the familiar package of fabric that Anne had brought with her.

"Adrien and Etienne have been called to Paris. And the concert is in four weeks. That's too soon for them to be back . . . if they ever return."

Janine's hand shook as she set down her cup. "Anne, you mustn't think that way. We have a gown to make. Come with me upstairs."

"You seem to think they'll be back in time," Anne said, following Janine up the stairs.

"I don't know for certain. What I do know is *you* will have a gown when they do return. And there'll be other events, even if you miss this one. Now, wouldn't Adrien be disappointed if he gets back and you don't have a gown to wear?" Janine opened the door to the sewing room. "Here we are. Let's get started." Janine picked up the measuring tape and asked, "When do they leave?"

Anne looked at the floor. "They left early this morning."

"Why is Adrien going with Etienne?" Janine began taking measurements and jotting them down.

"He's one of Etienne's men . . . his assistant."

His assistant . . . one of the men with Etienne at the Grand Hotel? "Did Etienne stay with him while I used his room?"

"Yes, how did you know?"

"I didn't, just guessed. Stop wiggling or we'll be here all morning."

"I'm sorry. I'm so upset."

"I know. Try not to worry so much." Janine closed the note pad. "That'll do for today. After I've cut the muslin pattern, I'll need you to come back for another fitting. How's tomorrow?"

"Fine. What time would you like me here?"

"Afternoon . . . about two o'clock?" She could finish in time to visit Cecile. Janine escorted Anne to the front door and gave her a hug. "Remember what I said. You need to be ready for Adrien when he returns." She waved goodbye and closed the door.

The deepening color on Janine's cheeks revealed her rising anticipation of the small dinner party. Yes, she was starved for a social life. She blotted her cheeks to remove any excess of her peach rouge . . . too much color. In less than an hour, the guests would gather in the salon before dinner. With a backward push of her slippered feet, she moved the bench away from the dressing table just enough to stand up. She picked up the dress of pale green, dotted Swiss cotton accented with gold dots. It had fashionable, short puffed sleeves, a high waist, and scoop neckline. After dressing, she approved of her reflection in the full-length mirror. The dress suited her well; she'd make a similar one for herself.

A soft tap at the door announced the arrival of Minette's lady-in-waiting, prepared to dress Janine's hair. She had come from their country home just for the event. *Hummm, Minette is grooming me with care.* "Come in. Madame de Bernay said you would be here to style my hair," Janine said after she opened the door. She worried the woman would delay her; she wanted to arrive on time to the salon.

"Oui. Come and sit. We begin." With deft fingers, the hairdresser swept Janine's hair to the right side of her head. She arranged it in a cascade of thick curls that resembled a cluster of round, dark chocolate swirls and added a final flourish of three yellow rosebuds. A scattering of ringlets finished her coiffure.

Janine gazed in the mirror, admiring herself as the woman packed her basket of hair supplies. "It's lovely. Thank you." With one last look in the mirror, Janine followed the woman out of the room. She'd be right on time.

As she approached the salon, she heard male voices in heated conversation.

"I warn you . . . don't trust Carnot or Tremeau." As she entered she saw General de Bernay bring his broad fist down on the wide arm of the silk upholstered chair, his rough-featured face scarlet.

Another man added, "You can't tell that to Bonaparte."

The general paused a moment and scratched his head. "Maybe not, but it doesn't mean my wife should get the vapors because those two men snub our social events."

Janine regretted having arrived during the exchange, but she'd been seen; there could be no turning back.

A look of relief banished the furrows from Minette's brow as Janine entered the room. She lost no time in introducing her to the stranger, a major general, who looked as though he and de Bernay had been cast in the same mold. Neither man wore his uniform with the suave confidence of Lieutenant Lenoir. General de Bernay scowled at Minette and through clenched teeth grunted a foul-smelling greeting to Janine.

Lieutenant Lenoir came forward. "Bonjour, Mademoiselle de Fleury. We meet again." He took her hand in his manicured one and raised it to his lips. He continued to hold it as his eyes wandered from her face and followed the lines of her body to her feet and back again. "You look divine this evening," he said with smooth, aristocratic charm.

At their first meeting Janine had found Lenoir to be in sharp contrast to the other officers. He was a gentleman, though somewhat vain. A dandy, perhaps? Several times he'd glanced at his reflection in a window as he regaled her with talk of his silk business and impressive list of clients. Now she found herself mirroring his behavior and slipping into the role of aristocratic lady. Surprised by the thrill she felt from the attention of this genteel man, she realized how lonely she was. She admired his regal posture and slender, uniformed body. *The man has style. A stark contrast to Etienne's rugged good looks*. She couldn't attribute her interest solely to the keen eye of the New Orleans tailor she had become.

He placed a light touch on her arm, escorted her to a settee, and sat beside her. "You've walked in on a political discourse," he said softly. "Emotions run high. I do hope we haven't distressed you."

"No, of course not."

Lieutenant Lenoir addressed General de Bernay. "Bonaparte is nobody's fool. He knows his officers."

"The devil you say," the general roared. "He knows their performance on the battlefield, but does he know what's in their hearts?"

The other man shook his finger at Lenoir. "You're too young and too naïve to remember how Carnot played both sides for his own gain. He received his military start in Prince de Conde's engineer corps. And then when the tide began to turn, he betrayed the Royals by voting for the king's death . . . without having been present at the trial."

"He's nothing but a self-serving chameleon . . . as is Tremeau as well, I think." The general lifted his bulky body from his chair and probed one ear with his finger. Then he walked from man to man, glaring at each one in turn as he pointed his stained index finger at them.

Janine turned away in disgust. How could Minette have married such an uncouth peasant? And why was he attacking Etienne? Janine's glance at her friend showed that Minette was subdued—so unlike her usual effervescent self.

The major general pulled at his scraggly gray moustache. "François, why do you waste your energy on Tremeau when there are many worthy officers who desire to be well-married and pay court to our leader?"

The lieutenant leaned toward Janine. "May I show you to the terrace and gardens? It is pleasant this time of day." Grateful to him, Janine nodded and rose. Lenoir offered her his arm as he spoke to the others in the room. "Please excuse us. I have invited Mademoiselle de Fleury to join me on the terrace."

Minette smiled at them. "What a wonderful idea. I'll send out some drinks."

A gentle breeze carried the sweet aroma of honeysuckle along the terrace as they sipped champagne.

"These gardens are only about five years old. The house and gardens that stood on the lot were destroyed during the Revolution." Lenoir waved his hand toward the parterre. "Would you care to take a stroll and see what they've done?"

"I would indeed." Janine took the lieutenant's extended hand. "It's a wonderful addition to the townhouse."

Lenoir stopped walking and faced Janine. "Especially tonight."

Janine smiled at him and breathed in the subtle woodland scent of him. She gazed into his unfathomable brown eyes. He was such a contrast to the two generals—a genteel man who knew how to treat a lady. She could only hope Charles would be equally polished. The lieutenant was the saving grace at this dinner party.

"What brings you to the Loire Valley?" He held her gaze.

Janine wondered how much she should reveal to him. He seemed genuinely interested. "I hope to reclaim my family home— Chateau Fleury."

"Eh. Chateau Fleury . . . Non. You must be Marquis de Fleury's daughter . . . are you? I can't believe it. I met the marquis while my father was imprisoned in Paris . . . in the Conciergerie . . . during the Revolution. Alas, he did not come home." His voice quavered and a hush descended around them.

At that moment Janine felt as much pain for him as she did for her own loss. "I'm so sorry. I do understand . . . my mother and my father were guillotined."

"Oh, my dear, please forgive my insensitivity. I had no idea your father hadn't been released from prison." Lenoir ran his hand through his dark, curly hair. "I recall hearing the family had returned from England and to their chateau."

Janine wanted to share her dilemma about her family home, but a nagging feeling stopped her. Prudence dictated she wait until she knew him better before asking him if he had information about the chateau. "It's all right. How would you know? I . . . I would like you to tell me, if you can, why are the generals so upset about Carnot and Tremeau?"

"Envy? Carnot is a man to be reckoned with. He has managed to survive and maintain positions of power throughout the upheavals since the king's execution. He's a brilliant man and a gifted military strategist. Most valuable to those in power." The lieutenant led Janine to a bench. "Carnot made the French Revolutionary Army what it is today. He introduced conscription to raise the necessary troops and used his organizational skills to supply the army."

"How is Tremeau connected with Carnot's organization?"

85

"Aren't you the inquisitive one?" His voice was teasing, but his eyes betrayed malice.

"My father served in the King's Army, and Colonel Tremeau's father was our gardener at Chateau Fleury. So you see, I have a number of reasons to be interested."

He took a deep breath. "Well, well." He continued, "Although a *peasant*, Tremeau is also a man of many abilities valued by Carnot. But more than that, his extreme devotion to the Republican ideas of equality and freedom for all men parallels that of Carnot. At one time another protégé of Carnot's was none other than Napoleon Bonaparte, who was promoted from captain to general by him." Lenoir stood. "We best go in before dinner is served."

"How long have you been in the Army?" Janine asked as they walked along the wide path toward the terrace.

"Two and a half years—since my older brother's death. Before that I'd served for three years without the responsibility of the family's silk business. I've had little more than four years to try to salvage our family's silk business since I took over. At first it seemed hopeless." When they reached the terrace, he cupped Janine's face in his hands and gave her a light kiss on the cheek. "I've enjoyed being in your company this evening." As they drew near the house, all was quiet in the salon.

When they came into the room, Minette lifted her chin and gave them a curious glance. "You must have enjoyed your time together. I was about to go looking for you."

Janine lowered her eyes. Flattered by his attention, nevertheless, she questioned his motives and still smarted from his attitude toward Etienne. "Yes, our time in the garden was pleasant." She couldn't shake the feeling that Lenoir wasn't genuine. Why would he lavish his attention on her? She had flattered herself in thinking Bonaparte had selected her for the lieutenant. Why would he?

Chapter 13

May 12, 1803—Paris

The great man sat with his back to the window, his face in shadow. What was his mood this morning? Etienne squared his shoulders and approached the desk. "At your service, General."

"Is all well with Colonel Tremeau today?" With a wave of his hand, Bonaparte indicated for Etienne to sit in the chair near the desk. "And how are you and the charming Mademoiselle La Roche getting on these days?"

Etienne quelled his impulse to say he had not spent any time with her yet. "All is well. We plan to attend a concert in a few weeks."

Bonaparte's sunny expression clouded. "A few weeks? What's the delay?" He lifted his chin and watched Etienne's face, shaking his head as if baffled. "At least you're one damn good military man."

"Thank you, General. You've answered your own question. For the next few weeks, I'll be engaged in active service with the Republican Army."

A rare smile softened Bonaparte's features. He stood and paced back and forth. "Etienne, I know I can count on you." A momentary silence intervened. "Do you have any idea where that royalist renegade, Georges Cadoudal, is today . . . or was yesterday, for that matter?"

After years of service together, Etienne and Napoleon had formed a deep friendship and respect for one another and Etienne had learned to expect his leader's sudden mood shifts. "Non, Monsieur *le General,* I do not." He appealed to the general's vanity. They had first met during their early years in Paris while they both were outsiders who proved themselves to the military establishment. "Cadoudal travels between Paris and London with a greater frequency than Louis XV deflowered young virgins," Etienne said.

"Ah, yes. He stays on the move. Rumors are afoot that he's hatching a plan to kidnap me." He stopped in front of Etienne. "Unfortunately, General Moreau has been implicated in the plot."

"This is serious." Etienne struggled to keep his voice level, although his shock was great. He realized that the success of this mission was critical to his military career—and might even allow him

87

to stave off Bonaparte's matchmaking efforts on his behalf.

"Your assignment is to gather information about co-conspirators across the Channel. You are to leave immediately for London. Duc de Bovet expects you. As usual, all of your arrangements are in place. Good day, Colonel." Napoleon returned to his desk and resumed signing papers as if there had been no interruption.

May 18, 1803—Calais

For three days rough seas delayed the sailing of the single-masted ship from the shores of Calais across the Channel to Dover. Finally, the ship's captain deemed it calm enough to depart, and Etienne relaxed as they moved into the rough seas, eager to get to work on his assignment. The ship rolled and tossed for the duration of the slow, six-hour voyage. The crew consisted of three sailors, the captain, and a scrawny cabin boy acting as steward. He'd begin by evaluating them.

The boy came across the deck. "I take good care of you."

Austrian? Yes, that's it. "I'd like wine. Can you get it?" Etienne reasoned he should avoid the boy as much as possible. The cabin boy could well be using his eyes and ears for the exiled French royals.

The boy scampered away and returned in a few minutes with a bottle, almost empty. "You see. I did."

"So you did. Do you carry many passengers on this vessel?" Etienne tipped the bottle and let the red liquid soothe his throat.

"One or two."

Etienne measured the risk and determined the information was worth it. He went ahead and asked, "I'm looking for my friend. He is tall, thin, and has gray hair. Have you seen him on board or on the docks at port?" Etienne removed a sketch of Cadoudal from his pocket, showing it to him

"Fortnight ago we have passenger. Him no talk to me. Says throw overboard if I not go away."

"This man?" The boy nodded. "During layovers in Dover, have you seen him since?" Etienne tossed the boy a coin.

"Once or twice. Could remember more for *ecu*."

"We'll see."

"Oui, monsieur. I see him in Jolly Englishman. Have a glass of ale, he did, and he sit with fancy man."

"How many days ago?"

"Four or five. Before we sail Calais."

Etienne released two coins to the boy's grasping fingers. At the sudden sound of men talking, the boy gave a guilty jerk and dashed in the opposite direction. Etienne didn't have a chance to talk to him again until the white cliffs of Dover came into view.

"If you be stayin' a while, I take you to where I see your friend," the cabin boy said, jingling the coins his pocket. "He a much good friend?"

"I'm the one asking the questions. Remember that."

The boy dashed off as the boat approached the dock.

Etienne pressed his hand to his chest to confirm the presence of his fake passport identifying him as Monsieur Descart. Fortunately, it had cost him nothing, unlike the extortionate sum—as much as ten thousand *livre*—paid by some of the émigrés. He'd spend no more than a day in Dover before making the daylong coach ride to London, where Cadoudal made most of his contacts.

Although Etienne had mixed feelings about Janine, his mother had embraced her as her long lost daughter. She'd urged him to help Janine. While in the city he'd make discreet inquiries about Comte de Fleury—had the imposter established himself in the émigré community?

An odd assortment of men crowded into the cramped quarters of the Jolly Englishman, leaving no seat unoccupied. Etienne made slow progress toward the bar, past rough men whose body odor overwhelmed the stench of the rotting fish debris on their clothes. A few well-dressed gentlemen sat at a long table by the window. He scanned the room for Cadoudal. *Not here*. He edged forward to the counter and caught the attention of the barman. Taking the sketch from his pocket, he said in English, "I'm looking for a friend of mine. Have you seen him?"

The barman squinted at the drawing. "Aye. He comes in once in a while. A man of few words."

"I'll have a pint of ale. When did you last see him?"

The attendant set the ale on the counter. "Been at least a week."

"Much obliged." Etienne handed him two coins, one for the tab and the other for the information.

London, England

The hackney moved along Marylebone Road and circled Portman Square before stopping in front of Duke de Bovet's nondescript residence on Thayer Street. The cash-strapped French nobility had to content themselves with frugality but sought to reside in as nice a neighborhood as possible.

Etienne paid the driver and approached the house, his tension building. All was quiet inside. He muttered an oath under his breath as he waited for a response to his knock.

When the door opened, a distinguished-looking man greeted Etienne by his passport alias. "My friend Monsieur Descart. I'm so glad you've come." He extended his hand in a welcoming gesture. "Do come in." Ever vigilant, he looked in both directions before he closed the door. "What brings you to London?"

"A social obligation." Etienne handed the duke a heavy envelope filled with cash. "I'm here to call upon your royal neighbor and to mingle with his guests."

"We must proceed with caution and not rush things. He's on tenterhooks these days. I think something's afoot. I've been keeping my ear to the ground," the double agent volunteered. He ran his fingers along the fruits of his betrayal of the exiled French Royal Court.

Etienne wiped his brow with his handkerchief. "So it's not just rumor."

"Doesn't seem so. You'll have to wait to see him until he decides to entertain us."

"I see. You and I will be left to pass the time playing whist?"

"I doubt that's all you'll be doing with your time. Of course, I'll play as often as you wish."

"You are perceptive. I do have other duties to attend to while I'm here. I'd like to know the whereabouts of Cadoudal and who he's visiting these days."

"I haven't seen him here, but I didn't expect to."

"Do you recall meeting the Comte de Fleury among the émigrés?"

He nodded. "What does he have to do with the suspected plot?"

"Nothing, so far as I'm aware. Tell me, what do you know about him?"

The duke shook his head. "Not much. He was here only a couple of years. It seems he remained in mourning for his family. He seldom attended social events, and when he did he spoke infrequently—and barely above a whisper at that—injury to his vocal cords, so he said."

It'll be hard for Janine to disprove his claim. "When did he leave London?"

"He suffered from fits of anger and was accused of stabbing a man. When the investigation got underway, he disappeared."

"How long ago?"

"About three, no more than four years," de Bovet replied.

"Had you met him before you left France?"

"No. I only knew his brother, the Marquis de Fleury, through his service at Versailles."

The imposter's luck holds. "If you think of anything else about him, let me know."

"Of course. And now for a glass of port." The duke poured the wine and handed a glass to Etienne. "Shall I arrange for an evening of whist tonight?"

"Tonight and each night until the Bourbon prince, our royal liaison, gives up an evening with his mistress in favor of our company."

Four days later Etienne relished the chance to play another game of whist—this time with the royalists. The house at 40 Baker Street didn't rival the elegant mansions a few blocks away on Portman Square, but the large drawing room was furnished in good taste in spite of the prince's lack of cash and heavy debts. Two guards in red uniforms stood a discreet distance from the guests. The Comte d'Artois, King Louis' brother, welcomed the duke and his friend, Monsieur Descart. He introduced them to the other five men present, one of whom was Baron Charles Dupré.

Mon Dieu, Janine's fiancé! A messenger from the king? Etienne puzzled as to whether Dupré and Cadoudal were plotting right

91

under his nose. He took an instant dislike to the man but couldn't be sure whether it was because of his favor with Janine or his close connection with the royalists. He hated to admit to himself that, although surrounded by royalists, he had selected Dupré as the object of his scorn.

The duke proceeded to explain to the group of six French aristocratic men that Monsieur Descart had been traveling in America. "Upon his return to France, he found himself a man without a home. His greatest wish is to see our king upon his throne in France."

The men took their assigned places at the gaming tables. Etienne was partnered with an eighty-year-old abbé; their opponents consisted of Duke de Bovet and Baron Dupré.

The old abbé addressed the duke. "*Monsieur le Duc*, why would Napoleon suggest that our king, Louis of France, surrender his claim to the French throne in return for lands in Italy?"

"I hear that Napoleon aspires to be the ruler of France— declared emperor."

The Baron nodded. "It is true he holds lofty notions of the sort. But our king rejected the suggestion. He told him in no uncertain terms that his rights couldn't be compromised."

Etienne listened with interest.

Duke de Bovet laid a card on the table. "Our general in Paris is looking out for our interests. But things are becoming dangerous for him. Bonaparte questions the loyalty of some of his distinguished officers."

Yes, General Moreau and others. Etienne played the ace of spades and took the trick.

His whist partner paid no heed to the card played. "I suspect Bonaparte had spies planted at Madame Moreau's Paris salon gatherings. He always blamed her, rather than his glorious Commander of the Army of the Rhine."

Dupré tossed the two of clubs on the table. "No doubt. I'm sure it's a real blow to come to terms with General Moreau's change of allegiance."

"I'm surprised King Louis agreed for you to leave Poland for New Orleans. When will you sail?" the duke asked the baron.

"When I can tear myself from the lovely ladies of London," the baron said with a smirk. "Actually, it's not surprising that King Louis desires that I build the family resources in the New World. Many who will serve him upon his return to the throne will be destitute."

"It sounds as if you've been promised a place in his court."

"The king knows my loyalty and devotion is constant in bad times as well as the good."

At evening's end Etienne had not gathered any specific information about Cadoudal, but they had openly discussed General Moreau. One thing for certain, the ultra-royalist camp remained steadfast in its opposition to Bonaparte. But were they plotting to kidnap him?

Chapter 14

Loire Valley

A verdant forest of gardenia bushes, orange trees, and rose garlands transformed the de Bernay grand salon into a lush, fragrant wonderland. Minette and Janine wove their way through the maze of greenery, making their final inspection. Within the hour, guests would begin to arrive for the elaborate fête. Minette snipped a bruised gardenia and turned the jardinière to expose the plant's best side. "I do hope Cecile's memory improves during your visits."

Janine stood on a ladder to get a bird's eye view of the garlands of ferns, dahlias, and lilies decorating the huge limestone mantle. "I'll keep trying to stir her memories, but I just don't know what to expect."

"That's all you can do." Minette gave her an inquiring glance. "Have there been other developments since I last saw you?"

"I spent a lot of time listening to Madame Parot tell me her life history." Janine climbed down. "And Anne was thrilled with her gown."

"Now maybe you're free to extend your visit with me."

"Oui."

Minette stepped onto the vacated ladder. "Etienne sent word that he would be here tonight. I thought you'd like to know." She pinched a rose from the arrangement. "Only time will tell if he does come."

Janine's pulse raced. "He's back?"

"You didn't know?"

"Non. I did not."

"Lieutenant Lenoir will be here too. I know he'll be pleased to see you again." Minette moved a fern away from the face of the clock. "It's almost five. We'd best ready ourselves for the evening."

Minette's pink silk gown shimmered as fleeting bits of light struck its random silver threads. She and her husband, in full uniform, received guests near a bank of flowers at the foot of the great stairway. The ballroom glittered with hundreds of candles in two huge chandeliers, their flames amplified in mirrors on two facing walls. Shifting throngs of people danced in the center of the room across the polished parquet floor while other guests arrived. Along one end of the salon, a group of women clustered together in conversation.

Janine stationed herself between a pillar and an orange tree to view the guests, trying not to be noticed. *Are Etienne and his lady here?* She scanned the faces in the crowd but didn't spot Etienne among them.

A light touch to her arm startled her. A jovial, portly man stepped into her line of vision. "My dear, you are far too lovely to be hidden from view. Come, let others feast their eyes on you." Before she could respond, the middle-aged man led her to the dance floor. At least she'd have a better view of the dancers twirling past them.

When the music stopped she excused herself and made her way to the sideline toward Lieutenant Lenoir.

"A pleasure to see you again, Mademoiselle de Fleury." The lieutenant kissed Janine's hand. "Shall we dance before the floor becomes yet more crowded?"

She nodded. *He is a charmer—too much so, I fear.* Her misty lavender silk gown garnered many an appraising look from the ladies and approving glances from the gentlemen. In the arms of the gallant lieutenant, she felt as if she were floating around the dance floor.

After the music ended, the general and Minette joined Janine.

"Shall we?" At the sound of music, General de Bernay propelled her away from most of the dancing couples.

As the last notes sounded, Lenoir positioned himself to claim the next dance and managed to keep possession of her for two more dances after that. Then, on a swirl of music, the crowd parted long enough for Janine to see Etienne across the room. He danced with a pretty, young blonde girl who gave him furtive glances and talked rapidly. *She's a mere child. Can she be the one?* They disappeared from view as suddenly as they had appeared and the magic of the evening faded.

Janine reached for Lenoir's hand. "I'd like a glass of champagne."

"Now or after the next dance?"

"Now."

They found chairs together along the sideline. Janine sipped the champagne for its steadying effect.

"Wait here." The lieutenant set his glass on a small table. "I'll bring a plate for us." He returned with a rainbow of appetizers arranged in an artistic pattern. The selection included butter-dipped asparagus, crisp pastry shells filled with chicken in a heavy cream sauce, and cream-filled pastries topped with strawberries and sugarcoated grapes. "I suggest we retire to the relative quiet of the conservatory to eat this."

"Excellent suggestion. I'm lucky to hear every other word in here." As the clock struck ten, Janine followed him to a secluded garden room. She welcomed a reprieve from the scene of her emotional conflict and forced herself to concentrate on the pleasant company of the lieutenant—an accomplished conversationalist—a man who clearly understood the social graces of interaction with a woman. She breathed deeply and tried to convince herself of her good fortune to be with him. "Is your silk business here in the Loire Valley?" she asked. She sought to ease her inner pain by listening to the tranquil sound of his voice, its hypnotic effect enhanced by that of the champagne. He was a charming companion, but he didn't melt her heart the way the brusque Colonel Tremeau did.

He swirled the champagne around the sides of his glass, lifting his eyes to hers. "Here . . . and in Lyon," he said, satisfaction evident in his voice.

She tilted her head. No question she could keep him talking on this topic. "Has it been in the family a long time?"

"Soon to be one hundred years. My great grandfather and his brother founded it in 1705; hence, the name 'Lenoir Frères'."

"I love silk velvet. My fifteenth birthday dress was made of *magnifique* green velvet from Maison . . . Your house of silk—Maison Lenoir Frères?"

"Oui."

"Your silks are the crème de la crème."

"You are very kind."

"I made the sketch for that gown, the first of many I've designed since."

He reached for her hand and brought it to his lips. "We've discovered something else we have in common . . . a love of working with fabrics. I create the patterns for most of our damasks and brocades." He looked upward, as though visualizing the fabrics. A pensive expression crossed his face. "I painted pictures of fabric patterns for our company while other men my age lost their lives on the battlefield."

Each of us orphaned in our youth. A feeling of kinship with this young lieutenant coursed through her. "You did what you had to, and now you're in the army." Janine gave him a wistful smile. "I'd love to learn about silk production."

"Are you just being polite or do you really want to get me started?"

"I'm most serious. Fabrics and fashion are dear to my heart."

"You must come to Maison Lenoir Frères and see the entire process."

"I'd love to. Do you keep silkworms or buy raw silk?" Janine held a strawberry in her hand, poised to take a bite. "You did say the entire process."

"We have a small mulberry grove and a raw silk production center on site. Much of our operation was destroyed in 1794. Fortunately, business is much better now that General and Madame Bonaparte are favoring fine fabrics in their homes."

"How will you meet the demand for silk with so little raw silk?"

"We augment our supplies with imports from Italy."

"Where is your business located . . . in town?"

"It's on the grounds of our family home near the quay . . . across the Loire about five miles from here. I do hope that you and Madame de Bernay will be able to come."

Minette won't pass the chance. "She shares my interest. I'll speak to her."

"If you would like, my sister and I will arrange for our coach to fetch you."

"I doubt that will be necessary, but I'm most grateful for your offer."

"You spoke about reclaiming Chateau Fleury. Have you and your uncle recently returned from England?"

Minette didn't tell him? "No, I've been in New Orleans for ten years."

He arched an eyebrow. "New Orleans! Whatever for?"

"I accompanied a family from Bordeaux."

"What about your uncle? Wasn't he successful in reclaiming the estate?"

"Contrary to the story that has been circulated, the man representing himself as my uncle is an imposter. My uncle was murdered before I left the country."

"I can't believe it. Have you met the man?"

"No, he's playing cat and mouse with me. His caretaker says he's in England."

"This is a serious situation. What do you plan to do?"

"I met with a notary who told me the seal had been removed from Chateau Fleury upon the request of the owner. The property has been returned to him. All the documentation is in order, so I have no recourse with the authorities unless I have proof that some irregularity took place in the process."

"Do you know of any?"

"Yes, my uncle is dead, so the whole thing in irregular. I need to have a court order to open our family crypt. Perhaps my proof lies there."

The lieutenant reached for her hand and caressed it. "A dreadful state of affairs. I was devastated when my father was guillotined. My mother lost her husband, witnessed the decline of the silk markets, and lost her will to live."

"But at least she had her children and home," Janine said.

"No, her home and the family means of livelihood were plundered." Lenoir rested his face in his hands. "She couldn't reconcile herself to her two sons' service in the Republican Army while the madman, Robespierre, committed endless murders of our countrymen."

"Why . . . did you join the army?"

"I had no choice . . . if I wanted to remain in France after Carnot instituted mandatory conscription."

"But you've returned to the army? Why?"

"General Bonaparte is a reasonable man and brings glory to France. If we are to survive, we must learn to look to the future rather than dwell on the past."

The past may well be the future. Janine nibbled a grape and kept her thoughts to herself.

In the distance the clock chimed the hour. The lieutenant gave Janine a studied look. "I've kept you from the party too long."

"We had best return so as not to offend our host and hostess." Janine edged her glass to the center of the table.

"Do you think they keep track of all their guests?"

"Maybe not all, but I'm sure they'll notice that you and I haven't been dancing."

"General de Bernay has requested a number of the officers meet with him a half hour before the midnight dinner. I'm among those summoned to the briefing."

Etienne too? "We have time for another dance before your meeting."

Lenoir's melodious voice interrupted her musings. "How is Monday morning for your introduction to silk production at Maison Lenoir Frères?"

"I'll speak with Madame de Bernay and let you know."

"*Bon.*" Lenoir rose and extended his hand to Janine. After kissing her cheek, he brushed his lips across hers. "A lovely woman makes for a lovely evening."

Although many couples danced, Janine noticed the general and a group of men in uniform stood in the corner nearest the library door. Etienne was not among them.

As Janine and Lenoir slipped among the dancers, she watched for Etienne and the blonde girl but didn't see them. Then, just as Lenoir started to lead her from the floor, she heard Etienne's rich, baritone, matter-of-fact voice.

"Mademoiselle de Fleury, what a surprise seeing you here. May I have the pleasure of the next dance?"

"I'd be delighted." She lowered her voice. "I didn't expect to see you here either."

Lenoir hesitated, looking toward the general and back at Etienne. "Good evening, Colonel Tremeau. It's clear you need no introduction," he said, an edge to his voice. He released Janine's hand and moved in the direction of the military men.

"Have you booked passage to New Orleans yet?" Etienne gave Janine a doubtful look.

"Non. I'm not ready to leave yet," Janine said. *Why doesn't he say something like 'you look beautiful tonight'?*

"I saw you earlier, but you vanished before I could speak with you. And now I must attend the general's private gathering."

"Perhaps we can talk after dinner."

"Not tonight. I don't plan to stay for dinner." A stubborn expression crossed Etienne's face, but his blue eyes glistened like royal silk, betraying a sincere regret.

Janine pressed his hand and tried to understand his unspoken words. "Are you home for long this time?" She wanted to tell him about her meeting with the notary. He'd have good advice for her.

"I never know how long I'll be in any one place." He released her hand and turned from her.

Why was he so elusive? With a twinge of resentment, she watched him until he disappeared behind the closed library door. It wasn't the warm reunion she'd desired and needed.

His companion appeared to be as distressed about Etienne's departure as Janine was. The jovial gentleman who'd danced with Janine earlier in the evening led the teary-eyed girl from among the dancing couples. A gray-haired woman joined them as they made their way to Minette. After they had spoken to her, they turned and went toward the door. The likeable gentleman spotted Janine and paused beside her.

"Mademoiselle de Fleury, I'd like you to meet my family. This is my wife, Madame La Roche. And may I present my daughter, Mademoiselle La Roche."

Chapter 15

Janine watched Minette fidget on the coach seat and purse her lips, a most uncharacteristic behavior for the usually composed woman. She had seemed eager to accompany Janine to Lenoir's home, so what had changed?

Wheels crunched on the gravel as their coach edged forward along the private road leading from the de Bernay country home toward Maison Lenoir Frères. Before they reached the main road, pounding hooves silenced the sound of those of their own horses. Two riders on horseback burst into view, rounding a curve and leaving a trail of dust in their wake.

"Who can that be? I hope they're not the bearers of unpleasant news." Minette leaned forward and squinted into the morning sun.

Janine's heart skipped a beat when she recognized Etienne's large gray horse. She quickly turned her head so Minette wouldn't notice her response. Had he come to see her—or General de Bernay?

"Bonjour." Etienne dismounted and approached the carriage. "Forgive our intrusion, but it is urgent that I speak with Janine at once."

An audible sigh of relief escaped Minette. "News for Janine. Can't it wait until later in the day?"

Janine's heart sank. There was no time to talk with him now. Minette and she were expected at Lieutenant Lenoir's home before lunch to tour the silk production facilities. "We have an appointment and can delay only a few minutes," she said, silently pleading for Etienne's understanding.

"In that case, it can await your convenience." He started to leave, returning when Janine called to him.

"Etienne, I have news and want to get your opinion. Can we meet tomorrow or Wednesday?"

Minette shook her head. "Better not schedule anything for tomorrow. Perhaps the lieutenant will want to see you again."

Janine wanted to strangle Minette. She'd said that on purpose to let Etienne know where they were going. She opened her mouth to protest, but Etienne had already retorted, "Madame, I should think it is Janine's decision as to whether she has a prior commitment." Etienne started to say something else but seemed to think better of it.

Janine gave Minette an icy look and spoke with emphasis. "I wish to meet with Etienne tomorrow. I will be unavailable for other activities." She turned to him to see the stubborn set of his jaw. Clearly he was displeased—but with whom?

"Perhaps it's best we talk when you return to Madame Parot's—where there are fewer distractions." Etienne remounted his horse. "I'll delay you no longer."

Janine watched him ride away. She'd have to go to Madame Parot's to meet Etienne. Irritation with Minette continued to build until Janine could no longer contain herself. "Minette, why did you interject Lenoir into the conversation with Etienne?"

As the coach got underway, Minette said, "Why, chérie, you looked at a loss as to what to say, so I came to your aid. That's all."

"Is it? I knew perfectly well what I wanted to say . . . and you didn't say it."

"Relax. You must be your usual charming self today at Maison Lenoir Frères."

"Of course I'll be gracious, but why are you so concerned?"

"Chérie, you've asked, so I'll tell you. You are wasting your time on Etienne Tremeau. If I didn't know better, I'd think you worshipped him . . . put him on an undeserved pedestal. Don't you know he considers your class of people his enemy?"

"Trust me. I do know Etienne, and he does care about me. I also know his political views, and believe it or not, I understand why he holds them."

Minette ignored Janine. She would not be deterred from the matchmaking role assigned to her by Josephine Bonaparte. She'd have to handle Janine with great care. Her job was to promote the lieutenant to Janine, who clung to Tremeau as the last vestige of her life before the Revolution. Those times were gone and Janine needed to come terms with it—just as she herself had done. *She's beating her head against a brick wall.*

"Isn't it wonderful that Maison Lenoir Frères survived the Revolution and is again thriving now that life is getting back to normal under Bonaparte?" Minette said. "Lenoir is one of the most desirable and eligible men in our social circle."

Janine raised her eyebrows. "I'm happy for the Lenoir family's good fortune. But in your praise of Bonaparte, you fail to acknowledge that the French king still lives in exile."

Minette placed her hand on Janine's arm. "Believe me, I know how hard it is to live through political upheaval and change—especially such a violent one. Let's not dwell on unhappy memories of those times."

"I'll never forget." Janine stared out the window.

"Of course scars remain, but the sooner you can move on with your life the better."

"I do agree with you on that."

"Let's change the subject and enjoy the day," Minette sought to soothe Janine. "I'm looking forward to the tour. My only knowledge of silk comes from selecting finished fabrics."

Janine mellowed. "Mine, too."

Janine's smile seemed to portend a pleasant visit. Minette settled back on her seat, no longer feeling the need to chatter constantly to lift her companion's mood.

"I think Etienne would be interested in silk production," Janine said. "I doubt he has visited a production center."

Minette bolted up in her seat. *Can't she forget him for more than a few minutes?* "I wouldn't think so."

"Just a thought."

Minette leaned back and hoped the subject was closed.

After the coach left the public road, a grove of mature mulberry trees nestled among acres of smaller ones came into view. In the distance the burned-out remains of what had once been an imposing chateau could be seen. As the coach drew closer, Janine gave a gasp of dismay, her heart sinking. This was nothing like she expected or what she had been led to believe.

An odd assortment of buildings sat on the periphery of the ruins: a strong storehouse and two cheap bungalows, which she surmised were the silk production centers of the lieutenant's supposedly flourishing business. Averting her eyes from the rubble, she watched Lenoir move toward the carriage, his face a mixture of pride and shame. Janine's heart twisted for him. He hadn't mentioned the loss of his home. She sought to compose herself as he drew closer and extended a hand to help her down.

"Welcome to Maison Lenoir Frères. Please accept my apologies that I cannot entertain you inside the chateau," he said in a resigned tone. "We've just begun restoring our home. It received severe damage during the Revolution." He pointed toward the arched opening in the tall cypress hedge. A scarred wall with boarded up windows and a crumbled chimney gave testimony to the extent of the destruction.

Placing her hand on his arm in a gesture of sympathy, Janine imagined how she would feel had Chateau Fleury suffered a similar fate. "I am so sorry. How dreadful to behold such senseless destruction." In the back of her mind, she recalled the elaborate coach Lenoir owned, no doubt an attempt to keep up appearances.

He shook his head. "When I returned home from the army, things seemed hopeless. Most of the mulberry groves were damaged beyond redemption, and two of the three production buildings were burned to the ground." He took a deep breath. "Enough of my tale of woe. Come this way."

He escorted the two women into a courtyard linking all three structures. At least half the white paint had peeled off the stone façade. Pieces of it lay on the ground like snowflakes among bits of gold gravel. Janine felt a sense of chagrin on behalf of the Lenoirs. So many aristocratic families shared their fate, if indeed they even survived to witness it.

Pausing on a carpet of velvety moss in front of the stone building, he opened the door and invited them inside.

When inside, Janine inhaled deeply and sniffed again. What was the delicious aroma? Cinnamon and cooked apples—that was it.

And then all thoughts faded. She felt as though her fairy godmother had waved a magic wand and propelled her into a prism of brilliant colors as she came farther into the huge barn-like room. She took no notice of the bare, rough-hewn, wood floor. All she saw was the beauty before her. Her eyes moved along the group of large, colorful illustrations lining the full length of the end of the room where she stood. Disappointed the other walls were bare; she took heart when she spotted display tables filled with a rainbow of gorgeous silk fabrics at the far end of the room.

Without thought she began to mentally rearrange the space to better display the silks—to give it a woman's touch. She observed that light from a row of clerestory windows across the north wall illuminated the framed designs but left the distant areas in shadow. She wanted to examine every detail—to study the design patterns and to run her fingertips along the seductive textures of the smooth and patterned fabrics, to see the rich colors unimpeded.

Janine pulled herself from her reverie and made a sweeping movement with her hand at the wall decorations. "They're beautiful. Are these your work?"

The lieutenant shook his head. "The one on the far end is my grandfather's—commissioned by King Louis for one of the salons at Versailles." Lenoir pointed in the opposite direction. "And that one is my father's work for Madame de Pompadour."

"And where are yours displayed?" Janine asked with genuine interest.

Lenoir hesitated as if at a loss for words, all the while holding her gaze. "A very special one of mine is an early design commissioned by your father for the green salon at Chateau Fleury." He spoke scarcely above a whisper. "I wonder if it is still there."

Janine was dumbstruck. She'd always admired it, but as she recalled, the design was by Père Lenoir, at least he'd so represented it. *If it is the lieutenant's design, Minette is justified in her praise of his talent.* She prided herself on her own designs and business success, but they paled in comparison to that fabric. "I remember it well . . . so long ago. Where are your recent designs placed?"

"You want to know if I am continuing to attract clients equal to those of my predecessors?" he teased.

"I'm sure you are, and I am interested to learn more."

"As you wish. Presently, I'm preparing fabric sketches for salon chairs and drapery at Malmaison, General and Josephine Bonaparte's country chateau."

Janine realized that with such a commission he was assured of recognition. "Maison Lenoir Frères continues to be a leading silk production house."

After Minette left them for the table of silks, Lenoir leaned close to Janine. "I'll wager your clothing designs would do justice to our silks. I would very much like to see your work."

"As you wish, but I'm sure you have seen the best Paris has to offer."

Minette returned to Janine's side but spoke to Lenoir. "I've found a number of your silks I wish to have made into gowns. I'll keep my dressmaker busy."

Lenoir smiled. "I'm gratified to hear it."

A young woman who looked to be an exhausted female version of the lieutenant appeared from the double doors to their left. She wore a plain cotton dress and apron. Lenoir introduced her as his sister, Aimée.

"Welcome. What a pleasure to meet you both," Aimée said after the formal introductions had been made. "I'm sorry to have kept you waiting. I've been putting the finishing touches on the salad." Her wistful eyes lingered on Minette's elegant dress. "I've prepared a light lunch for you before your tour begins." She led the way to an informal dining room with a long head table and six smaller ones, each covered with red-and-white-checkered cloths. The whitewashed walls brightened the expanse of the room. She excused herself for a moment and returned with a large bowl of salad, followed by a girl who carried a platter of chicken in one hand and a tray of assorted breads in the other.

"I regret this is our only dining area until the chateau restoration is completed," Lenoir's sister said as she took her place at the table.

"All of our resources went into rebuilding our business. But now we're able to start work on our home." Lenoir passed a plate to Janine while his sister gave one to Minette. After their meal, the lieutenant led them through the courtyard to the back door of one of the new buildings. "We'll begin with the sericulture area so that you can see where we get the raw silk."

Janine looked all around. "Where's Aimée?"

"She's in the kitchen I would imagine," he said with a shrug.

"She'll be joining us soon?" Janine asked.

Lenoir faced Janine, a questioning look on his face. "She isn't involved with this area. She keeps the home fires burning and the accounts in order."

"Isn't she interested in designing?" Janine asked.

Lenoir shook his head. "She expresses her creativity in

106

domestic areas." He stopped beneath clusters of silkworm cocoons hung from the ceiling.

Minette looked around the space. "Where's the silk?"

Lenoir chuckled and handed each of them a cocoon. "You're holding raw silk. Every one of these consists of just one very fine continuous thread."

Minette thrust the cocoon back at him. "Here, let me return this homely thing for you to work magic. All I care about is your fabrics fit for a queen."

"Is the silkworm still inside?" Janine asked, still troubled that Aimée seemed so far removed from the family business. Did she want it that way? She rolled the cocoon between her thumb and forefinger, an absentminded expression of her turmoil.

"Non." Lenoir carried on, oblivious to Janine's troubled thoughts. "The last step for the silkworm to turn itself into a moth is to make an escape hole. Let's move on." They passed women hand-reeling threads onto wooden spindles while other women worked with reeling machines.

"Machines are much faster. Why aren't they used for all of this work?" Janine asked.

"That's a reasonable question. With hand reeling we're able to get three grades of silk—two fine grades ideal for lightweight fabrics and a third, thicker one that serves for heavier fabrics." Lenoir moved closer to Janine. "Without even seeing your designs, I'm certain they'll require the finest silks."

Janine stared at him. "I'm impressed with your confidence in my abilities."

"I've noted your keen interest in things of beauty," he said, placing his hand on her arm. He looked around and spoke to Minette as they moved along. "Now we come to the weaving area. I'm sure you'll find this process much more enthralling. On each machine the warp is threaded on the loom according to the design. It requires two skilled workers, the weaver who inserts the weft and a draw boy who controls the pattern."

He paused. "I think you'll be especially interested in this new mechanical loom invented by Joseph Jacquard. I'm fortunate to have a prototype here to test. It can be adjusted to weave even more complex patterned textiles without the aid of a second worker. It promises to reduce production costs."

Fascinated, Janine watched the designs come forth from the loom. "What a time-saving device."

"Oui. I expect you'll want to spend time looking at the various patterns of finished silk fabrics. Before you leave I want each of you to select a fabric to take with you today as a token of our time together."

He was being very gracious, but as far as Janine was concerned, his carefully orchestrated presentation fell short—he'd treated Aimée in a cavalier fashion. Because of that Janine's impression of him diminished, but all she said aloud was, "Before we leave, I wish to thank your sister for the delicious lunch."

Janine found Aimée sketching at the kitchen table. "We're getting ready to go now. I want to thank you for the lovely lunch. I'm so glad we met."

Aimée quickly placed her hand over the drawing. "Don't mention this to my brother. He says it's a waste of my time."

Shaken by Lenoir's treatment of his sister, Janine couldn't get away from him soon enough. But as the carriage made its way past the mulberry grove, she caught sight of a lone rider lurking among the trees. He wove in and out, keeping pace with the coach. "Look over there," alarmed, Janine pointed in the rider's direction. "Do you see that man on horseback among the trees?"

Minette shook her head. "I don't see anything, but there's no need to worry. The coachman's armed."

Janine caught occasional glimpses of the man until the coach reached the main road. Was he spying on them or just one of Lenoir's workers?

Chapter 16

The miniscule window in Janine's small bedroom at Madame Parot's let in little light to brighten the drab space. *What a shame Etienne insisted we meet here.* A final glance at her reflection in the mottled looking glass provided no boost to her mood or self-confidence. She would need to use her feminine wiles as well as her wits to persuade him to help her through the legal maze to claim Chateau Fleury.

With a resigned sigh Janine left the oppressive room. She stopped, staring in disbelief at the pail of fresh cut flowers by the front door. Sounds of rapid footsteps in the kitchen blended with those of sizzling bacon. She went into the kitchen, savoring the aroma of fresh baked bread mingled with that of bacon. Madame Parot had gone all out to woo her tenant. The table was laid with rolls, jam, and bread.

"Good morning, dear," the older woman said as she brought the teapot and a plate of bacon to the table. "I'll be off to the market, but I've set out extra cups for Colonel and Madame Tremeau."

Janine succumbed to the woman's efforts to please, wondering how long it would last. "Thank you. You've thought of everything," she murmured, pouring herself a cup of tea.

"I know you'll have a pleasant visit. It'll do you good to have guests," Madame Parot purred on her way out of the room, so unlike her usual mournful self.

Janine lingered over her tea and thought of Etienne's visit. Seeing him again had awakened longings she had tried to deny after the signing of her marriage contract so long ago. Charles hadn't been a part of her life during the intervening years. He remained a two-dimensional image in her memory—not a living, breathing man who cared for her.

She'd need to steel herself to resist her attraction to Etienne. So vulnerable was she when he was near. She pressed her hand to her lips and indulged in remembering their indiscretion, the embraces and kisses.

She blinked and rose upon hearing a knock on the door. How long had she been sitting there? She lightly brushed her fingertips along her hair and adjusted the folds of her dress before opening the door for Etienne and his mother. "Please, come in."

Madame Tremeau slipped her arm around Janine's waist.

"How are you?" Her voice held a loving concern that made Janine long for her own mother.

"I'm well, *merci*." Janine led Madame Tremeau the few steps into the sitting room, followed by Etienne. "I haven't been sleeping well, though. I have a lot on my mind just now."

"How can we help?" Etienne kept his eyes on Janine, taking a chair facing her.

"You already have by coming today. Tea?" she asked after they were seated.

"Please," Madame Tremeau said.

"I'll assist you." Etienne ignored his mother's quizzical look and followed Janine into the kitchen.

She turned toward him, her eyes smarting with suppressed tears. "I'm feeling a bit overwhelmed with all that has happened since we last spoke."

He stepped closer and gently brushed a wisp of hair that fell across her cheek. "What has changed?"

She bit her lower lip to stop its quavering. She wanted to melt into his arms but stayed immobile. "I've seen a notary about Chateau Fleury. He told me that all of the ownership claim documents are in order as far as he can tell. I have no legal recourse for a challenge."

Placing his hand on Janine's shoulder, Etienne said, "There may be a way. If there is, we'll find it."

Janine looked away from him and found Madame Tremeau standing in the doorway. *How long has she been there?*

Madame moved around the table and fixed her gaze on them. "Let me take the tray for you, Janine. Will you be long, Etienne?"

"Not long, Maman." Etienne removed his hand from Janine's shoulder and watched his mother depart with the tea service. "It seems to me whoever this other Comte de Fleury is must have done extensive research about your family . . . unless he, or someone he knows, was closely associated with your father."

Janine pressed her hand to her forehead. "I can't imagine who he may be."

"Mull it over. You may think of someone." Etienne motioned to the sitting room. "Better not keep Mother waiting."

"Let's not." Janine and Etienne returned to the living room and sat. Janine accepted a cup of tea from Madame Tremeau, her mood lifted by Etienne's encouraging words. "I do have some good news. I

110

found my nanny, Cecile."

Etienne declined the cup his mother offered. "That is good news. I remember Cecile. She may be our best source of information right now."

Janine shook her head, doubting her nanny could tell them much.

Etienne ignored her. "She stayed on at the chateau after you'd gone and told me she intended to wait for you there."

"I doubt she can help us now. Her memory and health have deteriorated. It's strange . . . she's being called Gemma."

"She was still at Chateau Fleury when I left for the army. Maman, have you heard anything more about her?"

"Non." Madame Tremeau bowed her head for a moment. "Not much. Perhaps she wanted a fresh start and took another name when she left the house."

Etienne stood and moved to the window. "We have more questions than answers. When did she leave the chateau? Under what conditions did she leave? Did she feel threatened by anyone in particular?"

Behind closed eyelids Janine confronted the guilt she'd tried to deny. She recalled every word Cecile had said to her before she fled her home. "Nanny said, 'I will be waiting right here for your return until death claims me.'" Struck by how naïve she had been, Janine shuddered at the thought of how she'd left her there in spite of the danger. *I abandoned her that dreadful day.*

A gentle touch to her shoulder drew her back into the present. She opened her eyes, expecting to see Madame Tremeau, but when she raised her head, she found herself looking into Etienne's eyes—a calm and caring sea of blue—before he averted them.

After an awkward silence, Etienne's mother removed the tea service and took it to the kitchen. "Did something I say upset you?" Etienne sat down beside Janine.

"It's nothing you've done. I'm the one responsible for what has happened to Cecile. I could have ordered her to leave Chateau Fleury." Janine nodded as to if affirm her own statements. "Away from there she would have been safe."

"Stop thinking that way. It is *not* your fault. I heard the two of you talking before we left. One of the last things you said was for her to leave, but she refused. Believe me, you did all that you could to protect her." Etienne took her hands in his. "Look at me. You do know that, don't you?"

Janine longed to be held in his arms and not just because of the rational advice he offered. She rested against the back of the settee, her heart rebelling against the required decorum. "I do know. I'll try to use my energy more wisely. I just wish she hadn't suffered so."

"I trust you were able to carry on without me," Madame Tremeau said as she rejoined them.

"Oui, Maman." Etienne gave her a nod then turned back to Janine. "Of course you care about what has happened to her. Let's visit her this afternoon."

"I would like that. Madame Tremeau, are you free to go with us?" Janine asked.

"I am. But first I need to take care of a few chores at home. Afterward, we can leave whenever you like."

"Etienne, at the de Bernays' home, you told me you have information of interest to me. Is it about Chateau Fleury?"

"Oui. I know you're upset about the man who claimed the chateau. So I made inquiries about the Comte de Fleury and have found that a man who presented himself as the comtehad been in London for about two years before the claim was processed for the chateau."

"How could he succeed in passing himself off as my uncle?"

"He's a crafty one. He's adept at getting out of precarious positions. He was involved in an altercation resulting in the death of the other man, but he disappeared before completion of the investigation."

"That pretender made elaborate plans to steal Chateau Fleury . . . and prevailed. And got away with murder too," Janine said with bitterness.

"It seems that way."

"Did you find anything that might help identify him?"

"The distinctive thing mentioned is that he spoke in a whisper and claimed to have sustained an injury to his vocal cords. Of course that may have been an affectation to disguise his true voice while in London. We can only hope that's the case."

"If it's true, he should stand out like a sunflower in December." Janine said.

112

"Oui." Etienne looked at his mother. "Maman, we'd better go if you're going to visit Cecile this afternoon." He turned to Janine. "What time shall we get started?"

"Two. If you'll be ready then." Janine stood and accompanied them into the yard.

Madame Tremeau nodded and started walking home. Etienne paused and asked, "Are things satisfactory here with Madame Parot?"

Janine nodded. "So far. She talks a blue streak if I give her half a chance though."

Etienne smiled. "I don't doubt it. It'll be convenient having you close by while piecing together clues about the Chateau Fleury mystery."

"Oui." Along with her gratitude for Etienne's willingness to help her, she feared she would never have the chance to awaken the deep affection he had declared for her in his youth. Unreasonable, yes, but there was a connection between them—one she couldn't imagine being without. Before turning toward the house, she watched him stride away without as much as one backward glance.

To Janine's mind the scene at the half-timbered house seemed frozen in time. Nanny Cecile's emaciated body rested in a slatted chair, her head propped up on a pillow and her eyes closed, just as during her previous visit. Janine drew close to Cecile while Etienne and his mother stayed a few paces back. "Nanny Cecile, it's Janine," she said softly. "How are you today?" She received no indication of recognition. With apprehension she continued to try to reach her. "You remember Etienne Tremeau, don't you? He and his mother are here, too."

Cecile turned her head and stared at Etienne. "Come closer," she demanded with a sudden burst of conscious recognition. Etienne stepped forward until he stood within a few inches of her. Nanny peered at him. "Young man, you've arrived too late. Where have you been?"

"Too late for what?" he asked.

The old woman straightened and shook her thin finger at him. "I expected more from you. You earned my trust and then abandoned

Chateau Fleury and us. How could you? You loved this girl." She pointed to Janine.

Janine held her breath, wondering how Etienne would respond.

"I loved you *and* Janine." Kneeling on one knee beside Cecile, Etienne patted her arm. "Non, I didn't abandon you. I came when I could—until I went away with the army."

Nanny began to shake, her voice weakening. "You weren't there. I . . . waited as long . . . as I could. Soldiers left, other men came."

"What other men?" Etienne stroked her hair as he spoke until her trembling ceased.

"Bushy eyebrows . . . peg leg."

"What about the other men?"

Cecile opened and closed her mouth before running her tongue across her dry lips. "Water."

"I'll get a glass of water for you," Madame Tremeau offered.

"The others . . ." Cecile moaned and gripped Etienne's hand. "The . . . groomsman . . . can't remember name."

"The groomsman from Chateau Fleury?"

She slumped and began to slip forward. Etienne put his arm around her shoulders and eased her back against the chair. Her eyes glittered. "Oui."

Madame Tremeau returned with a damp cloth and a small cup of water. Janine patted Cecile's lips with the cloth before holding the cup to her parched lips. Cecile took a swallow and then sipped a little more. "No more," she said, pushing Janine's hand away.

Etienne returned to Cecile's side. "Did the groomsman return to the chateau after Janine went away?"

Cecile frowned at him. "How would I know the comings and goings of the staff?"

"What about after the family and staff fled?" Etienne prompted.

"What are you rambling on about? I mind my own business, not that of everyone else."

"Did you stay there alone for a while?"

"Non, I was the family nanny. Cared for the children."

"You stayed after the family left. While you were still there, three men came. Remember?"

"Go away. I've told you all I know." She closed her eyes and

114

folded her arms against her chest.

Etienne stepped behind Cecile's chair and shook his head at Janine, who nodded and spoke softly to Cecile, feeling utterly hopeless. Poor Cecile. She had to get away. She couldn't do anything for her dear nanny. "Do you want to stay out here or would you like me to take you inside?"

"Leave me alone." Nanny's voice was barely above a whisper, utter fatigue evident.

"You rest now. We'll come again soon." Janine adjusted the pillow before leaving.

After assisting Janine and his mother into the small carriage, Etienne climbed into the driver's side and took the reins. After they got underway, he tried to make sense of what Cecile had said. The man with the bushy eyebrows and peg leg matched the description of the man who had attacked Janine outside the Grand Hotel. Could it be that he and the murdering groomsman had driven Cecile from the chateau, disposing of a major obstacle to the false claim? The groomsman . . . how did he connect with the man in London who claimed to be Comte de Fleury?

"Cecile's description of the peg-legged man sounds a lot like the man who attacked you at the Grand Hotel." Etienne shared his suspicions with Janine and watched for her reaction. Without warning, Cecile's comment about his love for Janine interrupted his thoughts. He'd been so focused on getting information about the chateau that it hadn't fully registered at the time. He forced it aside.

"How would that man know where to find me?" Janine asked.

"Janine, we don't know for sure it's the same man," Madame Tremeau said in a soothing voice.

"While you went for water, Cecile identified the second man as your groomsman at the chateau. I don't think that's a coincidence. I believe the third man with them is the one who now occupies Chateau Fleury," Etienne said.

Janine gasped and put her hand over her heart. "The groomsman came back? But Cecile said he didn't."

"My word, what are you saying?" Madame Tremeau stared at

115

Etienne.

"That's what prompted Cecile's confusion." Etienne pulled back on the reins and stopped in front of Madame Parot's house. He climbed out of the carriage and assisted Janine. "As soon we get back home, I'll follow up with the jailer about your peg-legged attacker."

When Janine and Etienne started toward the house, Madame Tremeau called to Janine, "Plan on lunch with us tomorrow. Etienne can tell you about his findings."

When they reached the front door, Etienne paused momentarily and gazed at Janine. 'Loved her,' Cecile's words echoed in his ears. *I suppose I did . . . and still do. Cursed love, will I never be free?* He inched toward the carriage.

Chapter 17

The next day Janine's mood brightened while walking the short distance to the Tremeaus' cottage. Anticipation of being with Etienne again brought a free-spirited bounce to her steps. She laughed at her shadow caricature created by golden shafts of sunlight slicing through the gray fog. Brimming with optimism, she believed that Etienne would uncover the identities of the conspirators. Yes, she saw him as her knight in shining armor. His physical strength was daunting, and his mental agility a formidable challenge for his foes. *Stop.* She chastised herself for indulging in unabashed admiration for the man.

Soon she would know of Etienne's success with the jailer. What had he found out about the man who stole Chateau Fleury? She approached the house, hopeful of adding pieces to the puzzle.

Upon her arrival she tapped on the door, expecting to see Etienne. Instead, Anne opened it and gave her an enthusiastic hug. "Come. The table's set and lunch is almost ready."

Janine looked for Etienne as she went with Anne to the kitchen but found Madame Tremeau alone, paring an apple.

Madame set the knife and apple down and patted her hands on her apron before giving Janine a hug. "We're almost ready to sit down," she said, turning to place the last apple slices on a plate.

"I do hope Etienne doesn't keep us waiting," Anne glanced toward the back porch. "Sometimes he loses all sense of time when he's in the garden—says he goes there to think. Come, let's fetch him," she said to Janine.

As they reached the garden, Janine looked toward the lavender plants, a place he might work off some of his energy. "I don't see him."

"He's over there, grooming his horse." Anne watched her brother for a moment without moving then she whispered, "He's been quiet all morning. Something's troubling him."

"I hope it's nothing serious."

Anne shrugged and started toward him. "Lunch is ready," she called.

Etienne didn't look their way until the gate hinges squeaked. "Bonjour, Janine."

"Bonjour." Hesitating, Janine stopped a few paces from him.

"Are you about finished?" Anne walked to his side and patted the horse.

"Almost," Etienne said without looking up. "You go ahead. I'll be there in a few minutes."

Janine and Anne left and walked to the far side of the garden, pausing to pick a couple of sun-ripened tomatoes. By the time they reached the porch steps, Etienne was in step with them.

Madame Tremeau stopped fussing with the glass jar of red and white carnations and placed them on the table as they came into the kitchen.

They all sat down and began passing the various bowls and platters. "Everything looks delicious," Janine said, helping herself to sliced beef, a hardboiled egg, and bread.

"I didn't cook a hot meal because I didn't want to heat up the kitchen," Madame said as she took a chunk of cheese and several slices of apple. Then she frowned. "I'm worried about your nanny, Cecile. She's so frail."

Anne stopped buttering her bread and looked up. "Maman, how do you know?"

"Dear, your brother and I went with Janine to visit her yesterday."

"While I was in town?"

"Oui."

Anne held her mother's gaze. "I'm sorry I was gone longer than I expected." She broke a piece of bread and held it. "Janine, now that Adrien and Etienne are home, I'll be able to wear my new gown," she said, her voice full of anticipation.

Janine's heart skipped a beat. *The opera this weekend—Anne's big evening with Etienne and his lady.* "I'm sure you'll look lovely and will have a wonderful time." Janine watched Etienne and took some comfort in his apparent lack of interest in their conversation.

"I know we shall. Mademoiselle La Roche invited me to tea and surprised me with a pair of shoes to match my gown." Anne's face glowed with excitement.

The weepy Mademoiselle La Roche. "How did she know the color of your gown?"

"She took a sample of my fabric with her."

"She's cultivating you like one of her flowers," Janine said in an icy voice. She felt all eyes on her and altered her tone. "That's most thoughtful." She stole a look at Etienne and found him looking at her, a frown furrowing his brow as he reached for the wine decanter.

"Wine anyone?" After receiving no takers, Etienne refilled his glass. "I know Janine is anxious to hear what I learned about the man who ambushed her at the hotel." He tipped his glass and took a big swallow of wine. "I didn't get as much information as I'd hoped from the jailer." He paused for more wine. "And the prisoner has been released. A benefactor paid his fine for drunkenness in public."

"Released with no charges filed against him?" Janine asked, incredulous there had been no hearing or inquiry into his crime against her.

Etienne shook his head in disgust. "Apparently, the jail records contained a misstatement that no further charges were pending against him."

"Someone on the inside *deliberately* made the note that no further charges were pending?" Janine frowned.

"Unlikely to be a careless mistake."

"So the man has a benefactor who came to his aid?" Janine could hear the frustration in her voice. "Is that all you found out?"

"Not entirely. He gave his name as John O'Brien and claimed he came from Ireland to serve in the French army. There's no reason not to believe he told the truth. He carried a passport with . . ."

The beating of horse hooves sounded and then stopped outside the house. Etienne paused in mid-sentence and dashed toward the front door. Three sharp raps preceded the opening and closing of the door. Without speaking, the three women looked toward the street where muffled voices could be heard. Moments later the door opened and closed a second time, followed by footsteps inside the house.

"I'm sorry for the interruption," Etienne said from the kitchen doorway. "But I must leave immediately for a meeting with General de Bernay."

"General de Bernay? He won't spoil our opera plans, will he?" Anne wailed.

Her brother shot her an impatient look. "It's not likely." He paused. "Janine, I won't be free to follow up on O'Brien before Monday. As soon as possible we need to ask Cecile whether she knows of him."

"Shall we plan to call on her Monday morning?" Janine asked.

"Oui. I'll send word if there's any change in my schedule."

"I'll go with you. Poor Cecile must have suffered terribly at the hands of those awful men," Madame Tremeau said.

"Awful men. What men?" Anne said, alarm evident in her voice.

"No need for worry, dear. It's no one you know."

Anne appealed to Etienne. "I'd like to go, too . . . if you don't mind."

"I can't imagine whatever for," he grumbled, but then his expression softened. "We'll see at the time."

Etienne dismounted and patted the back of his gray stallion's neck, a ritual he had established for whenever they parted under uncertain circumstances. He hadn't anticipated another meeting with General de Bernay so soon; things had been quiet on the conspiracy front since his return from England. After hitching his horse alongside four others, he went to the front door of the townhouse.

The butler opened it in response to his knock. "Come in, Colonel Tremeau. The meeting has begun." He turned and led Etienne to the library and rapped lightly on the door.

"Colonel Tremeau, *entrez,*" General de Bernay said.

Etienne entered and quickly assessed the gravity of the situation. A second general, a lieutenant general, and another colonel—on special assignment for Bonaparte—sat around the table.

General de Bernay continued speaking. "The exiled Bourbon princes' pathetic Vendéan dissidents are on the move again—prowling around like the rats they are. Georges Cadoudal himself was spotted in Paris, and one of his closest confidants, François Carbon, has been seen in Le Mans. These sightings are most ominous. It suggests their plan to kidnap the First Consul is being readied. We must stop them before they can act. Each of you knows your responsibility. Now go and get it done." The general stood and opened the door. "Colonel Tremeau, wait here so I can fill you in on the details you missed."

Given what he had already heard, Etienne knew Bonaparte would soon order him to Paris until the danger passed.

General de Bernay closed the door after the other officers

departed, strode back to the table, and sat down across from Etienne. "Your orders are to spend the next few days here in the Loire Valley, scouring the area for any trace of Cadoudal's men and any other suspicious persons who may be part of a royalist conspiracy. After you're satisfied none of the conspirators are operating here, report directly to the First Consul in Paris at the Tuileries Palace. Any questions?"

Etienne pondered a moment before speaking. "Is this a precautionary assignment, or do you know of specific suspect activities here in the Loire Valley?"

"Since you asked, I'll give you a place to begin. I want to distance myself from this particular one. My wife's friend, Mademoiselle de Fleury, has been observed in clandestine conversation with various strangers. I told Madame de Bernay not to befriend the woman, but I was overruled because Josephine Bonaparte considers her an eligible wife for one of our officers. Huh. Upon the de Fleury woman's arrival here, she attempted to explain her presence by telling people she had returned to reclaim her family's property."

"Mon Dieu. Has she been under surveillance?" *Under whose orders? Why wasn't I informed?*

"Non, we haven't been watching her—at least not officially." The general tapped the table. "She's here more than anywhere else."

"Who observed her in these suspect conversations?"

"Three different people reported her to the local authorities," de Bernay said.

"Of course these accusations require immediate investigation," Etienne acknowledged. "But I can assure you she is serious about reclaiming her property, and there are people involved who want her out of the way." A pain, more intense than when a sword had seared his flesh, pierced his heart. Could it be true that Janine threatened the Republic? France, a land of opportunity for each individual, was a cause for which he would willingly lay down his life—as he would for Janine. *Is this why she ignores my pleas for her to leave?*

Etienne's training had taught him to put aside his own disquiet and to complete the mission. He couldn't take Janine's words at face value. "Reclaiming the chateau may well be a subterfuge to explain her presence while she is cooperating with the conspirators. God knows I hope it isn't true, for the sake of all of those who have befriended her."

"I don't have to remind you of the gravity of the matter, Colonel. Do not allow your personal sympathy for her to cloud your judgment. You're dismissed. Now get to work."

"Oui, Monsieur *le General.*"

The cloudless sky burned red as the heavenly ball of fire slid below the horizon. Janine mopped her brow as she walked along the dusty road toward the market square. She'd waited as long as she could to avoid the heat of the day before starting to town. Now she planned to loop around the market square and return to Madame Parot's before dark. By that time she could politely retire to her room and avoid her landlady's incessant chatter and bouts of wailing about her son. She just didn't have the patience for it tonight.

The main street was a beehive of activity. As Janine neared the square, she noticed the unkempt man again coming toward her, the one she had seen across the road at the edge of town. His soiled clothes were tattered and his long gray hair and scraggly beard were tangled. He was frightening, prompting her to dart through the open door of a bookshop and hide behind a bookshelf.

"*Bonsoir,* Mademoiselle. Good evening. May I be of assistance?" The shopkeeper, a non-threatening elderly man, startled her. Janine's head jerked in the direction of the voice.

"Non, just browsing," she said, turning her back to him. She leafed through a number of books before slipping out of the store. At least the bedraggled man wasn't waiting outside for her. She scanned the streets without seeing him. Only then did she move on, hoping to melt into the crowds at the marketplace.

Without stopping to look at the wares, she zigzagged between the booths, wending her way back toward the main street beyond a stand of trees. She must start back before nightfall.

"Don't be afraid," a pompous voice said while clamping a hand over her mouth and pulling her into the shadow of a tree. "Janine, I'm Charles Dupré—your future husband, risking my life coming to you. Don't let my disguise alarm you." He twirled her a half turn, just enough for her to see his profile while keeping a firm grip on her.

Her heart pounding, she stared at the disheveled man in disbelief. Could this apparent vagrant really be Charles? His arrogant manner and voice told her it could be. Yet she wasn't convinced. "Although your disguise fooled me, coming here is unwise." With a note of irritation evident in her voice, she asked, "Why *are* you here?"

Undeterred, he said, "To find you, of course. Have you settled the estate yet?" He loosened his grip a little.

"What do you mean?" He definitely needed to explain himself.

"Père wrote that you'd come here." He let go of her. "We may as well get comfortable and sit on that bench over there."

"All right." She agreed so as to avoid prying eyes. "What else did your father's letter tell you about me?" she asked, edging away from him.

"I know Merè can be harsh at times and I'm sorry. I'm aware that she gave you an ultimatum about our marriage contract."

"And she already has someone else in mind for you to marry," Janine felt a deep sense of indignation toward Madame Dupré, but now she began to wonder whether finding someone else for Charles to marry might not be for the best. She felt nothing for the man sitting beside her—the man she had kept herself for all those years in New Orleans. During those years, she hadn't wanted to renege on the marriage contract signed by her father and Monsieur Dupré, although she had certainly been treated poorly by the Duprés. But now . . .

"You know Mother," Charles' voice interrupted her thoughts. "She always keeps her options open. You shouldn't be offended. She's impatient for the marriage to take place . . . and so am I." He stretched his lanky legs in front of him. "I hope you've made good progress on closing the estate so that we can get that behind us."

Marriage, a chore? Disgusted and disillusioned, Janine wanted to tell him not to burden himself with chores—to just go away and leave her be. "It's not something I can accomplish with a wave of my hand, Charles. There are serious complications with my claim to Chateau Fleury. The marriage contract may well expire before I know whether I can regain possession of the chateau."

An intervening silence followed before Charles cleared his throat. "Of immediate concern are the desperate financial straits in which I find myself. Just give me enough money to get to New Orleans. I'll see you are repaid as soon as possible after my arrival."

Why was he short of money? "I have no extra money." Janine stood. "It's almost dark. I have to go now."

"Where are you staying?"

"Tonight I'll stay in the cathedral." It was an honest answer, although she wanted to evade the question. She would have to stay in town since he had detained her.

He reached for her arm. "I'll go with you."

"No, Charles. You're an enemy of the Republic."

"Have it your way . . . for now. I promise if you don't meet me tomorrow morning at this very bench . . . I will come to you."

Chapter 18

At the first light of dawn, Janine stepped softly along the stone slab floor, making her way past the huge limestone columns to the cathedral door. There was no time to linger and savor the transformation of the stained glass windows blossoming into full color like a flower kissed by the sun. She paused to look over her shoulder at the exquisite hues before continuing. An unwelcome complication, Charles' sudden appearance alarmed her. Although she had gone through the proper procedure to return to France, being seen with Charles could result in her arrest. She shuddered to think of her fate, as well as his.

Will Charles keep his word and leave if I give him a small sum?

The town had begun to awaken. Lights shone in windows and an occasional carriage passed along the street. A few people made their way toward the cathedral, but the center of town would be quiet for at least another hour. She thought of crossing the street when she spotted three men headed toward her. Dismissing the idea as a bad one, she continued on course. She'd attract less attention that way. As they moved closer she noticed one of them wore a wide brimmed hat, obscuring his face. He fell behind the other two and soon disappeared from view. The others passed by her without so much as a glance in her direction.

Where's the big-hat man? She whirled around and caught sight of him crossing the street, a slight hobble evident. "The peg-legged man," she muttered. Charles would have to wait. Feeling unsteady, she changed direction and followed behind the man in the general direction of Cecile's boarding house. Suddenly, he made a quick turn and began circling back toward the cathedral. He'd deliberately avoided her. Satisfied she knew where he was going, she started back toward the market square.

After taking several detours to lose anyone else who may be watching, she came to the stand of trees and bench where she'd left Charles the night before. There was no trace of him, yet she sensed the presence of unseen eyes upon her. *Where is he? I hope he hasn't been arrested?* The hairs on the back of her neck rose, and she turned just in time to see the caretaker from Chateau Fleury and a second man behind her. She held her breath. *How did I miss seeing them?* Hoping upon hope that *he* hadn't seen *her*, she left the square and started along the road leading from town.

An old woman pushing a cart came toward her. "Bonjour. We meet again." A powerful male voice—a voice she recognized—came from the stooped figure.

"*Pardonnez-moi?*" Janine studied every detail of the figure and tried to make sense of it.

"*Oui, c'est moi*, Charles."

Clearly, Charles was more experienced at evading prying eyes than she. "You're a man of many disguises. How do you manage it?"

"Ingenuity."

"We mustn't be seen together." Janine opened her handbag and removed a small linen pouch filled with coins. "This is all I can afford to give you," she said, handing Charles the bag. "Please, you must leave now."

Charles opened the bag and poured the contents into his free hand. He spread them in his palm and then dumped them back into the pouch and handed it to her. "This piddling amount won't get me out of town."

In desperation Janine said, "I'll bring more in the morning. Meet me at the park bench at seven-thirty . . . and be ready to leave town."

"Just bring the money. I'll decide when and where I go."

Janine fixed her gaze on the disgusting sight in front of her. Money. *If I don't give the Duprés the rest of my dowry, I'll be free of him and them.* She moved past him and called over her shoulder as she began to walk. "I'll be there."

As she walked along the dusty road to her boarding house, Janine was thankful to have started back before most people had left their homes. The morning was young and she wanted to be unnoticed. Why wasn't Charles in New Orleans? A rustling sounded from behind some bushes. *The peg-legged man!* Before Janine could react, a terrified rabbit dashed by, chased by a red fox. The rabbit froze when Janine gave a startled exclamation. The fox paused and the rabbit disappeared into another clump of greenery. A false alarm, thank goodness. Janine breathed easier.

She'd be within sight of her destination in a few more minutes, then she'd have to face Madame Parot and try to calm herself before calling on the Tremeaus. She had Charles to thank that she hadn't thought of Etienne and Mademoiselle La Roche for hours.

By the time she reached her temporary residence, the dawn gray had given way to a celestial dome of rich blue. She'd be back in plenty of time to call on the Tremeaus and change the hour for the visit with Cecile.

Knowing her landlady's inquisitive nature, Janine concluded there was little chance Madame hadn't noticed her absence during the night. She could only hope, and if by some miracle the woman had not, she'd try to slip into the house and let on she'd just been on an early morning walk. Either way she would have to appear for breakfast to find out. There would be no chance to catch up on her sleep until later in the day. All was quiet around the house. No curtains moved and the front door didn't swing open before she turned the handle.

As soon as Janine stepped inside, however, Madame Parot appeared from the kitchen with a petulant expression on her face. "Thank God you've returned. I suppose you stayed in town with the general's lady. But that doesn't excuse you for worrying me to death when you didn't come home." She gulped in a breath and continued. "I stayed up half the night before I realized what you'd done. Now come and eat your breakfast."

Following the woman into the kitchen, Janine said, "I'm sorry to have distressed you. I hoped you had gone to bed and wouldn't miss me."

"How could I sleep when I worried about you?"

Janine sat. "I'll try to be a better *pensionnaire* from now on." Janine did not enjoy being Madame Parot's boarder—the woman was simply too inquisitive about Janine's life—and she dreaded having to cope with the woman's ceaseless questions at breakfast. But after a bite of Madame's excellent scrambled eggs and cheese, she concluded the woman wasn't so bad after all.

"I should hope so." Madame Parot slid her chair away from the table. "Now you'll have to excuse me. I must get ready for church."

"Certainly." Janine welcomed the reprieve from the probing questions. She looked forward to getting some much-needed rest while the house was quiet. In the afternoon she would call upon the Tremeaus to reschedule their visit to Cecile for the next day.

After sleeping almost four hours, Janine left the house for the short walk to the Tremeaus. When she knocked, Etienne answered the door and showed her into the sitting room, where he sat across from her, an unfathomable expression on his face. "May I get you something to drink?"

"Non, merci." Janine felt as constrained as he appeared, she with her twinge of guilt and alarm at meeting with Charles, an enemy of the Republic. But what was affecting Etienne's demeanor? Mademoiselle La Roche or General de Bernay? A terrible third possibility crossed her mind. Charles? "We spoke of visiting Cecile tomorrow." She was surprised her voice sounded normal in her ears. "Shall we plan to go about two?"

"Eh, two tomorrow? I'm sure that will be acceptable." Etienne got up from his chair. "I'll confirm the time with Maman. Are you sure I can't bring you a glass of wine on my way back?"

"It does sound good. Thank you." Janine watched him leave the room and heard the outside kitchen door open and close. Apparently, his mother and, most likely, Anne were in the garden.

Before long Etienne returned with a bottle of vintage wine and two glasses and seated himself on the settee beside Janine. "We agreed on two tomorrow," he said, handing one of the glasses of red wine to Janine.

"Good." Janine sipped the smooth burgundy nectar and her pleasure turned bitter. Did the fine wine celebrate Mademoiselle La Roche and Etienne? She set her glass down and sought to steady her shaky hand. "What is the special occasion for such a rare wine?" She focused on the bottle rather than look at Etienne. The label read "Chambertin-Clos de Bèze 1787."

"It's in celebration of a remarkable woman." Etienne raised his glass in a toast.

Janine almost gagged, anticipating what she'd hear next.

"To Janine de Fleury, wherever destiny may take her."

Janine gulped. Is he saying goodbye? At least he hadn't said the dreaded name she'd feared he would. "Merci, you're too kind." She raised her glass. "To my dear Etienne, to whom I owe my life and for whom I have the deepest affection."

She rested against the back of the sofa and closed her eyes, pondering what he might say next. Instead of hearing his voice, she felt his muscular arms draw her against his lean frame for a brief moment. Her eyes flew open when he cradled her face in his hands. He didn't kiss her; he just searched her face with an enigmatic gaze.

"I want to remember you the way you look today," Etienne said, a gentle softness in his voice.

What does he mean? Her heart pounded against her chest. She didn't know how to respond to him.

Etienne edged his hands from her face and brushed his fingers along her hair as he sat back in his seat. In a husky voice he said, "Janine, as much as I would like it to be otherwise, you know there is no future for us together. I'm simply repeating what you told me years ago. And you were right. Your future is with Dupré and mine is in service to the First Consul of the Republic."

"Why are you telling me these things now?" *Get to the point.* "Are you telling me that you're going to marry Mademoiselle La Roche?"

He appeared to be annoyed. "I haven't told you anything about her. You're the one doing the asking. Right now my thoughts are of you. You must to return to New Orleans and marry Dupré before it's too late. Each day that passes becomes more perilous while you're here."

"Why do you keep telling me to marry Charles? I don't have to marry him even if I return to New Orleans?" Janine snapped. "Chateau Fleury is here. I must stay and fight for her."

"Do you wish to be a martyr?" Etienne gave no sign of being affected by her emotional outburst.

Janine stood, frustrated by his lack of response to her emphatic remark about Charles. She made an effort to be resolute. "Non, but I must do what I must do—*à-Dieu-va*. It is all in God's hands."

Etienne shook his head but made no response; he simply rose and led her to the door.

Janine folded the top sheet of her cot-like bed and climbed in, her mind racing between thoughts of Charles and Etienne, both of whom were troubling her at present. Her hope lay in giving Charles sufficient money to secure his departure from the Loire Valley. Depending upon how much he'd accept, she might have to dip into her return trip funds. If she could satisfy him before she saw Etienne again, she would breathe a little easier. What had brought about Etienne's heightened concern about her safety? If it had to do with Charles' appearance, no wonder he would distance himself from her and her activities. Or could it have to do with Mademoiselle La Roche? He *hadn't* denied he would marry her.

Meanwhile, Janine felt her life spiraling out of control—she no longer had a clear plan for her future. Charles and her marriage agreement had given her purpose after her parents were killed and while she made her way in New Orleans. Should she admit defeat and return to New Orleans? *Non, I won't give up on Chateau Fleury . . . or Etienne.*

Janine tossed and turned throughout the night, rousing numerous times, slipping in and out of restless, dream-filled sleep. She awoke in the morning to find the top sheet on the floor. Daylight signaled a need to dress in a hurry to meet Charles at the appointed hour. And this time she had the presence of mind to tell Madame Parot she would be in town for breakfast and would not be back until the afternoon. That should keep the peace between them.

Stillness enveloped the market square, although a few vendors had opened their stalls and begun unloading their goods. Janine preferred it that way so she would be able to see anyone who seemed out of place. She stayed some distance from the stalls, lessening the threat of attracting attention. She felt confident Charles would be discreet enough to keep out of sight. After passing the familiar group of trees and looking toward the bench, she saw no one sitting on it or anywhere around it. *He's being cautious. Better to be careful than punctual.* She removed a small book from her bag, opened it, and tried to read. At the end of each paragraph, she surveyed her surroundings.

Still no Charles. After waiting the better part of an hour, she concluded something was wrong. Had his identity been discovered? Had he been arrested? Could she hope that he'd decided to leave town? A cold sweat moistened her brow. She daubed her face with her handkerchief, her fingers like icy tentacles. She prayed that Charles would have the decency not to implicate her in any way. But he hadn't been above trying to extract money from her. Where would he go? After perusing her surroundings a final time, she left the square and walked toward the cathedral. Perhaps Charles had taken refuge there. She wanted to see for herself.

The number of people seated in the sanctuary chairs could be counted on the fingers of one hand, but several groups of people stood to the side in the aisles, absorbed in quiet conversations. She wandered by them, but they paid her no heed. Continuing onward, she started down the aisle on the other side of the church, scrutinizing the demeanor and face of each worshiper as she made her way to the back of the church. Charles wasn't there. *Could he be hiding in one of the small private chapels?* After assuring herself that the solitary person seen in the chapels could not be Charles in disguise, she deduced he wasn't there at all.

She exited a side door leading to the cloisters. The serene setting would afford her a place to sit and gather her thoughts. As she started along the path toward the arcade, she noticed two men scurrying in opposite directions—the abbé, his back to her, disappeared behind the colonnades; the other man came in her direction. The caretaker from Chateau Fleury! He gave a hurried look in her direction and stepped behind a trellis heavy with greenery. She turned away and retraced her steps. There seemed no point in confronting him. Perhaps he'd think she hadn't seen him. *They're up to no good,* she thought.

She returned to the church, waiting for the caretaker to leave— if that was his plan. Before she left the building, she lit candles in memory of her parents and uncle. By the time she left the church, coaches and carriages moved along the street as the town began the business of the day. Janine walked past them, wending her way to the main street of town on the return to her temporary residence. She paid little attention to the occasional passing coaches until one stopped beside her.

"Janine, I've been looking for you. Your landlady said you were in town. Get in. We'll give you a ride back." The footman opened the door before Minette finished speaking.

What a providential time for a ride. "Merci. Why are you looking for me?" She sat across from Minette, removed her hat, and set it on the seat beside her.

"We're staying at the townhouse for a few days, and I'd like you to spend time with me while I'm here. It's much easier when we're close together."

"I'd like that."

"I'll wait while you pack a few things. We'll go back together," Minette said. "I'm having a small dinner party tonight."

"I can't come back with you now. I have an appointment with the Tremeaus to visit Cecile this afternoon. But I'll be able to come for dinner."

"All right, get your valise ready now, and I'll take it back with me. My coach will pick you up about five."

"*Avec plaisir*. I'm looking forward to getting away from Madame Parot for a while. She means well most of the time but watches my every move."

"You need a diversion. And so does Lieutenant Lenoir. I'm afraid my husband is putting a lot of pressure on his men. They huddled together for hours yesterday—something big is happening. He won't talk to me about it."

Charles . . . or what? Janine nodded, determined to not let fear overwhelm her.

Chapter 19

A crack of the whip sent the horse galloping along the road, a wake of dust trailing the small carriage. Janine leaned against Etienne to avoid jostling Madame Tremeau. Frowning at her son, Madame gripped the side rail. With an apologetic glance at Janine, she muttered, "Etienne's in a hurry. He has a special meeting later this afternoon."

Mademoiselle La Roche! Janine's heart sank. "I do appreciate that he'd take time for me from his busy schedule." Janine managed a tight-lipped smile. "We won't be long. We mustn't tire Cecile."

Etienne pulled sharply on the reins, slowing the carriage as they came into town. The horse settled into a comfortable trot until they reached the old Tudor-style house. Janine's heart sank. *Where's Nanny?* She'd been outside on the porch or in the yard on each of their previous visits. Janine kept her fears to herself. She took a deep breath and waited for Etienne and his mother to disembark, biding her time until she could leave the carriage. As soon as her feet hit the ground, she released Etienne's helping hand and charged ahead, calling back to them, "Something's wrong. She's usually sitting outside."

After racing up the steps onto the porch, Janine peeked through the open door while she waited for Etienne and his mother. Alone in the room, the old man paid her no heed. Where were the women? Janine tapped on the door. The man looked at her, confusion written on his face.

Just then the red-haired woman came down the hall from the bedrooms. Putting a warning finger to her lips, she stepped onto the porch. "You won't be able to see Gemma today. A terrible thing has happened," the landlady said, her voice cracking.

"Don't speak in riddles, woman." Etienne stepped forward. "What are you talking about?"

The woman cringed and focused on a spot in the lawn. "I found her, unconscious and brutally beaten." She waved her hand. "Right over there on the grass."

"What?" Outraged, Janine grabbed the woman's arm. "How could you let such a thing happen? Why didn't you stop them?"

"How could I? No one heard a thing. She didn't even cry out." The woman pulled away from Janine. "I thought she was dead." Shaking, she collapsed into a chair, wringing her hands.

"Don't fear me. Just tell us what you saw and heard," Etienne said in a soothing voice.

She stood and gave Etienne a beseeching look. "That's what's so strange. We heard nothing. God only knows how long she lay out here," she shuddered, "and to think that beast could have been watching us."

"Did you summon a doctor?" Etienne asked.

"Mais, Oui. He did what he could and left instructions for her care."

"*Excusez-moi.* I want to take a look around the yard," Etienne said and left the women.

"I must go to her." Janine tried to brush by the woman. "Let me pass."

The landlady stepped in front of her. "Non. The abbé is keeping vigil over her. By his orders no one else is to enter her room. Only I am to enter to care for her."

Mon Dieu! The abbé? What's he doing here? Pushing past the woman, Janine dashed into the house and down the hall to Cecile's room. She paused a moment before turning the knob, hoping to slip in without alerting the abbé. As she eased into the room, before her eyes adjusted to the gloomy darkness, a hand seized her arm from behind and wrenched it upward until she screamed in pain. She fought back, scratching the air behind her with her free hand, hoping to find a target for her sharp nails. But her captor was too strong. "Etienne!" she cried out, "Help me!"

"What's going on here?" Etienne yelled, bursting into the room. Madame Tremeau and the red-haired woman stood in the doorway behind him.

The abbé released Janine's arm and stepped away. "I'm truly sorry, Mademoiselle," he said and turned to Etienne. "Colonel Tremeau, I'm relieved to see you. I ask your indulgence. When Mademoiselle de Fleury rushed in, I reacted to a perceived danger. I'm distraught about this poor woman's condition. I worry she may not make it through the night. We're all on edge."

Rubbing her aching arm, Janine wasn't fooled by the little man's rambling apology. He'd been in the dimly lit room and heard her voice. He had lain in wait for her. She went to Cecile's bedside and brushed the hair from the side of Nanny's bruised face. An ugly gash extended from her crown to just below her hairline. Her beloved

Cecile's face was deathly pale and her body limp. Janine reached for her hand. "Nanny. I'm here with you. I'm going to stay with you and care for you."

"Janine's here with you now." Etienne's gaze fixed on the old woman's bruised face. Lost in thought of Nanny, Janine flinched when Etienne spoke.

The abbé stood on the other side of Janine. "My child, this is a terrible shock for you. There's no need for you to stay tonight. Little can be done for her. It's in the Lord's hands now."

Madame Tremeau stepped forward and put an arm around Janine's shoulder. "I'll stay tonight and you can come in the morning to relieve me. We'll take turns." She looked at the abbé. "You're needed at the cathedral. Go and care for your flock," she said in a no-nonsense tone.

"*Merci.*" Janine kissed her friend's lined cheek, grateful for her intervention. "What would I do without you?"

"She is our friend too." Madame Tremeau turned to Etienne. "Let Anne know what's happened."

"Oui, *Maman.*"

The abbé looked to Etienne, "Will you be staying into the evening?"

"*Au contraire.* She is in good hands. I'll give you a lift to the cathedral," he said to the abbé and then motioned to Janine. "*Allez.*"

Janine bristled but kept her own counsel as she fell into step behind him. She was torn between gratitude to Madame Tremeau and disappointment at Etienne's apparent acceptance of the abbé's explanation of his aggressive behavior. True, Etienne wasn't privy to her damning information about the abbé's cozy relationship with the chateau caretaker. At any rate, Madame Tremeau's actions had—for the time being—squelched the priest's excuse for keeping watch over Cecile.

A subdued Abbé Dillon climbed into the carriage and sat by Janine. He remained silent during the short ride to the cathedral. Sitting beside the man was difficult enough, but having to wait to tell Etienne of her suspicions about him proved a greater challenge.

Upon arrival at the cathedral, the abbé lost no time getting out of the carriage. "Merci, Monsieur *le Colonel,*" he said and scampered away like a frightened mouse.

Janine moved to the far side of the seat and willed herself to be unemotional. "Etienne, the abbé can't be trusted. He meant to hurt and frighten me today." The more she thought about it, the more certain she was that the early morning meeting between the priest and the chateau caretaker had something to do with the attack on Nanny.

Etienne kept his eyes on the road. "Why do you say so?"

"You weren't present when the landlady said the abbé ordered her to allow no one into Nanny's room—that he would keep vigil. Why do you suppose he would want to do that?"

"I have no idea. That *is* strange."

"That's not the only odd thing. Early this very morning, I saw him in deep conversation with the Chateau Fleury caretaker."

"A coincidence?"

"What do you think? I saw them today before the attack on Nanny. When I approached, they went their separate ways. They meant to kill her," Janine said, more emphatically than she intended.

Etienne's brows drew downward into a frown. "We won't take any chances. I'll return and stay with Nanny tonight."

"Oui, please do." Janine relaxed against the seat. Nanny would be safe through the night even if the scoundrels did return.

They rode in silence until they arrived at Madame Parot's house, then Etienne turned to Janine. "We must have a serious conversation without interruption," he said, a chill in his voice. "How about at my house, now?"

Janine's mind reeled with confusion. Why was he so cold and aloof? Was he preparing her to accept his and Mademoiselle's relationship? "I can't stay long. I have a dinner party at Minette's this evening."

"The afternoon's early . . . not even three o'clock yet," he said with emphasis.

"Minette is expecting me right after our visit with Cecile. But everything is changed now. I need to let her know what's happened."

"She doesn't know our visit with Cecile was cut short." The corners of his mouth twisted with exasperation.

"I suppose that is so."

"Our talk *cannot* wait," he said with finality.

He was beginning to frighten her. "I . . . I'll need to leave before five."

"Keep an eye on the time and leave when necessary."

136

Etienne offered Janine a chair in the sitting room and called to Anne. Receiving no response, he said, "Make yourself comfortable. I'll see if she's in the garden." Glad for the reprieve from the distasteful task ahead of him, he headed outside.

Anne will wonder why I need to be alone with Janine. Shoulders slumped from the weight of his suspicions about Janine; Etienne was faced with conflicting loyalties to the Republic and to Janine. He often responded to her with his heart and not his head, and he felt an emotional need to protect her. But now he could no longer take Janine at her word. Had she returned to France solely because of Chateau Fleury? Understandably, her sympathies were with the deposed royal Bourbons. A royalist sympathizer, likely—but a spy? His gut feeling was that she was not. The attack on Nanny suggested a connection to Chateau Fleury and the threat Janine's presence posed.

After Etienne completed his rounds in the garden without finding Anne, he returned to the house. He sat in his favorite chair across from Janine, physically distancing him from her although unable to do so emotionally. "Sorry for the delay."

Janine stared straight ahead, looking ill at ease.

"As I see it, there's a well-organized group of people who will stop at nothing if you continue your quest for Chateau Fleury. You'll not prevail against them alone, and I'm not free to help you. In a few days I must return to Paris. I have received orders from the First Consul to work on a matter of national importance."

"You won't be here?" Janine's brow furrowed. "I feel so alone, struggling against those hostile people."

Etienne pressed on, "You'd be ill-advised to think that only one group of people wishes to discredit you. For instance, you've been observed in clandestine meetings with a number of unsavory characters." Emphasizing each word, he looked her in the eye. "What am I to make of those reports?"

"Whose observations . . . the abbé's?"

"Not only his, but several others as well. There are allegations that you're involved in a conspiracy of your own."

"I assure you I am not. As God is my witness, my sole purpose for being here is to recover what is rightfully mine."

"I want to believe you, and for the time being I will accept your word. I hope my trust isn't misplaced." When Janine looked at him with those mellow brown eyes, how could he remain unmoved?

"You must know it isn't," she said, holding his gaze. "A number of strange things have happened in the past few days. I wonder if the man and woman who approached me did so in cooperation with the abbé and his cronies. This morning at the cathedral, the abbé and the caretaker went to great lengths to stay out of view. They acted guilty."

Etienne nodded. "Go on. What other odd things happened?"

"Earlier this morning I caught sight of the man who attacked me at the hotel . . . he was with the chateau caretaker."

Don't lie to me, Janine. If you are in anyway involved with Cadoudal, I'll . . . "What business did the peculiar strangers with whom you were seen conversing have with you?"

Janine averted her eyes for a brief moment. "A beggar asked for some coins and another man asked directions to a place of lodging."

The break in eye contact led Etienne to conclude Janine had been less than honest with him. A deep sense of disappointment gripped him. What was she hiding? He had to face the possibility that he sat before an enemy of the Republic. Interrogating her this way pained him but must be done. "Two strangers approached you?" Etienne shook his head.

Janine nodded.

"What did you say to them?"

"I gave one man a coin and suggested to the second one that he inquire about lodging at the cathedral."

Etienne chastised himself for letting his guard down. He hadn't wanted to dwell on her sympathy for the royalist cause. "You neglected to mention the old peddler woman. Why did you prolong your exchange with her?"

Janine's face blanched. "Why do you speak in such in an accusatory manner? I have nothing to hide. She urged me to buy some trinkets from her basket. She needed coins to buy something to eat."

Had his voice hardened, reflecting his inner doubts? Etienne leaned toward Janine and held her gaze. "Is that the whole truth?"

"I wish you wouldn't look at me that way." Janine broke eye

contact and stood. "I must go."

Etienne didn't try to detain her. He walked her to the door and watched her retreat. *No answer is an answer.* His jaw set with determination. He would find the answer.

Chapter 20

Janine's head throbbed. She couldn't focus on the rippling, textured silk-covered wall without feeling dizzy. To keep from falling, she swayed and leaned against it.

"Steady there." Minette slipped her arm around Janine's waist and led her to a chair before tugging on the bell pull.

The butler responded carrying a tea tray. "Merci. And bring a glass of water for Mademoiselle, *s'il vous plait*." Minette kept her eyes on Janine. "You're unwell."

Janine pressed her hand to her forehead. "I've had a terrible shock today and I'm feeling sick."

"What happened?"

"Nanny is near death from a brutal attack by an unknown assailant. I'm frightened."

"What?" Minette paused as the butler brought a glass of water for Janine.

"Merci," Janine said and sipped it. "She's still unconscious and I am afraid she remains in danger."

"Who would do such a thing?" Minette poured the amber liquid into one of the cups and handed it to Janine.

"No one saw the attack." Janine sipped the tea before speaking again. "She was alone outside when it happened. I'm sure the abbé is involved somehow."

"The abbé? He's a strange man, but . . ."

"Yes. When I got there, he was in her room. He grabbed me and twisted my arm behind my back. Etienne rushed in when I cried out, and the abbé let go and apologized. Said he'd reacted to protect Nanny."

Minette scoffed. "He'd have to be blind not to recognize you."

"The room was darkened, so I suppose he thinks his excuse is good enough. Not for me though. I know he's up to something with the caretaker from Chateau Fleury. I saw them together again this morning at the cathedral." Just being able to verbalize her feelings to a sympathetic ear, she felt the tension subside. "I'm so worried for Cecile."

"You didn't leave Nanny alone with him?"

"For heaven's sake, no. Madame Tremeau is with her now, and

Etienne will go back tonight. I'll go in the morning to care for her."

"*Mon Dieu*, what a dreadful day. Try to rest." Minette rose. "I'll call you in plenty of time to dress for dinner."

Janine nodded. "I'll try to be better company tonight."

Janine forced a smile as she opened the door at Minette's tap. At least she'd dressed in plenty of time for dinner. Unable to slow her mind, she'd groomed with care for the evening, although not feeling festive.

"Aren't you the one?" Minette said lightly. "You look lovely and rested. I don't know how you managed it."

"Thank you. I'm better than when we last spoke."

"I must be off if I'm to be ready on time," Minette said, starting down the hall.

Janine closed the door after her and glanced at the gilt and rouge marble clock. She had an hour to herself before dinner. She sat in the pink brocade chair by the window, her mind in a quandary as to what the morrow would bring. Nanny, Etienne, Charles, the abbé, Chateau Fleury—any one of them challenging in and of themselves—combined, they threatened her will to fight. A gentle breeze from the open window cooled her hot cheeks. She closed her eyes, surrendering to the pleasant sensation.

What time is it? She blinked and stared at the gold hands of the clock. Six-fifty—no time to waste. She'd failed to hear the sound of the half-hour chime. She rose and hurried from the room, glancing in the mirror on her way out.

By the time Janine arrived at the salon, a small group of dinner guests had gathered there. Two military officers in uniform and their companions—none of whom Janine recognized—clustered around Minette and her husband. As Janine moved farther into the room, she wasn't surprised to see Lieutenant Lenoir making his way toward her. Had he been waiting for her? Of course. Minette wouldn't miss an opportunity to bring them together. After the emotional drain of the day's events, Janine had no will to cooperate or to object.

"It's a pleasure to see you again." Lenoir lifted her hand to his lips. "Shall we join the others?"

Janine nodded, accepting a glass of champagne from the

butler's tray. Usually, General de Bernay paid little attention to her, but tonight his doubting eyes lingered on her before he turned to the lieutenant. "I see my wife has paired you with Mademoiselle de Fleury."

All eyes focused on her.

Lenoir smiled. "So she has, and I am most honored to be in the company of such a charming lady."

Janine noticed the other men watching her as the women turned and peered at her.

"Mademoiselle de Fleury and I have been friends since we were twelve." Minette put her arm around Janine. "It's so good to have you here with us."

The group dispersed, leaving Minette with Janine and Lenoir. The other two women moved toward the fireplace, and the men gravitated to the table of appetizers.

"My dear, I'm ready for dinner," General de Bernay directed to Minette in a loud voice.

"We're waiting for the last of our guests to arrive. If they're not here in a half hour, we'll serve."

"Well then, I may as well see what's left of the appetizers before they eat them all," the general grumbled. He gestured toward a man standing by the table, filling two plates, then started across the room.

Minette looked after him. "He's testy if his meals aren't served on schedule. Please excuse me while I speak with him."

Lenoir nodded. "Certainly. It gives Janine and me time for a brief visit to your garden."

Grateful for the reprieve from prying eyes, Janine smiled at Lenoir. "Let's sit on the terrace while we finish our champagne." She would have more than enough time with the other guests at dinner.

On their way out, Lenoir picked up a leather portfolio. "I have something to show you."

"Now you've piqued my interest." *Chateau Fleury?*

On the terrace Janine slipped into the chair Lenoir held for her and set her glass down next to the worn leather packet he'd placed on the table.

"I'm glad we have this time alone," Lenoir said, drawing his chair close to hers. "I want your advice."

"I'm sorry, I'm not much of a military strategist," Janine said in jest.

"I had guessed as much." He kept a straight face. "In a serious vein, I do respect your opinion about design."

Janine couldn't resist teasing him just a little. "All you know about my talent is what I've told you."

"Wrong again. Minette showed me some of your sketches and fabric swatches you left in her sewing room."

Janine laughed. Lenoir had succeeded in disarming her in spite of her misgivings. Maybe she'd been hasty in judging him. He seemed to sense her moods and cater to them. She could benefit from more of that in her life, especially now.

He reached for the portfolio. "Do you want to see inside?"

"I thought you'd never ask."

"Are you sure you're ready to be serious?"

"Stop delaying. Show me." Janine feigned annoyance and reached toward the portfolio.

"Patience." He removed several sketches and handed them to her. "Here are a few preliminary drawings for an important commission awarded to Lenoir Frères. It's for a silk wall covering for Bonaparte's sister, Pauline. She recently acquired Hotel Charost in Paris. But I must warn you, she can be difficult to please."

Janine had heard stories about Pauline being widowed while in Saint-Domingo and sailing to France with her young son and her husband's corpse. Pauline was about her own age. What might appeal to such a woman?

Janine laid the five sheets of paper on the table and studied each one, taking her time to respond to the tinted designs before reading the notes printed below. She sought to put herself into the mind of the willful Pauline, a spoiled woman but one who appreciated beauty and perfection. She rearranged them in the order of her preference and pointed to the first one. "I think she'll choose this one. The delicate rose pattern is beautiful."

"Thank you for your opinion." Lenoir hesitated. "But that's not all I would ask of you. I'd like for you to submit several designs for her consideration. If one of yours is selected, it will give you the recognition your talent deserves." Pausing, he added, "What do you say?"

Janine couldn't believe the compliment he was paying her. Her head spun. Practically overnight, fantastic opportunities could come her way. But was she looking for opportunities to be involved in a bourgeoisie way of life? Although proud of her business, she'd started from need, not choice. Those thoughts collided with design images skittering through her head.

An image formed of sprigs of lavender on a silver silk background. The mere suggestion of the gray-green leaf stems, and the spikes of pale purple flowers with a touch of orchid repeated in a slightly raised pattern, made her think of Etienne. "I don't know what to say. Thank you for your confidence in me."

Lenoir sipped champagne and waited.

"I'd love to," she said after a few moments.

"Believe it or not, I was afraid you'd say no." Lenoir lifted his glass. "To your new designs and our working partnership."

Janine echoed his sentiment with a toast of her own. "To the success of our designs and Maison Lenoir Frères."

Lenoir rose and reached for her hand. "Now to dinner. Come."

Janine felt an optimism that hadn't been hers for years. It reminded her of emerging from one of Lenoir's silkworm cocoons.

Entering the salon, Janine drew in her breath and held it when she saw that Mademoiselle La Roche and Etienne had arrived. They stood in conversation with another colonel and his wife. Mademoiselle La Roche talked while the other woman occasionally nodded. The two colonels stood to the side without comment. At least Etienne wasn't hovering over his young companion.

Janine and Lenoir fell into line with the other couples and followed the de Bernays to the dining room. General de Bernay sat at the head of the table and Minette at the other end. To the general's immediate right, the lieutenant general's wife sat beside her husband, with Janine on his other side, followed by Lenoir, who sat nearest Minette. On the other side of the table, Etienne sat next to Minette, with Mademoiselle La Roche beside him.

Soup was the first course served and the usual light conversation and banter could be heard, mixed with the sounds of eating. After a few minutes, the lieutenant general edged his empty soup bowl to the side and turned to Janine. "Well, Mademoiselle de Fleury, what prompted you to leave New Orleans after so many years?" His gaze was hard and steady.

Janine's shoulders tightened, but she sat erect and looked him in the eye. "France is my country and I have returned to reclaim my ancestral home—Chateau Fleury."

"Reclaim it? Was it requisitioned by the Republic?"

"It was sequestered in 1793," she said in a dry tone.

"But it was not sold?"

"No." Janine turned to Lenoir, concluding the conversation with the disagreeable man. "The roast duck looks delicious," she said as the butler placed a plate in front of her. The lieutenant general was already chomping on the meat when she stole a sideways glance at him.

Her respite from his goading ended when he finished eating but before she'd eaten more than half her serving. "Have you family here . . . in the Loire Valley, Mademoiselle?"

She set her fork down and looked at him. "No."

He persisted in ignoring her nonverbal cue. "Old friends?" He eyed the fruit and cheese platter as the butler placed it on the table.

"A few," she said, grateful for the diversion provided by the butler's arrival.

After gorging himself on cheese, the man devoured a bunch of grapes. Before he finished chewing the last of his grapes, he leaned toward Janine, "You're involved in a variety of charities—at the cathedral helping the poor and the beggars, I understand."

"Not at the present." Janine glanced at Etienne. *Why wasn't he with Nanny?* He didn't seem to be paying attention to her or Mademoiselle La Roche. And neither he nor Lenoir gave any indication of concern about the rude officer at her side. She looked away and watched the server set small plates in front of each guest.

"Hmm. My source must be mistaken," her tormenter responded.

It was General de Bernay who unwittingly saved Janine from the incessant questioning. He stood as the butler wheeled in six bottles of Chambertin-Clos de Bèze. The manservant opened one of the bottles, poured a small amount into a glass, and handed it to the general. The general swirled his glass, tasted it, and—rather too quickly—nodded his approval to serve the guests. "The wine is compliments of the First Consul," he said, clearing his throat. "A token of his appreciation of the select group of men here tonight. He relies on our team to successfully complete the task we have before us."

145

The general returned to his seat and the guests were served, after which he signaled the butler with a tilt of his head. The butler placed a bottle of the wine and a white envelope near each man.

De Bernay gulped the last of his drink and set down his empty glass. He looked directly at each of the guests at the table then began speaking again. "As soon as we're finished here, my officers will adjourn to the library while the ladies retire to the salon." He nodded at Etienne. "The colonel and Mademoiselle La Roche regret they must leave us early this evening."

They had arrived late and would leave early, so it appeared Etienne intended to keep his word to watch over Nanny. Janine relaxed a little until confronted with Bonaparte's seal on Lenoir's envelope. *Rewards for what?*

She hoped it had nothing to do with Charles. A constant worry since he'd appeared in town. She dreaded being in the salon with Mademoiselle La Roche and the lieutenant general's wife. She had nothing to say to them—especially after the tone of the conversation at the table.

The general pushed his chair back and stood. Like clockwork, the officers and Minette did likewise. The women followed Minette into the salon and before the last woman was seated, the butler rolled in a cart of tiny crystal glasses and a selection of liqueurs.

During dinner, the salon chairs had been rearranged into a small conversation area. Janine hung back—to no avail—in the hope Etienne would let her know he would return to see Nanny. Because Janine was the last to arrive in the salon, she sat in the only empty chair—beside Mademoiselle La Roche. She nodded to her then turned to listen to the lieutenant general's wife chattering about an upcoming celebration at the Tuileries Palace in Paris.

Mademoiselle La Roche leaned toward Janine, her big blue eyes wide with wonder. "Père told me about you. It's so sad your parents were guillotined. And you fled to the New World. What is it like there? Did you see many savages? What did they look like?" She paused for a fraction of a second as she sucked in a breath. "We went to London and stayed until it was safe to return. Why didn't you go there?" She looked expectantly at Janine.

"Mademoiselle, you've asked so many questions. Which shall I answer?"

"Too many questions? I'm sorry. Père says I talk too much and

146

that I must learn to listen."

Janine looked at the girl, scarcely older than she'd been when she lost her parents. "Be thankful that life has been kind to you." *Her jabbering will drive Etienne to distraction.*

"Why are you shaking your head?" the girl asked with a puzzled look.

"I was thinking about how much I miss my family." Janine gave Minette a weak smile when she moved her chair closer after the lieutenant general's wife excused herself to visit the powder room.

"Think of us as family now," Minette soothed and patted Janine's hand.

"My dear friend, you are most kind."

"Did you hear our conversation about the invitations to the celebration at the Tuileries?"

Mademoiselle La Roche gave Minette a quizzical look but said nothing.

"Non, we've been talking," Janine said. "What about the celebration?"

"The invitations were distributed tonight at dinner, and I expect our bachelor officers will be inviting you ladies as their guests." Minette nodded in agreement with her own comment. "Isn't that exciting?"

"It is. It is. It's divine." Mademoiselle La Roche leapt from her chair and danced in front of them.

Under different circumstances, Janine may have shared the young lady's enthusiasm. *Am I to be considered a friend or a foe?* "We must wait for the invitations to be extended."

"You can count on it." Minette readjusted her chair as the other woman returned to the room.

Mademoiselle La Roche leaned toward Janine and lowered her voice. "Are you and Lieutenant Lenoir going to be married? I like him. I think Colonel Tremeau and I will marry. Père says the First Consul wants it."

Her voice returned to a normal conversation level. "I like his sister, Anne, too. She's sweet. You made a beautiful gown for her. You must like to make dresses. I love to go to parties and wear lovely gowns and accessories. Are you going to make your gown for the party in Paris? I know you won't have time to make my gown this time, but when I get married, I'd like for you to make my wedding dress." She stopped her monologue and waited for Janine's response.

Lenoir came through the library door just in time to relieve Janine from the girl's inane conversation. As he came toward them, Mademoiselle La Roche didn't take her eyes off him.

The lieutenant stopped and spoke to Minette before continuing toward them. "Have you ladies enjoyed the evening?" He looked at Janine and then at the blushing Mademoiselle La Roche. "I will be leaving shortly, Mademoiselle de Fleury, but I am looking forward to seeing your designs. I bid you ladies *bonne nuit,* good night."

Janine had no desire to linger with the other women—including the rather scatterbrained Mademoiselle La Roche. Nor did she want to think about what the girl had said about Etienne. She'd concentrate on her work for Lenoir Frères and Bonaparte's sister. Lenoir's offer of a new opportunity beckoned her. Would it materialize and solve her financial problems?

Chapter 21

A slight click of the door latch satisfied Janine she hadn't disturbed the de Bernay household on her way out. With such an early start, she would arrive at Nanny's bedside before the sun peeked over the horizon. As she walked, the sky transitioned from dark to light shades of gray until surrendering the night to the day. A chorus of songbirds relieved the monotonous tap-tap of her heels on the cobbled street. Worried, she pressed her icy fingers to her warm face. Had Nanny regained consciousness? *God forbid she . . .*

Not until she passed the police station did she hear loud footsteps approaching from behind her. Frightened, she attempted to hurry away but was stopped by a pair of strong hands turning her around to face two *gendarmes.*

A Goliath-sized man held her fast and began to pull her toward the station. "Citizen Janine de Fleury, you are coming with us for questioning," he said with a note of spiteful satisfaction.

Her worst fears were realized. Who had given these orders? Had Charles Dupré been captured? Had he implicated her? She might be thrown into prison and not be heard of again, or worse yet—shot at dawn. She prayed Madame Tremeau would sound the alert when she didn't arrive at Nanny's house.

"You've made a serious mistake. I'm not guilty of any crime." Janine didn't bother to ask why she was to be questioned—the lieutenant general had given her a clue at dinner the previous night. But she was taken by surprise at how quickly action had been taken. Etienne had tried to warn her. Would he be able to help her?

"Keep moving, you royalist traitor." The man tightened his vise-like grip on her arm. "We'll see about that at the jail." The two men took long strides, pulling her along with them. She stumbled once, but they didn't slow their pace. She struggled to keep upright, not wanting to give them the satisfaction of her further humiliation.

Mercifully, they didn't pass anyone during the short walk to the jail. When they reached the stone building, the hefty man rushed up the three steps, dragging her along with him. Once inside, he released his grip and pushed her into a dingy room. "Sit." He gestured to one of three chairs near a battered table.

She hesitated, taking time to avoid sitting on the most offensive splinters on the rickety chair.

"I said *sit*." He lowered his voice, "I give the orders. You are a nobody around here." The man glared at her as she obliged him. He turned and left the room, soon returning with a silver-haired man in uniform. " Commissioner Le Bec here will deal with you."

"Mademoiselle, do you know why you are here?" the commissioner asked, his attitude polite, unlike the vulgar Goliath.

"Non. To my knowledge I have committed neither crime nor indiscretion."

He tapped the fingertips of one hand on the sheets of paper he'd brought to the table. "I have sworn statements from six people who have seen you consorting with unsavory characters—meeting in secret and holding long conversations with them—most suspicious. It is a crime to plot the overthrow of the Republic or to harm any government official."

The seriousness of the charges began to dawn on her. Her parents had been arrested and taken to prison, never to return home. Beads of perspiration erupted along the top of her upper lip as she fought to control the panic threatening to overcome her. Charles must have implicated her in some way. When he'd appeared in Tours, she'd been afraid the authorities would find out.

"I am not involved in any kind of plot. May I see those statements? It seems the plot is against me."

"You may not see them unless charges are brought against you. Let me assure you, if there is a conspiracy against you, it's all in the family—Comte de Fleury and his caretaker are two of those who signed statements."

The imposter is here in Tours. Had the abbé also accused her? He seemed intimately involved with the Chateau Fleury caretaker.

She looked her inquisitor in the eye. "My uncle, Comte de Fleury, is dead. The man making the charge is an imposter. These people intend to harm me and have a motive to make false statements about me."

He responded with a dismissive wave of his hand. "A tall tale if ever I heard one. I warn you not to waste my time with such nonsense. I won't be deterred from doing my duty. Is there anything else you want to say in your defense?"

"There is no truth to the charges." Janine stood, feigning confidence while her knees felt as if they would buckle any moment.

"Am I free to leave?"

He gave her a withering look. "Be seated. You are *not* free to leave. Because of the serious nature of the threat you pose, we must detain you until we have completed our investigation."

He nodded to the large man. "Lock her up. She needs more time to recall the purpose of her clandestine meetings."

Janine instinctively flinched when the formidable jailer rattled his huge keyring near her ear. He pushed her toward the first cell down the narrow corridor. The heavy key grated in the lock, followed by screeching hinges when he pulled the door open. Placing his hand on the small of her back, he hurled her into darkness. As the door slammed shut, she heard his heavy footsteps and jangling keys fade as he walked away. For the first time in her life, she was in a jail cell. *I don't want to die.* Etienne had helped her survive the Revolution, but would he be disposed to help her again?

In the darkness, despair and hopelessness closed in around her. She stood frozen, although her head felt as if it would explode. She felt faint at the thought of what the future might hold. *What can I do to get out of here?*

As her eyes adjusted to the dim light from the slit of a window, she looked around the small space. The cell contained a straw mat-covered metal bed, washbasin on top of a stand, and a chamber pot in the corner. What had her mother's cell been like? And her father's? Her stomach lurched at the stench of perspiration and urine and heaven knew what else. With trepidation she sat on the bed and began to wrack her brain for a solution.

A best she could, she tried to ignore the low murmur of voices in the interrogation room and the sound of loud snoring in the next cell. Loud peals of laughter erupted in the outer room and the jailer's voice carried down the passageway. "Who'd have thought we'd catch such a big fish? An *aristo.*" The excited chorus of voices grew louder with each word.

Another voice reverberated. "There'll be a big reward for us. Maybe we'll be commended by Bonaparte himself."

"Why not? He doesn't want to die any more than anyone else does," the jailer said.

"We put our lives at risk to capture a dangerous enemy." More hoots and hollers followed.

Janine covered her ears to close out the jeers from her captors. *They speak the truth. If it concerns Bonaparte, there'll be no waiting before an execution.* Her shoulders slumped and her arms dropped to her side. *I have to get out of here. Now.* Just as all hope vanished, an idea came to her as if by divine intervention. She jumped up from the bed and went to the barred door. With all the strength she could muster, she rattled it and shouted. "I'm ready to talk to the commissioner now. NOW!"

The footsteps coming nearer her were not as heavy as they'd been earlier and she saw it was the smaller gendarme shuffling toward her. "So yuv had a change of heart, have ya?" He leered at her. "You kin wait here while I tell 'im."

After a few moments he returned with the keys. He fumbled and tried several before he found the right one. Finally, he managed to get the door open, and Janine recoiled at the strong alcohol odor on his breath. He reached for her arm and pulled her through the open door. "It's about time ya confess and tell the commissioner all ya knows." Janine followed but wouldn't give him the satisfaction of a response.

Commissioner Le Bec sat in a faded upholstered chair at the table, and Janine took the chair she had used earlier, no other being available. The silver-haired man eyed her with evident interest. "You asked to speak with me. Have you remembered information that is of interest to us?"

She took a deep breath. "Oui, Monsieur, I have."

"And what is it?"

"Last evening I was handed a note by a stranger. It said, 'Be at 44 Place Plumereau first thing in the morning. Your life depends on it. Will meet you there and tell you more.' I was afraid to disregard it because a group of three men have been shadowing me near the cathedral and market square."

"Let me see that note."

"I can't. I destroyed it."

"Why?"

"I didn't want anyone to know where I was going."

He shook his head. "Did you recognize any of the men you claim followed you?"

"Oui, one of them is the caretaker at Chateau Fleury."

"What about the others?"

"I don't know who they are." Janine thought better of

mentioning Etienne's help in identifying her attacker outside the hotel. "I was on my way to the address given in the note when your men detained me."

The commissioner pursed his lips. "Hmm. I see. Perhaps you and I aren't too late for your mystery rendezvous. Do you agree, Mademoiselle?" Janine nodded. "No time to waste then," he said and turned to the jailer. "Ready a carriage."

With wobbly legs and sweaty palms, Janine got up and followed the commissioner to the door. So far her plan had worked. By the time they got under way, the morning sun in the eastern sky had climbed toward the treetops.

"Mademoiselle, upon our arrival at the location, you are to carry on as you had planned earlier today—before we delayed you. Remember, I'll be observing you at all times."

"I understand." Janine didn't want to aggravate him in any way; she needed him to accompany her to the place where Anne and Madame Tremeau watched over Cecile.

The short ride seemed an eternity. When the carriage finally stopped in front of the house, Janine stared at its facade and feigned curiosity, her near panic genuine.

Le Bec surveyed the surroundings while the driver assisted Janine from the carriage. "No sign of anyone out here. You lead the way to the house."

Janine ascended the steps and tapped on the door. When the resident old man shuffled to the door and peeked through the screen, Janine said, "You wanted to talk to me? Well, I brought the police commissioner, too." She pushed the door open and shouted in a manner contrary to her upbringing and repeated, "I'm here with the police commissioner so that no one gets killed."

A startled look changed into one of terror on the elderly man's face as he cowered in a corner. The commissioner stepped in front of Janine and shook her. "Calm down, Mademoiselle de Fleury. This harmless old man isn't going to kill anyone."

The old man seized the opportunity and disappeared toward the bedrooms as fast as his shuffle would carry him. "Help me," he shrieked in terror.

Janine regretted having frightened him—especially after the attack on Nanny—but her plan had worked so far. Madame Tremeau,

Anne, and the flame-haired landlady rushed from Nanny's bedroom. The old man collapsed into the landlady's arms and allowed her to lead him toward his own room.

Madame Tremeau and Anne stared in stunned silence at Janine and the commissioner.

"On my way here this morning, I was detained and taken to jail. It seems several people, including the caretaker at Chateau Fleury, have signed sworn statements to the effect that they've seen me with suspicious . . ."

Before she could complete the sentence, Commissioner Le Bec interrupted. "Madame Tremeau, I believe. Please excuse the interruption. It appears this woman brought me here under false pretenses. I'll get her back where she belongs." He turned to Janine, gripped her arm, and moved her toward the door. "You have some explaining to do, Mademoiselle."

Janine twisted her head to the side to catch Madame Tremeau's attention. Where was Anne? Had she gone for help?

"What is the meaning of this? Who has made such accusations?" Madame Tremeau faced the commissioner. "I shall ask my son, Colonel Tremeau, to get to the bottom of this."

"Madame, six people have signed statements, and I have no choice but to follow procedures."

Anger clouded Etienne's thinking. Emotionally, he wanted to rush to the jail and threaten the commissioner's job for being over eager to go after Janine without further investigation. *He's ignored standard procedures for selfish reasons.*

After assuring Anne he would take care of it, Etienne headed to the stable and saddled his horse. He mounted and, with a snap of the reins, rode toward General de Bernay's house. A horseman raced toward him, leaving a trail of dust in his wake, and passed by before Etienne recognized him as one of de Bernay's messengers.

Etienne turned back toward the man and saw him coming to meet him. "The general requires your presence immediately." The soldier said, handing Etienne an envelope bearing the de Bernay seal.

"As it happens, I was already on my way there." Etienne ripped

154

open the communication and verified the message. "Let's go."

When Etienne entered the library, he was surprised to find the general wasn't alone. The other officers assigned to the conspiracy investigative team also waited around the table.

"Colonel, pour a drink and be seated. It seems the locals are anxious to make arrests based on little evidence." The general looked at Etienne. "I don't suppose you know anything about this."

"I heard about the arrest of Mademoiselle de Fleury this morning."

"From whom?"

"My mother."

De Bernay looked at the lieutenant general. "Apparently, Madame Tremeau is as well informed as you are." The man made no response, but his jaw tightened. The general went on. "Bad timing. Bonaparte looks forward to meeting Mademoiselle de Fleury at the Tuileries in two weeks." De Bernay turned to the younger man and said, "Lieutenant Lenoir, I want you to take this message to the local commissioner."

Etienne hadn't seen this coming. He viewed the assignment as being part of his responsibility to work with the locals. *I don't outrank the matchmaking orders.* He remained silent.

The general continued. "I'm sure Mademoiselle de Fleury will be promptly released to us. You are to wait for her and bring her here. She'll need to be with friends—and be questioned with discretion."

"Lieutenant, I trust your skill in this regard," de Bernay said and turned to Etienne. "Colonel Tremeau, you are to get started interviewing the people who signed the statements against her. Depending upon what you find, you may have to report your findings to the First Consul . . . and Madame Bonaparte."

Next, de Bernay addressed the glum-faced lieutenant general. "As for you, carry on with your own work. We'll meet again tomorrow morning at nine unless you hear otherwise. That's all, men."

155

Chapter 22

Janine turned to the commissioner as he led her from Nanny's house. "You're hurting my arm." She saw a flicker of anger in his eyes and feared what he would do next.

He tightened his grip. "Mademoiselle, you've confirmed my suspicions. You are a liar ... and most likely implicated in a conspiracy." Upon reaching the carriage, he motioned to the waiting officer who doubled as the driver. "Handcuff her. She lied to us and is a flight risk. She took us to Colonel Tremeau's mother, of all things." His cold gray eyes seemed to pierce hers. "You're a vindictive traitor and will pay a high price for your transgressions."

When back in the jail cell, Janine worried Etienne wouldn't be home when his mother arrived. Had Anne reached him? When would Madame Tremeau be able to tell him about her arrest? She paced the small area. Doing so did little to relieve her agitated state. She longed to avenge herself on the man who had stolen her ancestral home—and now her freedom, maybe even her life.

She had alienated the commissioner by misleading him and embarrassing him in front of Madame Tremeau, the mother of one of Bonaparte's confidants. She'd been willing to take the risk and had played her high card. Was it a winner or loser?

Janine's heart leapt at the sound of Lenoir's familiar voice. But where was Etienne? How did Lenoir know where she was? She clutched the bars and waited for him.

"Take me to the prisoner before I meet with the commissioner," the lieutenant spoke with authority to the guard. Janine waited impatiently for Lenoir to be led to her cell.

"Mademoiselle de Fleury, you have a visitor." The guard, his voice surly, took a step back and waited.

Lenoir turned to him. "Leave us," he said in a rough tone so unlike him. The jailer jerked to the side as if afraid of being struck before rushing away. With no trace of his previous irritation, the lieutenant spoke quietly. "Be assured you'll be leaving with me after I talk to the commissioner."

"Praise the Almighty, you've come." Janine made the sign of the cross and pressed her body against the iron bars.

Lenoir reached his fingers between the bars and brushed her cheek. "This must be a terrible time for you. It should never have happened."

Tears stung her eyes and a lump lodged in her throat. The compassion she saw in the lieutenant's eyes warmed her heart. She slipped her hand through the bars and reached for his hand. "Commissioner Le Bec said I'd be kept here while they complete their investigation."

"Their investigation? What have they told you about it?"

"They have signed statements to the effect that I've been seen talking with suspicious people."

"Signed statements by whom?"

"The commissioner wouldn't let me see them, but he said Comte de Fleury—the one who falsely claimed the chateau—and his caretaker were among them. He said only if charges are brought against me will I have access to their statements."

"He has overstepped his bounds. After I clarify the matter with him—it won't take long—I'll take you to the de Bernay's townhouse." Lenoir squeezed her hand before returning to the interrogation room. Janine couldn't hear what he said to the guard before they left the outer room, presumably for his private meeting with the commissioner.

Lenoir had told her with utmost confidence that he would take her away from this awful place. How could he be sure? Had Etienne sent him? At any rate, she couldn't relax while locked up. She made a diligent effort to slow her irregular breathing and hoped to banish the dizziness threatening to overcome her.

In reality, she waited no more than ten minutes, but it seemed like hours before she heard Commissioner Le Bec say, "Release her into Lieutenant Lenoir's custody."

This time she welcomed the sound of the jailer and his noisy keys coming toward her. He stopped in front of her cell and stared at her for a moment before he unlocked her cell door. "You're being transferred to the charge of one of General de Bernay's officers." He glowered at her.

She didn't care. She was free. Hurrying along the corridor, she soon reached the dingy interrogation room.

Upon her arrival, the commissioner stopped talking to Lenoir but didn't look at Janine. "Mademoiselle de Fleury is here," he said grudgingly.

The lieutenant turned his attention to Janine. "Come." He lightly touched her elbow and guided her to the door.

As they emerged from the poorly lit jail, Janine squinted at the bright sunlight. It took a moment for her eyes to adjust enough to see the de Bernay coach. Had the general made all the arrangements for her release? Why would he?

After they were seated in the plush coach, Janine asked, "Did General de Bernay arrange my release?"

"He did."

"Do you know why?"

"Oui. When the commissioner received the signed statements, he should have immediately contacted the general about this matter of concern to national security. There was a breakdown in communications."

"I think the commissioner decided I was guilty of some terrible crime."

"I agree he was overzealous, but I believe he felt it was his job. There is legitimate alarm about royalist plots."

"He can't seriously believe I'm involved in a royalist conspiracy, can he?" Janine sought reassurance from the young officer who shared a background similar to her own.

Lenoir looked uncomfortable and gazed at her for a moment before speaking. "I can't say." He looked away. "Perhaps I've said too much already."

Janine felt as if she'd been kicked in the stomach. What was going on here? What kind of reception would she receive at the de Bernay household? If she asked would Lenoir take her to Madame Parot's? Afraid of the answer, she remained silent.

The coach stopped in front of the townhouse. The coachman helped Janine out and the Lieutenant took her arm, leading her inside.

As they entered the house, Minette came toward them. "*Chérie*, thank goodness you're back. Come, tell me, how is Nanny?"

The general glared from at the library door and said to Minette, "There'll be no chitchat."

"François, can't it wait until Janine and I have a cup of coffee?

She's been through hell."

"Madame, don't interfere in these affairs. Get back to your menu preparation." The general glowered at her before looking at Lenoir. "Lieutenant, I'll brief you and Mademoiselle de Fleury now. Close the door behind you."

Minette pivoted and her skirt swished behind her as she disappeared toward the kitchen without another word. Janine had never before seen her friend so chastened, but apparently, she knew when to pick her battles. Janine cringed at what awaited her in the library.

"Come on." Lenoir placed his arm on Janine's shoulder and with some urgency encouraged her to move along.

Closed doors and secret meetings—not the typical use of a library. But this library had little to do with books and relaxation; rather, it served as the general's military headquarters. De Bernay's lack of good manners did little to put her at ease. After an awkward moment, Janine took her cue from Lenoir and sat down, although she hadn't been invited to do so.

The general sat at the head of the massive table; his face expressionless, his eyes cold. "Mademoiselle de Fleury, consider yourself fortunate to be here. The least hint of involvement in a royalist plot will not be ignored. However, it's probable the First Consul wants you given the benefit of the doubt. While the investigation is in progress, you will be a guest here and at my country estate. Until the inquiry is complete, your freedom of movement will be limited. I have assigned Lieutenant Lenoir the responsibility of ensuring you do as directed. If you have questions, ask the lieutenant." He turned to Lenoir and said, "She's all yours, Lieutenant," then he stood and went to the bar. He poured himself a glass of brandy and returned the bottle to its place.

Lenoir stood and motioned to Janine to follow him. They left General de Bernay in the library and went to a secluded corner at the far end of the salon. "We can talk here," he said softly.

"So I'm to be sequestered." Janine gave a disingenuous laugh and glanced at Lenoir. When she saw his mouth tighten, she added," I couldn't ask for a more compassionate guard though." She knew he had no more choice in the matter than she did.

"Most of the time you will be," he said in a bland tone. "But I think you'll be able to accompany my sister, Aimée, and me to Lenoir Frères to work on our design project. This will be a good time to prepare a portfolio of sketches for Pauline Bonaparte's approval."

She nodded. That's what she'd choose to do, whether or not her mobility was restricted.

"Now that the general is in charge of the investigation, it should progress quickly and be wrapped up soon."

"I hope so. Is anyone safe from such denouncement by others? I suppose they can attest to anything as often as they wish."

"Don't worry. It's not like it was during the Revolution. When it's been shown there is no substance to the allegations, those making them will lose credibility."

"I hope so." Janine stood. "I'd like to freshen up now—if that's permitted."

"By all means. Consider yourself a guest here and at the country house."

Minette's home. Janine rose and started toward the kitchen to look for her friend, but she turned back toward Lenoir. Noting his thoughtful expression, she asked, "Will I see you at lunch?"

He gave her a ponderous look. "Oui. You'll being seeing a lot of me."

Oh well, she'd leave him to his thoughts. She'd like a word with Minette before going to her room—the room she'd left before dawn that morning. It seemed like days ago.

She popped her head into the kitchen, but no one was there. Perhaps the upstairs maid could help her she thought as she hurried along the corridor and up the stairs.

In keeping with the general's orders, Lenoir accompanied Janine and Minette to the country house. General de Bernay remained at the townhouse to keep close tabs on his elite investigative team, or so Janine concluded. That suited her just fine. Minette and she could have a cup of coffee and talk freely without fearing his ire, she reasoned. At the townhouse Minette had spoken only briefly with her and had seemed tense while doing so.

Somehow this whole thing had deeply affected Minette. She

remained the gracious hostess, but she was distant, no longer the chatty Minette that Janine knew. The desired invitation for coffee together hadn't been received. Minette spoke to Janine in short, impersonal sentences when necessary. Perhaps a day or two away from her husband would change all of that. In the meantime Lenoir showered her with attention and his companionship helped pass the lonely hours.

While Janine sat alone in the salon, wishing Lenoir would look in on her, Minette stepped into the room. She remained standing, an indication she didn't plan to stay for long. "Is there anything you need or want?"

"Non, merci. You've thought of everything . . . almost. I have missed our long talks over a cup of coffee."

Minette shook her head. "I'm sorry to be neglecting you. It's because of the upcoming trip to Paris. I have a hundred and one things to get done. But all is not lost; you and the lieutenant will get things accomplished on your project."

Janine nodded. "Just keep in mind I'll always have time for coffee with you."

"I will. But now I have to get busy. Please excuse me." Minette moved toward the door.

"By all means." Janine noticed the slight tremor in Minette's hand that clutched a cut-crystal glass. She remained seated on the carved walnut canapé and pondered what could possibly have such an effect on Minette. Was there something more than her house-arrest guest? Were the de Bernays having marital problems? Did he have a mistress—if so, in Janine's opinion that could be a cause for celebration.

Lenoir's sudden appearance pulled her from her heavy thoughts. "Why so serious? Feeling cooped up in here?" He held out his hand to her. "Let's get some fresh air and talk about how we can change that."

"Confinement has a sobering effect on my mood. I'm for fresh air and a sense of freedom."

"It's worth a try." Lenoir tugged on the bell pull. Shortly, the butler appeared and the lieutenant instructed him, "Mademoiselle de Fleury and I will appreciate chilled wine and cheese served at the pavilion."

Lenoir's assignment appeared to include acting as co-host during Janine's enforced visit. Had he spent the night there too? He was there when she arrived for breakfast, that much she knew. At least he talked with her, and for that she was grateful. The silent treatment was especially painful at this time of emotional turmoil.

On their way to the pavilion, the lieutenant walked beside Janine along the graveled path, bordered on each side by expansive emerald lawns. Rounding a curve, she caught sight of it, a lacy iron skeleton canopied with a profusion of yellow roses.

Janine could contain her curiosity no longer. "You surprised me by requesting wine and cheese from the butler. Has Minette asked you to see to my comfort?"

Lenoir nodded. "Yes, under the circumstances I have been asked to see that your every need is anticipated."

"You seem quite at home here and at the townhouse. I suppose that comes from your responsibilities to General de Bernay. Are you with him often?"

"I spend a great deal of time assisting him. But tomorrow I'll take you to Lenoir Frères for a day of design work. A change of scene will do you good."

"I have designs dancing in my head but have yet to capture them on paper." Janine waited for the butler to depart after setting the tray of wine and cheese on the table. "I look forward to getting started on them."

"Keep them dancing until tomorrow." Lenoir placed his hand over hers. "I know this investigation is difficult. Do you suppose the complaints against you will crumble under scrutiny? Or do you think there is an organized plot against you?"

She sipped the wine Lenoir poured for her. "I expect the caretaker and the fraudulent Comte de Fleury planned their stories. I have no idea who else is involved, but I suspect they're part of a conspiracy to destroy me."

"Is it true that a number of strangers have approached you and engaged in conversation?"

Janine wanted to be truthful with Lenoir, but she couldn't tell him that only one person had approached her in various disguises. "Yes, I was most distressed by the ordeals."

The lieutenant refilled their glasses. "I can imagine. I'm sorry to have brought up the subject."

"It's better to ask than to continue to wonder whether there is any truth to it," Janine said.

"You're most gracious, one of your many admirable qualities. I'm sure it's no secret I want you to accompany me to Bonaparte's celebration in Paris, but this dreadful business forces a delay in my asking."

"Merci, I'm pleased you thought of me. I know circumstances are affecting my friends. I am truly sorry to put you through this."

"It's you who is suffering. You have no need to apologize."

"Something seems to be troubling Minette. I hope I'm not the cause of it."

"Of course she is concerned about you. But she is also anxious about preparation for the Paris event. Madame Bonaparte depends on her to fulfill certain obligations."

"I'd like to be useful in some way. If you think of anything I can do to help, let me know."

"We'll all feel better after the investigation is completed. Until then it's a waiting game. I can tell you one thing of interest though. Josephine Bonaparte is eager to meet you. She was deeply moved when she heard about the loss of your parents during the Revolution. As you may know, she too was imprisoned. Her first husband died on the scaffold."

Janine started to say something but turned to follow Lenoir's gaze instead. In the distance a dust plume followed three men on horseback racing toward the house. "General de Bernay," Lenoir murmured. He stood and reached for Janine's hand. "We have to go inside—let's hope he brings good news."

Chapter 23

Etienne rode toward Chateau Fleury, noting its impressive profile bore the tarnish of neglect. He sought information in his official assignment, as well as for Janine. He regretted being unable to communicate his concern to her, but he couldn't risk allowing his sympathy for her plight to cloud his judgment. Instead, he directed his irritation toward the derelict rose garden, observing scraggly bushes dangling over its damaged brick walls. His father would have been appalled at the sight. On the approach to the residence, his horse gave an appropriate snort. Etienne pulled back on the reins and sat for a time. How long had it been since he was last there—three or more years?

"You're right, this place doesn't look inviting, does it, boy?" He stroked the horse's mane as he recalled the beauty of the estate's manicured gardens and flourishing vineyards when his father, the head gardener, had overseen their care for the Marquis de Fleury. Many a day he had worked alongside his father, developing his keen interest in botany.

Etienne felt a pang of remorse for his resentment directed at the marquis because of the class system they had all lived under. Limitations had been placed on his father's talents because of his birthright. The best his père could hope for was to work for an aristocratic family who reaped the rewards. In retrospect he realized the marquis had been generous to the Tremeau family and shown goodwill toward them. Etienne owed his rapid rise in the Revolutionary Army to the education and knowledge he'd gained from Janine's tutor and the marquis. He had taken what they had to offer, believing his future would be much different than his father's.

Etienne shook his head at his memories. Just a boy when the rumblings of the Revolution had begun, he had welcomed a part in the fight for equality. He'd held a vision of enlightened thought ushering in the much talked-about Age of Reason.

But little had he known the cost. Reason did not prevail; rather, brutal mob mentality had gripped the nation. Blood had flowed freely, with little distinction of the innocent from the guilty. Five years later Janine had lost everything save her life. Did it have to be so? Unanticipated violence had reigned during the upheaval. Yet he shared some of the guilt for her misfortune.

And now he returned to Chateau Fleury, a colonel in the Army of the Republic and a special emissary for Napoleon—soon to be general and owner of a confiscated chateau of his own . . . *if* he married Mademoiselle La Roche.

Today, he sought answers about men who represented the ugly part of the Revolution. They manipulated the chaos of the Revolution for their own devious purposes rather than its lofty ideals. His eyes fell on the weed-choked remains of the kitchen gardens and moved on to the imposing stables where he and Janine had sought to save the life of her uncle, the mortally wounded Comte de Fleury. Under the cloak of the Revolution, the marquis' groomsman had plunged a dagger into her uncle's heart before escaping on the prized steed, Le Diamant.

With a heavy heart, Etienne hitched his horse to a post and continued on foot to the chateau. After persistent knocking on the door brought no response, he called out, "Open in the name of the Army of the Republic." Would the fake count appear?

A diminutive man answered the door, his white hair falling to his shoulders. "What is the nature of your business?"

Etienne stepped inside without invitation. "I am here in response to the sworn statements of Comte de Fleury and Monsieur Jean O'Rourke regarding Mademoiselle de Fleury."

"Oh . . . the count has suffered a serious accident and isn't able to receive visitors. Monsieur O' Rourke may be grooming the horses. Please have a seat while I go and see." The little man started down the long hall.

Etienne followed alongside him. "What sort of injury?"

The man stopped and looked up at him. "Serious head injury. Riding accident."

"I'll show myself out to the stables and look for Monsieur O'Rourke myself, but before I do, I want some answers from you." Etienne loomed over the slight figure, moving within a hairbreadth of him.

The man backed up against the wall. "Oui, Monsieur." He paled and stared past Etienne toward the stairs.

Etienne whirled around, hand on sword, confronting a black-robed figure with shoulder-length, salt-and-pepper hair moving toward them. A thick black beard and moustache—clearly not his own—

covered the bottom half of his face. The top of his head was bandaged like a mummy except for openings for eyes and nose. A ridiculous disguise hastily put together, yet it accomplished the purpose of obscuring his real features. *Who is he?*

"Colonel, you have questions for me?" The man addressed Etienne in a raspy voice barely above a whisper.

The little white-haired man rushed forward and grasped the man's arm. "Non, Monsieur. You must go back to bed."

Etienne took his other arm. "Have I the pleasure of speaking to Comte Alexandre de Fleury?"

"Oui."

"I'll help you back to your bed."

The man exhibited remarkable strength as he tried to free himself. "I'll answer your questions right where I am."

Etienne led him toward a bench in the reception hall. "Have it your way. I'll be as brief as I can. Your affidavit is signed Comte Alexandre de Fleury, yet in your statement you make no mention that Mademoiselle Janine de Fleury is your niece. Why not?"

"I am a loyal Republican. I do not want her to sully my good name. Now, after ten years, she has returned to conspire with the enemy. Not just once. Not by chance, but on a regular basis since I've been watching her. I have no choice in the matter. It is my duty to report her."

"You are of noble birth. How long have you been loyal to the Republic?"

The man jumped up, almost tripping over his robe. After he regained his footing, he sat with his fists clenched before opening his mouth. "I've always been an eg . . . egali . . . ."

Etienne completed the word for him. "Egalitarian." Was the man an aristocrat who choked on a hated word or an uneducated peasant? Who was this imposter?

"No privileged classes or kings for me . . . you understand?"

"Have you served in the Army of the Republic?"

"I wanted to volunteer, but I was forced to emigrate because of the hostility toward aristocratic families. I came back as soon as I was able to lend my support to our Republican government. I want no part of the Bourbons' plan to rule again."

Egalitarian, ha. Conniving opportunist. How familiar was this imposter with the day-to-day lives of the de Fleury family? "Refresh my memory. What crime was the marquis, your brother, charged with during his trial?"

"I . . . don't know exactly. I suppose . . . his service to the king."

"And what crime were you accused of?"

"None."

"That's peculiar. Comte Alexandre de Fleury, captain in the King's Army, was accused of a crime in 1793." The mummy-count fidgeted without responding. Etienne's gaze bored into the man's shifty eyes. "In what year did you emigrate?"

"1793."

"Why did you leave your niece behind?"

"She was already a traitor to the Republic."

"As were you. But unlike you, she was but a child."

"Non, Non. I wanted to help but they refused to believe me."

"You coward. You abandoned your dead brother's daughter. You endangered her life and you are still a threat to her well-being. You disgust me." Etienne moved closer to the man. "In 1793 I'm sure the authorities did not issue you a passport to emigrate. How were you able to leave the country?"

"I used a false name."

"What name was that?"

"I don't remember."

"Comte—or whoever you are, I don't believe you. This reflects poorly on your credibility because you did not disclose your poor memory in your allegations against Mademoiselle de Fleury."

"Why are you so hostile toward me?"

"I am seeking the truth and you are evading my questions."

"I am answering them as best I can."

"I doubt it. Tell me, did the Marquise Marie de Fleury attend her husband's trial?"

"Oui."

"In spirit? She was already dead."

"Stop trying to confuse me." The count clenched his hands before pressing them on his knees and lowering his head.

"Perhaps your memory will allow you to answer my questions about your allegations against your niece. If not, your assertions will be discounted. How many days have you followed and watched

Mademoiselle de Fleury?"

"About three weeks, off and on."

"Within that time you saw her in conversation with three people whom you deemed unsuitable—that's one per week. Is that correct?"

"Non. It's not like that. It's just been in the past few days that she's been meeting them. Even more suspicious, because she doesn't usually talk to people she meets on the street. Wouldn't you agree?"

"Not necessarily. You've said you observed her off and on. After you saw her speak with a questionable person, did you spend more time following her?"

"Well, uh, maybe a little."

"Did you overhear her conversations?"

"Not everything. They talked in low voices and kept looking around to see if anyone was near."

"What did you hear?"

"I saw them exchange money."

"You saw her accept money?"

"Eh . . . Oui, and she passed something to the man."

"Your statement says that she gave the man a small sack but makes no mention of money or of her receiving anything in return. Are you aware you are deviating from your report?"

"I am not. I am explaining it to you."

"Did you or didn't you see an exchange of money?"

"I heard coins clink."

"Let's get this straight. She gave the man a sack that you think contained coins, is that right?"

"Oui. I already told you so."

Serious questions plagued Etienne. He had to separate past wrongs this man had committed against Janine and his present accusation against her. Had she given or received money? "How many times did you witness her in compromising circumstances?"

"Many times. I don't remember exactly."

"Would you estimate six or more?"

"Oui. I believe so."

"Really? Your affidavit cites three occasions. I warn you there is more than a slight breath of scandal here today."

The man pressed his hand to his head. "All right, three. My head isn't very clear since my accident."

"Or could it be you are deliberately making misleading statements. No further questions today, but you are directed to remain available for further questioning until after the hearing or until you are notified by General de Bernay that there will be none." Etienne turned to the little man. "I'll go to the stables now. Good day."

Etienne needed to conclude his report to General de Bernay and to the First Consul quickly while the imposter was still under orders to remain available for questioning. Much investigation remained to be done at the chateau, as well as more questions for the count-impersonator.

The little servant skittered away like a frightened fawn, leaving Etienne to show himself out. Silence surrounded the mummy-like count as if he were sealed in a tomb.

The informal gardens and stables stood to Etienne's right. Blinded by the sun, he shaded his eyes. He imagined the cornucopia of mouth-watering vegetables, the scent of lavender, and the rainbow of colors of perennials and annuals as they had been when he and his father nurtured them. His father's voice emerged from the recesses of his mind. *Son, put aside your dreams of revolution and work with me here on the estate. The marquis is ready to sponsor your training in botany. Your future will be bright right here.*

He banished the memory and took the long way to the stables to avoid passing the derelict gardens where he and Janine had heard the scuffle that led to Comte de Fleury's death. Approaching the stables, he found them maintained in pristine condition, unlike the neglected chateau and abandoned gardens. When he stepped inside the freshly painted structure, the pleasant scents of fine leather and aromatic hay welcomed him. He surveyed the stalls, surprised to see ten fine horses. Two men brushed and groomed the horses, and a third one with shaggy red hair sat on a stool, polishing a saddle.

"Monsieur O'Rourke?" Etienne approached the man nearest him.

"What are you doing here?" The red-haired man jerked his head up in Etienne's direction. The words appeared to escape his mouth before he saw Etienne's uniform. "Uh . . . Colonel, I beg your pardon. I am O'Rourke."

There were advantages to being in uniform. The power of the military was not to be questioned in Napoleon's France. Etienne savored the moment and held the man's gaze. "I have questions about your statement against Mademoiselle de Fleury."

O'Rourke shifted in his seat. "Everything I know is in my statement."

"Some clarification is needed. You seemed to cross paths with her frequently. Was that by chance?"

"I'm in town quite often and chanced to see her in deep conversation with a suspicious-looking man. I felt it my duty to watch her and report the matter. That's when I saw her meet with other unkempt characters."

"How did you know who she was?"

"She came to the chateau with the abbé and Madame de Bernay. She asked to see the comte. I let her know it was impossible because he was in England at the time."

"Did you invite her to stay here at the chateau, her family home?"

"God forbid I should do so without the count's permission. He left strict orders that nothing was to be disturbed in his absence."

"Hospitality for his niece should be an exception."

"The household is essentially closed down when the count and his family are away."

"I can't imagine one guest would require a large staff. Surely, you could have called in sufficient help without permission."

"Non, I could not deviate from my instructions. Just think of the trouble I would have brought to the count by harboring an enemy of the Republic."

"Be careful about making defamatory statements not supported by definitive evidence."

O'Rourke cast his eyes downward at the saddle in his lap.

While Etienne waited for a response, he studied the horses in the stalls and was astounded to see Le Diamant, the dead Comte de Fleury's blue-gray stallion, in the far stall. The distinctive white diamond shape on his forehead—for which he was named—identified him. Etienne took leave of O'Rourke to take a closer look at the animal. He stroked the horse's neck and spoke softly to him, "Le Diamant."

The stallion whinnied and nuzzled Etienne's outstretched hand. He pressed against the timber barrier that prevented an unfettered reunion with a long lost friend.

170

O'Rourke rushed forward and screamed, "What are you doing?"

Etienne ignored him and opened the unlocked stall door. He climbed onto the horse's back and rode him bareback around the stable, followed by O'Rourke trying to catch them. He halted the animal with a word and turned to face the man.

"What does this horse have to do with your investigation?" the red-haired man asked after catching his breath.

"You don't want to know. Be assured, he does." Etienne continued to sit astride the horse and look down at O'Rourke. The man appeared as though he might explode at any moment, his face almost as red as his hair. "I'm not here to answer questions, rather to ask them. How long has this stallion been here?"

The caretaker wiped beads of sweat from his brow. "Please, if he's your horse, understand I know nothing about it. He was here when I came into the count's service."

"In that case, I'll have to ask the count," Etienne called over his shoulder as he rode Le Diamant from the stables, past the gardens and away from captivity. Yes, the Army of the Republic had a place for such a fine animal.

The stallion galloped in response to his liberator's directions around the vineyards and back toward the chateau. Finally, reluctantly, Etienne dismounted and released his own horse to follow them home. *The count can wait.*

He settled Le Diamant into the stall next to his own horse and prepared to leave for town to seek the others who had signed statements about Janine. It was of utmost importance to conclude his report before the day's end. Time was of the essence. Would he receive Bonaparte's approval for his next move to expose the fake count?

Chapter 24

With a flourish of the quill, Etienne inked his name at the bottom of the parchment sheet and affixed his seal. His report to Bonaparte and de Bernay, brief and to the point, concluded that none of the men signing statements against Janine provided compelling evidence for further investigation. When interviewed, Comte de Fleury and Monsieur O'Rourke had contradicted their signed allegations, while another man had confessed that the count had promised to give him a horse in exchange for his statement against Janine. The count had assured him he had seen his own niece, a royalist sympathizer, talking with the strangers. There was no mistaking it had been Mademoiselle Janine de Fleury. Another witness acknowledged that, although he had been with the count, he had not noticed her at all but had taken the count's word she was there. The fifth man, John O'Brien, who had assaulted Mademoiselle de Fleury, had been released from jail while charges pended from his attack on her—an administrative mistake, so the jailer had said. He had not been seen since. The abbé's statement simply said he'd seen Janine speaking to a stranger in town.

"Based on your investigation, these witnesses don't seem reliable to make a case." The general affixed his signature to the document. "You'd best get started to Paris in the morning."

"I plan to leave this afternoon." Etienne blotted the signatures before rolling and tying the parchment.

"I suggest you stay for dinner and a game of chess tonight. Leave for Paris early in the morning. I'll send my letter to the First Consul with you."

Etienne swallowed his frustration at the delay. "In that case, I accept. If you will excuse me, I'll leave you to your letter writing," Etienne wondered why the general wanted to write a separate letter to Napoleon.

General de Bernay tapped his pipe on the side of his desk and pressed tobacco into it. He lit it, puffed, and puffed again before he spoke. "Stop by to see me before dinner. I may have some more questions for you."

So much for his well-laid plans. He'd check on Le Diamant at the stables and let the groomsman know of the change of plans.

Janine was crestfallen to hear from Lenoir that her case was not concluded; General de Bernay had returned to await the reports of his officers. "This means I'm still under house arrest." She shook her head in disappointment.

"Cheer up, I do have approval for you to spend the day at Lenoir Frères tomorrow. We'll devote the time to working on designs for Pauline Bonaparte." He gave her an encouraging smile. "And whether or not the investigation is finished, we can use the next few days to work in the studio. You won't need to be here if you don't want to be."

"Since I must be under someone's watchful eye, I'm glad you're the one," Janine said, noting his satisfied expression. She meant what she said, grateful for his kindness, a marked contrast to her treatment in the jail. "I'm going to my room to capture my design ideas before they fade. I'll see you at dinner."

"What choice do I have?" Lenoir gave her a weak smile. "Request granted."

The next morning Janine hummed as she dressed. She was looking forward to the day with Lenoir. Was it because anything was better than staying at General de Bernay's holding facility? No, excitement coursed through her veins at the thought of creating designs of beauty with the gallant lieutenant. She patted the portfolio of sketches she'd worked on before dinner and afterward late into the night. An opportunity like this wasn't likely to present itself again. Besides, she found talking about her work with the lieutenant filled her with hope. If things went well, she might even become an associate designer for the company—and if she wanted, perhaps she could live in Paris and have her own elite group of clients from the new Bonaparte-designated royalty. She chastised herself for indulging in such a fantasy. These days her life allowed only for planning one day at a time.

With a final glance in the mirror, and after an extra dash of rouge to her cheeks, she picked up her vignettes and left the room. After breakfast she'd go to work at the prestigious Maison de Lenoir Frères design studio. She reveled in the thought. With an eager bounce in her steps, she entered the morning room.

Although early in the day, Lenoir was already seated, devouring a plate of sausage, eggs, and bread. A half-filled glass of juice sat beside his cup of coffee. "Good morning, Mademoiselle. We have the room to ourselves. May I prepare a plate for you?"

"No, thank you. I can't think about eating just yet. My thoughts are filled with designs, not food. I'll start with coffee and see if anything looks tempting."

She set the portfolio on the table. Following him to the buffet, she picked up a cup and poured herself a cup of the steaming beverage. Six silver chafing servers lined the table like treasure chests hiding a variety of precious gems. After lifting three monogrammed lids, she decided on a boiled egg.

The lieutenant took the silver cover from her hand while she removed the egg. "Don't you want a piece of ham, too?" He replaced the cover and moved back toward the pan of ham.

"Non, just some bread and jam."

Lenoir moved to her side, took her plate, and carried it to the table.

"Merci." Janine seated herself, lifted her knife and lopped off the top of the egg before placing it in the holder. "Do you know why Minette wasn't at dinner last night?"

He shrugged his shoulders and then swallowed with a thoughtful expression. "I think she's distressed about this investigation. I saw her maid take a tray to her room. You do realize you're like a sister to her, don't you?"

Janine set her spoon on her plate and lifted her eyes to Lenoir. "I hope she doesn't get sick because of me."

"I don't think this inquiry will go on much longer. I certainly hope not." He pushed aside his plate.

Within the hour they were on their way to the design studio. The coach rumbled along the rough road, a trail of dust swirling behind them. "I want you to accompany me when I present our designs to Pauline Bonaparte . . . eh . . . Madame Leclerc." Lenoir glanced up from a small sketch he'd been working on while the carriage moved along.

Since she'd been in the Loire Valley, Janine had overheard critical remarks about the First Consul's younger sister, Pauline Bonaparte Leclerc, and she had wanted to learn more. "I know so little about her. What can you tell me?"

174

"Bonaparte arranged her marriage to General Leclerc and named him to the office of Commander-in-Chief of the French Army in Italy. After Bonaparte pronounced himself First Consul, he appointed General Leclerc Governor-General of Saint-Domingue."

"Pauline and Josephine have both experienced life in the Caribbean colonies."

"Things didn't go well on the island for the Leclerc family. All three of them suffered from the effects of yellow fever. Less than a year later, Leclerc died of the disease. Pauline and the boy still have bouts of its ill effects."

"Since I've been here, I've heard some wags say Pauline had numerous lovers, in spite of her illness."

"That wouldn't surprise me. She's extravagant, as is Josephine, but without Josephine's gentle, caring nature. So be prepared, she'll let us know if our designs don't suit her. We'll be fortunate if she gives us a second chance—it'll depend on what kind of day she's having."

As the coach rounded the curve and turned into the private lane, Janine caught sight of the familiar grove of broad-leafed mulberry trees leading to the silk production facility and the Lenoirs' home.

"I suggest we present many beautiful choices so she'll find something to her liking," Janine said.

"You're a woman, so you should know."

By the late afternoon they had narrowed the sketches from fifty to a final five—and five more for good measure—for presentation to their patron. Lenoir arranged to have fabric samples of the final patterns made up, the six of Janine's he had selected and four of his own. "We have enough variety here to suit the tastes of all of France." He stood beside Janine and placed a hand on her shoulder. "I'm honored to introduce you to my Paris clientele."

Janine felt a deep camaraderie with the lieutenant. She felt appreciated and valued—and almost optimistic about the future. "Thank you. Your belief in me means a lot."

He took her hands in his and gave her fingers a gentle squeeze of acknowledgement. "I'm glad." After a brief pause, he added, "You'll enjoy the soirée at the Bonapartes'. I'm pleased you accepted my invitation to be my guest."

Janine wondered whether he spoke with certainty that she

would be free to attend or whether he said it to cheer her up. "I'm sure I shall."

"We'd better get started back to the de Bernays' or we'll miss dinner."

Janine and Lenoir bid farewell to Aimée and climbed into the waiting coach. During the ride, they talked about their plans in Paris. After their arrival they strolled in the de Bernay garden until the dinner hour, not so much to avoid going inside but by an unspoken agreement to prolong their time together,

The evening was pleasant and Janine enjoyed abandoning herself to the free-flowing conversation with him. She wanted to be with him and found herself hoping it would continue after his assignment ended. She slipped her arm through his as the sun dropped behind the horizon. "It is so beautiful. I wouldn't mind doing without dinner to stay here."

"Later on you might regret it. Never mind, we'll make garden walks a habit." He took her hand and drew her toward the house.

When inside, Janine stopped for a moment and faced him. "I'll change for dinner and meet you there."

"Come to the salon when you're ready. We'll go to dinner together," he said.

"Is that an order?" Janine asked with a straight face, hoping his words meant he wanted to be with her.

"Non, Mademoiselle. If the thought displeases you, I will see you in the dining room."

"I shall look for you in the salon." Janine raised her hand in a half wave and went to her room.

The clock stood at a quarter to eight, leaving fifteen minutes until the dinner hour. Etienne had spent the entire afternoon in the library with General de Bernay, receiving minute instructions about his meeting with Bonaparte. In his view it was a waste of time, but he understood de Bernay hoped for a reward for a successful mission. He had been bored to the point of exhaustion until there was a light tap at the door.

Minette's face glowed as she came into the room. "I'm here as you asked, *mon chér.* I'm so relieved for Janine that your investigation is completed." She kissed her husband on both cheeks. Turning to Etienne, she wrapped her arms around his neck and kissed him on both cheeks as well, a bit too enthusiastically in his opinion. "Colonel, you've done a wonderful job ferreting out the lies about Janine. Merci. There's joy in my life again."

The general studied his wife. "You are so right, my dear. We've done a thorough investigation. I'm sure our report will be well received by the First Consul." He poured three glasses of champagne. "To Colonel Tremeau's distinguished service to the Republic."

The hands on the clock crawled for the next fifteen minutes as Etienne endured small talk about plans for the trip to Paris and the Bonapartes' fete. He would much rather be well on his way to Paris than sitting here. He excused himself from the table as soon as good manners allowed.

Following Minette and the general into the dining room, he turned to see Janine come from the salon on the arm of Lenoir. Of course Lenoir had been the bearer of the good news about the completion of the investigation and that a report would soon be on the way to Bonaparte.

Janine looked ravishing in a long lavender gown, her cheeks the color of rose petals, her lips like red rosebuds. He swallowed hard and mustered the strength to suppress the passion threatening to overpower him. Why was he reacting this way? This was no surprise. He knew Napoleon's plans for Lenoir and Janine. Lenoir he understood, but he hadn't expected Janine to fall into line so quickly. Perhaps the shock and uncertainty of her arrest had hastened it. He sat down, his shoulders tense.

Minette bordered on giddiness as she rushed to Janine and hugged her. "Chérie, thank God it's over . . . this silly investigation. We have so many plans to make for the soirée." She took her husband's arm and spoke to the others. "Let's be seated.

Lenoir sat next to Janine. "Madame de Bernay, you will need to make an appointment to see her. Mademoiselle de Fleury is in high demand these days."

Minette frowned. "Oh, how so?"

"Six of her designs will be presented to Pauline Bonaparte Leclerc while we're in Paris."

"Chérie, you didn't even tell me you knew her," Minette said to Janine with a pout.

Janine looked at Lenoir and then at Minette. "I haven't met her."

The lieutenant gazed at Janine. "I'd better explain. Mademoiselle de Fleury's designs are included in the portfolio that Madame Leclerc has commissioned from Maison Lenoir Frères."

Janine glanced at Etienne before staring at her plate.

Minette set her fork and knife down. "I had no idea you'd made so much progress, chérie. That's wonderful. I suppose this means you won't have time to design my gowns."

Gowns. Good God. An acidic burn rose into Etienne's throat.

Lenoir reached for his wine glass. "All of Paris will love her designs. I want you to know we're fortunate to be in the company of a very talented artist."

Minette put her hand to the side of her face. "*Bien sûr.* But, of course."

Etienne pushed his plate to the side. "I have a long journey before me in the morning. Will you be so kind as to excuse me tonight?"

"Indeed. *Bonne nuit.*" General de Bernay stood and walked with him a short distance, while behind them Etienne could hear the ladies murmuring their own goodnights to him.

Etienne took the packed breakfast from the cook's outstretched hand. "Merci." He paused a moment to watch the cook stir a steaming pan over the fire. A hot breakfast would have to wait for another day.

"*De rien*, it's nothing," she answered without turning from the stove.

Outside, the pre-dawn night was inky black and a chill hung in the foggy air as Etienne walked with determination to the stables and saddled up Le Diamant for their trip to Paris. He would leave earlier than planned to avoid seeing Janine. Disgusted with the turn of events, he had no interest in telling her about his findings at Chateau Fleury.

Things were moving quickly now. She'd fallen into Lenoir's hands like a ripe plum and most likely succumbed to the lure of Bonaparte's marriage plans for her. It was an offer she'd find appealing. He shook his head, annoyed with her *and* with Bonaparte, who shouldn't be encouraging artificial class distinctions contrary to the Republican principle of equality for all. He placed his cold breakfast in the saddlebag with his extra clothes. A second saddlebag, reserved for important papers, contained the rolled parchment and General de Bernay's communications to the First Consul. He smiled at the irony of the fact that his report enabled Janine and Lenoir to chase after the Bonapartes and their vision for the future. Why should he do more than required to expose the phony count?

Chapter 25

The farther Etienne traveled from the Loire Valley, the darker the sky became. Gray fog gave way to black sheets of pelting rain by the time he and Le Diamant reached the forests approaching Orleans. Muddy waters carved crevices in the earthen road and obscured hazardous stones beneath its murky path. He appeared to be the only mortal within miles. But in case he wasn't, Etienne kept a tight rein on his mount, his muscles tensed to react to hidden dangers. He'd have little notice if he needed to change course to accommodate unseen riders or other obstacles.

As he brushed water droplets from his face and sleeves, he noticed his horse's ears perk forward, alert. Then Etienne heard it, too—the crack of snapping branches. In the shadows of the woods alongside, he saw the outline of a rider keeping pace with him. *Odd place to travel.*

"Halte!" Etienne shouted, giving the reins a tug to the right. Without a word the horseman turned and disappeared into the dense forest. Etienne gave chase but soon lost sight of the receding figure. Given this development, he regretted sending his aide, Adrien, ahead to Paris in preparation for his arrival. At a time like this, two men were better than one.

Clearly, the rider and his horse were familiar with this area to be able to maneuver with such skill through the thicket. The man either lived in the area or was part of a renegade group—most likely the anti-revolutionary Chouans—who roamed the forests and preyed on travelers along the road. He made a mental note to explore the area and make inquiries on his return trip.

Today, he couldn't spare the time for pursuit. His primary concern was the delivery of the parchment to Bonaparte. Astride his muscular stallion, Etienne resumed his journey to Paris to brief Bonaparte on the conclusion of his investigation. Yet a nagging question haunted him. What had Janine failed to tell him about the conversations she'd had with the strangers she'd acknowledged being seen with? Did the shadow man in the forest have a connection to the strangers she had talked with? How had the man happened to be following him and for how long? Only a handful of people knew he'd be making the trip.

Did General de Bernay also have doubts about Janine's innocence, or was Etienne reading too much into the sealed de Bernay letter he carried? He had no choice but to tell the First Consul about his concerns. He was well aware the Bonapartes planned to bring Janine and Lenoir together with the hope they would lend the legitimacy of the old aristocracy to their regal court. Based on his report, their goal would move full speed ahead. There would be no changing their minds *unless* Janine was guilty of treason. Woe unto all of them if she were.

As Le Diamant and he wended their way along the desolate road, he was reminded that his value to their court was not because of birth but by a combination of his loyal military service, coupled with a marriage into a titled family as decreed by the First Consul. The whole thing ran contrary to his commitment to equality for all. He didn't want a magic wand waved over him to become part of an elite group. He lowered his head. There was no telling what Janine wanted— whether she yearned for the Bourbons to return to the throne or whether she'd be content to serve as lady-in-waiting to Josephine Bonaparte. Before the Revolution she had every reason to expect such a royal lifestyle. He drew in a deep breath and slowly released it. As he thought about it, he knew he couldn't compromise his principles and marry Mademoiselle La Roche, but he expected Janine would marry Lenoir as a path to an aristocratic lifestyle.

First, he'd try to solve the problem with Chateau Fleury and the fake count, and then he'd ask for an assignment in the renewed war with England. That was the one way he could in good conscience serve Bonaparte and the Republic—he would distance himself from Bonaparte's palaces and his resurrected royal court at the Tuileries and Saint Cloud.

After three rainy days of travel, Etienne entered Paris under a sun-splashed sky. The jagged outline of Parisian rooftops glistened in the distance. Etienne put his handkerchief over his nose to dull the stench from the still-muddy streets and tightened his grip on the reins, carefully guiding his mount to avoid splattering the putrid slush of excrement, mud, and decayed garbage. In spite of the hazards of the streets, elaborate coaches ventured forth among the throng of horses, carts, and people.

He'd have to clean up at the Tuileries stables before going to his apartment at the palace to change into fresh clothing before meeting with Bonaparte before lunch. He well knew the First Consul's custom to eat his midday meal alone while entertained by actresses, artists, or other special guests.

By the time Etienne entered Bonaparte's office, the noon hour neared. The First Consul appeared to be in a good humor. *"Mon cher ami, come in. What news do you bring?"* Bonaparte strode forward, his hand extended, and eyed the parchment in Etienne's hand. He led him to a casual seating arrangement consisting of four overstuffed chairs and a small table near the enormous fireplace. He gestured to a chair and sat in one beside it. "Show me what you have there." He poured two glasses of sherry from a crystal decanter and placed one in front of Etienne, studying him as if seeking a clue. "Good news, I hope. I've had my share of bad this morning. Those damned Englishmen."

"My report regarding allegations lodged against Mademoiselle de Fleury." Etienne handed Bonaparte the parchment. "The good news is that there doesn't seem to be any substance to those accusations."

The First Consul fingered the rolled paper and looked at Etienne. "I'm glad to hear it. As you well know, since the English violated the Treaty of Amiens and are now at war with the Republic, I have proof that they are funding royalist plots against us."

Etienne noted Bonaparte's creased brow. "We must be ever vigilant against the threats. After you've read my report, I want to make a few unofficial comments."

Without waiting for a response, the First Consul unfastened the document and proceeded to read. When he finished, he rolled it up with a hint of amusement in his eyes. "If your thoughts have anything to do with Mademoiselle de Fleury's attendance at the upcoming fete, I suggest you express them in the presence of Madame Bonaparte, as well as to me."

Etienne had to smile at Napoleon's savvy assessment of the topic on his mind. He wasn't surprised in the least. "Oui, it is about that event."

With a nod of his head, Napoleon said, "I thought so. In that case, you're invited to dine with Josephine and me this evening. She will want to hear what you have to say."

"I'll be there."

Bonaparte looked up at Etienne and held his gaze. "Why would Comte de Fleury make such serious allegations against his niece?"

Etienne weighed how best to answer the question without going into detail. "I'm certain that the man who calls himself Comte de Fleury is an imposter who may well be a spy."

"What evidence do you have?"

"Comte Alexandre de Fleury was murdered ten years ago by his groomsman."

"How can you be sure your information is accurate?"

"I saw it with my own eyes—and I laid the count's cold body in the family vault."

"You?" Bonaparte stared at him with a look of shock. "You weren't among the roaming peasants going from estate to estate to mete out mob justice, were you?"

"Non. To the contrary. I was working in the garden near the estate stables and heard Mademoiselle de Fleury's cries for help. We both reached her uncle at the same time and saw the groomsman ride away on the count's horse. I calmed the young lady and assured her I would take her uncle's body to the vault—which I did."

"How long had you been the de Fleury's gardener?"

"My father had been their gardener for more than twenty years. From time to time I helped him."

"After all the time I've spent with you through the years, I had no idea." Bonaparte shook his head. "That explains your infatuation with the fair Mademoiselle de Fleury."

Etienne ignored the barb. "I don't know who has assumed the identity of the dead Comte de Fleury, but I do know he was in England among the French émigrés until he disappeared five years ago after killing a man. The man who reclaimed Chateau Fleury on behalf of the family fits some of the distinguishing traits of the man seen in England."

"Such as?"

"He barely spoke above a whisper—injury to his vocal cords,

so he said. He exhibited hostile behavior and a violent temper."

"Are his physical characteristics the same?"

"According to the émigrés' descriptions, he was of the same general height and build as the Comte de Fleury they knew in France."

"I read in your report that the proprietor of the chateau went to great lengths to disguise his appearance when you interviewed him." Napoleon's knit brows revealed his effort to understand. "That is peculiar. I'll rely on you to continue your investigation of him and any illegal activities he may be involved in . . . and whether he poses a risk to Mademoiselle de Fleury."

"While taking a look around the property, I found that someone had sealed the de Fleury burial vault. The opening is filled in with brick. I request your permission to open the tomb."

With pursed lips Napoleon fell silent before responding. "I hope that won't be necessary. If the return of the property to him conformed to all the legal requirements, I don't want to appear to disregard my own policy."

The clock chimed a quarter to twelve. Both Etienne and Napoleon stood with military precision. General Bonaparte's itinerary was sacrosanct.

Merde! He'd have to wait until supper to tell the First Consul about the forest incident.

A few minutes before seven Etienne arrived at the Bonapartes' private quarters, aware Bonaparte and Josephine would return from their customary evening carriage ride on the hour. Likewise, the household staff would have the supper table laid for their arrival. Any delay with the set routine sent the First Consul into a fit of anger and was to be avoided at all cost.

Etienne stood when Josephine, wearing a simple yet elegant blue gown, glided into the small salon adjoining the dining room. A few minutes later her husband followed. Napoleon had changed into a silk brocade smoking jacket.

With a casual motion of her hand, Josephine smoothed her long dark hair and repositioned the band of red roses adorning it. "I am pleased you've joined us for supper."

Etienne accepted her outstretched hand and kissed it. "Madame, the pleasure is mine."

"Enough small talk, Madame." The First Consul pivoted on one foot and then the other before leading them into the dining room. "The food is getting cold and I'm ready to eat." He gestured for Etienne to be seated to his right.

Etienne bristled as Josephine meekly took her place at the table. Things had certainly changed after seven years of marriage. Now Napoleon was the self-assured one. Over the years he had watched Napoleon's physical health and strength improve in concert with his military and political successes. Etienne recalled when the Bonapartes had married in 1796; the relatively unknown General Bonaparte had been puny, penniless, and his future precarious. Josephine had brought him respectability and had served as his goodwill ambassador.

Etienne ate his soup in silence and waited for Napoleon to set the tone of the conversation. After a few minutes Bonaparte pushed his bowl aside and addressed Josephine. "Mademoiselle Janine de Fleury will be the topic of discussion tonight. The colonel's investigation of complaints lodged against her concludes the witnesses are unreliable."

"I'm relieved to hear so." Josephine's expression brightened.

"The colonel has voiced some reservations about giving her clearance to attend the gala with Lieutenant Lenoir."

Josephine gave Etienne a quizzical look. "What are they?"

An unjustified sense of betrayal swept over Etienne like a rogue wave over a ship. "I'm not one hundred percent sure she has been completely forthcoming with me." He tried to assure himself that his personal feelings for Janine had nothing to do with what he had to say. "We must be confident that neither she nor any of her close associates pose a threat to you personally or to the Republic."

Bonaparte squinted at Etienne. "To what associates do you refer?"

"She has a history with Charles Dupré, a royalist who keeps company with the exiled Bourbon princes. While their ships blockade our coasts, the English are also funneling money to the Bourbons."

Josephine shifted in her chair. "Her marriage contract must have expired by this time. Surely, she has no contact with him."

"To my knowledge she has not," Etienne assured Josephine.

"Nevertheless, the unsubstantiated reports about her meeting with strangers are sufficient to hold off giving her access to the First Consul."

Bonaparte remained silent while the butler removed the soup bowls and replaced them with the main course of roast capon. Napoleon dissected the fowl and took a bite. Before he'd finishing chewing, he said, "Given our intelligence capabilities, I see no reason why she should not accompany Lieutenant Lenoir to the gala." He washed down the remaining food in his mouth with a gulp of wine and pierced another chunk of chicken with his fork. "Besides, she'll be under your watchful eye."

Etienne gripped his knife until it felt like the design on the handle would transfer to his palm. He didn't appreciate being the recipient of chastising remarks but had little choice as to how to react. "There is another mystery that needs to be pursued. Few people were aware of my plans when I departed from General de Bernay's house with my report to you. Yet near Orleans I discovered a rider in the woods, keeping pace with me. When I called to him, he retreated into the forest. I gave chase without success."

"I don't like the sound of that. Take a detachment of our best men and comb the area from stem to stern for any trace of a renegade campsite." Bonaparte gave the stripped carcass a contemptuous push to the side of his plate. "Report back to me on your findings." He shoved back his chair, stood, and started walking. "I have work to do in my study." Then he stopped and faced Etienne. "Mademoiselle de Fleury comes to the celebration unless I receive conclusive evidence she is a danger. You are to do nothing to impede the blossoming romance between the young lady and Lieutenant Lenoir." He held Etienne's gaze for a moment. "I'll have letters for General de Bernay and Lieutenant Lenoir for you to deliver. *Adieu.*"

When the sound of Bonaparte's footsteps faded, Josephine's voice broke into Etienne's thoughts. "I'm sorry my husband was testy at dinner. But I take comfort in knowing you understand him almost as well as I do." A look of pain marred her expressive eyes.

"Madame, you have nothing to apologize for. I knew he wouldn't be pleased to hear what I had to say. If you will excuse me, I'll prepare to leave at daybreak."

"Certainly. God's speed to you, mon cher ami."

186

Chapter 26

Etienne and Mademoiselle La Roche married in Paris? Disoriented, Janine sat up in bed with a start. A dream? Where was she? Of course, the de Bernays' country house, awaiting Etienne's arrival with Bonaparte's decree for her freedom. Etienne, always Etienne. Why couldn't she dream of Lenoir? Her head told her it would be a wise choice, whether she learned to love him or it remained a union of convenience. Her contracted marriage was out of the question now that she recognized Charles to be self-serving just like his parents. Etienne was out of reach. He had made it clear her desire for him should remain unrequited. Decision time was at hand.

Cypress tree shadows reached across the table like fingers of a giant hand. The afternoon tumbled toward tomorrow, unnoticed by Janine. While she and Minette relaxed in the garden, time seemed to stand still in the peaceful surroundings.

Lieutenant Lenoir strode toward them, interrupting the quiet. "Bonjour," he called as he approached and stopped beside Janine.

"Won't you join us?" Minette gestured toward a chair. "What have you there?" She pointed to the rectangular package he set on the table.

"Dear lady, a thing of beauty—a token of my appreciation of Mademoiselle de Fleury's creative designs for Maison Lenoir Frères." He placed the package in front of Janine and sat. "Please, open it."

"How kind of you." Janine removed the twine from the muslin cover, revealing a bolt of French blue silk embellished with fuchsia and silver peonies.

Minette gasped.

"It's one my designs," Janine said in a whisper to Lenoir. "It's exquisite. Thank you so much."

"*C'est magnifique.* Did you really design it, Janine?" Minette ran her forefinger along the cloth.

"She did indeed. I took the liberty of changing the colors for her gown to wear to the gala." Lenoir said, his voice filled with pride.

"You're very sure of yourself. We don't even know whether

187

I'll be able to go to the event. But I love it, whether I go or not." Janine held Lenoir's warm gaze.

He reached for her hand. "I'm sure this unpleasant detention will be behind you by nightfall and you'll have many happy tomorrows."

Minette patted Janine's other hand. "He's right, you know."

"How can I doubt the word of two of my favorite people?" Janine replied.

Lenoir released her hand and stood. "I'm sorry, but I must excuse myself. General de Bernay will wonder what has delayed me. He wants me there when Colonel Tremeau arrives with Bonaparte's dispatch."

Minette's eyes followed him as he progressed along the path toward the house. "Chérie, you're loved by a wonderful man." She smiled at Janine. "You must have a fairy godmother."

"I'll believe it when I hear that Bonaparte accepted the report and ordered my release."

"There is no reason for him not to."

Minette's worries seemed to have vanished, but Janine still felt the sting of her withdrawal during this terrible ordeal. Would a true friend have done so? "I hope you're right."

Less than an hour passed before two men on horseback passed by the garden, riding toward the house. "They're bringing word from Bonaparte." Minette rose and placed the cups and saucers on the tray with the silver tea service. "We'd best go inside and wait for word from François."

"Oui, the moment of truth." Janine stared transfixed when she saw Etienne ride by on Le Diamant. There was no mistaking the steed's distinctive diamond marking. Where had he found her uncle's horse? The last time she'd seen the animal, the murdering groomsman had raced away from Chateau Fleury on him.

"You look like you've just seen a ghost. What's wrong?" Alarm sounded in Minette's voice.

"The horse . . . how did Etienne get him?"

Minette stared at Janine, her brows knitted. "What do you mean?"

Janine shook her head. "Never mind. I'm just thinking out loud, that's all." Had Etienne found him while in Paris? Had Bonaparte given him the horse? Had the assassin groomsman entered the Army of the Republic, and if so, how did the imposter figure into the puzzle? Did Bonaparte know him?

After slipping the silk fabric back into the wrappings and fastening it, Janine stood and followed Minette.

The two women went inside into the salon and Janine chose to sit on a settee facing the door to watch for Lenoir's return with news for her. She wasn't sure whether to expect Etienne or de Bernay to accompany him. Minette remained standing with the tray in her hands.

"Wait for me here while I drop this off in the kitchen. Be right back," Minette said on her way out.

Janine placed her precious package on the settee next to her and tried to harness some degree of patience.

After a few minutes Minette returned and looked with longing at the package beside Janine. Sitting on a chair across from her, Minette said, "Now that you have your fabric, I must see the new ones at Maison Lenoir Frères before I make the selection for my own gown."

Janine felt lightheaded when the library door opened and de Bernay, Etienne, and Lenoir entered the salon. She found it hard to bear the stifling suspense. She struggled to maintain her composure and, without conscious thought, sought answers from Etienne's face. Dark circles under his eyes and the stubble on his unshaven face obscured his expression. She diverted her eyes to Lenoir, who in marked contrast looked rested and confident. His smile hinted at the good news Etienne must have delivered.

General de Bernay broke the silence. "Mademoiselle de Fleury, you are released from house arrest. I hope Lieutenant Lenoir treated you with kindness while you were here."

"Oui, he did. Merci." Joy at her release was tempered by concern for Etienne.

Lenoir stepped closer and spoke in a low voice. "Do you accept my invitation to the celebration in Paris?"

"You already know my answer. Yes." Acutely aware of Etienne's presence, Janine rose and followed him when he moved toward the door. "Wait. Don't go yet. I have a question for you."

"I'm sorry." He turned and gave her a distracted glance. "I can't delay."

The general reinforced the remark. "He's under orders from

Bonaparte and must leave immediately."

"I see." Janine stood, her feet frozen in place, and watched as de Bernay and Lenoir saw him out. With a sinking feeling, she returned to her seat.

Oblivious to Janine's distress, Minette walked to the liquor cabinet. "This calls for a celebration."

Janine toyed with the package at her side. Etienne's devotion to his service to the Republic and to Bonaparte had been demonstrated this day. He belonged to Napoleon. She may as well accept it. In contrast Lenoir remained a creative artist and businessman who happened to serve in the Army, free to court a woman.

Minette returned with two glasses of champagne and handed one to Janine. "May you have much happiness and success throughout your life." She said, lifting her glass and touching it to Janine's.

Janine responded by lifting hers and drinking to the toast. "Thank you, *m'amie.*"

"That's better. Has it registered that you're free again?" Minette set down her glass and stood. "Let's take another look at your gift from Louis."

Janine nodded. "Let's." The familiar way Minette used Lenoir's given name wasn't lost on her. Had she and Lenoir had a love affair?

Janine rose and carried the silk to a large table by the window. Removing it, she unrolled a length. The hand-embroidered gold threads and silver peony leaves glittered in the light, emphasizing its beauty. Clearly, he had had a great many women working on it.

Minette touched a silver leaf. "First thing in the morning, we'll go to Maison Lenoir Frères to select something beautiful for my gown. I imagine Louis is having fabric made up from a number of the newest designs the two of you have worked on."

Louis, is it? Irritated, Janine said, "I won't be able to go with you in the morning. I must get back to Madame Parot's. She must think I've fallen off the edge of the earth."

"What difference will a couple hours make? I'll take you there in the afternoon on our way to the townhouse. We'll stay there until our gowns are ready. The dressmaker will send a seamstress to work with us."

Janine resented Minette's disregard for her wishes but had to admit she couldn't come up with a better plan. "Agreed."

190

"*Bon.* Imagine, in two weeks' time, we leave for Paris."

Etienne rode directly to Captain Martin's residence in Tours with written orders to organize an elite contingent of twenty-five experienced men in accordance with the First Consul's decree. He'd select the soldiers because of their experience in battles against the remnants of the warring royalist sympathizers in the northwestern regions of the country. Etienne recognized that his own strength as a warrior—not unlike Bonaparte's—centered on strategizing conventional battles. He'd rely on the captain if engaged in an irregular, disorganized battle with Cadoudal's royalist men in the forest. His gut told him the renegade was involved in some way.

Satisfied Martin would have their men ready for departure in the morning, Etienne left him and started home. Frustrated that he couldn't look forward to much-needed sleep for many hours yet, his irritation turned to Bonaparte and his grand plans for a royal court of his own. Instead of rest he'd need to bathe, shave, and dress in civilian clothes to call on Mademoiselle La Roche and invite her to accompany him to the gala in Paris—not by choice but to pacify Napoleon. He fumed along the way. Why hadn't he confronted the First Consul's wrath head-on and put an end to any thought of an alliance between him and the young lady? He had no intention of marrying anyone not of his own choosing.

An image of Janine drifted into his thoughts. *If I can't have her, I'll marry no one!* He'd always felt that way and had believed he'd learned to accept the disappointment.

Up early the next day, Etienne rode to the forest. The mingling odors of decaying leaves and the pungent sap of the trees carried him back to his early days in the Republican Army. He placed his hand on the ugly scar on his cheek—a reminder of a moment of hesitation in his first battle with the *Vendéen Militaire*, an assemblage of sixty thousand untrained and ill-equipped royalist insurgents, who fought for their king and religious freedom. In spite of the great superiority of the

191

Republican Army, battles raged, with the brigands winning some skirmishes until forced to retreat. They would scatter into the dense growth of trees and underbrush and regroup in hidden underground lairs they'd built beforehand.

The conflicts had continued for two months until the rebels were defeated at Le Mans. Two of their generals had been killed and a third seriously wounded on the battlefield, but still they hadn't given up the cause. Off-and-on skirmishes continued until two years later when the armies of the Church and the exiled Bourbon princes joined forces under the command of Georges Cadoudal.

In retrospect, Etienne realized many of the insurgents fought for their beliefs and freedom to worship in the Catholic Church.. Before the Revolution, the Church and the Bourbon kings had enjoyed a symbiotic relationship and the new Republic threatened to annihilate both. Early on, the ruling National Convention in Paris banned priests who refused to take the Ecclesiastical Oath under the Civil Constitution of the Clergy of 1791. Public worship was prohibited; Catholic churches were closed and their properties confiscated. Deeply religious and loyal to the Bourbon king, these peasant farmers would rather die fighting for their personal freedom—not unlike him. In his youth he had accepted the ideals of freedom featured in the proliferation of revolutionary pamphlets.

Would this be the day he'd corner the elusive Cadoudal in this forest? Etienne regretted he'd be without Le Diamant this trip. He'd pushed the stallion hard on the Paris trip and noticed a slight limp upon their arrival home.

Upon arriving at the agreed-upon meeting place, he briefed his cadre of men and handed a map to the captain. "Your territory is outlined in red. I'll work the area in green. Report back to me at this location at four." The soldiers dispersed.

Etienne, accompanied by his aide, Adrien, charged into the forest, followed by their cavalrymen. The men fanned out on either side of them like tines on a huge rake.

"With the recent rains we'll have little to go on. Tracks and other telltale signs are likely washed away," Adrien said.

Etienne nodded. "We'll also need to be vigilant about the storm damage and not get mired in a swamp while searching for evidence."

The troops progressed into the depths of the forest until the carpet of pine needles gave way to rotting oak leaves. Trouble began when three horses lost their footing on the mossy, leaf-coated terrain, slowing their progression.

Although they avoided known marshy areas, one of the animals took a wrong turn and became hopelessly mired in the murky waters. Etienne fretted over the crucial minutes wasted. By the time the horse was rescued, the sun stood at the apex of the sky, and his team had found no trace of a campsite. In situations like this, Le Diamant's instincts and brute strength would have saved valuable time. In little more than an hour, they'd have to start back for the rendezvous with the captain and his team. Etienne drew alongside Adrien. "Let's hope the captain is having more success than we are."

A slight change of course to the west brought them to higher ground. They passed an outcropping of rocks and continued to climb. At the top of a crested hill, they saw a craggy wall of rock on the downslope about one hundred yards ahead. Etienne and Adrien rode down to the wall and followed alongside it.

Peering intently at the rock of wall ahead of them, Etienne spotted a darker area in the limestone in the distance. Could it lead into a cave? He gestured in the direction of the color variation. "Do you see that? Come on." He brought his horse to a canter in anticipation of finding clues.

As they drew closer, an opening in the rock came into view. *A cave?* A surge of energy coursed through him. Who and what might they find inside? He slowed his horse and brought him to a halt near a clump of trees some distance from the rock barrier. He and Adrien tethered the animals and crept stealthily toward the opening.

"When we get inside, assess how far the cave extends," Etienne instructed Adrien.

The first thing they saw upon entry was evidence of a recent campfire. Behind a nearby rock Etienne found a sack containing a pair of men's trousers, shirt, faded red cape, and a gray wig. A disguise? One of Cadoudal's favorite tricks! Most distressing, the clothes bore a similarity to those described in the sworn statements against Janine. Stricken, Etienne felt as if iron pincers tightened across his chest. *Not Janine!* She'd been accused of meeting with a stranger, an old, gray-haired man wearing a red cape.

He took a deep breath and turned with a start when a slight movement came from behind him. Adrien stepped from the shadows.

"I went just a short distance. Didn't see anyone, but there's no end in sight either."

A horse's whinny sounded. Adrien and Etienne drew their sabers and waited inside, out of sight, one on each side of the opening.

The newcomer clomped across the ground, singing in time to each step. He called, "Anybody here?" and poked his head inside. Letting go of the box he dragged with him, he jumped back. "I mean no harm. I bring supplies."

Etienne sheathed his sword and stepped forward. "Bonjour, citizen." He extended his hand to the burly peasant. The calloused hands and the leather-skinned face suggested a man who barely eked out a living from the land. "Colonel Tremeau of the Army of the Republic. You'll need to answer a few questions."

"Oui, Monsieur. But I only bring goods to men here."

"What sort of supplies?" Etienne, followed by Martin, walked to where the man had dropped the box and opened it. Its contents consisted of four chickens, vegetables, and candles—those items couldn't be considered contraband.

"You see. Only food and candles," the man said, his brows drawn together.

Etienne examined the box and satisfied himself it contained no secret compartment. "Tell me about the people you're supplying."

"Don't know names. They three see me feeding my chickens and asked to buy four and some garden vegetables. I say it cost five *ecu* for poultry and basket of vegetables."

"The three men arranged for you to deliver more supplies to them?" Etienne asked.

"They did that very day. They pay me half and say meet them at side of road ten miles toward Orleans. I did and they bring me here. They already pay for things I bring today."

"How long ago did you first meet them?"

"Three . . . four weeks now."

"Did they say how long they plan to be here?"

"Non. I tell you they pay me to bring supplies for two more weeks."

Mindful of the position of the sun, Etienne allowed for another question or two. "What do you recall about them?"

"One I swear was *aristo*. Arrogant he was and shouted at other two. Strange, hair long and gray, but piercing eyes of younger man."

194

Features of Baron Charles Dupré. This might explain his presence in London . . . and Tours? He hoped not for Janine's sake. "What about the other two?" Etienne glanced skyward.

"One live in village, but leave. Just boy he was. The other, Briton wearing breeches of coarse cloth and thick cord yarn. Old man, his hair long and gray, too. Hard to know what he say."

"You've been most helpful. Where will I find you in the village?"

"Come to town, my house first on left."

"You're free to go now," Etienne said, dismissing the man.

Chapter 27

As protective as a mother of her newborn infant, Janine's eagle eyes followed the path of the dressmaker's scissor-wielding hand. It had to be perfect, her precious fabric transformed into her gown for the lavish ball in Paris. While designing and working on other women's gowns, Janine had daydreamed of the time she'd wear one of her own. And now her turn had come. She'd relinquished control to Minette's dressmaker with an exact pattern, complete with written notes, but she continued to look in on its progress more often than pleased the other woman.

In front of the full-length mirror, Minette postured and posed in her silk frock fastened together by pins and basted stitches. She stretched her body and pulled back her shoulders, glancing at the seamstress. "Perfect . . . if I can breathe in this darned corset. I don't want to resort to swooning for attention." Minette watched the dressmaker for a moment. "Careful. Don't cut too close to the pattern."

Of course, Minette didn't understand and was forgiven her infractions. Janine and the dressmaker exchanged knowing looks and ignored the comment.

Changing the subject, Janine said, "Maybe one inch off your waist isn't worth it."

"You poor innocent. You're about to find out how important an inch is. Why Pauline Bonaparte reclined on a sofa all evening after making her entrance at the last Tuileries fête." Minette flashed Janine a patronizing look.

Perhaps she did have a few things to learn about Parisian high society. How could court life be more extreme and competitive than when her mother had served as a lady-in-waiting to Queen Marie Antoinette? Janine had memorized entries from her mother's diary describing the court intrigue and rivalry.

There was a soft rap at the door to the sewing room and Janine turned to see Minette's maid standing there, awaiting recognition. "A letter from Madame Bonaparte." The girl held up an envelope. "I thought you'd want to see it right away."

"Merci." Minette reached for the letter, opened it, and after reading a few lines, she looked at Janine. "We've been invited to visit Malmaison, the Bonaparte's country home, on the way to Paris. Do

196

you know what this means?"

Before Janine could answer, the dressmaker sighed. "I'll have the gowns ready within two days. That's the best I can do."

"Good. We'll have to hurry to be ready by then," Minette said, turning to the seamstress "Get me out of this thing and finish it."

The dressmaker placed the scissors on the cutting board and gave Minette an exasperated look. "You know you can rely on me."

"You haven't yet failed to please me," Minette said, slipping into her peignoir. "I know you won't this time."

Janine smiled at the woman. "You'll do a beautiful job, I'm sure."

As the de Bernay coach rounded a curve, the low profile of Malmaison nestled against the tree-lined horizon. Janine sensed serenity about this manor house surrounded by nature and manicured gardens. To her left she saw two black swans gliding across the silvery-blue water of a large pond. A rabbit scampered under a flowering shrub. What a welcome respite from the monotonous bouncing and jiggling of the coach ride toward Paris.

Lenoir caught Janine's eye as she looked from the sleeping Minette. "You'll enjoy your visit here. Madame Bonaparte takes great pleasure in her gardens, as you can see. She's a gracious lady."

"So I understand. I'm looking forward to making her acquaintance." Janine brushed a lock of hair from her cheek.

"I'll wager she invited us here to give you a proper welcome," Lenoir said. "At the Tuileries she'll have little free time."

Upon their arrival the butler met them at the door. He ushered them to the salon before leaving to announce their presence. In a short time a graceful, dark-haired woman made an entrance.

Lenoir stood, as did Minette and Janine. "Madame Bonaparte," Lenoir said, stepping forward, "it is my pleasure to present Mademoiselle Janine de Fleury."

"*Beinvenue à Malmaison.* I look forward to this time together," Josephine said in a soft voice, a trace of her Creole accent evident. She turned to welcome Minette and Lieutenant Lenoir. "Do be seated while I pour the tea." After passing a tray of chocolate wafers and lemon tarts, she asked, "Has General de Bernay gone on to Paris?"

Minette shook her head. "Non. He'll be along later."

"I left him working on a report for your husband," Lenoir added.

After finishing their tea, Josephine said, "I expect you're tired from your trip and would like to rest a while or perhaps stroll in the garden. Dinner will be at seven." She motioned to the butler. "Please see our guests are shown to their rooms." Josephine stood and paused by Janine. "Plan to meet with me at four. I'll have my *demoiselle* escort you to my apartment so we can have a quiet tête-à-tête. I so regret the short time we have here together. But I know you must get an early start in the morning."

Janine relaxed and breathed in the pleasant floral essence of the gracious lady. "It's kind of you to set aside time for me." She looked forward to four o'clock.

A knock sounded at Janine's door. Opening it, she came face to face with a young woman whose pursed lips and dour expression didn't extend the warm welcome that Janine expected. The woman looked Janine up and down as if evaluating her importance. "I'm Madame's demoiselle," she said in a curt manner. "Come with me. I'll escort you to Madame Bonaparte."

They walked almost to the end of the hall before turning to the left. Continuing along the passageway for a short distance, the woman stopped and entered an anteroom. "Take a seat. Madame will be with you shortly." With an abrupt turn, she left Janine sitting alone.

Janine looked at her surroundings with interest. A round, multicolored rug covered much of the parquet floor and complemented the Roman design of the furnishings and the frieze around the ceiling. A teacart held a silver tray and tea service awaiting the arrival of the hostess.

Little time elapsed before a door opened. Josephine glided into the room and sat in a matching chair beside Janine. "Here we are . . . the two of us, kindred spirits." She poured tea and passed a platter of pastries. She paused as if weighing her words. "I imagine it's been difficult for you to return to France. Many terrible things have happened here. I want you to know my husband is working very hard to bring order out of the past chaos." Josephine leaned toward Janine. "We are friends of all of the people of France. Be assured, we care about you."

"Merci. We all have adjustments to make in our lives. That's why I returned."

"I understand. The future of France is bright, as yours can be. Lieutenant Lenoir is very impressed with your design talent. He is most eager for you to become associated with Maison Lenoir Frères." Josephine leaned back in her chair and smiled. "Tell me, have you always been interested in artistic endeavors?"

"Oui, at Chateau Fleury I used to spend hours in the gardens sketching flowers. I'd often use them for my needlepoint designs."

"Chateau Fleury . . . you probably don't know you and I have many things in common. I hasten to add that drawing isn't one of them." Josephine fell silent for a moment.. "I had the pleasure of meeting your mother, Marquise Marie de Fleury, before the Revolution. You have every reason to be proud of her. She was a beautiful and wonderful woman."

Reeling from the emotional impact of talking with someone who had known and admired her mother, Janine fought to maintain her composure. This was unfair. Madame Bonaparte had disarmed her and entered her world. Unshed tears burned Janine's eyes as she blinked and willed them away. "You knew my mother?"

Josephine reached for Janine's hand, holding it while she spoke. "Upon hearing about her death while I was imprisoned in the Conciergerie, I wept for you, as well as for the loss of her life. I, too, was a mother and wanted desperately to live for my two children." Tears glistened in her eyes. "Their father was guillotined. By the grace of God, I was spared."

Caught off guard, Janine could no longer hold back her tears— tears she had delayed after she'd arrived in New Orleans. What a strange twist of fate. Josephine was truly of the *ancien régime*—and of the new Republic. *Can she be trusted?* Josephine had changed with the times as Minette urged Janine to do.

Janine wanted to ask how she could marry a Republican general so soon after her first-hand experiences during the Terror of Robespierre. But her genteel upbringing didn't allow for such personal questions.

"Enough of this talk. We must not look back too often." Josephine released Janine's hand. "On a brighter note, my love of flowers and plants brings me much peace. Roses are my real passion. Here at Malmaison I'm able to indulge in beauty—and to forget."

"I saw the lovely gardens as we arrived," Janine said.

"Three years ago I built a heated orangery large enough for three hundred pineapple plants. Now I am cultivating new plants."

"How rewarding."

"I've kept you long enough." Josephine rose, as did Janine. "I'm sure you would like to spend some of the afternoon with Madame de Bernay and Lieutenant Lenoir."

"I confess your gardens sound very tempting." Together they walked to the door. "Thank you for speaking of my mother to me."

Bonaparte frowned as he read Etienne's report about the three unidentified men in the Orleans forest. He threw the pages across the room and moved in front of Etienne, shaking his forefinger at him. "They're here; ready to make their move at just the right moment. You must find them first. Search all of Paris, building by building if necessary."

Etienne maintained a calm demeanor during the tirade, despite the turmoil he felt inside. Bonaparte was right to be alarmed. Etienne faced another challenge from Cadoudal and his conspirators. Relentless, the man knew not defeat except in death. "I'll flush them out unless they've fled to England. As we speak, Captain Martin and his men are following up in the village and at the campsite."

"They're in France—not England! Get out of here. Stop wasting precious time." Bonaparte turned from Etienne and looked out the window, his shoulders hunched.

Etienne left Napoleon's office and went directly to the Tuileries military guard area. There he issued specific orders to continue the search for conspirators in the city, giving the soldiers the description of the three men who had abandoned their campsite in the cave.

"We'll begin in the heart of the city," Etienne said. "We'll work in pairs to comb each street, starting with the Île de la Cité and Île Saint-Louis. Each of you has your specific assignment as outlined." Etienne pointed to the map on the wall. "Report back here each afternoon at five for an update unless you discover something suspicious—then, as you know, report back immediately."

Chapter 28

The uneventful trip from Malmaison to Paris allowed time for speculative conversation about the fête and the excitement of the city. Janine looked forward to going with Minette to places of interest there. Listening to the talk of Paris, she tried to picture the de Bernay house on Rue Saint-Honoré—a wedding gift from Bonaparte, according to Minette. She tried to banish the thought that it was probably from the spoils of the Revolution. Her difficulties with establishing ownership of Chateau Fleury prompted bitter feelings on behalf of others in similar circumstances.

Minette's mood changed as the coach turned from the street into the enclosed courtyard of the house. She didn't speak but fidgeted in her seat while waiting for the footman to open the door.

"Do be seated until the butler shows you to your rooms," Minette said as she led her guests into the salon. "I apologize I won't be with you this afternoon. I have a prearranged appointment I cannot reschedule." With an eye to the mantle clock, she spoke to Lenoir, "Please see that Janine and Aimée, when she arrives, feel at home."

"*Avec plaisir.*" Lenoir exchanged a subtle look of familiarity with Minette.

"Merci. Dinner is at eight." She rushed from the room as if pursued by a demon.

Two days after their arrival in Paris, the Lenoirs and Janine concluded their appointment with Pauline Bonaparte at her recently acquired palatial home. Janine closed her eyes while the coach rumbled along the cobbled streets returning them to the de Bernays' home. Lenoir and Aimée sat across from her, their muffled voices indiscernible. *Mon Dieu. What have I done?*

Pauline Bonaparte's selection of her silk design had brought Janine stunned elation. The Lenoirs and Pauline expressed delight at the decision, but a brief glance between Lenoir and Pauline before she made her choice raised questions in Janine's mind. What significance, if any, did it have?

The possibility of Pauline's selection being based on a

prearranged agreement with Lenoir left Janine feeling as helpless as a silkworm bound in its cocoon. Her commitment to the commission sparred with thoughts of independence forfeited, exploding into a throbbing headache—a headache begun upon their arrival at the de Bernays' residence. She hadn't seen nor heard from Minette for two days. When asked about Minette's whereabouts, Lenoir said she was not feeling well and was taking her meals in her rooms.

Had she offended Minette in some way? Janine longed for a trusted confidante to help her review her options. Out of necessity she lived her life one day at a time. But she realized her decisions of the day impacted her tomorrows. And now it seemed events had taken on a life of their own. If not careful, she would become a helpless pawn in Bonaparte's matchmaking plan.

She had returned to France for Chateau Fleury, and she must not allow herself to be diverted from that purpose. What choice did she have in the matter? The answer would have to wait. She forced herself to listen to the conversation between Lenoir and Aimée as they talked about calling on various merchants and artisans while in Paris.

"We'll stop by the tailor's to pick up the waistcoat I've ordered. It's on our way." Lenoir added, "I plan to wear it to the fête."

Aimée sighed. "Where is the tailor's shop?"

"About two blocks from Notre Dame."

Notre Dame Cathedral. She'd heard it had recently reopened upon orders from Bonaparte after having been closed for many years. Alert to the opportunity, Janine said, "Do you suppose I could go to the cathedral while you pick up your garment?"

Lenoir smiled at her. "If you wish. You'll have about thirty minutes. Will that be sufficient?"

Any amount of time would be enough at this moment. "For today, Oui." Her need for divine guidance, or any kind for that matter, had never been greater than now.

"We will come for you when I am finished at the tailor's," Lenoir said.

Janine looked up, their eyes meeting. She halfway wished he would come in with her. No doubt he would if she suggested it. "Perfect," she said, rejecting the thought.

It seemed like yesterday and yet so long ago when Janine had gone to the great cathedral with her parents during one of her last visits to Paris in 1789—before the rumblings of the Revolution erupted with the storming of the Bastille prison. She longed to recapture some sense of the security and purpose she'd experienced then. Could she find solace there again?

After crossing the bridge over the Seine onto the Île de Cité, the coach came to a halt by the Place de Purvis Notre Dame. Janine stared up at the almost-square façade of the centuries-old house of worship. People milled in front of it; some hawked assorted wares and others engaged in conversation. An occasional uniformed man walked among the crowd, pausing once in a while as if on the lookout for suspicious behavior. Most people remained in the square, with few entering the church.

After the carriage stopped in front of Notre Dame, the footman opened the door. Janine hesitated before accepting his outstretched hand, an uneasy feeling assailing her. Again she considered asking Lenoir to come in with her. She brushed it aside and stepped down into the warmth of the sun. She hurried past the crowd and followed an aged man and woman inside the church.

The couple sat and bowed their heads while Janine made her way along the nave toward the transept. A red-haired man and a dark-haired boy sat side by side, their heads bowed, their lips moving in whispers. Her instinct told her to keep moving. Lenoir wouldn't return for nearly thirty minutes.

She steeled herself and moved along the aisle. Despair tore at her heart. Tears formed at the sight of the desecration inside Notre-Dame de Paris. She'd seen scars from the Revolution in the Cathedral of Tours, but she hadn't been prepared for the extent of the destruction that lay before her. Holes gaped and huge cracks zigzagged on the great stone walls. A few mutilated—some headless—statues remained in place, while many she remembered with reverence had disappeared. The statue of the Virgin, Our Lady of Paris, was gone; only its pedestal remained.

As she neared the high altar in the chancel, she sensed an unwelcome presence. A quick look behind her revealed three sets of footprints in the dust—hers and two others that branched off a little farther back behind hers. Whose were they? Where were the people who had made them? Listening, she heard not a sound nearby?

Retracing her steps to the place where the other footprints changed direction, she followed them past a huge pillar to a door into a small antechamber. A boy and man stood inside, still as statues. The Chateau Fleury caretaker! Mortified, Janine trembled. *He's here!* Her heart thumping, she scampered down the aisle as quickly as her long skirt allowed, her heels clapping on the stone floor. She dared not look back. The slap of boots behind her told of their aggressive intentions.

The boy's voice grew closer each time he called, "Madame, stop! You dropped your scarf."

She wasn't wearing a scarf. *I can't outrun them.* Beads of sweat blanketed her face. Without glancing around, she reached the door and fled onto the square. *"Excusez-moi."* She panted and pushed past people, not knowing where the men were. Panting, she continued to run as fast as she could. And then an excruciating pain shot through her foot and ankle. Dazed, she struggled to sit up and adjust her skirt. She had fallen over a heavy wooden crate.

"Are you hurt?" A bearded vendor looked up from his cart of leather goods.

She focused on the question. How badly *was* she hurt? She gave an involuntary, startled response at the sound of her name being spoken.

"Janine, what happened? Are you injured?" Lenoir crouched beside her.

"My ankle hurts. I don't think I can stand on it."

"We'll get you to a doctor," Lenoir lifted her into his arms and carried her to the waiting coach.

After riding through the streets of Paris all morning, Etienne patted the stallion's neck, an unconscious gesture in preparation for battle— enemy seen or unseen. Three days into the methodical search through Paris, he didn't have any new leads as to the whereabouts of the suspicious characters camped in the Orleans forest. Waiting for a report from Captain Martin in Orleans tested his patience. All the while Bonaparte became testier as each day passed.

Etienne turned to Adrien, riding alongside him. "Notre Dame Cathedral warrants a second look."

Adrien nodded. "Location and anonymity. They move around."

They rode in silence, engrossed in thought, until they drew

close to the cathedral.

"This assignment may be more difficult than getting an audience with the Pope," Adrien said as he secured his horse to a hitching post.

"You take the north side, including the bell tower, and I'll take the south," Etienne said as they walked along. He stood and watched as Adrien turned to the north before he started toward the church. He stopped at the sound of shouting and noticed a commotion at the far end of the square. He saw Adrien on his horse, moving through the throng shouting, "Make way!"

Losing no time, Etienne ran to his horse and rode to Adrien's side. "What happened here?" He addressed two men who chattered excitedly while keeping an eye on their leather goods.

"A fine lady ran from the cathedral, pursued by a man and a boy. So terrified was she, my warning went unheeded. She ran right into my stand and hit the ground with a thud. The man and the boy stopped and waited a little distance behind her. They ran when we had surrounded her."

A bystander waved his hand and said, "Maybe they planned to rob her."

"What did she tell you?" Etienne asked the vendor.

"Nothing. A man she knew appeared and called her by name. She told him she couldn't stand on her foot and he carried her to a waiting coach."

"Describe the men who frightened her," Etienne prompted him.

"Muscular man of medium height with a full head of shaggy red hair. An Irishman, I'd say from his accent. The other one . . . hum . . . just a ruffian street kid. Skinny. Maybe ten or twelve."

Sounds like the Chateau Fleury caretaker. Could this woman have interrupted a meeting between him and one of Cadoudal's Parisian informants? Etienne wondered. "If you see either of them again, notify the Prefect of Police to get word to me." Etienne took one of his cards from his pocket and handed it to him. "Merci. You've been most helpful."

"Oui, Monsieur le Colonel," the two men said in unison as Etienne and Adrien moved away.

"We'll search inside. Then we'll comb through the crowd out here and expand our hunt outward." Etienne said to Adrien, gesturing toward the cathedral as the people stepped aside to make way for them.

After they separated and began their pursuit, Etienne glanced at the south tower and decided to leave it for last. He wasn't looking forward to climbing all 368 stairs to the top. He knew he'd confront rats—both animal and human. He thought of the indignities visited upon the church during the Revolution. Once used by Robespierre as a shrine for his Feast for the God of Reason, the cathedral had served as a food storage warehouse after he abandoned his grand plan in 1793. Robespierre's harebrained and sacrilegious idea hadn't caught on with the Parisians, but the local vermin loved the locale, and rats of all kinds had proliferated during the intervening years.

After a thorough inspection of the nave, chancel, and transept areas, Etienne climbed the spiral stairs leading to the top of the south tower. He took his time, not only to be sure nothing escaped his attention but also to rest his easily tired left leg—a reminder of protecting Bonaparte at the siege of Toulon early in their military careers. His sacrifice had earned him favor with the First Consul, but he paid for it at times like this.

Resuming his climb after pausing, he sliced the air with his sword to keep aggressive rodents at bay. When Etienne reached the bell ringer's chamber with the one remaining bell—the largest of all the cathedral bells—he stood still and listened. He detected a rustling movement ever so slight in the dank, dark space. Sword at the ready, he stepped forward . . . straight into a spider web. He stopped, waiting a moment before pulling his hand back. A skinny youth edged around the side of a large crate and froze when he saw Etienne.

Extending his arm, Etienne moved swiftly and pressed his weapon against the boy's chest. "Do as I say and I won't harm you. Sit down right where you are."

With fear in his eyes, the boy dropped with a thump and protested. "I didn't do anything."

"Answer my questions and we'll see about that. What were you doing with the red-haired Irishman?" Etienne pictured the chateau caretaker as he described the man, although he hadn't seen him in the square.

"Nothing. He's not Irish. He's my uncle," the street urchin said, shifting to survival mode.

"I see no family resemblance." Etienne leaned close to the

olive-skinned boy's face and stared into his brown eyes. The captive broke eye contact and looked up at the thick ropes fastened to the huge bell, as if wondering how he could escape. "I know you're lying. Given time you'll change your story."

Etienne removed a reel of heavy twine from his pocket and bound the lad's arms. After cutting another length of twine, he fastened it around the boy's waist and left an extra length to form a knot at the end. "Downstairs." He tugged on the braided twine knot.

By the time he located Adrien—who had found nothing out of the ordinary—the better part of the afternoon had passed.

"Let's see if this fellow's *uncle* is waiting for him outside," Etienne said in a sarcastic tone.

Adrien raised an eyebrow. "His uncle?"

"That's his story."

If possible, the square held more people than it had in the morning. As luck would have it, few had red hair. As they worked their way toward the street, Etienne spotted bright red hair about twenty feet ahead of them.

"Adrien, he could be our man. Go after him. I'll wait here with this one." Etienne tugged on the lead fastened to the boy.

About ten minutes later, Adrien returned empty-handed. "He eluded me and jumped on a horse before I could get to him."

"At least we have one. He comes with us." Etienne handed the light rope to Adrien and mounted his horse. "Hoist him up."

With a swift heave, Adrien lifted the boy like a sack of feathers into Etienne's waiting hands. The lad squirmed while Etienne set him in front of him and secured the binding. The horses moved forward two abreast into the street and continued the short distance to the police station. After Adrien hitched the horses, he lifted the boy from Etienne's steed and the three of them climbed the stairs to the Prefecture of Police.

Adrien and the boy stayed in the waiting room while Etienne spoke to Chief Inspector Catellan, with whom he worked closely while in Paris. He explained the boy might be a witness of importance.

The chief inspector located an interrogation room for their use then he and Etienne waited in the room while an officer fetched Adrien and the boy from the waiting room. The officer pushed the boy into the room, removed the binding from the child, and led him to a chair.

With a look of fatherly disapproval, Chief Inspector Catellan glared at the boy. "What have you gotten yourself into this time, you little whippersnapper?" He turned to Etienne. "He's one of our informants. Looks like he's in over his head this time."

"It does indeed." Etienne turned to the officer. "We haven't had any lunch. Do you suppose you could send for some bread and cheese?"

"Consider it done," the man said and left the room.

Etienne questioned the boy while the chief inspector made notes and listened in silence. The boy persisted in saying the man was a distant uncle. He swore he hadn't met him until about a week ago and could tell them nothing more about him.

After the officer returned with a loaf of freshly baked bread and slab of cheese, Chief Inspector Catellan took a knife from a drawer. He cut chunks of cheese and gave the plate and bread to Etienne.

Etienne took a bite of cheese and addressed the boy, "If you want to join us for lunch, you must convince me that you're telling the truth. I have no doubt that a cunning fellow like you, who lives by his wits, is up to the challenge."

The boy sat with a sullen look and watched the others eat.

"Chief Inspector, it looks as though our guest wants to spend the night, hoping to have a more substantial meal than we can offer him now. Lock him up."

"Non." The boy leapt from the chair so fast it tipped over. "The man's not my uncle, but I did just meet him a week ago. He paid me to deliver a note to another man and to wait for a response. I delivered that to him at the cathedral this morning."

"What was the response?" Etienne asked.

"The party has begun."

"Where did you deliver the note to the other man?"

"Place de Châtelet . . . by the fountain."

Etienne passed bread and cheese to the boy, who gobbled it down. Then Etienne motioned for the Chief Inspector Catellan to step outside. "Keep the knave here for the night. In the morning, I'll send two of my men to see where he goes after he's released."

"Leave him to me." The chief inspector shook his head. "These street kids."

Chapter 29

Lenoir approached the coach, Janine in his arms, and called to the footman. "Open the door."

Aimée looked up. "What happened?" she asked, concern etched on her face.

"She had a bad fall." Lenoir placed Janine on the seat with her back toward the window, her legs elevated to the front. "We need to remove your shoe," he said.

Janine moaned, no desire to speak. Pain radiated from the bottom of her foot, along her lower leg, and around her kneecap. How seriously was she hurt? When Lenoir touched her foot and started to remove her shoe, a curtain of blackness sweep over her. She stirred at the sound of his voice.

"I'm sorry. I tried to be gentle." He turned to his sister. "Take a look at her leg while I tell the driver to hurry to the palace. Let's hope there is some ice remaining in the frozen-water house."

Janine's memory of what had happened began as a trickle and grew into a roaring torrent, threatening to push her into the oblivion of escape from her pain and fear. She struggled to speak. "The caretaker . . . the man behind . . . my arrest. He followed me . . . in Tours, too."

Aimée stared at her as if she were delusional.

Janine clasped her hands together and nodded. "Oui. He followed me in Tours." Her voice broke. "And now he's here . . . at Notre Dame."

"How can it be?" Aimée asked.

Janine shook her head and grimaced. "There's a stabbing pain in my ankle . . . my knee aches." She moaned when she leaned forward to watch the young woman fold her skirts away from her leg. Puffy, discolored patterns marred her skin from knee to ankle. Was it broken? How long would she be disabled by her injury? She could ill-afford such a setback.

"If the doctor has something cold, it will slow the swelling." After placing her shawl over the leg, Aimée touched Janine's forehead in a gesture of comfort. "You're safe now. Try to stay calm."

When Lenoir returned, Janine closed her eyes and listened to his sister recount the story about the caretaker while the coach swayed and jolted along the cobblestone streets.

Fortunately, Lenoir knew his way around the Tuileries Palace and directed the coachman to take them to a private entrance near Bonaparte's apartment. Janine breathed a sigh of relief. She would soon see a doctor, with as little commotion as possible.

The coach came to a full stop. Lenoir got out of the opened door and spoke to the footman. "I'll ask in the kitchen for something cold. You go ahead and have a stretcher sent out for Mademoiselle de Fleury."

Janine appreciated the advantages accorded Lenoir through his silk dealings with the Bonaparte family.

"Oui, Monsieur. Is that all?" The footman hesitated.

"Send a messenger to Madame Bonaparte in her quarters to advise her that Mademoiselle has severely damaged her ankle and requires the attention of a doctor right away."

Preparing herself for a long wait, Janine rested her head against the makeshift pillow.

"You'll get the best care possible here," Aimée said in a reassuring tone.

Janine trembled. "The caretaker wasn't alone, either."

"You told no one about him following you in Tours?" Aimée sounded incredulous.

If Janine continued her relationship with the Lenoirs, she realized admitting her reliance on Etienne wouldn't be appreciated. "Minette knows."

Lenoir's return to the coach ended the conversation. Several men came with him, carrying a stretcher, and the footman followed.

"Take your time. Be careful when you move her," Lenoir cautioned the men as they moved forward holding the caretaker.

Inside the building the men's feet glided along the smooth marble floors and provided a more comfortable ride than had the uneven stones outside. Janine occupied herself by looking up at the ornate ceiling as she lay on the stretcher, wondering where they would stop along the seemingly endless corridors. Her thoughts shifted to her convalescence and whether she could return to the de Bernays', considering Minette's frequent absences. She'd need to be cared for while she healed. She would rely on the lieutenant and Aimée, if need be; they had shown a willingness to care for her.

Rounding a corner, they entered a large room. The men stopped and waited. Janine looked across the room and saw that just one of four doors stood open. She watched as Lenoir, followed by his sister, moved ahead of the stretcher and led the way through the open door.

A doctor stood beside a long table while the men lifted Janine onto it. The two attendants stepped aside and stood the stretcher on end against the wall. The doctor nodded as he examined her ankle, causing Janine to gasp when he pressed firmly on the noticeably swollen and discolored areas. "Bad sprain. No broken bones." He wrapped it and said without looking at her. "Stay off your foot for at least two weeks."

"Aren't you going to apply a cold compress?" Lenoir scowled at him.

"One can be applied later in her room."

"What about my knee? It hurts, too." Janine winced.

"Let's take a look." He gave it a sudden jerk to the side.

"Ouch!" Janine heard a clicking sound as the knee seemed to go back into place.

"Take it easy," Lenoir spoke up. "Mademoiselle de Fleury needs something for pain."

"Yes, yes, of course." The man's back stiffened as he whirled around toward a shelf nearby and removed a large bottle and a small one. He transferred a portion from the large one to the smaller container. "Laudanum to be taken as needed . . . and a wheelchair for the lady." He pushed the chair toward Lenoir and busied himself with straightening the bottles on the shelf.

Lenoir lifted Janine and transferred her to the invalid chair. "Merci, Monsieur *le Docteur*. That will be all for now." The lieutenant demonstrated how to steer the control handle at the front of the chair, gave it to her, and began pushing the chair from the back. Leaning close to Janine's ear, he said, "Madame Bonaparte has made available a suite near her own quarters. She asked Aimée and me to stay to watch over you."

Janine turned to look up at Lenoir. "Madame Bonaparte is truly compassionate."

Lenoir rolled Janine's chair into a beautiful guest room overlooking the gardens. The bed, complete with a silk-flowered canopy, brightened the inside of the room. The bedside table held a pink pitcher and glass on a tray.

"You'll want to take some of this." Lenoir removed the bottle of laudanum from his jacket pocket and set it on the table then rummaged in the table's drawer until he found a spoon. After administering the medicine, he spoke to his sister, "Stay with Janine while I let Madame Bonaparte know Janine is resting in her room."

Aimée nodded to her brother and began to fold back the bed covers. "Would you like to lie down or sit for a while longer?" she asked Janine.

"I'd like to sit here by the window until the medicine takes effect. And I must speak with Minette about arrangements to find a place to stay. I can't remain here."

"I'll leave word for her." Aimée came to Janine's side and followed her gaze into the garden. "Look at those beautiful roses." When Janine didn't answer, Aimée left the room, calling over her shoulder, "I'll be in the next room should you need me."

Approaching footsteps sounded outside the bedroom. Janine looked around and saw Josephine and Lenoir at the door. "I brought this cane and a book for you." Josephine leaned the cane against the table by the bed, crossed to the window, and handed the book to Janine. Pulling up a chair, she sat beside her.

Lenoir gestured toward the cane. "Use it sparingly until your ankle is stronger. My sister is in the adjoining room to help you as needed."

"How is your ankle feeling now? You must stay off it for two weeks, I hear," Josephine said in her calm and soothing way.

Strange as it may seem, Janine found comfort in hearing her soft Creole accent. In New Orleans she'd found a genuine concern for others among the Creoles—unlike the self-importance of Charles' parents, who prided themselves on speaking untainted French. "I'm feeling better already. The laudanum is dulling the pain."

"I'm glad to hear it."

"If you will excuse us," Lenoir broke in, "we'll go to the de Bernays' and pick up Janine's bag." He called for Aimée to come with him.

"Madame Bonaparte, thank you for all you're doing for me. I'll make other arrangements as soon as possible," Janine said.

"I won't hear of it while you are incapacitated like this. It's the least I can do for Marie de Fleury's daughter. I have no doubt the marquise would have done the same for my children had the occasion arisen."

A chill crept up Janine's back and spread to her arms and legs as she thought about the time of danger that had deepened the friendship between the two mothers who feared for their children. "I'm deeply grateful to you."

Josephine placed her hands together. "*Il n'y a rien.* It is nothing. I want to get to know you better, and I value the time we will have to do so."

The effects of the medication and of Josephine's soft voice lulled Janine into drowsiness and she felt her eyelids growing heavy.

"Let's get you to bed so you can rest." Josephine pushed the chair to the side of the bed and helped Janine onto the silken coverlet. "I'll stop by for an hour or so every afternoon. As you know, Aimée is here to help you. I'm sure she and the lieutenant will keep you company as much as you like. I regret that I must leave you now."

Where am I? Janine awoke with a start and began to stretch her legs but stopped as the pain refreshed her memory. She opened her eyes and saw Minette sitting in an armchair in the corner of the room.

"Chérie, how dreadful. I am so sorry." Minette stood and moved to the side of the bed. "I should have been with you and it wouldn't have happened."

"Thank you for coming." To keep the peace, Janine didn't mention her disappointment with Minette's absence. She lay still, afraid of reawakening the pain in her leg.

"I came as soon as I heard. I know I've been a poor hostess, but I haven't come to Paris as often since connecting with you. When I arrived, I tended to business that couldn't be delayed." She paused. "Forgive me?"

Janine nodded. "Madame Bonaparte insists I stay here until I'm healed."

Minette's face brightened and her shoulders relaxed. "Ah, you'll get excellent care." She seemed to be deep in thought and said, "Be assured, if for any reason you want to stay with me, I'll see your needs are met."

"Thank you. That's very kind."

"I should leave now. You need rest, and so many things need my attention." Minette moved toward the door and stopped. "I'll stop by again."

After she left, Janine gingerly raised herself to a sitting position and lifted her skirt enough to see her bandaged ankle. She ran her finger over it and felt swelling all around. Inching her skirt higher, she looked at the bruises on her knee. The lump seemed to be a bit smaller, or was it just wishful thinking?

A sharp rap sounded at the door. Janine adjusted her skirt before calling, "Come in."

The door opened and Josephine's demoiselle came toward the bed. "So you've had an accident and want to be pampered?" She gave Janine a patronizing look.

Janine's checks burned at the young woman's rude and hostile behavior. "Pampered in what way?"

The woman's defiant black eyes bore into Janine's. "Madame asked *me* to see if you want to be wheeled around the garden this afternoon—as if I have nothing better to do."

"I must decline your offer." Janine turned her head and looked out of the window. Without a word the demoiselle left the room and closed the door with a thud.

To take her mind off the insolent behavior of the woman, Janine picked up the book of poetry and read. She was halfway through when Aimée and Lenoir brought her evening meal on a tray. They visited for a time and saw to it that she had another dose of laudanum, after which they bid her goodnight.

The next morning Janine awoke to the sound of birds outside her window. A blend of distant city sounds reached her ears. Wanting to look out of the window, she reached for the cane, slid her legs out of the bed, and managed to get into the chair. If she stretched herself as tall as possible, she could see a portion of garden from where she sat by the bed.

Her attention turned to sounds outside her door. After a cursory tap, a pretty maid came in with a washbasin of warm water. The boudoir maid set about sponging Janine's face and arms after she had removed the bandage and placed a cold pack on her ankle. "We must ready you for your breakfast. It will be here soon . . . and none too soon for you, I'll wager."

"I'm ready for breakfast and to get back on my feet." Janine's spirit responded to the girl's sunny disposition and she smiled. She did enjoy the pampering. She slipped her arms into the fresh blouse and the maid guided them into the sleeves.

"Beautiful hair," the girl said as she began brushing and arranging curls around Janine's face. She hummed as she worked. "We're almost ready." Removing the cold pack, she placed her hand on Janine's ankle, scarcely touching it. "Good. It's not fevered." She dried and rewrapped it with nimble fingers.

"Thank you. I feel much, much better." Janine smiled at the maid with the healing hands.

"I'm glad to hear it. Now to get this table set up for breakfast." She crossed the room to the small drop-leaf table, removed two placemats from the drawer, and put them on the table. Returning to the bedside and gathering up the bath items, she said, "All is ready for you and your guest."

Alone in the room, Janine wondered who her guest would be. Which Lenoir would it be? Or was it someone else?

Chapter 30

Bonaparte's expression predicted a storm brewing inside of the First Consul's office. The renewed war with England and rumors of an impending attack on his person had begun to wear on him. "If you don't have something of substance to report, don't try to appease me with generalities. I want specifics!" Bonaparte glared at Etienne without offering him a chair.

"Regarding the campsite in the Orleans woods, Captain Martin found evidence of the presence of Cadoudal's men. Whether they have entered Paris or not is of utmost importance."

Bonaparte jumped up from his desk and rushed to Etienne. "That's your job. What have you found?" He turned and paced before returning to his desk. "Well, sit down. We'll be here awhile it seems."

Sitting across from Bonaparte, Etienne proceeded to tell him about the caretaker and the boy at Notre Dame. "We can't rule out the Irish caretaker and the boy as being connected with Cadoudal's conspirators. We're keeping a close watch on the lad in anticipation he will lead us to others of interest."

Bonaparte frowned and gave Etienne a thoughtful look. "What other leads do you have?"

"My men are following up on two other suspicious activities. One involves meetings of known dissidents at Madame Moreau's salon. The other includes a stockpile of explosives discovered at the shop of a Marseilles innkeeper who makes frequent trips between there and Paris. I've assigned teams to investigate them here and in Marseilles."

"Do what you must to get to the bottom of these treacherous plots against the Republic."

"As soon as I know where the caretaker is, I plan to trail him, whether he stays here or leaves. Perhaps he's a roaming contact for the conspirators."

Napoleon leaned back, his chair squeaking, a hard edge forming around his mouth. "Etienne, you must be back in Paris in time to attend the ball. And you must make time to propose to Mademoiselle La Roche before then. I wish to announce your upcoming marriage, as well as that of Lieutenant Lenoir, at the event."

So Janine accepted Lenoir's marriage proposal. A deep sense

217

of disappointment swept over Etienne. "I must respectfully decline, as I do not wish to marry anyone at this time."

Bonaparte stood up and shook his finger. "Damn you, Tremeau. *Mon Dieu*, why are you resisting matrimony when you know it will help unite the French nation? You understand as well as I, our people desire pageantry and celebration. They're sick of death and tragedy."

"You know I wish to be of service to you, on and off the battlefields, just not in my bedroom."

"Is that your final answer?"

"Yes."

"Rethink your position. If you're not married in three weeks' time, I have an assignment for you. It will provide an ample period for you to reconsider marriage to Mademoiselle La Roche."

"Assignment? Where?"

"Your services may be needed in New Orleans. You'd assist the Colonial Prefect, Baron de Laussat, during the transition and transfer of the Louisiana Territory to the United States. As you know, the Baron is disappointed about the sale, as are the Spaniards. Unrest is likely . . . and I can think of no better soldier than you to protect our interests there." Bonaparte gave Etienne a triumphant stare.

Expecting Bonaparte would send him to Italy to face Lord Nelson's naval blockade, Etienne felt a rush of enthusiasm to be banished to Louisiana. Although he deeply regretted that France's financial situation forced Napoleon's decision to sell the colony, he admired the determination of the Americans to fight for a land of liberty, equality, and justice for all. Bonaparte's push to be absolute ruler of France, and for the establishment of a Bonaparte dynasty, ran counter to Etienne's desire for a people's Republic. Yes, he looked forward to taking part in this historic event in the New World. He would have time to be involved in the production of his sugar crops— and the freedom to court whomever he pleased.

I've been duly chastised and must seem to be chagrined. Etienne kept a straight face. "As you wish. When do I begin?"

"Some weeks or a month. I'll let you know." Bonaparte began reading and signing papers on his desk—a sign of dismissal.

Before Etienne started for the door, Bonaparte glanced up. "You've helped me make a difficult decision. You are my best choice for the Louisiana assignment, but I need you here too." The First

Consul resumed work at his desk.

With or without a wife, I'll be going to New Orleans for a time. The question remained would he return to France? Etienne understood the workings of Bonaparte's mind. The leader had already made his decision. Etienne mused that a twist of fate would take him to Louisiana. Adrien had told him that Pauline Bonaparte had commissioned one of Janine's fabric designs for Lenoir Frères. How did his aide keep up with all the latest news? How ironic; he'd be in Louisiana and Janine would not. A twinge of regret enveloped him. *Why should I care?* By the time he reached the end of the long corridor, he acknowledged the truth: he *did* care.

Turning the corner, he made his way to the Command Center for a progress report from his staff. A surge of energy shot through him at the sight of one of his men deep in conversation with Adrien, his aide-de-camp.

When the man saw Etienne, he rushed to him with Adrien close on his heels. "We've spotted the red-haired man leaving and returning to a boarding house. The house is under surveillance, so he won't be able to elude us."

"Give me five minutes and be ready to take us to him," Etienne said. Turning to his aide, he instructed, "The major and I will keep watch for the next twenty-four hours. You stay here. I'll keep you informed of tactical changes."

Her stomach rumbled with hunger as Janine anticipated breakfast with her unnamed guest. Having been groomed by the maid and helped to her chair, she felt much better and looked forward to sharing breakfast with a visitor. She brightened at the sound of voices outside her door. Responding to a light tap, she called, "Come in."

The door opened and Lenoir walked in, followed by a butler pushing a cart filled with silver-covered servers—a veritable breakfast buffet, no doubt.

"I hope you're feeling as well as you look this morning." Lenoir placed the steering handle in Janine's hand and pushed the wheelchair to the table before sitting in the chair across from her.

"Merci." Janine's head bobbed up and down. She did feel

better. "I do." She smiled inwardly. No doubt Josephine had arranged the feast for the two of them.

Proceeding in an orderly manner, the butler removed the cover from each of the silver dishes. After their selections had been made and their plates filled by the butler, he poured champagne into their glasses. Placing the tray beside Lenoir, he said, "If that will be all, Lieutenant, I shall take my leave."

She and Lenoir were being given the utmost privacy. Why? Janine's head spun. She wasn't ready to make any important decisions. "Where's Aimée this morning?"

"She's with Madame Bonaparte to share ideas for new draperies in her boudoir."

Janine set her fork down and raised her eyes to Lenoir's. "Does Aimée also design silks for Lenoir Frères?" She already knew the answer, of course, but she hoped that Lenoir had seen what Aimée could do and changed his mind about excluding her from the design process.

"Her duties don't allow her time to do so. And she's good at what she does. We each keep busy."

Janine tried again. "Much of the design work must fall on her while you're away in the military."

"Fortunately, I have a good man who covers for me when I'm unable to travel on business matters. Aimée stays home to manage the day-to-day business operations."

He gives her little credit for all that she does! But aloud, all she said was, "I had no idea until you told me. Does she have any designs I'd be able to see."

"Not that I know of." Lenoir stood and placed his plate on the tray. "Would you like anything more, or may I take your plate?"

"Nothing more, merci."

The lieutenant removed Janine's plate, refilled their glasses with champagne, then moved his chair around the table and sat next to her. "You're a wonderful lady and I'm elated you've come into my life." He paused, lifted her left hand, and held it between his palms. "It's a beautiful morning. How does a visit to the rose garden sound?"

"Wonderful. I've been admiring it from the window."

After finishing their champagne, Lenoir wheeled Janine's chair along the corridor and through a door leading into the gardens. They moved slowly along the winding grassy paths among the roses.

"Stop here. Look at that one." Janine gestured to a delicate pink rose.

"It matches the blush of your cheeks" Lenoir snapped it from the bush and handed it to Janine. "What a lovely etching I can imagine of you sitting on a garden bench with the rose in your hand."

Continuing around the garden, Lenoir suggested scenes and various roses he thought would make nice designs. "Perhaps we can come out tomorrow and make sketches."

"What a pleasant way to spend a morning," Janine agreed. Sketching would be pleasant, whether or not she chose to use the ideas for silk designs. Her mind raced ahead to places in the garden she'd like to draw. Perhaps she could work on watercolor paintings during the long hours of her convalescence. "Do you suppose you could arrange for me to work on a watercolor while I'm here?" She looked over her shoulder at Lenoir as the chair moved along.

"I'm sure I can." He stopped by a bench near a parterre of red rose bushes and lavender plants. Taking a deep breath and exhaling slowly, he raised his head before turning to Janine. "Let's sit here and enjoy the fragrances and the view."

After a moment's hesitation, Janine looked up at him and nodded.

He lifted her to the bench but remained standing. Only after furtive glances along the path in both directions did he sit beside her. "What do you think of that shade for a red silk wall covering for Pauline Bonaparte's dining room?"

The gentle breeze carried lavender scent their way. It reminded of her of the Tremeaus' garden. *Etienne.* How she longed to see him. Janine's eyes blurred. She shrugged her shoulders while trying to banish her wandering thoughts. She needed to get ahold of herself.

Lenoir sat in silence for some time before he said, "You haven't answered me. Don't you agree that red would be ideal?"

"I'm sorry. What did you ask me about it?"

Lenoir pointed to a perfect red rose. "It's not important. What I want you to know is that this beautiful flower represents my love for you."

Janine's heart flip-flopped. Why hadn't she seen this coming? She liked him, but she didn't entirely trust his motives.

"You take my breath away," he said softly.

She looked into his eyes and saw a charismatic man who used his gift to further his ambitions. What did love mean to him?

"Janine, I want to marry you. I am asking you to be my wife."

"You're a wonderful man. I . . . I mustn't give you a hasty answer. I'll need some time." She couldn't look at him and focused instead on the lavender plants.

"Our marriage will be good for both of us. I don't want to wait, but if you need time, wait I will," he said, pulling a face.

"Thank you. You've had the advantage of thinking about this longer than I." Janine laid her hand on his.

He put his arms around her and kissed her on the cheek. "How long will you keep me waiting?"

"Not long. A few days." The lavender swayed in the breeze, its haunting scent—always associated with Etienne—threatening to overcome her. She feared her tears would flow like water rushing from a ruptured dam. "Please take me inside now," she said in a weak voice. "I tire easily."

"Of course, my dear."

Chapter 31

Janine sat by the window, faced the garden vista below, and pondered Lenoir's proposal. *Why hesitate?* Deep in her heart she knew she clung to a hopeless dream and must face the truth. She tried to focus on all the reasons she should accept the proposal—none of which involved passion. She would have married Charles, a man she knew little about, had he come to New Orleans and claimed her. But he hadn't, with little regret on her part. Her heart yearned for Etienne. She knew she should harbor no interest in anyone other than Louis if she was serious about accepting his marriage proposal, but she could not stop her thoughts of Etienne. And yet he wanted to send her back to New Orleans. She'd heard he was at the Tuileries, but he hadn't even bothered to come to see her after her accident. In the past he always seemed to appear when trouble darkened her door. Not this time; rather, Lenoir was the one by her side.

"There you are, by the window. I'm glad to see you're feeling better and enjoying this beautiful day." Josephine came in through the open door. "I stopped by to see if there is anything I can do for you."

Janine turned and smiled. "Oui, I am better." Josephine's presence brightened the day.

The regal woman came forward and sat in the chair next to Janine. "I'll have my demoiselle take you out for fresh air anytime you'd like."

"Non." Janine shook her head resolutely. "I don't know how to say this . . . the young woman has made it abundantly clear she doesn't want anything to do with me."

A look of disbelief crossed Josephine's face. "In what way?"

"She told me she didn't have time to pamper me."

Josephine sighed. "I've known for some time she is not loyal to me."

"Why do you keep her on?"

"Her family is Corsican, old friends of the Bonaparte family. When she first came to me, she was eager to please. Things changed a couple of years ago, and when I wished to dismiss her, Mère Bonaparte interceded with my husband on her behalf."

"Please forgive me, I didn't mean to pry."

"I know. I needed to tell someone, and I trust you." Josephine wiped an errant tear from her cheek. "My husband's family is trying to turn him against me."

"He won't let them," Janine said.

"I know he loves me." Josephine took a deep breath. "But in our case, love may not be enough. He desperately wants—needs—an heir, and I cannot give him one."

"I am so sorry."

Josephine stared out of the window. "His mother doesn't let an opportunity pass without reminding him or me about it." She returned her attention to Janine, a serene expression on her chameleon face. "Enough of this unhappy talk," she said with a smile. "How was your morning with Lieutenant Lenoir?"

"He proposed marriage." Disarmed by Josephine's openness, Janine confessed she was still considering his proposal. "I haven't given him my answer."

"Oh?" Surprise flickered across Madame Bonaparte's face. "You and he are so well suited. Besides, he's a dashing young aristocrat with a bright future. If I were you, I wouldn't keep him waiting."

"I won't."

"I'm glad. I know you'll have a good life together."

I didn't say I'd accept. "I'm not sure what I'll decide." *I'd be a fool to refuse.*

"My dear, I know this will please you." Josephine's eyes held the sheen of purpose. "My husband and I agreed that Chateau Fleury would be an ideal wedding present for you and the lieutenant."

Chateau Fleury. She had returned to France to claim her ancestral home and now it was being offered to her. How could she say no to the proposal with such a temptation? Overcome with the prospect, Janine said, "I promised him an answer soon. I'll say yes."

"You won't regret it. I'm happy for you—a tiny bit envious too."

Her decision made, it seemed a great weight should be lifted . . . but it was not. Janine's mind raced from her wedding to Chateau Fleury. She'd sealed her fate. *Oh, God, Etienne will despise me.* "He won't care. He rejected me," she murmured, clenching her hands. She and Lenoir would live at Chateau Fleury right away, with Aimée and her family living in the Lenoir home after its repairs.

Josephine didn't let on if she noticed Janine's distress. "Unfortunately, you won't be healed enough to attend the fête on Saturday. Don't worry, I'll stop by and tell you all about it."

"I so wanted to attend. My gown is ready—made of a beautiful silk, a gift from the lieutenant."

"How romantic. You're one lucky lady." A satisfied smile curved Josephine's mouth.

Preparing to depart from the Palace Military Headquarters, Etienne turned from Adrien at the sound of Lenoir's approach.

The lieutenant squared his shoulders and stopped in front of him. "How's your investigation progressing?" he asked with a smug demeanor.

"Why do you ask? Do you have information of importance?" Etienne moved around him and continued toward the door. Lenoir followed. The lieutenant usually avoided him, so why seek him now? What motivated him—love or war? Irritated with the delay, he wanted to get to the boarding house. Since Lenoir reported to de Bernay, and he reported directly to Bonaparte, there should be no reason to talk unless de Bernay had information relevant to his investigation.

"I do but not about your investigation. I'm here as a gesture of friendship. Now that Mademoiselle de Fleury and I are to be married, I hope we can let bygone rivalries be forgotten."

Etienne seethed but did his best not to show it.

Lenoir persisted. "I know you and she were childhood friends . . . and I can't blame you for your interest in her."

Etienne kept walking. Damn nerve of the little weasel—thanks to Bonaparte's meddling. He strode away without a response. He couldn't blame Janine for being seduced by Bonaparte's offers, whatever they were. She'd live the aristocratic life that she valued so highly.

Lenoir followed him outside and called, "Will I see you at the big event on Saturday?"

Five soldiers, three in civilian clothes and the other two in uniform, stood in the shadows of two large elm trees. The boarding house where O'Rourke had been spotted was just a remnant of its pre-Revolutionary elegance; the building on Rue Saint Honoré needed major repairs.

As the afternoon sun slid low, Etienne still waited for Jean O'Rourke. "You're sure he didn't leave the building last night?" he asked one of the men.

"He didn't go anywhere. We took turns standing watch, and even in the dark we couldn't miss that red hair." He laughed at his own attempt at humor. "A man and a woman went in about ten. The man left alone about three this morning. That's the extent of the activity here."

"That is if O'Rourke didn't wear a wig," Etienne countered.

As the uneventful night gave way to the first light of dawn, the red-haired Irishman stole from the house. He stood for a moment, and after furtive glances in each direction, he stepped forward, picking up his pace along the street.

Etienne raised his hand in a gesture of silence and spoke softly. "Give me a few minutes' head start and then follow."

The caretaker turned a corner, disappearing from view before Etienne rounded the curve. He searched the street, frantic because he'd lost sight of his quarry. Passing a church, he noticed a slight movement in its side garden. Man or beast? He squinted until a human backside, partially obscured by a tall bush, came into focus. Etienne backed up, looking over his shoulder until he saw that his captain and the others stood well behind him. Moving to a position directly behind the bush, he waved his men forward. They waited as silent sentries for his next hand signal.

Etienne strained to hear the muffled conversation behind the screen of green.

"Cursed be that woman. What was she doing at Notre Dame?" A hushed voice said. "We're going to have to wait awhile before we make another attempt to nab the pesky de Fleury woman. She's holed up at the Tuileries."

Mon Dieu, they're planning to abduct Janine. Another person, perhaps the boy, spoke too softly for Etienne to hear.

O'Rourke spoke a little louder, his Irish brogue more evident in his agitation "I'll be goin' home now. In a week, we'll meet again, same place, same time."

Etienne motioned for his men to retreat farther away from the hedge. He stepped sidewise into the dark recess of the shadows, signaled for them to follow the caretaker, then Etienne and his captain returned to the boarding house by a street less traveled than the one they'd come on. When they arrived at the house, the other three soldiers informed them that the Irishman was already inside.

Etienne said to one of them, "Return to the Tuileries and have my aide-de-camp, Adrien Fortier, send a report to Bonaparte. The five of us will follow these men."

Stopping only to eat and relieve himself, O'Rourke, followed by Etienne and his contingent, rode hard for two days and nights directly to Chateau Fleury. Encouraged that O'Rourke didn't digress to report to another party along the way, Etienne surmised he wasn't part of Cadoudal's information-gathering organization.

As soon as the caretaker had stabled his horse and entered the chateau, Etienne led his men inside the stable, where they fed and watered their horses. After splashing their faces with water and washing their hands, the men rested on the hay.

After a few minutes of rest, Etienne stood and stretched. "I'll go for food and other supplies. The rest of you keep watch. Better take turns enjoying the respite while I'm gone." He requisitioned a fresh horse from one of the stalls and rode toward town. He'd stop to check on Nanny before going to the market square.

As he rode along, he wondered whether Nanny Cecile had regained consciousness and how his mother and Anne had managed to juggle their time while keeping watch over her. Perhaps Madame Parot had relieved them. She could be trusted. If they hadn't enlisted her help, he'd suggest it.

All was quiet in front of the old plaster and timber convalescent home. Etienne hitched his horse to a post in front of the house and climbed the porch steps. The red-haired landlady stood by the door and opened it. *Red hair, no Irish brogue.* Did the red hair alone tie her to O'Rourke? He hadn't considered it before because nature didn't bestow hair that shade on anyone. And to his knowledge, nothing she'd done warranted investigation.

"Colonel Tremeau, come in. Your mother's with Gemma now."

Not stopping to inquire about Gemma's condition, Etienne made a beeline for the bedroom and met Madame Tremeau in the hall.

"I thought I heard your voice." She threw her arms around him. "I'm so glad you're here."

He hugged her in return. He moved his hands to her shoulders and took a step back. Her face was drawn, a sign of her hectic schedule. He reached for her hand and led her back into the bedroom. "How is she?" Nanny Cecile lay motionless on the bed, face pasty white, giving no indication whether she slept or was still unconscious.

"Not good. Sometimes she opens her eyes and looks at me. But when I talk to her, she doesn't answer." His mother shook her head. "Once, she squeezed my finger."

Leaning close to the inert figure, Etienne slipped his forefinger into her hand and jiggled it. "Nanny, can you hear me?" No response. "Nanny, it is Etienne," he said in a more urgent voice. "Let me know if you hear me."

She gave a slight squeeze to his finger and opened her eyes.

"Et . . . Etienne, I waited for you," she said, her voice faltering.

"I'm here now."

"Janine?"

"She's in Paris. All is well."

Nanny watched him; her eyes clear and fiery. "You must hear me." She held his gaze without speaking. She gulped, swallowed, and then spoke in a weak voice. "A long time after Janine left, the groomsman came back to Chateau Fleury." She paused and took a deep breath. "He tried to convince me he was Comte de Fleury returned." She closed her eyes and pressed her lips together.

Etienne stroked her arm. "Take your time. I'll wait."

Some minutes passed before she spoke again, "I knew he couldn't be. The count was dead, but the man seemed familiar."

"Why did you think he was the groomsman?"

"Voice was different than before, but he pointed his finger in my face and called me Nan like the groomsman used to do." She squeezed Etienne's finger and nodded her head.

"The murdering groomsman is the imposter," Etienne said. "I understand. You can rest easy now."

"Non. More, more." The old woman increased the pressure on his finger. "I looked for groomsman's Z-shaped scar on his neck. It's there. I called his name. He hit me across face." She moaned. "I don't remember more." Her eyes closed, her grip on his finger relaxed. Her body drooped like a rag doll, appearing lifeless.

Etienne squeezed her hand farewell. "Bless you, Nanny." He stood and led his mother from the room. "I'm afraid she won't last the night. I've seen too many critically injured soldiers rally just before they die."

"Poor dear. Soon she'll be at peace."

Etienne nodded. "I'll stop by in the morning. Now I must go and get supplies for my men. We'll be here for a few days at least."

He mounted his horse and rode the short distance to the market square. Although he felt the accumulated fatigue of the last week, he pressed onward. After selecting the necessary staples, he stopped by the Loire Valley military headquarters and spoke with the officer on duty before riding back to the chateau.

When he arrived at the stables, the major met him and stood beside the horse. "No sign of any activity around here." He gestured to the three men sleeping on the hay. "No doubt they'll awaken when they know food is here."

Etienne chuckled. "I'm sure of it." He dismounted and tethered the horse before removing the bundle of supplies, then he and major broke pieces of bread from a loaf and cut a block of cheese into smaller pieces. Devouring their sustenance, they washed it down with wine.

"Tomorrow, I'll need your help to break down the walled-up entrance to the Fleury crypt," he said to the other man. An explanation for the strange happenings at Chateau Fleury no longer eluded him. It was now or never if he wanted to see whether the rightful count's body had been disturbed. Ten years ago, after the murder, he'd taken the body to the family vault and placed it in an empty coffin, hoping to protect it from desecration by marauding bands of lawless villagers roaming the countryside during the height of the Revolution.

"The crypt. What's in there?"

"The body of Comte de Fleury *should* be. I can't tell you what else." Etienne returned his cup to his mess case before he lay his weary body down on the hay and slept.

"Wake up, Colonel, someone's coming."

When he awoke to the major's plea, long shadows foretold the approach of night. For an instant he wondered where he was and was irritated at the disturbance, but he was on his feet before O'Rourke came into view.

"What the devil are you lot doing in here?" the Irishman stared from man to man in disbelief. "Get off this property right now," he growled.

Etienne sauntered to the man, lowered his head until their faces almost touched, and looked him in the eye. "If you don't want this property sequestered, you'll show us your best hospitality. Go tell your master to prepare quarters for us and a decent meal."

Recognition passed over O'Rourke's belligerent face as he eyed Etienne. He trembled and rubbed his ears as if they ached, but he could not move. It was as if his feet were fastened to the ground. "Oui, Colonel Tremeau," he finally muttered.

"Go!" Etienne gestured toward the sword at his side.

Losing no time, the caretaker dashed toward the chateau and the soldiers laughed and patted each other on the back.

"Two men are to keep watch at all times. Unless sleeping, each of us must be vigilant about our surroundings and what is going on around here. Any questions?"

"Non, Colonel," they said in unison.

On their way to the chateau, the men seemed relaxed and talked of comfortable beds and gracious dining. "When are we going to question O'Rourke?" The major asked as he strolled beside Etienne.

"Not while we're here. We can't reveal we're on to him. He's arranged another meeting in Paris in one week. I want him to lead us to his contacts."

O'Rourke delayed them at the door until the butler arrived. "Come with me. Your rooms are prepared," the butler said grudgingly.

One of the men and the major were stationed outside to keep watch. Inside the house the butler showed them to their rooms. "Where are the others?" he asked, his eyes searching, alarm sounding in his voice.

"They'll be along," Etienne assured him.

The man scowled. "Your men will be quartered in this wing. I'll show them to their rooms. I have placed a tray of fruit and cheese and a bottle of wine on each bedside table." He turned to leave, calling over his shoulder, "Dinner will be brought to your rooms at seven."

"Just a moment." Etienne stepped in front of him. "We plan to dine with your master."

"I'm sorry, that won't be possible. The count is indisposed and takes his meals in his room."

"In that case, escort me to him. I'll personally extend our appreciation."

"He was sleeping when I left him. I'll awaken him. Wait here for me." He rushed out the door as if pursued by a demon.

True to his word, the servant returned in a short time and led Etienne to the bedroom. He tapped lightly on the door but there was no response.

Etienne tried the door. It wouldn't budge. He tried again. Bolted. He kicked and kicked until it gave way and he was propelled forward into the room. A tray of food sat on a table by the empty bed. Etienne turned to address the butler. He wasn't there. A quick search of the room confirmed his suspicions—the count had used the delay to escape.

Etienne dashed down the stairs and out the front door to where his men stood guard. "The count has disappeared. Have you seen anything?"

"Nothing."

Sprinting to the back of the house, Etienne received the same answer from the second guard. Where was the count? He must be hiding somewhere inside the house. They'd have to remain on watch so he couldn't leave without being noticed while the others conducted a thorough search inside.

Chapter 32

The promise of possessing Chateau Fleury consoled Janine to some extent. She lay in her bed, twisting and turning, unable to sleep. She'd been hasty in telling Josephine she would accept Lenoir's marriage proposal, though she most likely would. The answer she gave Lenoir in the morning would determine the direction of the rest of her life.

Why hesitate? She'd gone to New Orleans under difficult circumstances and drawn on her love of design to survive and build a successful business. Her shop, Très Chic, had thrived under her guidance, and with the influx of Americans, its future looked bright and she saw many possibilities in her future in New Orleans. But if she returned, she could well remain a spinster—not appealing to a woman who loved children and wanted a family.

On the other hand, she feared Lenoir Frères would limit her to design work and allow her little say in the business decisions. The lieutenant certainly limited his sister's role. Yet he offered Janine a market with the royalty of Europe for her creative work. Très Chic would never have access to such clientele. By marrying Lenoir she'd be in possession of her beloved Chateau Fleury and have a family of her own. She'd have everything . . . *except* the husband she longed for—Etienne Tremeau.

What was she thinking? Whether she married the lieutenant or not, she wouldn't have Etienne. He'd dismissed her and urged her to return to New Orleans, perhaps to spare her feelings when he wed Mademoiselle La Roche and received his professional reward—promotion to general in the Republican Army, most likely. Minette had told her of the plan. She'd pointed out that Bonaparte held him in high regard. Would they each be bought for a price? She thought she knew the answer. Didn't Bonaparte always win?

She could sleep now, her decision finalized in the quiet of the night.

Waiting by the window the next morning for Lenoir and their time in the garden, Janine decide to tell him of her acceptance. There would be wedding plans and, later, talk of Chateau Fleury. She turned at the sound of footsteps outside her open door.

"You look lovely this morning," Lenoir said as he approached her and raised her hand to his lips.

"Thank you. It's good to see you," she said, overwhelming sadness threatening her composure.

"Are you ready to smell the roses?"

"Oui. Today is the day," she said, making an effort to sound cheerful.

"Your wish is my command." Adjusting the guide handle for her use, Lenoir pushed Janine along the garden path they had followed the previous day. When they reached the place among the roses and lavender, he gently moved her onto the bench and sat beside her.

Cupping her face in his hands, he looked into her eyes. "My dearest Janine, I love you and will cherish you always." He lowered his arms and gave her a hug and a kiss on the cheek.

"I have my answer." Janine smiled at him.

"Don't keep me in suspense."

"I won't." She lifted her eyes to his. "Yes, I will marry you."

He wrapped his arms around her and pressed his lips to hers, a slow, exploratory, demanding kiss. Suddenly, he moved away and jumped up without saying a word.

Puzzled, Janine wondered what had happened. "Is something the matter?"

He slapped at his neck. "Must have been a bee."

"Did it sting you? Let me look."

"Non. It's all right." He sat back down. "Our engagement will be announced at the gala. I'll escort you there."

"I won't be able to go."

"Of course, you will. I'll bring you in your wheelchair. You'll enjoy the fanfare and festivities. The only thing we won't be able to do is dance together."

I don't think so. Hadn't Josephine promised to tell her about the fête since she couldn't attend? And she had told her about the special wedding gift. Maybe he didn't know about that either, since he hadn't mentioned it. Confused, Janine said, "We'll see."

"Yes, we shall . . . at dinner tonight with the Bonapartes." He pulled her toward him and planted a rough, bruising kiss on her mouth.

Romantic this was not. She pushed away and licked her lips; the metallic taste of blood shocked her. She felt nauseous, the aroma of lavender overpowering as whispering memories of Etienne's gentle touch, and the taste of his lips swirled through her head. Moody he was but never rough with her.

Lenoir grasped her wrists as if to restrain her. Where did he think she could go? "Don't play coy with me. I don't fancy such games."

"Take me inside now."

"Not yet. I have more to say."

"Then we need to move. The lavender is overwhelming."

He scowled. "The lavender? What changed since yesterday? You said you could stay here forever."

"I can't say. Suffice it to say, it has changed," Janine said, puzzled by his abrupt change of mood.

"The lavender hasn't changed. You have!" He got up, paced back and forth, then stopped moving, his face composed in a genial expression.

An apology seemed in order. Janine waited. Nothing. She turned to see what had distracted him.

"Good morning, Lieutenant." Josephine's demoiselle sauntered toward them, swinging her hips.

"Mademoiselle, it's a pleasure to see you." Lenoir kissed her hand.

She lowered her eyes for a moment and looked back up at him. "Indeed." She ran her tongue along her lips. "What are you doing here? I'm sure you have many important demands on your time?"

"Mademoiselle de Fleury and I are enjoying the beauty of the day," he said glancing at Janine.

"It is kind of you to bring her outside. If you would like, I'm going inside and can take her with me."

Janine spoke up. "That won't be necessary. We're just leaving."

The young woman looked at Lenoir and back to Janine. "Good day."

Lenoir stared after the demoiselle as she sashayed along the path until she disappeared around a curve. "Let's get you back to your room. Hopefully, a few hours' of sleep will put you in a better temper for tonight's festivities."

Lenoir's deliberate indifference toward her hadn't been lost on Janine. She would like to boot him with her good foot. "I doubt I'll rest. I would like to work on some watercolors. Did you get watercolor supplies for me?"

"I'm sorry, it slipped my mind."

They retraced their route to the palace and on toward her room.

Upon entering her room, Janine caught sight of Madame Bonaparte standing by the window. A fresh bouquet of flowers sat on the table, a cream-colored envelope propped against the vase.

The First Consul's wife turned. "I didn't expect you back so soon." Walking over to them, she reached for Janine's hand and placed her other hand on Lenoir's arm. "What a handsome couple you are. May the gods bless your union."

"Merci, Madame Bonaparte," Lenoir said, charm dripping from his lips.

"I won't keep you. I stopped in to leave your dinner invitation. We'll visit then," the lady said.

"And I'll be off to meet with General de Bernay now. But I look forward to dinner tonight." Lenoir gave Janine a peck on the cheek. "Do get some rest this afternoon." He said and lost no time leaving.

Josephine waited until the sound of footsteps faded into nothingness, her brow furrowed. "Is there anything I can get you before I go?"

"The beautiful gardens inspire me. If possible I would like some watercolor supplies to record my impressions of them. And som crutches so I might try to walk on my own."

"You shall have them today." Josephine's eyes searched Janine's face. "Don't expect men to understand women. They don't. A quick peck on the cheek and it is back to work for them."

"I didn't expect him to change so quickly . . . we're not even married yet," Janine said as Josephine helped her to the bed.

"He's been under a lot of strain lately, waiting for your answer. Now he's relaxed and able to think of other things. It doesn't mean he doesn't care for you. You'll see."

Watching Josephine leave the room, Janine kept her thoughts to herself—afraid she had made a dreadful mistake.

True to her word, Madame Bonaparte had her congenial maid bring Janine crutches and an assortment of watercolor supplies.

235

"Madame sent these for you. I know I'll find you painting when I come to get you dressed for dinner," she said, arranging the supplies on the table. "You'll be all set up for work before I leave."

"Merci. Help me to my chair, *s'il vous plaît*. Let me lean on your arm and try out my foot a little." Janine winced, clung to the woman's arm, and placed a little weight on her ankle. She yearned for the use of her foot, feeling a burning need for independence raging in her bosom. She hated feeling helpless.

Involved in painting, Janine escaped into a timeless realm. She flinched at the sound of the maid's voice and glanced at the clock. Where had the afternoon gone? She put a last stroke of the brush to a small painting of Chateau Fleury before setting it aside. Another picture sat to the side on an easel—a street scene in front of her shop in New Orleans. She'd painted a likeness of Etienne and then tore it to pieces. It wouldn't do for anyone to see it.

The maid carried a cornflower blue dress over her arm. "Madame Bonaparte thought you might like to wear this tonight."

"I would. How nice of her." Janine packed up the art supplies.

The woman moved them to a corner of the room and began applying rouge to Janine's cheeks. "Is that your home?" She pointed to the easel.

Janine watched in the mirror as the maid colored her lips. After a long moment, she said, "Chateau Fleury, the home of my family." She couldn't bring herself to claim ownership of it yet.

"It's beautiful." The woman stood back and looked at Janine. She arranged one last curl before declaring, "There. You're ready for your young man." She gathered her basket of rouges, powders, and hair-styling paraphernalia and left.

Sitting by the window, Janine waited a short while for Lenoir's arrival. She dared to hope he would be the gentleman she had come to know over the last few months. Perhaps, unbeknownst to her, she had somehow contributed to his behavior earlier in the day. She chided herself to be more sensitive to his feelings.

Within fifteen minutes, he appeared, only a few minutes late, appearing at first to once again be the thoughtful escort. "You look ravishing."

He came closer, his face flushed and his breath reeking of liquor. He leaned forward, kissed her lips, and nibbled at her neck. He paused as if uncertain before lifting her from the chair and starting toward the bed.

She trembled, fearing his intentions—surely, he wouldn't dare be late for an appointment with Napoleon. "Have you lost your good sense?" she asked.

He stopped and looked at the clock. "Damn, we'll be late." His gave one last glance toward the bed before taking her back to the chair and rolling her into the hall, slamming the door behind them.

What had come over him? Did he drink to drunkenness often? The chair rumbled along the floor, traveling at a fast clip. As they neared Bonaparte's private quarters, the demoiselle came in their direction. Seeing them, she turned and rushed the other way.

"Trollop!" Lenoir muttered under his breath.

What brought that on? Janine wondered, relieved to see they had arrived at the dining room.

Bonaparte stood beside the table, talking to Josephine, but he stepped forward when Janine and Lenoir entered. "Lieutenant, what took you so long—you're five minutes late . . . and tipsy."

Lenoir didn't move, appearing confused, but finally murmured, "I apologize."

Josephine came to her husband's side, putting her hand on his arm. "You haven't met Mademoiselle de Fleury." She continued with the introduction. "May I present my husband, Napoleon Bonaparte."

Bonaparte focused on Janine for the first time. "Mademoiselle, my pleasure. I trust you'll teach this man to be punctual." He slapped Lenoir on the back. "Now let's be seated and eat." He sat down at the head of the table and left it to his wife to direct Lenoir and Janine to their places. After one and all were seated, the butler served bowls of steaming onion soup.

Napoleon dove in as if famished, slurping spoonful after spoonful until emptying his bowl. He pushed it aside, the spoon clattering, and nodded to the butler, who looked at the others.

Madame Bonaparte slipped her half-empty bowl to the side. Lenoir and Janine followed her cue. "My husband and I regret we must wait to announce your engagement until the upcoming Military Honors Gala."

Lenoir spoke up, "There's no need to delay. Janine and I plan to be at the fête on Saturday and look forward to your announcement of our upcoming marriage there."

The butler brought the main course and served while the conversation continued.

Josephine's mellow voice wafted across the table like a breath of fresh air. "We want everything to be perfect for such an important announcement. Janine and you must dance in celebration and allow us to share the moment." Her tone changed and became matter of fact. "It's already on the program for the Military Gala. In three weeks Janine should be as fit as can be."

Lenoir looked down at his plate. "I understand."

"This is a joyous occasion, and my husband and I have a wonderful surprise for your wedding."

Lenoir straightened his shoulders, his eyes brightened. "May I ask what it is?"

"Of course you may. Our wedding gift to Janine and you will be Chateau Fleury."

"Wh-what . . . th-thank you," the lieutenant stammered.

Bonaparte set down his fork and knife. "Lenoir, you seem hesitant. What's the matter? Aren't you pleased?"

"I am. It's just . . . I thought for a moment it could be a restoration of Chateau Lenoir."

Bonaparte jumped up from his seat. "Lieutenant, this is not about you. It is about the glory and future of France. Janine's heritage and Chateau Fleury are an important part of the history of the old aristocracy of France. Lenoir Frères may be an important component of the future economic success of this country, but that's all. This lapse on your part demonstrates why you are still a lieutenant . . . not a general. Do you understand me?" He sat down and stabbed the slab of meat on his plate.

Josephine looked at Lenoir. "I believe we have covered the topics of importance tonight. My husband will leave us in a few moments to return to his office, and I'm sure you've already had an eventful day. We'll talk with you both later."

Chapter 33

Etienne returned to his room following his night watch outside Chateau Fleury. After a quick splash of water on his face, he selected a piece of cheese and a chunk of bread from the meager breakfast tray by his bed. Standing by the window facing the rear of the house, he saw no movement outside. The phony count still must be inside . . . but where?

Torn between staying with his men to search the chateau again or going to see if Nanny Cecile had survived the night, Etienne decided to go into Tours, confident that his men had sealed the chateau. If the Nanny had survived, he'd seek a reliable person to relieve his mother and Anne. He should be back to assume command within the hour. The difficult decision made, he went to the stables, saddled up his horse, and rode home.

Madame Tremeau met him at the door, her expression saddened. "Nanny took her last breath about an hour after you last saw her."

Embracing her, Etienne said, "It's a blessing."

"I know. She suffered so for her loyalty to the de Fleurys."

"She was a brave woman." He wondered about how best to tell Janine. What could he say to lessen her pain?

"I'll fix breakfast."

"Non, Maman. I must get back to Chateau Fleury. How's Anne?"

"Sleeping. We stayed up until after midnight, talking." Madame Tremeau went to the kitchen, accompanied by her son. "Sit down. At least have a cup of coffee with me."

Etienne sat. The time had come to tell her about his new assignment. Watching her fill his cup, he realized how much he'd miss his family. "Bonaparte is sending me to New Orleans in a few weeks."

Biting her lip, his mother looked away. "You're Bonaparte's man now."

She's right. What can I say? "For the time being at least." He swallowed the last of his coffee, stood, and gave his mother a prolonged hug. Reaching into his pocket, he took out several gold coins and set them on the table. "See that Nanny gets a proper burial. I must go to Paris in the morning. I'll try to be back by Thursday. If not,

239

don't delay her service on my account."

Madame Tremeau nodded. "While you're there, let Janine know about the service."

"I will." He gave his mother a quick kiss on the cheek and left.

Within the half-hour Etienne rode past the chateau and down the sloping hillside garden to the stables. O'Rourke was there, grooming one of the resident horses. A quick tally of animals assured him none were missing. No one had escaped with one. He ignored the caretaker and led his stallion to the tool shed. Retrieving heavy sledgehammers and battering rods, he continued toward the chateau.

The major met him as he approached. "Still no sign of him . . . inside or out."

Etienne inclined his head. "Leave your man on guard here and help me examine the de Fleury crypt."

After a word with the other soldier, the major climbed on his horse and drew up by Etienne. They rode together down the sloping ground past outbuildings and a grove of trees until the classical edifice of the de Fleury family vault came into view.

Passing through an open iron gate, they rode beyond neglected gravesites, overgrown with weeds and tangled vines outside the large main crypt. The two men dismounted and carried the tools to the bricked-up entrance door of the temple-like structure and lost no time starting on the laborious demolition.

Beads of perspiration flowed freely as bricks crumbled and pieces of damaged stonework gave up a man-sized opening. Etienne laid down his battering rod and wiped his forehead. "I'll take over from here. Go on back to the chateau."

"Yes, sir." The major wiped the back of his arm across his own wet brow.

When inside, Etienne waited for his eyes to adjust to the dark space before he lit his torch and descended the stairs to the main burial chamber. Standing in the center of the room, he rotated the torchlight around the space, bringing clarity to ghostly shapes and shadows. He paused at the vaults of the Marquis and Marquise de Fleury—Janine's parents—giving a sigh of relief when he saw no obvious vandalism inside the main area of the crypt.

He didn't stop to look at the other elaborate de Fleury tombs on his way to the second flight of stairs that descended deeper into the earth. He had taken the murdered Comte de Fleury's body to the lower level that dreadful day years ago. As soon as he stepped into the smaller room, his breathing became more labored in the damp and musty air, but he moved deftly around the room. Where exactly had he placed the count's body? Which container had he used? He closed his eyes a moment and tried to recall the scene before moving forward. Stepping over fragments of stone and around broken statuary, he came to a row of caskets, all but one unoccupied, he believed.

Recalling he had passed by the first one when laying the count to rest, he placed the torch in a nearby holder and heaved aside the stone lid of the second one. He peered into a black abyss. He leaned forward and squinted—empty. The stone slab covering the third one was askew, leaving the receptacle partially open. He pushed it enough to look inside. A spider web created a strange pattern over the opening and he used a marble arm from a broken statue to remove the web and probe the interior. It met with no resistance. *Unoccupied.* Had someone discovered the body and removed it? He'd been in such a hurry to care for the remains and get back to help Janine to safety. Maybe he hadn't closed it completely.

With a sinking feeling, he moved to the next stone box, anxious to examine it. A thick, dank odor assailed his nostrils. He'd found him. The white skeleton rested inside, his riding clothes still in place. At that moment Etienne was again the seventeen-year-old lad overcome with shock and grief. The young count, larger than life to Etienne, had taught him to ride a horse and had rewarded him for his progress by allowing him to ride his own horse, Le Diamant. Back then his was the first human corpse Etienne had ever handled and buried. In the intervening years, however, he'd lost track of the number of men he'd laid to rest.

He steeled himself and reached for the bony hand, looking for the signet ring the count had been wearing. Finding it, he slipped the cold metal circle from the finger. The de Fleury ring was rightfully Janine's. He would take it to her.

He put the ring into his pocket and replaced the stone cover. "Rest in peace," he murmured. Moving with care around the statuary fragments and broken tomb debris, he followed his footprints in the dust to the stairs.

⚜

Napoleon surprised Etienne by greeting him at the office door, hand outstretched in a welcoming gesture. "Does this visit mean you've decided to propose to Mademoiselle La Roche?"

"Not today. I've come to report on my investigation."

Bonaparte clapped him on the shoulder and led him to the informal seating area by the fireplace. "Unless your report is a matter of life and death, I want to discuss your engagement to Mademoiselle La Roche."

"The last time I saw you, I told you I wasn't ready to make my decision. Nothing has changed," Etienne said. "I plan to leave for New Orleans as soon as you issue orders to do so."

"Perhaps you won't need to do that. You'll have two additional weeks to think about it. I have decided to make the announcements at the Military Gala rather than the fête because of Mademoiselle de Fleury's sprained ankle."

Perplexed, Etienne asked, "When did that happen?"

"A few days ago at Notre Dame. Lieutenant Lenoir brought her here for treatment and now she's under Josephine's watchful eye."

The pieces of the puzzle began to fall into place. Etienne rose and paced the floor, his brow furrowed.

"Calm yourself," Bonaparte urged, "She is mending well. Come. Sit."

Etienne complied. "Are you saying Janine was the woman chased at Notre Dame?"

"You didn't know?" The First Consul sounded incredulous. "I ordered Lenoir to send you a report."

"Which he didn't do," Etienne said with rancor. "A clear breach of policy on his part."

"I'll take care of him." Bonaparte frowned. "He's not much of a military man, I'm afraid . . . but I have to say, he knows the silk trade. That's where his value lies."

Napoleon slapped the arm of his chair. "You really should give more thought to an alliance with the house of La Roche. Since we last

242

spoke, I have decided upon your wedding gifts—a chateau in the Loire Valley, befitting your new rank of general. General Tremeau. How does that sound?" He gestured toward his black leather case embossed with distinctive gold letters, *Premier Consul.*

Etienne recognized the case as the one in which important papers were kept. If he said the right words, he'd be General Tremeau with the stroke of the pen—the chateau be damned.

Bonaparte waited for Etienne's response. Receiving none, he went on to say, "The sooner you and Mademoiselle La Roche are married, the sooner your promotion to general is effective and the chateau is yours. She'll like that."

"I appreciate your confidence in my ability to serve my country well."

"Does that mean you've come to your senses?"

Etienne paused as if considering the question. "Mon ami, you know me well enough to understand I am a simple man who places little importance on a lavish lifestyle."

Bonaparte rose, clasped his hands behind his back in his deep-in-thought pose, and walked back and forth before stopping in front of Etienne. "I expected better from you. You should know I don't care about your personal preferences. My generals deserve respect and recognition for their contribution to the welfare of France. Lavish living, as you call it, is a visible sign of their value to the nation."

Napoleon sat back down. "I suggest you open your mind to what I have said. We'll discuss this again in a few days. If you remain undecided, plan to leave for New Orleans the day after the gala." Bonaparte jumped up. "I'm losing patience with you, Tremeau. I'm giving you an order. You and Mademoiselle La Roche are to marry before the New Year. If not, you'll be guilty of insubordination and no longer worthy of my trust. You of all people know I do not tolerate anyone disobeying my orders." He glared at Etienne. "Now what have you come to tell me?"

Etienne knew he had tried the First Consul's patience, and his report, of necessity, would be brief. "So far we've found no evidence that O'Rourke, the Chateau Fleury caretaker, is part of the conspiracy against you. But he *was* heard plotting to kidnap Mademoiselle de Fleury. It's unclear why."

Concern etched on his face, Napoleon said, "With her

upcoming marriage, he could be planning to kidnap her and extort money for her release. Continue to keep him under surveillance." He pursed his lips. "He acted without knowing of our plans to gift Chateau Fleury to her upon her marriage to Lieutenant Lenoir."

"What?" Etienne hadn't anticipated that development. All of Janine's prayers had been answered. He breathed deeply and clenched his teeth. It was his turn to rise and pace. No wonder Bonaparte had refused to interfere in the phony count's claim to the property. He planned to use it to lure Janine into marriage to Lenoir, and only then would he oust him. Disgust for the complicated game Napoleon had designed consumed him. Napoleon considered people to be pawns to be moved around a chessboard in furtherance of one man's game plan.

"This concludes my report. I'll keep you informed," Etienne stood, waiting for dismissal.

Bonaparte remained seated. "I expect you give me good news before the gala."

Etienne followed Josephine's maid toward Janine's room. The hollow sound of his boots echoed along the marble hall, mirroring his empty feelings. He wished he could feel unbridled happiness for Janine's good fortunes. He couldn't. He'd rather not see her again, but duty demanded this last meeting. He accepted his responsibility to tell her of Nanny's death and the revelations she'd shared in her final hours. He'd also assure Janine that the family crypt had not been vandalized. Her uncle's tomb and body were undisturbed. He regretted having removed the signet ring and, for that matter, battering the walled-up entry to the crypt. His efforts had been for naught. Since he had the ring, he had asked Josephine for a velvet-lined box in which to present it to Janine—a wedding gift of sorts, he thought with distaste.

Janine's heart leapt at the sight of Etienne. Why had it taken him so long to come? Thank goodness, the woman had helped her dress for the day. She couldn't have been happier had the fabled genie popped out of a bottle and offered to fulfill one wish.

244

The maid stood to the side. "A gentleman to call on you, Mademoiselle. May I bring some tea and coffee?"

"Non, merci. I won't be here long," Etienne answered for Janine, his eyes moving to her feet and ankles. "How is your ankle?" he inquired, his abruptness having vanished.

"It's so good to see you." Janine gestured to the chair beside her wheelchair. "Do sit down."

He shook his head and stood beside her chair. He looked toward the window for a moment before he turned and faced her. With a tight smile, he said, "It's nice to see you too. You haven't told me how your ankle is healing."

"It's a slow process, but each day is a little better. I test it every morning but still can't put much weight on it." With a nervous laugh, she added, "I don't do well being an invalid, I fear." She feasted her eyes on his familiar bronzed face and probing eyes of sapphire blue.

"You'll get the care you need here." Etienne averted his gaze. "I've come from Tours with sad news for you." He placed his hand on her arm.

"What is it … not Nanny?"

Etienne leaned forward and reached for her hand. "She passed away peacefully three days ago. I've taken care of her burial arrangements. I'm sorry your mishap prevents you being there." After a long pause, he said, "I saw her the day she died. She was lucid and said she'd waited for me."

Janine could no longer bear it and held out her arms to Etienne. "Please hold me," she whimpered between sobs. Etienne had buried her uncle without her, and now he'd taken care of Nanny without her.

He hesitated and then did as she asked. He leaned forward and drew her to him, holding her face against his heart and gently stroking her hair. "It's best this way. She's free of worry now."

Taking comfort from the rhythm of Etienne's heartbeat, steady and strong, she asked, "What did she tell you?"

Etienne stepped away from her. "The groomsman returned to the chateau some years later and tried to convince her he was your uncle. She knew that was impossible since Comte de Fleury was dead. But she noticed something familiar about the imposter. At some point she realized his mannerisms were those of the groomsman. She looked for the distinctive scar on his neck and called him by name. That's when she was brutally beaten."

"Mon Dieu. The groomsman . . . is the imposter?" She caught herself before she went on to say he'd soon be thrown out of her chateau. She could not yet bring herself to tell Etienne she had sold her soul simply to regain Chateau Fleury.

Etienne sat down, putting distance between them. "I'm sorry for your pain, Janine. I do know Chateau Fleury is yours—not that I approve." He removed an elegant box from his pocket and handed it to her. "I brought you something."

Janine wanted to hide her face. He knows what I've done. *A ring! Non. What can it be?* Her hand shook as she opened it. She gasped. "The de Fleury signet ring." She had early memories of it on her grandfather's finger, and after his death her father wore it. The last time she'd seen it was on her uncle's hand as he lay dying. Overwhelmed by its significance to her family, she said, "Did Nanny have it?"

"Non. Nanny wouldn't have it. I opened the crypt to see if your uncle's body was where I placed it after the groomsman killed him. I thought you should have the ring and brought it for you—before I knew the chateau was to be returned to you." Etienne gave her a contemptuous look.

What could she say to explain how complicated things were— that she hadn't accepted Lenoir's proposal without much soul-searching. "I hope I've made the right decision. I didn't give him my answer without days of thought."

"Is that so? The lieutenant told me you had accepted before I left for Tours, a day so after you hurt your ankle."

"That's not true." Janine whacked the side of the chair. "Lenoir lied to you."

"It doesn't matter," Etienne said and turned away from her. "Before I leave, I need to ask a couple of questions about what happened at Notre Dame."

Perhaps it didn't matter since they both would soon be married to others. "All right," she said.

"Begin by telling me what happened."

Janine pressed her lips together. *Where to begin?* "I went to the cathedral alone while the lieutenant and his sister went to the tailor's shop. I hadn't realized the terrible condition of Notre Dame. So few people were there. I just walked along the aisle until I reached the chancel. That's when I noticed a man and a boy following me. I recognized the caretaker from Chateau Fleury and rushed back down the aisle and out into the square, hoping to disappear into the crowd. The two of them chased me, and I tripped over a heavy crate and fell to the ground. I couldn't stand on my foot. I was afraid I'd be abducted and killed. About that time, Lieutenant Lenoir arrived and carried me to the carriage. He brought me here to be seen by a doctor."

"Did the caretaker say anything to you?"

"Inside, he tried to lure me back by saying I had dropped my scarf. I was afraid of him. He didn't say anything else and I just kept running."

"Did you tell Lenoir you recognized the caretaker?"

"I think so. I don't remember."

"You did the right thing. The caretaker was up to no good." Etienne rose. "I've kept you too long. I must go now."

"Thank you for coming." She looked into his divine eyes and wondered when or if she would see him again.

"You know you're special to me." He leaned forward and kissed her cheek.

She wrapped her arms around his neck and moved her lips to his and on along his face. "You'll always be my hero, Etienne Tremeau," she murmured in his ear.

He stepped away and shook his head. "I've overstayed my visit." He turned and walked briskly from the room.

She mourned the loss of his presence, shaken by the intensity of her feelings for him. Why had he allowed this to happen to them? Why had he kept her at arm's length while they were free to love? Feeling utterly hopeless, she made no attempt to stem the stream of tears rolling down her cheeks.

Chapter 34

"Your services aren't needed at Nanny Cecile's burial. I've arranged for another priest, one who is untainted by his behavior and associations—you know what I mean." Etienne waited for a response from the man facing him.

Seated in his lavish apartment, Abbé Dillon studied the gold ring on his finger, his voice quavering, "Colonel Tremeau, I did nothing to harm the de Fleury's nanny. I was the only one there for her. I took her to the boarding house and paid for her care."

Etienne noted the elaborate, tooled leather-covered books filling the bookshelf behind the churchman. Five pairs of fine leather shoes rested beneath the bottom shelf—his weakness for expensive leather evident. "You listed her name as Gemma. Why? You didn't want her out of your sight after the recent assault. Why?"

"I was afraid they'd come back and kill her."

"They? Who are *they*?"

"I don't know. I'm afraid for myself too."

"Why should they want to harm you? Considering your odd behavior, you're in more danger of being shot at dawn as an enemy of the Republic."

Twisting the gold ring on his middle finger, the abbé said, "I beseech you not to breathe a word of what I am about to tell you."

"Go on." Etienne stared at the man and rested a hand on his sword.

"About six years ago Comte de Fleury returned from England, a changed man. He'd been badly injured after he left the chateau. I saw him at the marketplace and spoke to him. He didn't answer so I stepped closer and said, 'Bonjour' in a loud voice.

"He scowled at me and put his hand to his throat, responding in a whisper, 'Go away,' then he took a few steps from me before stopping. He returned and regaled me with a harrowing tale of his torture for defending the church.

"When I asked about his niece, Mademoiselle Janine de Fleury, he waved his hand in a dismissive way. "Lost her mind," he said, "in an insane asylum."

Doubting the prelate's version of the story, Etienne thought it more likely he had colluded with the imposter to support his lust for

248

financial gain. "How did you come to be Nanny Cecile's benefactor?"

The cleric's eyes darted from Etienne to the crucifix on the apartment wall. "A parishioner brought her to me. Cecile had been wandering the streets, bloody and bruised. She didn't know her own name." The abbé lifted his eyes to Etienne. "She couldn't tell us what had happened. I took her to the nurse's house and arranged for her to stay there."

The abbé's eyes betrayed him. Etienne knew he'd have to probe deeper to get the true story. "Why didn't you contact Comte de Fleury about the nanny?"

"I did. I went to the chateau to see him." The priest seemed to relax. "He released his dog on me. I barely escaped being torn apart, saved only when he whistled for the dog at the last minute. He apologized and said he wasn't responsible for the nanny.

"While walking with me to my coach, he asked if I could recommend a good caretaker for the estate." The man of the cloth shifted his eyes to a window. "I . . . I hesitated until he added he would make it worth my while. Money being scarce since the Revolution, I gave him the name of Monsieur O'Rourke."

"Do you keep in touch with O'Rourke?" Etienne asked in an even tone.

"Oui. He brings me a small monthly contribution from the count."

"What does the count receive in return?"

The man bowed his head. "I give him a monthly report about Cecile . . . and about Mademoiselle de Fleury; that is, since her reappearance."

"Do you have any idea why the count and Monsieur O'Rourke might wish to harm Janine de Fleury?"

"I don't. Maybe the count is embarrassed by her mental state. He may worry about how it reflects on the family and wants to frighten her away."

Etienne leaned close to the abbé. "Do you expect me to believe that?"

The prelate clutched his chest, his face flushed. "I really don't know what he's thinking."

Etienne stood. "You know as well as I do that Mademoiselle de Fleury is as sane as either of us—and much more so than O'Rourke and his master. Why are you defending them?"

Abbé Dillon shook his head. "They threatened to beat me and tell the town I'd accepted bribes from them. They knew my weaknesses. I was deeply in debt and used the money for myself." He rested his head in his hands. "God help me."

"Is that why you signed a sworn statement against Mademoiselle de Fleury, accusing her of meeting in secret with suspicious characters?"

"I did see her sneaking around with a stranger."

"Where did you see them?"

"I . . . I don't remember exactly. Inside the cathedral, I think. You're confusing me. But I did see them."

"Did you report it to the authorities immediately?"

"No. I didn't know what to make of it until . . ."

"The count prompted you what to say?"

"I swear it wasn't like that," the abbé said, blotting beads of sweat from his brow.

"Do you? The two of you signed statements the same day, making identical accusations. Explain that to my satisfaction, or you will be tried for conspiring for pay against Mademoiselle de Fleury. Your reputation will be ruined and you'll be deemed unfit to remain in your position in the church."

The abbé fell to his knees at Etienne's feet. "Have you no mercy on an old man who has suffered through the Revolution. Sometimes my memory fails me, but I am not dishonest. Please, please," he sobbed, "don't ruin me."

Walking toward the door, Etienne turned to the pathetic figure for one last look. He had a duty to notify the church authorities of the unfit man's sins. Perhaps they'd just retire him, showing him more forgiveness than he deserved.

By the time Etienne reached his mother's house, he concluded that his work in the Loire Valley was almost done. He'd leave it to Bonaparte to return Chateau Fleury to Janine and Lenoir and to deal with the fraudulent actions of the phony count and O'Rourke. As for the abbé, he would live out his final days in disgrace.

After Nanny's service he would say goodbye to his family and pack a few things to take with him on his assignment in Louisiana. When he reached Paris, he'd inform his aide about the change in command and instruct him to relieve the major at the chateau until ordered otherwise. *Let's get on with it.* Restless to be on his way to New Orleans, he bridled at the delay required by the First Consul's gala.

Two weeks had passed since Janine had sprained her ankle. Reaching for her crutches with confidence, now she walked back and forth between her bed and the armchair by the window. Day after day she'd seen Lenoir and the demoiselle rendezvous midday in the garden. They didn't linger long enough to draw attention to themselves—unless someone with nothing else to do watched from a window. Feeling betrayed and helpless, Janine wondered what was going on between them. *What can I do?*

She sat in the armchair and with her good foot pushed the wheelchair away. It struck the wall with a thud. "I won't need you anymore. Next week at the gala, I won't even need these crutches," she said aloud.

She'd make sure to wait sedately in her chair for Lenoir's cursory late afternoon visit. She hadn't shared with him about her progress on crutches and he hadn't asked. As the time drew closer for the party, he'd likely focus again on his charade with her.

Feeling brave, Janine ventured out for a longer walk along the marbled hallway. She carried a watercolor of Josephine's garden in her pocket, with the intention of surprising her with it. The gracious lady had visited every morning without fail. They'd laughed and cried together. She had no reservations about calling on her while the lady's disagreeable companion strolled in the garden.

Beginning to question the wisdom of walking all the way to Josephine's quarters, Janine sat down on a chair to rest next to a life-sized Roman statue. She'd been there for a short time when a man came out of a room farther down the corridor. *Lenoir.* What was he doing in one of the chambers in the private wing? She stared at him as he walked briskly away from her toward an outside door leading into the garden. She waited a few more minutes before getting up. As she stood and adjusted her crutches, the door opened again. The demoiselle glanced up and down the hall before she rushed toward Josephine's apartment, adjusting her skirt as she went.

Lenoir's audacity shocked Janine. After their tryst in the garden, had Lenoir and the demoiselle met in her room—on a daily schedule? This was more than a simple flirtation while Janine's ankle kept her housebound. They weren't even married yet and already he was deceiving her.

Janine retraced her steps to her own room, so preoccupied she didn't give a thought to her ankle. She went inside and sat in the armchair, so furious she decided she would make no effort to appear serene when Lenoir called. *Cursed be the man if he comes in and tries to handle me again.* As she calmed down, she realized the throbbing in her weakened ankle had grown stronger. She'd tired it more than she'd realized. She hoped Lenoir wouldn't come, but the clock warned he'd be there any minute. She had no wish to see the deceitful man. He would learn she was a woman to be reckoned with.

One tap and her door opened. Not even waiting for permission to enter, the lieutenant came in, carrying a bottle of wine. His face was slightly flushed, most likely from his illicit encounter. He set the bottle on the table. "My dear, why is your wheelchair in the corner?" He came toward her and leaned down to kiss her.

She turned away. "Non. I may have said I will marry you, but I did not say you can treat me like property." She stood up without her crutches, steadying herself against the chair. "Don't you ever put a hand on me unless you have my permission. Doubtless, Josephine's treacherous lady-in-service is a willing participant!"

His expression sobered. "You're mistaken. I honor you. You are to be my wife."

Emotionally and physically exhausted, Janine sat down. "You have an exceptional way of showing that honor."

"Darling, I have respected your need for rest. I've gone to great lengths not to be a bother. You need your strength for the gala. I want you to know it will be the happiest night of my life."

"You lie! Right now, I'm of no mind to discuss this with you. Leave me, please."

" Shall I come for dinner?" he asked contritely.

"Non. I've lost my appetite."

"I'll look in on you tomorrow." Nonplussed, Lenoir turned on his heels and left.

⚜

Janine and Minette assembled in Josephine's intimate sitting room off the boudoir. Josephine poured tea for her guests after dismissing her maid. This was a time for private conversation among friends. They sipped tea and talked about the guest list and the gowns they would wear to the military celebration the following night.

Although the lively conversation suggested an air of excitement about the upcoming event, Janine was keenly aware of a tense undercurrent. She couldn't dismiss her own contribution; she must immediately inform Josephine of her decision not to marry the lieutenant.

She had wandered the halls and gardens, pondering her dilemma, and she had determined to not go through with the marriage, no matter the consequences. It had been a bad decision made for all the wrong reasons. As much as she wanted Chateau Fleury, she wanted Etienne Tremeau more. If she couldn't have him, she'd have no one. She had finally come to realize she had to live her own life, not the one her father had sought for her. Times were different now, and she'd begun to understand why Etienne fought for changing a system that put a value on a person based on an accident of birth.

Minette, unusually pallid, lacked her usual enthusiasm for talking about beautiful gowns and grand celebrations. "I'm feeling poorly," she admitted to her hostess. "Please excuse me if I rush off."

Josephine tilted her head. "Why certainly. You've been a great help with the preparations. Tomorrow's the big day."

"Thank you for understanding. I'll come early tomorrow to assist any way I can." Minette turned to Janine. "I'm sorry I haven't been able to spend more time with you. Forgive me?"

Janine nodded, saying, "Of course," and she watched Minette leave. Turning back, her eyes met the compassionate lady's and saw concern in them. As much as she dreaded to speak of her decision about Lenoir, she forced herself to do so. "I have something I must tell you, and I ask that you forgive me."

"You look as if you have lost your best friend. What has happened?"

"I cannot marry Lieutenant Lenoir. He is not the man I believed him to be."

253

"My husband will not understand . . . no matter your reasons." Josephine shook her head. "You did accept the lieutenant's proposal and your engagement is to be announced tomorrow."

"I know this is serious and that Chateau Fleury is lost to me. I also know Lenoir neither loves nor respects me. I no longer have esteem for him."

"How can you say such things?"

"He's having an affair with your demoiselle. Day after day I see them meet in the garden, then I saw him coming out of her chamber. As soon as I accepted his proposal, he began to neglect me, and when he *was* with me, he forced his attentions on me."

Josephine's eyes opened wide. "He violated you?"

"Non. It happened when he was in a drunken state. Our dinner appointment with you saved me. But he did change after I accepted his proposal, showing a lack of sensitivity to my feelings. You commented on it yourself."

"I'm shocked. He's always so polite and charming."

"That's the side of him that he always showed me—until I agreed to marry him."

"This is dreadful." The First Consul's wife persisted, "There has to be a way if you love him. Do you?"

"Non, I love another. Regardless, I have come to terms with my decision to marry him."

Josephine's brow creased with worry. "I suppose you are in love with Charles Dupré." After a momentary pause, she said, "I don't expect you to tell me."

"No, it isn't Charles. I decided some time ago not to marry him. He is not the sort of man I wish to marry."

"For God's sake, who is it?"

Janine shook her head. "I shouldn't tell you. He's promised to another."

"Oh, dear, how tragic." Madame Bonaparte grew silent before she said, "I'd like to know anyway."

The urge to tell her about Etienne tempted Janine. What would be the harm? Afterward, there'd be nothing more to say about it.

Taking a deep breath, she said, "You probably don't know Etienne Tremeau's father was the head gardener at Chateau Fleury. My father saw potential in Etienne and allowed him to be tutored in my classes. Over the years I became greatly attached to him." She paused to gauge the other woman's reaction.

Josephine placed her hand over her eyes and lowered her head. "A true Romeo and Juliet story. I've known Etienne for some time and am fond of him. He's loyal and trustworthy. I think of him as a friend and believe the feeling is mutual."

"After my husband advised him he should think of marriage to Mademoiselle La Roche, Etienne came to me and asked that my husband and I consider you as a suitable wife for him."

Etienne asked for my hand. Janine's head spun.

Josephine continued, "I spoke to my husband about it."

Janine's heart leapt. "You did? Then why is Etienne going to marry Mademoiselle La Roche?"

"Napoleon was adamant that a union between you and Etienne would be a threat to his vision for the Republic."

Her moment of hope dashed, Janine asked, "In what way?"

"He said Colonel Tremeau is an idealist, not always practical. His rigid philosophy, coupled with an *ancien régime* wife who lost her parents to the Revolution, might well appeal to dissidents of all sorts. Mademoiselle La Roche is a scatterbrained girl without a political thought in her empty head. She'd be of no help if he should be tempted to make trouble. When I saw Etienne again, I told him he must put you out of his mind."

Janine looked through misty eyes. "Thank you for telling me. I'll arrange to leave as soon as I can. I'll ask Minette to help me prepare for the journey."

"You're welcome to stay with me as long as necessary. At least stay long enough to complete the watercolors of my exotic plants. Say you'll accept a commission for the portfolio."

Janine was suspicious. Did the First Consul's wife hope she'd change her mind and accept the lieutenant? She would accept him under no condition, of that she was certain. At the same time, she needed all the money she could muster to get back to New Orleans and to reestablish her partnership in Très Chic. Chateau Fleury wouldn't be paying her way. "I'd be honored to do so."

"I'll inform my husband of your decision and, of course, no marriage announcement will be made. However, you will be expected to attend the gala with Lieutenant Lenoir. After that you will have fulfilled your obligation."

"I understand." Janine longed to see Etienne once more. "Will Etienne be there?" she asked in a small voice.

"I'm sure he and Mademoiselle La Roche will be in attendance." Josephine added with uncharacteristic sternness, "It would be most unwise for you to mingle with them."

Janine felt compelled to let Etienne know she was not going to marry Lenoir. She *would* speak to him at the gala. It didn't matter whether Bonaparte had announced his engagement to Mademoiselle La Roche. Before she left France, she must tell him of her love for him.

Chapter 35

Upon their arrival at the Tuileries, guests paused to watch fireworks light the sky while cannons boomed in the distance. Janine stood beside Lenoir near a window, observing elegant coaches deliver France's military elite and their companions to the festive front lawn. The military *soirée* had begun. Many men wore uniforms—what woman could resist a man in uniform—some of whom would be honored for their bravery during the ceremonial celebration.

Ladies made the most of their grand entrance, posturing to show off their gowns and themselves to best advantage. Brimming with pride, Janine felt equally as elegant as any of them in her beautifully designed gown made from Lenoir Frères silk. Tonight she'd bask in the enchantment—for tonight was make-believe. Tomorrow, the spell would be broken.

Glimpsing General de Bernay and Minette across the room, Janine slipped her arm through Lenoir's, hoping to gain his cooperation. "Come, let's greet the de Bernays. Over there." She gestured with her free hand. Lenoir wrapped his arm around Janine's waist along the way and she shuddered at his possessive familiarity—her peace offering had worked too well.

As they approached them, Minette's husband stepped aside and huddled in conversation with another man. Janine noticed Minette's rouge-covered cheeks failed to conceal the pallor of her skin; her lack of vitality was accentuated by her dark blue gown.

"Good evening, Lieutenant . . . and to you, Janine. You're absolutely gorgeous in your *magnifique* silk." Minette turned to Lenoir. "Would you be so kind as to bring us a glass of champagne?"

After he left, Minette stepped closer, her hand trembling as she slipped a small envelope into Janine's hand. "Keep this safe. Read it after the gala," she whispered. She wrapped her arms around Janine and clung to her for a moment before stepping back. "Have a wonderful time tonight. In this sea of humanity, I may not get to speak with you again," she said, her eyes filled with sadness.

Janine tucked the paper under the linen handkerchief inside her pearl-encrusted evening bag and watched Minette vanish into the crowd. She briefly puzzled over the written message until Lenoir intruded on her musings.

"Where's Madame de Bernay?" He glanced around, passing one of the glasses to Janine and staring at her as if she were to blame for Minette's behavior.

"I don't know." Janine gestured to the champagne. "I guess it's yours now."

"Why would she leave after asking for it?" he said in a peevish tone. "At least she could have waited and taken it with her."

"Perhaps she needed to join her husband."

"Forget about her. There's a good crowd here already. Shall we make the rounds?"

"There's no better time," Janine said, wanting to escape Lenoir's questions and hoping to meet acquaintances of her parents.

Her escort paused to introduce her to people who seemed to hold him in high esteem and who lavished praise on Lenoir Frères silks. Did he hope to impress her sufficiently to change her mind about him? She needed no convincing about the prestige of his silk business. His military achievements were another matter, and his prospect as a husband dismal. She'd already formed her opinion of him and grew weary of his efforts.

She searched the crowd for Etienne until she found him. Her heart skipped a beat. There he was in full military dress—sky blue uniform with silver buttons on the jacket, the scarlet collar and cuffs with a single row of silver embroidery delicious next to his bronzed face. For the first time she saw the military hero in his element. An air of authority and purpose emanated from him. No longer was he the gardener's son with the mesmerizing eyes. He was a man to be reckoned with, like Bonaparte.

And of course Mademoiselle La Roche stood at his side and watched his every move. He seemed unaware of her as he and Bonaparte stepped aside, engrossed in deep conversation. A burning resentment toward the girl threatened Janine's composure. Her dear, brave Etienne deserved a wife of his own choosing—not one to serve Bonaparte's political purposes. And what about her own contribution to his decision? She must tell him she loved him and valued him so much more than fame or fortune.

The lieutenant saved her from gawking when he gripped her arm rather too tightly and led her to the center of the room, away from Etienne and Bonaparte. Just as well, because she didn't want to further displease Bonaparte. The First Consul already knew she'd decided not to marry Lenoir; besides, Josephine had warned her to stay away from Etienne. She'd have to be more discreet when she told Etienne of her decision not to marry Lieutenant Lenoir.

By the time Janine saw the First Consul again, *sans* Etienne, he was close enough to reach out and touch her.

Bonaparte stepped closer, looked her in the eye, and said in a low growl, "Your decision to deny a union with the great house of Lenoir Frères is foolish." His tone lightened as Lenoir tilted his head toward them. "It's the perfect place for your talent to blossom among those who appreciate the finer things of life." He waved a dismissive hand and shrugged. "I don't understand women." Janine was left speechless as the First Consul moved away.

Musicians assembled at one end of the room and Bonaparte and Josephine led the way to the dance floor at the first musical strains of a minuet.

"If you wish to dance, we should do so now, before the floor gets too crowded." Lenoir stepped toward Janine.

"Let's do," she said to fulfill her dancing obligation. As they moved around the floor, Janine watched a bevy of waiters, carrying trays filled with glasses of champagne and various hors d'oeuvres, weave their way among the guests.

As the music faded, a cotillion was announced as the next dance.

"I need to rest and would like to sit," Janine said.

"That's fine. Champagne?"

"Non, merci."

Lenoir located a chair for her and went to get champagne for himself, stopping to greet the disagreeable lieutenant general she'd met at the de Bernays' dinner party. She watched the Bonapartes leave the dance floor.

Josephine seemed to float toward her on clouds of white organdy. Her dress contained yards of the fabric, and a garland of pink roses adorned her dark hair. "I saw you dancing. How is your ankle?"

"Very well, thank you."

"Are you enjoying yourself?"

"Very much."

"Is your escort being a gentleman?"

She has an ulterior motive, Janine thought. "He is." She forced a smile.

"Good," Josephine said. "Please excuse me. I must circulate among the guests."

While Lenoir made the rounds, Janine watched for her chance to speak to Etienne.

Clusters of military officers gathered when not otherwise in the company of beautiful women. As guests continued to arrive, freedom of movement diminished and small groups began to congregate around the room. Waiters circulated among the cliques and kept the champagne flowing.

Janine searched the crowd until she saw Etienne. Bonaparte was to his left, a short distance away, greeting others. *This is my chance.* She stood, her legs unsteady. She'd have move quickly.

She inched forward, every fiber of her being taut with anxiety while her eyes darted back and forth between the two men. People moved in front of her, forcing her to go around waiters and guests alike, her heart pounding as if it would explode.

A man turned abruptly, colliding with Janine and spilling his champagne. *"Pardonnez-moi."*

Ignoring his apology, she pushed past him and caught sight of Etienne and Bonaparte within a few feet of each other. She'd have to wait until Bonaparte separated from him.

Janine froze in place at hearing a loud clatter, followed by the sound of shattering glass. Had a waiter dropped his tray? Time seemed to stand still. What was the waiter doing? A flash of steel betrayed the blade in the waiter's hand as his arm raised and began its descent toward Napoleon's chest. Janine watched in horror, her breath caught in her throat, expecting to see the First Consul fall. She'd seen just such an exotic Persian dagger in Bordeaux at the Duprés' home. There was no mistaking the ornate, hilted, undulating blade.

Etienne reacted quickly and deflected the Khanjar dagger into his own arm. The crowd gasped in unison at the sight of his blood-soaked sleeve. Holding the bloody weapon in his left hand, Etienne thrust his right fist into the assailant's face. The waiter staggered and the white wig tumbled from the man's head. Both men disappeared from Janine's view but not before she recognized Charles.

Great God, how did he get in here?

Hushed voices rose to a loud buzz, indistinguishable as a few listened and many vocalized their questions. People jockeyed for position. A woman next to Janine dropped her hand from her mouth. "What happened?" she asked her companion.

Janine and others pushed to get closer to the crime scene. She stifled a cry when a man's boot landed on her foot. Her only thought was to get to Etienne. She watched the palace guards merge into the scene and escort Bonaparte and Josephine from the room. More guards swarmed and kept onlookers at bay, preventing Janine from seeing Etienne or Charles. She looked for Lenoir but didn't see him either.

Janine's head throbbed from worry about Etienne—and uncertainty as to whether she might be implicated by association with Charles. She searched the sea of faces for Minette to no avail. *The envelope. Charles.* No, it couldn't be. She leaned against the wall, her head spinning. Had Charles passed the note to Minette? Surely not . . . what if . . . she must get rid of it at the first opportunity.

After the chaos subsided, the guards positioned themselves around the room, ordering no one leave unless they had express permission or until dismissed.

It seemed an eternity before she overheard General de Bernay say, "There's been an attempt on the First Consul's life. He's unharmed. The perpetrator has been subdued and taken away. No, I don't know who he is. Or how he got in here."

Lenoir rushed up, out of breath. "The First Consul is unhurt."

De Bernay gave him a smoldering look. "How do you know?"

Lenoir squared his shoulders and gave him a smug look. "I took Madame Bonaparte to her husband."

Another general remarked, "I saw it all. If it hadn't been for the quick action by Colonel Tremeau, Bonaparte would have taken the blow. Tremeau saw it coming and pushed Bonaparte to safety with his left hand and deflected the knife with his right arm. The blade went into his arm and still he drove his fist into the man's face." The officer pantomimed the action as he spoke. "The assailant tried to run, but the colonel subdued him until the guards took the prisoner away."

Another officer said, "The unfortunate fool won't live to see dawn."

"Any accomplices?" a man asked.

Confined with the other guests, Janine felt like a caged animal. The more she thought about the note, the more agitated she became. She feared it as much as if she carried an explosive in her handbag. In her misery her eyes wandered to Mademoiselle La Roche, who clung to her father, wailing at the top of her lungs. Janine walked over, reached for the girl's hand, and spoke with an assurance she didn't feel, "Don't worry so, I'm sure the colonel is not seriously hurt."

The young woman turned to her, hope in her eyes. "You think not?"

"Of course I do. He's a skilled and brave soldier. He knows how to take care of himself." *And others,* Janine thought, as wistful memories tugged at her heart. "He'll soon be as good as new. You just wait and see."

Monsieur La Roche patted his daughter on the shoulder. "She's right, you know." He turned to Janine. "Thank you for comforting my daughter. I just don't know what to say to her at a time like this."

"It's been a terrible shock for all of us. It's especially frightening for a young woman who hasn't been exposed to such violence."

He nodded. "That is so. Still, I am indebted to you for your compassionate response. If there is ever any way I can return the favor, please call upon me."

Janine swallowed and hoped the lump in her throat would subside. "You are most kind." She wondered on whom she could call after Charles' identity became known.

Mademoiselle La Roche looked up at her father. "When can I see him?"

"I don't know, dear."

She turned to Janine. "When do you think?"

The girl's innocence touched Janine. "I suppose it depends on Colonel Tremeau."

"Oh. What about you? Will you come to visit with me?"

"Perhaps I can." Janine felt sympathy for her in their common concern for Etienne. She edged away and looked for a place to sit. Finding none, she stood by a wall and waited with everyone else.

The First Consul's personal doctor worked feverishly to stop the bleeding from the ugly gash on Etienne's arm. After more than twenty minutes of compression on the wound, the flow slowed to ooze. While bandaging the arm, the doctor said, "You're lucky the knife didn't hit the bone. You'll need to stay here until morning in case the bleeding gets heavier. Keeping still is important, too."

The immediate danger past, Etienne's thoughts went to the breach of security. The royalists had come too damn close to succeeding in their mission. How had Charles Dupré—the pompous man he'd met on his recent trip to London—been cleared as a waiter in the Tuileries? It had to have been instigated by someone within the palace who was trusted. But who? He drew a blank. He must get to the interrogation of Charles as quickly as possible.

Now that the rush from the emergency had subsided, Etienne struggled to stand. "There's a pressing matter," he said. "I'll be back as soon as I can."

The doctor raised an eyebrow. "You've lost a lot of blood. You know the risk."

Ignoring his lightheadedness, Etienne reached for the clean, oversized shirt the doctor offered. The other man guided his arms, shaking his head all the while.

Hearing voices in the outer room, Etienne waited and listened.

Bonaparte stuck his head in the door. "Thank God, you're able to stand. It must be your peasant stock." He laughed and then turned serious, staring at the bandaged arm. "I want to talk to you . . . over here." He motioned to the medical supply room and closed the door behind them.

"The situation is serious. I have no doubt that Cadoudal and the Bourbons sent Charles Dupré here to murder me. Dupré has implicated General de Bernay's wife in this plot. The palace and grounds have been searched, with no trace of her. He insisted she was his only contact within these walls. A contingent is fanning out in the city, searching for her."

Minette! She had made a fool of all of them. *What about Janine?* "Does General de Bernay know?" Etienne asked.

Etienne chastised himself for missing clues that must have been there. With Minette's involvement, everything fell into place. It explained Dupré's movements in Tours, at Cadoudal's campsite in the Orleans woods, and at the Tuileries.

"Not yet."

"I don't understand how she was able to deceive everyone."

Bonaparte shook his head. "In light of this, I must ask, do you wish to revise your report on Mademoiselle de Fleury?"

"Non. Her troubles began most likely when Minette told her royalist contact about Janine being in Tours. The imposter at Chateau Fleury may have seen the disguised Dupré as an opportunity to denounce Janine, persuading others to do so as well. After the sworn statements were signed, I did a thorough investigation. I found no evidence of conspiracy on Janine's part. To the contrary, her accusers conspired against her with well-rehearsed statements, some of which were outright lies. As for the pre-revolutionary marriage contract between Janine and Dupré, the terms were not met." Etienne gave Bonaparte a sly look. "You must have known that when you selected her as a suitable wife for Lenoir."

"That's true. Dupré was in England and she in New Orleans. Josephine and I did look into that aspect."

Etienne sank onto the cot. "If you need more convincing, consider that Janine has no authority to make palace staffing decisions. Besides, she was lame and incapacitated while her ankle healed, right here under the watchful eye of your household. She wasn't at liberty to conspire with anyone."

Bonaparte rubbed his temples. "I see your point." He took a deep breath. "This is the second time you've saved my life. I want to thank you for your loyalty. Within a year I'll be crowned Emperor of France, and I want you appointed as my *Intendant General de la Grande Armée*. If you still refuse to marry Mademoiselle La Roche, you will find yourself a traitor to the Republic. Think long and hard about it. You have a choice—share in the future glory of France or face a court-martial."

Etienne clenched his teeth and nodded. *If I do as I'm told.* Consul-for-Life should satisfy Napoleon. But no, he planned a Bonaparte dynasty to dictate to the citizens for generations. *No different than the royal Bourbons.* Etienne saw his fight for the rights of man failing right before his eyes. "I'm honored to know of your confidence in me," he said, buying time to get his affairs in order before he left the country.

"In spite of the disruption, I will go on with the awards to our brave heroes, among which you rank with the best of them." The First Consul clapped Etienne on the shoulder. "After the event, I'll bring your award to you."

Disappointed not to have been present at the interrogation of Dupré, Etienne acknowledged that his arm needed a rest—a troublesome red spot had already spread along his sleeve. Time for the bandage to be changed; not a good sign. As he and Bonaparte walked out, he wondered how the despicable affair affected Janine's marriage plans. He would do everything in his power to avoid any adverse effect the royalist attack might have on her getting Chateau Fleury back, although the means were contrary to his own interests.

With a sigh, Etienne went in search of the doctor to change his bandage.

By the time Janine reached her bedchamber, she could hardly wait to lie down. She'd thought the evening would end after the attack and was amazed Bonaparte returned to the gala to bestow the military awards. When he announced Etienne's name, she was much relieved to hear the assurance that Colonel Tremeau was not seriously injured.

Attendants poured champagne from freshly opened magnums while musicians played lively music. Fireworks followed a midnight supper served in the Gallery of Diana, ending the evening on a celebratory note.

Lenoir had escorted Janine to her bedroom, but now, outside the open door, he didn't even try to kiss her goodnight.

"Bonne nuit." She avoided eye contact with him. Why didn't he go?

After an awkward silence, he said, "Try to get some rest. I'll visit you later?"

Janine, rather too quickly, closed the door. Pushing a small table against it, she took the envelope from her evening bag. With clammy fingers she removed the handkerchief and let it fall to the floor. She waited a moment before opening it, stepping to the flickering candle on the nightstand. After she removed the seal, she sighed at the sight of Minette's monogram—it *wasn't* from Charles.

Chère Janine,
By the time you read this, I will be
out of your life forever. You will be the

265

*one in Bonaparte's court—not me. I
cannot live a lie and have made my
choice, regardless of the outcome.*
May God keep you safe and happy.

Minette

In disbelief Janine stared at the words. Minette, a royalist? She
had seemed so loyal to the Bonapartes. Janine was unable to control
her shaking hands as she clutched the incriminating paper. Would she
be suspected because of her friendship with Minette, let alone her
relationship to Charles? What should she do? What *could* she do? As a
first step, destroy the damning evidence. She carried the candlestick to
the fireplace and edged the message into the flame. Waiting for it to
turn bright orange, she watched its writhing contortions until the note
crumbled to ashen gray dust.

Chapter 36

Arms flailing, Janine broke free from the tangled bedclothes, alarm alerting her. Again her senses were assaulted by a rumble of thunder followed by a jagged bolt of lightning. Fully awake by this time, she dashed to the open window and closed it. Jumbled memories tumbled around in her battered mind. One by one they paused before moving on like invading Republican guards. Things had gone terribly wrong at the gala. Etienne wounded. Charles likely executed by now. Minette viewed as an enemy of the Republic—too much to fathom.

How long had she slept? She squinted at the clock—a few minutes after six, no more than three hours of fitful sleep. Torrents of rain pelted the window; storm clouds blackened the gray morning sky, obscuring her view of the gardens. Would she be interrogated or, worse yet, arrested and . . .

Intolerable suspense!

By the time Josephine's *femme de chambre* brought her morning coffee and a sweet roll, Janine had dressed and was waiting for Lenoir. She paced the floor, unable to quell the fear she felt for Etienne. Had the bleeding been stopped? Had he survived the night? Would she ever see him again? And if she did, would he blame her for the harm Charles had done?

"Is there anything I can do for you?" the maid asked.

Snapping out of her self-inflicted torment, Janine pasted what she hoped was a bland look on her face. It wouldn't do to give the servants fodder for gossip. "Nothing more. The coffee is perfect." Janine searched the maid's face for a clue as to what she knew about the gala.

"You did your hair yourself? It looks nice," the woman said.

"Oui, I did. I didn't know whether you'd come today."

"Mais, oui. I didn't expect you to be awake and dressed so early."

At least the maid had planned to treat her as a guest—not a villain. "The storm awoke me and I couldn't go back to sleep."

"The rest of the household seems to have slept through it. I best get back to Madame Bonaparte."

"Is she still sleeping?"

"She was when I left her," the woman said over her shoulder on her way out.

Janine looked out the window at the rain-freshened flowers and greenery. Although the conversation with the femme de chambre had served to assuage her anxiety, she knew she couldn't place too much faith in it. The woman had seen very little of Josephine since the gala.

After drinking the last of the coffee, Janine took her sketchbook to the chair by the window. She outlined the scene of lavender and roses near the bench where she and Lenoir had sat. The activity helped take her mind off the uncertainty as to whether Josephine would revoke the art commission. *Where is Lenoir?* She laid aside the pencil and pad, stood, and moved aimlessly around the room.

Still waiting at three in the afternoon, Janine picked up her art supplies and left her room to go into the garden to further work on her picture on site. Not far along the hallway, she saw Josephine come out of a room and turn in her direction. Frozen in place, Janine didn't know which way to turn. In spite of her trepidation, she forced herself to keep walking.

As Madame Bonaparte drew closer, she said in a curt tone, "Follow me," and led Janine into an unoccupied bedroom.

Janine sat down in the chair facing her hostess. "How is Colonel Tremeau?" she asked, her voice breaking.

"He's recovering. That's all you need to know," Josephine said, a chill in her voice. "After the disturbance last night, I'm sure you have some idea what I'm going to say." Dark circles under Josephine's eyes gave her stony face a foreboding appearance.

Janine dreaded what she would hear. "Non, I do not," she answered in a weak voice.

Josephine nodded. "Don't make this any more difficult than it already is." After a brief pause, she said, "General de Bernay's wife, in whom I had complete trust, has betrayed me. I'm forced to accept that it's true—which brings me to you."

Mon Dieu, has Minette been arrested? Janine's eyes burned

with unshed tears for her friend and her own perceived guilt by association.

Madame Bonaparte shifted in her chair and raised her voice in emphasis. "Last night the man you were once contracted to marry attempted to assassinate my husband. When I took you into my home and my confidence, I believed you to be falsely accused of conspiracy." Josephine shook her head. "I am no longer sure and will not risk being deceived by you."

A vision of the guillotine flashed through Janine's mind. Trying to control her emotions, she forced herself to seek eye contact. Josephine turned away. Saddened, her voice soft, Janine said, "Your trust in me was not misplaced. I want you to know that I'm most grateful for your kindness."

Josephine rose. "Enough. I don't want to hear any more. By tomorrow at this time, I want you gone from here."

Janine understood that in Josephine's eyes she was guilty. She'd lost a friend and defender. She wouldn't remain free long. At a loss for words, Janine stood and departed. Where could she go on such short notice? Was she free to leave France? How soon would she be interrogated? Clearly, there would be no money from the commission for watercolor prints. Should she chance asking for Lenoir's advice? Or should she risk trying to contact Adrien, Etienne's aide-de-camp?

⚜

Lenoir didn't arrive until the dinner hour. He waited to be invited in and genuinely appeared surprised by Janine's warm welcome. "Do come in," she said.

"Thank you." He seemed subdued as he followed her into the room, keeping a respectful distance. "You look lovely this evening," he murmured.

Janine ignored the empty compliment. "It's good to see you. May I serve you a glass of wine?"

The lieutenant raised an eyebrow. "Merci. After the recent events, I expected you'd be quite distressed." He shook his head. "I've been with General de Bernay most of the day. There's still no word about his wife's whereabouts."

"This must be a most difficult time for him."

"*Oui.*" Lenoir took a swallow of wine, avoiding Janine's eyes. "I don't suppose you've heard that Dupré was executed this morning."

Will I be next? Janine shuddered. "I hadn't." Charles, gone—a casualty of the Revolution and his own rash behavior.

"It's better than rotting in prison," Lenoir said.

"I suppose." Janine sipped wine, bracing herself to speak about her immediate dilemma. As long as she had a breath left in her, she'd fight for her freedom. "Madame Bonaparte informed me I must leave here tomorrow. She's upset about Minette's role in the attack on her husband. And I am guilty by association."

Lenoir appeared startled. "I'm sorry I can't invite you to stay with Aimée and me. I'm sure you know I would if Lenoir Frères' reputation weren't at stake. There'd be whispers and doubts about our loyalty to the Republic. I just can't take the risk."

"I understand." What had she expected? He owed her nothing.

"Please believe me, I do want to help. Is there anyone I can contact for you?"

Shaking her head while she pondered the question, Janine thought of Baron La Roche's invitation to call. Could she possibly bring herself to ask to stay with them for a few days? She could hope. "Will you take me to call on Mademoiselle La Roche in the morning?"

Lenoir stared in disbelief. "Your nemesis for the affection of Colonel Tremeau?" he asked with a note of sarcasm.

Janine chose to ignore his remark. "Last night Mademoiselle La Roche and I shared our concern about the colonel's health. Have you heard how he is?"

"I'm sure he's in no danger. I hear he's in the care of Bonaparte's personal physician."

"You didn't answer my first question. Will you take me to see Mademoiselle La Roche?" Janine cringed at the evident irritation in her voice.

Lenoir didn't appear offended by her curt manner. "Oui, I will . . . and if you will accept, I'd like you to dine with Aimée and me this evening."

He's up to something. "That's most kind. I accept," she said, knowing she had little choice. She hoped no harm would come to her as a result.

They walked the short distant down the hall to Aimée's room, where dinner was laid out for three. During the meal, Lenoir revealed the purpose of his invitation. "I venture you plan to return to New Orleans as soon as possible. Is that so?"

Janine nodded. "I'm eager to get back to Très Chic and to utilize the inspirations I've gathered here." She added, "I'm much indebted to Lenoir Frères."

Aimée excused herself and left the room and Lenoir resumed the conversation. "I'm pleased you feel that way. I respect your talent. We'd like to maintain our association with you and expand our business to the New World. Take some of our designs with you. I'll send a supply of silks for you to gauge the response of your clients."

Pleased by the respect Lenoir accorded her, Janine felt less resentment toward him. "You won't regret your confidence in me."

Patting her hand, he said, "I'm sorry I acted like a scoundrel after you accepted my proposal of marriage. I admit I asked for your hand for the good of Lenoir Frères. I don't want to end up like Bonaparte—without a son. For two years I have wished to marry the young demoiselle who serves the First Consul's wife, but each time I ask, Madame Bonaparte has refused my request. Everything depends on the Tuileries' approval—as you probably know. The demoiselle and I have a one-year-old son already. In my frustration, I overindulged in libations. I tell you this not to excuse myself but so you'll know the circumstances. I wasn't myself when I misbehaved. I didn't want to hurt you."

Janine nodded. "At least we've avoided a disastrous marriage."

"You're a courageous woman. You dared to say no to Bonaparte."

The next day, true to his word, Lenoir accompanied Janine to the La Roche home on the Rue du Faubourg Saint-Honoré, several miles from Bonaparte's palace. The noon sun stood overhead as the coach, with her valise and boxed silk gown safely stowed inside, carried Janine away from her ill-fated visit at the Tuileries Palace. Fortunate to still have her freedom, she'd have to leave France at the first opportunity.

As the carriage rumbled along, Lenoir looked up from the ledger he studied. "This morning the baron and his daughter were enthusiastic about your visit. I wouldn't be surprised if they invite you to stay with them for several days. If so, you'll have time to make other arrangements."

Afraid to get her hopes up, Janine shook her head. "Why would they?"

"The baron is sympathetic because of his own past experience. Besides, it helps that his daughter adores you."

With a dismissive wave of her hand, she said, "I must temper my expectations."

Lenoir returned his attention to the ledger, and almost as an afterthought, he said, "Of course."

They rode in silence until they arrived at their destination. When the carriage stopped, the lieutenant gestured toward a house fronted by smooth green lawns and blazing red and orange flowerbeds. "How welcoming."

"It is inviting."

In response to Lenoir's knock, the baron himself opened the door. "Welcome. We're gratified you've come." He led them into the salon. Large windows revealed a pleasant terrace and garden at the back of the house.

By the time they were seated, Mademoiselle La Roche and her mother had joined them, followed by the butler with a teacart. After giving Janine a hug, Mademoiselle La Roche served tea. "I'm practicing being a good hostess," she said with a self-conscious giggle. "Père says I mustn't talk so much."

The baron spoke to Janine, his brow creased with worry, "Lieutenant Lenoir told me of your precarious situation. And through no fault of your own. My family and I know how devastating it must be."

"Oui, it is distressing." Janine set down her cup and focused her attention on him.

"What are your plans now?"

"To return to New Orleans as soon as possible."

"I can help arrange your passage, as I have several friends who captain their own ships. They helped me in my time of need. I've repaid them handsomely now that I'm home again."

Janine sighed. "Merci. I can't tell you how grateful I am."

"I'm happy to do so. My family insists you stay with us until it's all arranged."

"That's most gracious of you."

272

Lenoir gave Janine an I-told-you-so look. "I must be going as soon as I send your things in. Later, I'll return with silk fabrics for you and Mademoiselle La Roche."

Baron La Roche stood. "Plan to stay for dinner upon your return." He and Lenoir went to the door and talked a moment before the lieutenant left. The baron waited at the door for Janine's valise and box to be brought inside.

"It's our turn to talk now," Mademoiselle La Roche said to Janine, glee evident in her voice. "The lieutenant is such a nice man." She gave Janine a curious glance.

Janine smiled and nodded.

Admiration shone in Madame La Roche's eyes. "He's charming—not aloof like Colonel Tremeau."

Janine reacted as if she'd been criticized herself. "I've known the colonel since childhood. I can assure you he has a heart of gold." She hoped to ease the woman's concerns about her future son-in-law.

"Well, I wish he'd show it to my daughter," Madame said.

" Maman!" The girl shrieked, "He does."

"I'm glad to hear it." Madame La Roche gave her daughter a patronizing look. "Perhaps our guest would like to see the house and gardens before dinner."

"Oui, Maman." Mademoiselle La Roche seized the chance to be away from her parents. "Now we can talk without Maman correcting everything I say and do," she said when they arrived at the garden.

Janine listened with one ear and gave an occasional nod while the young lady talked on and on about her fantasy of married life and her independence from her protective parents. Janine's thoughts turned to her own family life at Chateau Fleury. *Young lady, you don't know how lucky you are.*

Rounding a corner to the street side of the house, Janine watched Adrien approach and turn toward them.

"Bonjour, Mademoiselle La Roche. Please excuse Mademoiselle de Fleury and me. I have a confidential communiqué for her. We'll be just a few minutes."

Janine almost gagged, her breath caught in her throat. *Etienne!*

Adrien kept silent until Janine and he were alone. "I've brought a message from Colonel Tremeau," he said in a hushed voice. "The

273

lieutenant general, the one you met at General de Bernay's home, suggested that Bonaparte have you interrogated, overriding Etienne's recommendation."

"Oh, non." Her mind racing, Janine realized she'd have to sail before Bonaparte's men arrested her. *I won't see Etienne again.* Adrien turned to go and Janine laid her hand on his arm. *"Un moment, s'il vous plaît.* Thank the colonel for me." Without taking a breath, she added, "How is his arm?"

"A little better today. The doctor keeps a close eye on it. Colonel Tremeau hopes to leave for the Loire Valley tomorrow." Adrien appeared uneasy. "I really must go now," he said and rushed fleet-footed toward the street.

Chapter 37

La Havre Harbor, France—July 1803

Janine traveled by coach from Paris to the coastal harbor with the ship captain's sister and her husband, courtesy of Baron La Roche. During the voyage, she took her meals with them in the skipper's quarters. More often than not his duties kept him away at mealtime. The baron had taken a fatherly interest in Janine and prevailed upon the captain to accept a minimal fare for her voyage. Well aware that he charged her less than anyone else would have paid. Janine wanted to be helpful while on board; however, whenever she offered, he replied, "I won't hear of it."

Although he said it in kindness, she felt let down. There were things she could do if he would only allow it. How would she occupy her time during the six- to eight-week voyage?

The days at sea passed slowly for Janine and the nights were almost intolerable. Had it not been for her love of drawing—and the occasional company of the captain's sister—she would have gone mad. As it was she spent her days on deck with her sketchpad and her evenings alone, thinking of Etienne. She realized too late that he had the same qualities she had respected and loved in her father. The title her father had held was not a measure of the man he had been. Neither was Etienne's lack of a noble title of real importance. She'd been superficial in her judgment of people. Her elitist ideals had clashed with Etienne's egalitarian philosophy—and rightfully so.

Two weeks into the trip, after the captain's sister and her husband had excused themselves for the evening, Janine continued to sit at the table with a glass of wine, hoping to dull the gnawing ache in her heart and thinking of Etienne. Why should leaving him this time be more painful than the first time? Definitely, absence and renewed time together had resulted in her heart growing fonder. She sighed. She'd never see him again, for she'd not willingly return to France. And if by chance fate intervened, he'd be a married man, their friendship forever changed.

Interrupting her thoughts and appearing unusually relaxed, the captain came in and began preparing his plate. "The stars are *magnifique* tonight."

Brought back to the moment, Janine wondered how long she'd been sitting there. "Oh, I don't want to miss seeing them," she murmured, standing up to leave.

"What's the hurry?" He poured himself a glass from the decanter. "The stars aren't going anywhere for many hours. Stay, enjoy your wine."

She sat down while he ate, the silence palpable. "You must have mending that needs to be done," she ventured. "I come highly recommended by my patrons."

He looked askance. "Patrons?"

She hastened to explain, not wanting him to get the wrong impression. "I have a dress shop in New Orleans, and while in Paris I designed silks for Lenoir Frères."

"I'm impressed. They're the very best house of silks in France. Bonaparte and his family patronize them."

"Oui, I know. His sister, Pauline, selected one of my designs for her gown worn at the recent Military Gala."

"Beautiful woman, that Pauline."

Janine nodded. "I've been commissioned by Monsieur Lenoir to introduce their designs and silks in New Orleans." One thing led to another, and before evening's end she'd arranged for the silver-haired ship's captain to deliver Lenoir Frères' silks to her shop when business took him to New Orleans.

After that night, whenever by chance they met on deck, he asked to see her most recent sketches. Often they talked into the early hours of the new day.

One evening the skipper was especially jovial at dinner. "We've crossed the Tropic of Cancer and will soon arrive at the island of Saint-Domingue. We'll take on fresh water and a supply of fruits and vegetables."

The next morning the ship entered the harbor of Cape François, dropping anchor near a larger vessel. Janine went on deck with the others and forced herself to record the mountainous skyline scene, but the sweltering day quickly sapped her energy. Unable to overcome her languor, she returned to her cabin. Opening the port window, she reclined on her bunk and soon drifted into a fitful sleep.

In a poignant dream, Etienne caressed her and urged her to wait for him. So real was the sensation that when she awoke to the familiar rocking motion of the ship, she wondered whether, somehow, their minds had actually communicated. But how could they? It was her desire alone, not his.

Suddenly restless in her small cabin, Janine made her way to the galley. She found the captain already there with an assortment of exotic fruits he'd placed in various baskets. "What's that?" She pointed at the large green fruit he'd sliced in half, its striking black seeds crowded together in the orange flesh like a large cluster of caviar on a plate.

"Papaya or *Lechosa*. It thrives here, growing year round, producing fruit."

"What a blessing to know the fruit is always here."

"The locals also use the leaves as an antidote to fish poisoning," the captain said. "I always take some with me, just in case."

The meals of tropical fruits were the highlight of the long monotonous days. The ship's course took them along the island of Cuba, where the night moon seemed paler and the stars brighter. How she'd like to share the experience with Etienne. Shifting winds created periods of calm during which the sails hung limp, frustrating all on board but freeing the captain to regale her with seafaring stories. After some days the winds picked up, and she saw little of him until they passed the Cape of Saint Antoine at the western end of Cuba.

The skipper brought Janine good news one clear morning. "We've passed the final milestone and have crossed back over the Tropic of Cancer. We're now in the Gulf of Mexico—the short deep waves are an indication." He gestured toward the sea.

Looking deep into the water, she noticed the color of the sea had changed. "We'll make good time now? No more days of little wind?"

He nodded. "Fortunately, no storms appear on the horizon. Lady Luck is with us, for August is a month of frequent storms."

New Orleans, Louisiana—August 1803

Awestruck by the panoramic view of the city from the deck of the

277

small brig, Janine reached for her sketchbook. From the waters of the Mississippi River, New Orleans looked grand with Saint Louis Cathedral anchored on each side by the Cabildo, the city hall, and the Presbytère, the ecclesiastical-purpose building. Facing the public square, the elegant buildings of the Place d'Armes occupied the entire waterfront between St. Peter and St. Ann streets.

Janine thumbed through her earlier sketches of inky-blue seawater breakers, drawn as they had approached the mouth of the river downstream. They had entered through the muddy, tree-littered waters of the Mississippi River, and continued their tedious voyage up its slithering body. And now the city lay before her, shown to its best advantage. She must capture its beauty in one last sketch. With great care she penned in the massive form of the cathedral and deftly placed the equally impressive colonnaded side buildings on the page. After adding distinct shades of blue for the water and sky, she set in several trees and a suggestion of the French flag on its high pole before closing the book. She had intentionally left the flag undefined, as the Spanish banner still waved. She looked forward to the French flag replacing it.

As the ship dropped anchor, Janine experienced mixed emotions of anticipation and anxiety. The occasional brief letters she'd received from Angélique gave no clue as to the fortunes of Très Chic during her absence, but the enclosed love notes from Angie's brother Antonio troubled her. He'd always disregarded her marriage contract to Charles. Now she didn't even have that to hold him at bay.

Uncertain as to whether she and Angie could resume their partnership, she hoped Angie's assurances in her letters held true. But Antonio's romantic notions could change their relationship. She'd need to guard her affiliation with the prestigious Lenoir Frères and keep it a separate business. Whether she continued with Très Chic or not, she must focus on repayment of her loan. She counted on her enterprise with Lenoir to do so.

Waiting on deck with the captain's sister, Janine turned to her. "Are you sure that giving me a lift won't inconvenience you?"

"Not at all," the congenial woman assured her. "For goodness sakes, it's on our way home."

Janine clutched her valise, pleased she'd have an hour or so before the skipper delivered her bulky items, her gown, and the silk fabrics supplied by Lenoir. She'd have time to catch up a bit with

Angelique before he arrived. *Let's hope she's expecting me.* Had her letter to Angie arrived ahead of her?

From the coach window Très Chic appeared unchanged. Encouraged, Janine accepted the footman's hand as she stepped onto the street. She turned to thank the captain's sister and her husband once again then entered the shop and acknowledged the greeting from a young girl, unknown to her, working behind the counter. "I'm Janine de Fleury. Is Angélique in?" she asked while noting two dresses featured on mannequins. Her memory of gowns at the Tuileries gala overshadowed the small shop's work. They'd have to spruce up their displays. All of the New Orleans society ladies desired the latest fashions from Paris.

"Mademoiselle de Fleury." The girl's eyes widened. "Oui, she is. I'll let her know you're here."

While waiting for Angélique, her mind raced with plans for the shop. Her new designs and Lenoir's silks would keep her busy. She'd enlarge her sketches to life size and dress mannequins with her clothing designs. Right away she'd set up an exhibit of the Lenoir-gifted silk gown she had worn to the gala at the Tuileries. What better way to promote Lenoir Frères fabrics and designs and at the same time increase business for the shop?

Footsteps on the stairs announced Angélique's approach. She rushed to Janine. "You're here already. I just received your letter two days ago. I didn't expect you for another week, but I prepared your room just in case."

"We had an uneventful voyage, thank goodness."

"Come upstairs. Antonio is here for lunch. Please join us."

Oh, no. Janine had little choice and with reluctance followed Angie up the familiar stairs, through the sitting room, and into the dining area.

Angie's brother rose when they entered. "The wayfaring traveler has arrived. Welcome back," he said and kissed Janine on each cheek. His eyes were as black as coal, revealing his father's Spanish heritage.

After Janine spoke of her experiences in France, she assured them she had returned to stay. "I want to meet with you both to discuss repayment of my loan and tell you of my new business venture. I have many new ideas and suggestions for the success of Très Chic."

"I'll plan to be here for lunch tomorrow." Antonio ogled Janine—he'd scarcely taken his eyes from her during the meal.

She hoped he wouldn't make a scene about courting her. "Oui. We'll plan on it," Janine nodded.

Antonio rose. "Please excuse me, I must get back to the exchange."

After pouring another round of wine, Angie leaned back in her chair without lifting her glass. "Does this mean you have given up all hope of taking possession of Chateau Fleury?"

Janine sighed, sadness filling her heart. "It's hopeless now. When it came right down to it, I couldn't marry just for a house."

An expression of empathy settled on Angie face. "My heart aches for you." She brightened. "Everything will work out now that you're back here. You add elegance to our shop. Antonio and I adore you."

"I appreciate your confidence in me. I'll tell you all about my plans tomorrow."

"Since you can't fulfill your part of your marriage contract to Charles, I wager you and he won't marry."

"Non, we won't. Charles is dead."

"Dead? What happened?"

"He made an attempt on Bonaparte's life."

Angie got up, coming to Janine and embracing her. "I hadn't heard. I'm so sorry."

"I'm sure the Duprés have been notified by this time."

"Will you call on them?"

"I plan to do so."

"While you settle in, I'll get back to work." Angie dashed off, leaving Janine to adjust to being back home in New Orleans.

November 15 already. How quickly the days had flown for Janine. The Lenoir Frères liaison generated so much new business that Janine hired three seamstresses to keep up with new orders for "Janine's Parisian

Fashions." Her displays attracted and appealed to the society ladies, each one wanting to outdo the other. They'd stop by to ask about galas and events at the Tuileries and express their pleasure at the talk of Louisiana's return to France. The amiable truce with Lenoir worked well for both of them.

With her business booming, she expected to repay her loan within a few months. Whenever she saw Antonio, she reaffirmed her projected time for full repayment. And in turn he asked her to have dinner with him or to be his guest at some upcoming social event.

A week later Janine and Angie had caught up on their work enough to linger over lunch. The past weeks they had skipped lunch to complete their backlog of gown orders in time for the new French Commissioner's grand ball. All of New Orleans wanted to meet de Laussat, the man appointed by Bonaparte to serve as the Colonial Prefect after Spain retroceded Louisiana to France. The city buzzed; the gala was the main topic of conversation among women of all social strata.

Angie placed her knife and fork on her plate and pushed it aside. "You must attend Baron de Laussat's party. You'll meet most of the society ladies within a hundred miles of here, women you won't see again for a long, long time—all of whom look to Paris for things of quality."

Squirming in her chair as well as inside, Janine found no reasonable way to refuse. Angie spoke the truth. "I can't commit now. We still have unfilled orders."

Frustration in her voice, Angie said, "We'll get it done. I'll tell you what I think. It's not the work—you're still in love with Etienne Tremeau . . . a married man by now."

Stung by her words, Janine excused herself. "I'll think about it on my way to the market." She had to get away from Angie. She didn't need to be told how hopeless things were for her. How many nights had she lain awake, suffering because she'd lost Etienne?

Slipping into her jacket, Janine stepped into the street and walked briskly toward the marketplace. She must give Angélique and Antonio an answer about attending the baron's gala. Of course she needed to go and mingle, wearing her spectacular Parisian gown. Everybody that was anybody would be there. She just couldn't face it—not yet. Vexed by the crowds on the street, Janine changed course, pivoting toward the harbor.

A man nearby was caught unaware and bumped into her. "Excuse me," he said, a note of irritation evident.

She gave no notice and dashed across the street, her full attention on the profile of a tall man in the distance. *Etienne!* Gazing in disbelief and afraid to hope, she tried to keep sight of him while hurrying after him. Unable to keep pace, she must have taken a wrong turn. He'd disappeared from view. *It was Etienne. I know it.* She turned back toward the market in desperation. Doubts began to mock her. It couldn't be him. How could her wishful thinking be so cruel?

Chapter 38

Fervent feelings filled the small apartment above Très Chic during the contentious conversation about the future of New Orleans. Antonio's dark eyes glittered in the flickering candlelight, giving them a predatory appearance. He raised his glass. "At last they're finally going to act on the Treaty of San Ildefonso. A date has been set for the return of Louisiana from Spanish to French rule."

"About time," Angie said, "They signed it three years ago."

Janine nodded. "The lengthy delay created a great deal of talk in Paris."

Antonio's head snapped around toward her. "Since you've just returned from France, I suppose *you* know everything about it." Irritation racked his voice. "In that case you'll also understand that its implementation depends on all the provisions being worked out."

"You don't need to shout at me to make your point," Janine spoke with quiet firmness. "I don't know about its provisions. I'm just pleased it's going to happen," she added, hoping to soothe his bruised pride.

"Is the date set?" Angélique placed her hand on her brother's arm and turned to include Janine. "I think we all agree business will flourish under French rule."

"By the end of the month." Antonio lifted his sister's hand from his arm and continued, somewhat mollified. "I admit, under Spanish dominion business has languished."

Tensions in the room vaporized like fog on a hot day with the new topic of conversation. Antonio's mood continued to mellow with each refill of his wine glass.

"My dear Mademoiselle de Fleury, Angie told me of Charles Dupré's demise. She said that you're not yet ready to accept invitations from gentlemen. I do understand." He continued in his most persuasive manner, "But I can think of no reason you should hesitate to attend the commissioner's ball with Angie and me. What do you say?"

Anxious to avoid a confrontation, Janine agreed to go with them, but she'd have to tread a fine line so as not to offend him. She could ill-afford to rile him. Antonio's advice and financial help, as well as his contacts with city leaders, were valued assets. "Oui, I wouldn't miss the celebration for anything."

Antonio's look of surprise changed to one of victory. "A wise decision." Satisfaction puckered his mouth.

December 1, 1803

Etienne stood by a window inside his small house, watching workers harvest fields of sugar cane, satisfied he'd selected an excellent foreman to care for the crops during his absence. He'd hired his able and experienced plantation overseer when in Saint-Domingue and brought him to New Orleans before he left for France. Drawn outside to take a closer look at the progress of the workers in the fields, he left the house and breathed deeply of the crisp autumn air. He'd invested heavily in his land, using much of his military pay. Now he could pursue the life he desired—to live simply and enjoy freedom of expression as he saw fit. In time he'd send for Anne and his mother. They'd help ease the transition. Perhaps Adrien would follow Anne, but that would be his decision.

The sugar master looked Etienne's way and rode to meet him. "This year's crop is the best yet. Each year gets better."

"The cane looks healthy. I can see I have a lot to learn from you."

"Together, this plantation will be *par excellence*." The man tipped his hat and turned back toward the field.

"I'll have more time to spend with you after the first of the year. At last I'll be able to participate in the entire season from the planting through the harvest." Etienne nodded and gazed over his fields.

"Good. You'll be here for the entire cycle," the overseer said, nudging his horse forward.

A gray cloud slipped over the sun. Feeling very much alone, Etienne's mood darkened like the sky as he fought his somber thoughts of life without Janine. His shoulders slumping, he turned back to the house. He must dress for yet another ball tonight in celebration of the return of the Louisiana Colony to France. Etienne steeled himself at the thought of the busy social season ahead.

⚜

Commissioner de Laussat edged close to Etienne. "Why the long face? You should be dancing with a beautiful lady."

"I need time to decide which lovely lady to select. You must agree that's a serious matter."

"Decide while you dance with my wife." De Laussat motioned his wife to his side.

Etienne responded as good manners required, "Madame de Laussat, may I have the pleasure of the next dance?"

"How can I resist such a handsome partner? Colonel Tremeau, the pleasure is mine." The middle-aged woman lifted her eyes to his, feigning the coyness of a smitten young lady.

Relieved to blend into the crowd, Etienne led her to the dance floor. She pressed her ample body against him, her hand quivering at his touch. He took comfort in knowing protocol required that she dance with her other guests, freeing him to seek another partner . . . or not. While twirling her around the room, he surveyed the young women, expecting to find none to his liking. And then a couple halfway across the room caught his attention. Without seeing her face, he was captivated by the grace of her movements, her beautiful dark hair stark against her porcelain neck and shoulders. She danced with a short stocky man. His eyes followed her, watching to catch a glimpse of her face while preparing for disappointment.

Madame de Laussat pressed his hand. "I wish I could dance with you all evening, but I cannot."

He blinked as they drew nearer the beautiful woman. *Janine!* He couldn't believe it. Without looking at his partner, he said, "Don't concern yourself on my behalf."

Unobtrusively, he led her closer to the dark-haired beauty, propelled by a mixture of joy and jealousy. How could Janine be here? Had she been implicated in the Charles incident yet escaped somehow? He had to know.

The music ended and he thanked Madame de Laussat for the dance. As soon as he freed himself, he followed Janine and the man to the sideline. Janine sat down while her companion remained standing, boasting to a group of men. Etienne wasted no time approaching to ask her for the next dance. With a tight grip on his emotions, he tried to shield himself from the dread of disappointment and rejection.

"Mademoiselle de Fleury . . . or is it Madame Lenoir . . . what a surprise to find you here."

A soft gasp escaped her. "Etienne!" Her gaze was clouded with tears. "I thought I saw you in a crowd here in New Orleans. I believed my eyes must have deceived me. I thought it just my imagination." Janine raised her hand to her lips, emotions written across her lovely face. Her eyes strayed to the sleeve of his jacket. "How's your arm?" she said, concern written on her face.

"Honor me with the next dance and I'll explain everything," he said, extending his hand to her. Was his face as revealing as hers? It didn't matter.

She rose, still looking at him as if she was seeing a ghost. "Oui. What are you doing here?"

He led her some distance from the man she had danced with. Not to mince words, he asked, "Did you marry Lieutenant Lenoir?"

"Non. When it came down to it, I could not—not even for Chateau Fleury."

"Your wedding gift upon marriage to Lenoir." Etienne tightened his grip on her shoulder as they waltzed around the floor. "When Bonaparte told me, I thought he'd found a way to ensure your union with Lenoir. That I'd lost you forever."

Janine frowned. "What about your marriage to Mademoiselle La Roche?"

"I had no intention of marrying her," he responded. Indignation at the thought of Bonaparte's attempt to manipulate him was no doubt evident on his face.

Janine's brows drew together. "I was under the impression you had proposed to her."

"I did not. I told Bonaparte I would not. That's how I happen to be here."

"It will break her heart."

"Why should it? Bonaparte will find someone else for her."

"You need to let her know."

"In that case, I'll write to her."

"How long will you be here?"

"I have no idea. I plan to resign from the army and return to work with the land, as did my father. I'm trying my hand in the sugar cane business." Etienne nodded with resolve and led Janine from the dance floor as the music ended. "Now, back to my questions to you. What is your relationship to the man you're here with tonight?"

Janine shook her head. "Antonio is my business partner's brother. They urged me to come with them tonight. That's the extent of it." The music ended. "Speaking of Angie, here she comes now. You better watch out, she's looking for a husband."

Angie, hips swaying, slowly ran her tongue across her lips. "Who have you here? Please introduce me." She stared at Etienne; her eyes devouring him from head to toe. "I'm Angélique and you're . . ."

"Etienne Tremeau," he responded.

Janine slipped her arm through his. As if unaware of anyone else around her, she tilted her head, tears like sparkling diamonds in her eyes. "Etienne Tremeau, *je t'aime.* I love you."

Angelique stared at her in disbelief before turning to Etienne, a slight flush on her cheeks. "I'm sorry, I didn't know who you were."

"Don't give it another thought." Hesitating and cursing his reserve, he found the strength in the depth of Janine's eyes to kiss her on the cheek. Like metal in a blacksmith's smelting fire, her signature gardenia scent softened his iron will. The crowd be damned.

"*Mon précieux amour,* I'm not going to lose you this time," he whispered in her ear.

Angie stepped away and met Antonio just as he reached them. "Can you imagine, Janine's with Etienne Tremeau, her childhood friend from France?"

"What do you mean she's with him? She is with *us,*" Antonio snapped. He turned and confronted Janine.

Etienne sensed danger before he caught sight of the stocky, balding man's uplifted arm. He spun around in time to deflect the man's hand before it struck Janine. "It's time for you to leave," he said, pinning Antonio's arms behind his back and pushing him away from Janine.

"How dare you touch me? Do not interfere with my lady and me, or you'll regret it." Antonio lifted his shoulders and thrust his chest forward.

Appearing startled by his claim and bravado, Janine stared at Antonio, "I beg your pardon. I am *not* your lady."

Fury darkened the man's features. "You will find you cannot

toy with my feelings whenever it suits you." He turned to Etienne, "I know who you are. I suppose you had carnal knowledge of this woman while she was in France. And here you are, back for more. Well, we'll see how much of a man you really are."

"Antonio! Stop this madness," Angie cried as she rushed over.

Shoving her aside, he glared at Etienne. "You've dishonored me in front of all these people. I hereby challenge you to a duel."

Chapter 39

The unexpected excitement died down after Etienne and Antonio left the room with de Laussat and a small group of men to confirm arrangements for the duel. Most of the guests returned to the festivities—eating, drinking, and dancing. Janine was not among them. She sat on the sidelines between Angie and Madame de Laussat, awaiting the men's return.

"I don't want this terrible affair to change anything between us." Angie reached for Janine's hand and pressed it.

"I know you deplore this as much as I do." Janine shook her head. "Why does Antonio want to hurt me so?"

"Because he is a hotheaded fool." Angie made a fist. "And is blinded by his passion for you."

A cloud of fear settled over Janine. Etienne could die. Danger loomed ahead of him. "Nothing good can come from this," she said.

"It's in God's hands now." Madame de Laussat looked at Janine. "Stay here tonight with us. I know you and Colonel Tremeau need time together before he goes home."

"Merci, I will. Each moment I'm with him is precious." Janine wiped a tear from her cheek.

Angie nodded. "I'll bring a change of clothes for you in the morning."

They fell into the silence of despair. Janine had no idea how much time had passed before she heard footsteps and looked up to find Etienne coming toward her. She didn't notice whether the other men had returned—she had eyes only for her beloved Etienne.

She rushed to meet him and fell into his outstretched arms. Not wanting the moment to end, she raised her lips to his and saw longing in his eyes. The woodland scent of him filled her nostrils as he kissed her with a gentle yet hungry passion.

He reluctantly released her at the sound of the soft voice of their hostess. "Follow me. You need privacy," she said, showing them to a small study at the rear of the house.

Alone with her hero, Janine tried to discern the meaning of Etienne's serious expression. What had transpired between the men? Anxiously, she waited for him to say something.

Etienne reached for her hand and led her to a large sofa.

Drawing her into his arms, he kissed her forehead and cheeks with tenderness before reaching her lips. He probed her mouth with a fiery urgency she had never before experienced—even in her most passionate dreams of him. She responded with complete abandon. Time stood still as their pent-up love at last broke free like torrents of water breaching a dam.

After some time Etienne leaned back and looked into her eyes. "I want you to know that finding you here tonight and knowing you really care for me makes this the happiest day of my life."

Janine gazed at him in wonder. "You can't imagine my joy in finding you here and even more so at hearing your words of love. I've dreamed of this for ten years." She sobered. "Damn that oaf Antonio. I'd like to wring his neck with my bare hands. I've never encouraged his advances."

Resting her head against Etienne's chest, she heard the rhythmic sound of his heartbeat—the life force within him—steady and strong. The possibility of losing him was unbearable.

"Since I'm the one challenged to the duel, I've arranged for it to take place in two days," Etienne said, self-assurance reverberating in his resonate baritone voice. "It's best to dispense with this unwelcome confrontation as quickly as possible."

Janine sat up and looked deep into his beguiling blue eyes, concern still clawing at her heart. "What is your weapon of choice?"

"Saber."

"Have you used one since your injury last summer?" she asked, a lump forming in her throat.

He pressed his face to hers. "I'm a soldier and I'm prepared for the enemy." Then he whispered in her ear, "Have no doubt, I will return to you."

"Don't underestimate him. Five years ago Antonio ruthlessly killed a man, a mere boy. He'd won the duel and could have spared the lad's life but chose not to. Promise me you'll be careful. He'll show you no mercy."

Etienne nodded. "I know. De Laussat's assistant already warned me that Antonio is an accomplished swordsman. Trust me, I'll be ready."

She felt the same kind of terror as when she had been told of her mother's arrest during the Revolution—the thought of losing Etienne threatened to overwhelm her. She must not let him see her raw emotions. She snuggled her head against his chest and savored the comfort of his nearness.

He seemed to sense her mood. He cradled her in his arms, gently patting her shoulder. She relaxed more and more against his warm body and listened to his rhythmic breathing. Time stood still. She was with her beloved Etienne.

A sharp rap at the door startled her, pulling her from her reverie.

Etienne squeezed her hand. "Shall I answer it?"

Janine sat up and ran her fingers across her forehead. "So soon?"

Etienne called out, "Just a moment." and let go of her hand, giving her a quick kiss before going to the door.

Madame de Laussat stood there. "I'm sorry to have to disturb you." She tilted her head until she could see Janine. "It's getting late. I'll show Janine to her room now."

Her husband stayed near her, watching Etienne. "We have a few things to go over before you leave."

Janine complied and walked to Etienne's side where, ignoring the presence of the onlookers, he gave her a lingering kiss.

Quite unlike my hero, Etienne—and perhaps lacking good manners. Janine smiled inwardly when she saw Madame de Laussat reach for her husband's hand and whisper in his ear.

Though a bone-penetrating fog obscured the sun on the morning of the duel, Etienne didn't feel the chill. His blood boiled in anticipation of his upcoming match with Antonio, and he fought to calm the flood of energy pulsing through his body. He'd decided to disarm his opponent without inflicting serious injury, and he would hold himself to that for the sake of Janine, as well as for Antonio's sister, Angie. He knew his self-imposed stricture put him at a disadvantage because Antonio would extract the maximum penalty, given the chance. But he'd accepted this inner challenge and would do his best to live up to his commitment.

Over the last two days, he'd worked hard to strengthen his weakened saber-wielding arm. Training had gone smoothly, but still his arm wasn't as powerful as he'd like. Keeping control of the confrontation would be one of his toughest battles.

De Laussat's assistant, serving as Etienne's second, led him across a stone bridge to a grassy opening among the cypress trees. Antonio and his second were already on the field. Carriages lined the edge of the dueling site. Faces of women and children pressed against coach windows, and crowds of people, mostly men, waited along the sidelines for the spectacle to begin.

A quick look around assured Etienne that the ground was level but the grass damp and slippery. "All we need now is for de Laussat to bring the sabers," he said to his second.

Upon de Laussat's arrival, the seconds dropped handkerchiefs to mark the boundary of the dueling square. Etienne and Antonio took their positions, as instructed, twenty paces apart. They threw their jackets to the ground and postured while their men continued to review the instructions of the duel. The seconds and the four official witnesses readied themselves for the event.

"The Code Duello states that if swords are chosen as weapons then the combat continues until one of the participants is either bloodied, disabled, or disarmed," a second said in a loud voice.

Battle calm settled around Etienne with each step toward his opponent until they were two swords' length from one another. When the starting signal sounded, Antonio lost no time and thrust his sword at Etienne's chest, only to miss his mark because of Etienne's quick defensive lateral parry and step back to disengage. Again Antonio rushed at Etienne with a sweeping attack at his lower body. And again Etienne evaded the blow with a side step.

After warding off a third offensive attack, Etienne noticed that Antonio was panting and beads of perspiration covered his brow. Still his adversary lunged forward, only to be met by Etienne's defensive stop-hit maneuver. Antonio's own momentum worked against him and helped deliver a stunning blow to his weapon. Etienne was ready to draw blood and end the match. This time he took the offensive with a diagonal slice of his sword and nicked Antonio's left arm. A telltale crimson stain spread on his opponent's slashed white shirt sleeve.

"Blood has been drawn. The duel is halted," Antonio's second called.

Enraged, Antonio glared at the man and then at the seeping blood before swinging his weapon at Etienne's face. Etienne avoided the blow and parried. Using all the strength he could muster, he struck Antonio's sword, knocking it to the ground.

Disbelief distorted Antonio's face. Etienne held the point of his weapon against his opponent's right arm. Antonio twisted and strained to reach his weapon, but Etienne kicked it well out of his reach.

Success. He'd brought an acceptable conclusion to this ridiculous affair.

Antonio's coterie of men gathered around him while his doctor examined his superficial wound. He struggled against them as they restrained and reasoned with him. Gradually, his stream of profanity diminished and his shoulders drooped.

Etienne caught sight of a man dressed in black darting from behind a tree with a revolver in his hand—a man he recognized. *What the hell—the fake Comte de Fleury*. He dropped to the ground the instant before a shot rang out, the bullet whizzing over him. He was an open target with no means of defense against a gun.

Pandemonium broke out on the field. One of the duel officials reacted instantaneously, shooting the assailant in the chest, fatally wounding the Chateau Fleury groomsman. Antonio bellowed obscenity after obscenity at Etienne.

Surrounded by his team, Etienne had turned to pick up his jacket when he saw Janine and Angie running toward him. He sprinted to Janine, unable to contain his euphoria to be alive and with the woman he loved.

She fell into his outstretched arms, tears running down her cheeks, and murmured, "Thank God, you're safe." They clung to each other without moving for a long moment.

He stepped back, cupping her face in his hands and kissing her forehead, her cheeks. Finally, their lips met. He savored the heat of her eager lips until the fire within threatened to consume him.

Angie waited quietly a few paces away until Etienne acknowledged her. "Thank you for sparing the life of my brother. He didn't deserve it. I had no idea that stranger was dangerous. I've seen him with Antonio several times," she said. "I'll leave you now and see to my brother."

Etienne dropped to his knee, took Janine's hands in his, and looked deep into her eyes. "Janine de Fleury, will you be my wife?"

Chapter 40

December 11, 1803

Adorned in her white silk wedding gown, the bodice embellished with seed pearls and embroidered rosettes of silver thread, Janine clung to Baron de Laussat's arm. Moving down the long aisle of Saint Louis Cathedral, she beheld her groom. Etienne, the priest, and Angie waited in front of the Altar of the Most Blessed Virgin of the Rosary. For a moment Janine pressed her hand against the gold locket she wore around her neck, remembering it had been a wedding gift from her father to her mother. How she wished they could be here for the happiest day of her life.

Still she counted her blessings for Angie and for the de Laussats, who had become like family to her during the preparations for the wedding. As she approached Etienne and the altar, she felt as if she were floating six inches off the floor—as if it were all a dream. Her heart overflowed with love for her groom. All she could manage was to give him a shy smile.

Standing by Etienne, Janine reassured herself she was indeed awake and the Mass recited by Père François was for their wedding. Later, during the ceremony, the priest spoke briefly of having known Janine for ten years and having recently met Etienne. He expressed his approval of their union. Etienne and the priest, also a man of simple tastes, had found a common ground for friendship. They each believed strongly in freedom and opportunity for all mankind. She too had come to value freedom for all, regardless of their circumstances. She had known times of plenty and times of want in her own life and understood the universal value of hope.

At hearing the words, "Do you take this man to be your husband?" she felt as if time stood still and all of eternity belonged to them.

"I do," she said in a strong voice for all to hear.

Pleased that the priest had kept the ceremony as brief and simple as she and Etienne had requested, she anticipated with joy life with her new husband by her side. The past was just that—past. The future belonged to them. They would build a new life together in this new land.

Etienne slipped a gold band on the fourth finger of her left hand. She glanced down at it and then at her engagement ring on the other hand before locking eyes with the man of her dreams.

The priest turned to Etienne. "Do you take this woman to be your wife?"

Janine saw tenderness in Etienne's eyes as he said, "I do."

With a twinkle in his eye, the white-haired father said, "I pronounce you man and wife," and looked to the guests. "I present Monsieur and Madame Etienne Matthieu Tremeau."

The organ sounded. Janine and Etienne joined hands and walked together down the aisle, smiling and nodding to their friends, most of whom they'd visit with at the reception immediately following at the de Laussats' home.

After leaving the church, they paused for a moment and watched the French tricolors flutter in the breeze atop the flagstaff in the Place d'Armes. They'd been fortunate to marry under the banner of France, for in nine days the French colors were to be lowered and the American flag of seventeen stars and thirteen stripes raised.

Etienne slipped his arm around Janine's waist. "I don't want my wife to get chilled. Come, the coach awaits."

As they hurried to the enclosed carriage, Janine snuggled closer to the protection afforded by the warmth of her husband. *Monsieur and Madame Etienne Matthieu Tremeau!*

The wedding reception filled the night hours like a dream. After breakfast at dawn, Janine and Etienne climbed into their coach and made the short ride home. Etienne jumped down, extending his hand to his wife as she alighted. Almost before her feet touched the ground, he lifted her into his arms and carried her across the threshold into the entry hall of their home. Janine had seldom experienced such abandon to happiness. Like in a fairytale, when all seemed lost, she and her Etienne had found each other and declared their undying love, only to have Antonio and the murderous groomsman threaten it. Her hero hadn't failed her. And now they were united as man and wife.

"Come, my love." Etienne took her hand and guided her into the modest salon. "Please." He motioned to an overstuffed sofa. After she sat, he settled down beside her. "Welcome to *Rose Aube*."

"Rose Dawn." Janine spoke slowly. "Nice." She frowned, "You didn't tell me the plantation had a name."

"That's because it didn't before this morning. I named it for the beautiful rose-colored sky on our way home. It portends well for our marriage. Do you agree?"

"Wholeheartedly. It's perfect."

"I want you to love this place as much as I do," he said.

"I will. I will always love being with you . . . any place."

He put his arm around her shoulders and drew her to him. "You make me very happy, and I will work hard to ensure your happiness forever." He released her and stood to add a log to the fire before pouring a glass of wine for each of them and sitting back down. "Vouvray from the Loire Valley for this happy occasion."

Janine sipped the pleasantly sweet liquid and set her glass down. "*A la bonne heure*—I'm reminded of happy times at Chateau Fleury. Our home here is warm and welcoming too." Reminded of her father when she saw a small chessboard in a corner, she knew he would approve of their union. Hadn't he been the first to recognize how exceptional Etienne was? If it hadn't been for him, she and Etienne wouldn't have been brought together. Merci, Père. Contented, she snuggled against her husband.

Etienne lifted his glass. "A toast to our love and happiness in our new life here in New Orleans."

"And to my husband, the man I've always loved and will forever more," Janine said as they touched glasses.

After the toast, Janine wrapped her arms around Etienne's neck. Looking into his mesmerizing sapphire blue eyes, she ran her fingers through his thick, sun-kissed hair. "Do you realize we've been up all night?"

Etienne kissed her on the tip of her nose and stood. Reaching for her hand, he said, "Come, *mon précieux amour*."

Historical Note

The birth of the new Republic of France emerged and morphed out of the lengthy struggle to overthrow the Bourbon dynasty, as well as the privileged church and aristocratic classes, by inciting neighbor to betray neighbor.

The bloody Reign of Terror began in the spring of 1793, in part in response to the counter-revolutionary revolt begun in March in the western region of France known as the Vendée. The French armies also suffered a major defeat that same month in the Austrian Netherlands, thereby flaming the fears of the revolutionary government.

At that time the ruling National Convention formed the Committee of General Security. Its members included Danton, Carnot, and Robespierre. Within a year, a second committee, the Committee of Public Safety, assumed dictatorial powers over France through Robespierre's control of the two committees.

Both Robespierre and Danton were bloodthirsty; Danton and his collaborators were sent to the scaffold for abuse of national justice. Carnot, an engineer with military responsibilities, posed no threat to the virtual dictator. Robespierre's frenzied use of the guillotine on both foe and friend ended when he too faced the blade in 1795. Carnot went on to become a member of the newly formed Directory in 1795 and later served during Bonaparte's rule.

General Napoleon Bonaparte rose to power as First Consul in 1799 after staging a coup d'etat and overturning the Directory. By the end of 1804, he had made himself Emperor of France.

For more than a decade, the royalists resisted the Revolutionaries and attempted to return the exiled Bourbon princes to the throne. The royalists included the Catholic and Royal armies, Vendeans, Chouans, and emigrés. Nobles and religious leaders led the Vendeans of the Vendée—generally from areas south of the Loire River on the west coast of France—and lived on good terms with the peasants. They resorted to violence when the Revolutionaries attacked the Roman Catholic Church.

An army of peasants exceeding 50,000 cleared the region of Revolutionary authorities. They marched toward Paris, but the poorly disciplined men were defeated at Le Mans in 1793. Greatly weakened, the group continued to fight for religious freedom until the overthrow of Robespierre, when the governing National Convention granted amnesty and freedom of worship to the Vendeans in 1795.

Georges Cadoudal, a French royalist conspirator, was a commander of the Chouans, a disorganized group of peasants from northwest France—areas north of the Loire River, including Brittany—that opposed the new revolutionary government in 1793. That independent spirit is evident in Brittany today. The Celtic language of the Breton people is taught in the schools and its many traditions are apparent.

The Chouans and Vendeans joined forces in 1794. Cadoudal was perhaps the most capable leader of the counter-revolutionists in the Vendée. After 1795 he continued to lead resistance to the Republic. He fled to England in 1801 and received financing to continue the resistance. He returned to France in 1803, spearheading yet another plot to drive Napoleon from power and restore the French monarchy. In 1804, after a failed attempt on Bonaparte's life, he was arrested and sent to the guillotine.

Further Reading on this Time Period

Listed below are source books I found useful as reference material for *Silk or Sugar*:

D.M.G. Sutherland. *France 1789-1815: Revolution and Counter Revolution (*1986).

Memoirs of Madame de Rémusat, 1802-1808. Translated by Mrs. Cashel Hoey and John Lillie (1880).

Memoirs of Madame de La Tour du Pin. Edited and translated by Felice Harcourt (1971).

Pierre Clément de Laussat. *Memoirs of My Life.* Translated and introduction by Agnes Josephine Pastwa, O.S.F., Edited with forward by Robert D. Bush (1978).

George J. Hill, M.A., *The Story of the War in La Vendée and The Little Chounneirie.* (n.a.).

Honoré de Balzac, *The Chouans.* Translated with introduction by Marion Ayton Crawford (1972).

Imbert de Saint-Amand. *Citizeness Bonaparte.* Translated by Thomas Sergeant Perry (1900).

Imbert de Saint-Amand. *The Wife of the First Consul.* Translated by Thomas Sergeant Perry. (1893).

Carolly Erickson. *Josephine: The Life of the Empress* (1999).

Diana Reid Haig, *Walks through Napoleon & Jospehine's Paris* (2004).

The Life and Times of Napoleon. Edited by Enzo Olandi. Text by Mario Rivoire. Translated by C.J. Richards (1967).

The Life and Times of Robespierre. Edited by Enzo Orlandi. Text by Luigi Mario Pizzinelli. Translated by Barbara Thomas (1968.)

www.ingramcontent.com/pod-product-compliance
Lightning Source LLC
Chambersburg PA
CBHW060533180626
46817CB00002B/547